PRAISE FOR JOHN LINCOLN

'Cardiff has never been so vibrant as in these seductive and strangely moving novels' – *Sunday Times*

'Williams' writing animates the city in much the same way Nicholas Blincoe managed with his Manchester novels and Armistead Maupin with his tales of San Francisco' – *Time Out*

'Williams has an extraordinary imaginative grasp of under-represented minorities' – *Guardian*

'A synthesis of thriller and literary fiction, teeming with dangerous Cardiff lowlifes' – *Independent*

'John Williams's *Into the Badlands* opened up the world of American crime fiction for me and a generation' – **David Peace**

'Drives a rugged path through the twisted badlands of the British wild West' – **John Harvey**

'I learned a few things. There is vital sociological and moral comment here too' – **Patricia Highsmith**

T0018387

Other Books by John Williams/Lincoln

Non-Fiction
Into The Badlands (Paladin 1991)
Bloody Valentine (HarperCollins 1994
& Oldcastle Books 2021)
Michael X: A Life in Black & White (Century 2008)
Miss Shirley Bassey (Quercus 2010)
America's Mistress: The Life and Times of Eartha Kitt
(Quercus 2013)
CLR James: A Life Beyond The Boundaries (Constable
2022)

Fiction
Faithless (Serpent's Tail 1997)
Five Pubs, Two Bars and a Nightclub (Bloomsbury 1999)
Cardiff Dead (Bloomsbury 2000)
The Prince of Wales (Bloomsbury 2003)
Temperance Town (Bloomsbury 2004)
Fade to Grey (No Exit 2019)

As Editor
Wales Half Welsh (Bloomsbury 2004)

GREY
IN THE DARK

JOHN LINCOLN

NO EXIT PRESS

This edition published in 2023
by No Exit Press,
an imprint of Bedford Square Publishers Ltd,
London, UK

noexit.co.uk
@noexitpress

ISBN
978-0-85730-516-9 (print)
978-0-85730-517-6 (epub)

Typeset in 11.1 on 13.35pt Sabon
by Avocet Typeset, Bideford, Devon, EX39 2BP
Printed and bound by CPI Group (UK) Ltd, Croydon, CR0 4YY

For more information about Crime Fiction go to
crimetime.co.uk / @crimetimeuk

For my mum and dad, Gillie and David Williams

One

GETHIN DIDN'T MIND THAT THE guy was lying. All his clients lied to him. Even the ones who were actually innocent.

He didn't mind that he was sure Karl Fletcher was guilty. Most of his clients were. When they claimed to be innocent, they didn't generally mean it in the civilian sense. They weren't saying they didn't actually do the crime they were convicted of. They were talking about being innocent in the professional sense – that the evidence against them wasn't strong enough to justify their conviction, that they'd spotted a loophole. That kind of innocent.

No, the thing that was really bothering Gethin, as he sat in the delightful visiting area of Long Lartin Prison, was that the guy stank. In prison most people shower pretty regularly – apart from anything else it's a disciplinary offence not to. This guy though – it wasn't even that he was obviously dirty, he just smelt rotten. There was no other way to say it. Gethin tried and failed to put out of his mind some of the sordid stuff that had come out at his trial – the huge collection of pornography and all that. So when Karl put his hand out to shake, Gethin just pretended not to see it.

The third person at the table, Mrs Kendall, didn't seem to mind, though. She took Karl Fletcher's hand all right, and stared at him like he was Nelson Mandela in Robben Island, strong and noble.

Gethin sat back in his chair and looked at the pair of them with frank bewilderment. It really does take all sorts.

Karl was lank and greasy and hunched over. Even his clothes, the chinos and the striped shirt he always wore, looked like they were coated in grease. In the photos of him from the trial he'd looked handsome enough after a fashion. A preppie psychopath in his late twenties. Ten years of jail time later he looked like hell. Prison has a way of ruining people.

Mrs Kendall, though, was rather more of a puzzle. For starters what modern woman in her mid-thirties insisted on being called Mrs at all times? Her name – he'd seen it on the cheques – was Hayley but woe betide you if you tried using it. Nor was there any sign of a Mr Kendall. Whoever he was, he was long gone. She was, Gethin figured, one of those people who live their whole lives like they are starring in their own movie. And in her own head she was doubtless a mysterious blonde called Mrs Kendall.

It was just that this presumable inner life didn't manifest itself on the outside. To look at she was a neat, compact person, dressed in an older woman's twinset, with her hair in a carefully coiffed helmet. She was a good-looking woman, seen in the abstract, but there was nothing overtly sexual about her, just a sort of grim determination occasionally lit up with love for her great cause in life, Karl Fletcher.

Not that Mrs Kendall's peculiarity mattered to Gethin. What mattered was that she was rich. Rich enough to keep paying Last Resort Legals to look into the conviction of her beloved. A conviction which she, and a very few other people, believed to be a miscarriage of justice. Gethin himself was frankly dubious about this, but he had learned not to look a gift horse in the mouth.

'So,' he said, once Mr Fletcher and Mrs Kendall had had their fill of gazing at each other adoringly, 'first the good news. We found the postman.'

'You did?' Mrs Kendall turned to look around at him: 'That's fantastic.'

'Took quite a bit of doing,' said Gethin. 'He quit the job three months later. And you won't believe how many people called Matt Edwards there are in this country, but we found him eventually.'

'Well, that's what I pay you for.'

Gethin nodded. It was a fair enough point and in reality it had taken Bex about five minutes to find Matt Edwards on Facebook. He just hoped he was storing up a bit of credit before delivering the bad news. 'He's living in the Peak District these days, working as a property investor.' Which was a polite term for a bloke who'd watched way too many episodes of *Homes Under the Hammer* and finally bought a couple of little terraced houses in Stoke which he rented out to unfortunate students. Anyway Gethin hoped it all sounded like he'd been earning his fee, given that Mr Edwards had been last heard of living in Chislehurst, Kent.

'So?' said Mrs Kendall.

'Unfortunately, he doesn't remember seeing your brother at any time that morning.'

'Oh,' said Karl. 'Fuck. You're sure he didn't see anything at all?'

'No,' said Gethin. 'I mean it's ten years ago and obviously it was a big deal at the time so he remembered the morning pretty well, but he didn't see a man in a blue Audi TT at any time and he likes cars, so he thinks he would have remembered.'

'Is he absolutely certain?' asked Mrs Kendall. 'Did you get him hypnotised?'

Gethin looked at her in amazement. 'No, I didn't get him hypnotised.'

'Well, why not? For God's sake.' She swivelled round. 'See, I told you they were incompetents.'

Gethin took a deep breath. Reminded himself that he needed Mrs Kendall rather more than she needed him. If she wanted him to eat shit he would grin and ask how much.

'I'm sorry. Of course I considered the hypnotism option' – yeah right – 'but I thought I would report to you first, before incurring the extra time and expenditure, given that Matt Edwards – the postman – did seem to be quite a reliable witness.'

'He's not that reliable, is he? He didn't see James drive by.'

'Well, no, but of course he might have been delivering a parcel at the moment in question.'

James was Karl's brother. Karl's defence case was based around the idea that he, James, was the man responsible for massacring the family. The only problem being that no one had ever placed James within three hundred miles of the scene of the crime. Hence the interview with the postman.

'Exactly,' said Mrs Kendall. 'That must have been what happened. He would have been on the doorstep, pushing letters through the box or whatever, when James drove by. His brain will have noticed it subconsciously and once you have him hypnotised he'll remember it.'

* * *

Gethin managed to keep it together until he was back in the car. Then he banged his forehead repeatedly on the steering wheel. For Christ's sake! Surely there had to be a better way of making a living than this – taking a deluded woman's money in the vain hope that he might somehow find the evidence that would free an obvious scumbag like Karl Fletcher. That wasn't why he'd started Last Resort Legals. He had been full of idealism then – keen to ride to the rescue of victims of miscarriages of justice across Britain.

A few months ago he'd really thought they were finally getting somewhere. They'd taken on the case of Izma M, the poster boy for moderate Islam, and that was a proper battle for truth and justice. They did a hell of a job getting to the truth, but unfortunately the way it had all played out meant that most of it never made the press and, while there had been an uptick in business, and the wolf was currently having a nap some way from the door, there hadn't been the surge of new cases he'd expected. So Karl Fletcher remained a valued client.

He put the car into gear. Maybe he'd make it back to Cardiff before the rush hour choked up the M4. Reaching over to check Google Maps on his phone, he noticed a message.

It was from Cat and it just said 'Call me'.

Gethin put the car back into neutral. What did his just-about-wife want now? She'd left him three months ago for reasons he still didn't really understand. Surely the mid-life crisis was a male thing? Not for sensible, professional, super organised women like Catriona. But then a lot of things you never hear about happen all the time. Innocent people go to prison, guilty ones don't. He still couldn't quite believe it though, still expected she'd be back soon.

Anyway the question was, what did she want now? Probably to bend his ear about Hattie, their daughter and only child. That was the hardest part of it all. Hattie was thirteen, with all that entails, and she was absolutely livid with Cat. Partly, Gethin figured, it was simple outrage at having her family unit ripped asunder, and partly it was super-strength adolescent embarrassment – how could her mum show her up like this? Running off with Nils bloody Hofberg, like she was a teenager herself.

So Hattie absolutely refused to visit Cat where she was living, some rented flat in Roath. Instead Cat would come over for a few hours every weekend. Gethin would do the weekly shop and maybe have a pint in the Gwaelod Y Garth Inn and Cat and Hattie would have their mother and daughter time. Gethin almost sympathised with Cat over that – being the full focus of Hattie's fury for an afternoon

JOHN LINCOLN

couldn't be much fun. But she had made her bed and she was most certainly lying in it.

He waited till he was on a clear stretch of the M4 before calling her on the hands-free.

'Hi,' she said, then went quiet, presumably moving to somewhere more private. 'You okay?'

Gethin bit back the urge to ask what business it was of hers and just gave a noncommittal grunt.

'Listen, this isn't about Hattie.'

'Oh?' Dear God, was she going to launch into a big relationship chat? 'Can it wait? I'm driving.'

'Yeah, I mean fine, call me later, but it's about a case you might be interested in.'

That was a turn-up. Cat had never brought him any work before. She was an NHS psychiatrist specialising in drug rehab in the South Wales valleys and, while she dealt with plenty of criminal types, none of them had a pot to piss in and most of them saw prison as a kind of economy rehab scheme. 'What sort of thing? I'm not doing any pro bono for your junkie fuck-ups.'

'No,' said Cat, 'nothing like that, not really. It's the Morgan Hopkins case.'

This was interesting. The Morgan Hopkins case had been all over the Welsh news for the past few months. Hopkins had been convicted of murdering a woman called Kelly Rowlands. It was a horrible, brutal murder and there'd been lots of lurid details about the dead woman's lifestyle that had kept the tabloids salivating. Hopkins had always protested his innocence. 'So, what's your connection?'

'He was in one of my rehab groups – though you mustn't tell anyone that.'

'Oh great,' said Gethin, 'so you want me to take on another case for no money?'

Last Resort Legals was not a charity. Gethin liked to

think they were on the side of the angels, working for people who believed they were wrongfully imprisoned, but they had to make a living, so a rich, innocent man was always going to be a more appealing client than a poverty-stricken junkie.

'Don't worry, he's got money. He is, he was, a builder. Got his own business. He's happy to pay your fees.'

'How d'you know?'

'The family. His sister got in touch. I met her before and she's at her wits' end, trying to find someone to help. Says that Morgan's lawyer was an idiot.'

'So you put in a word for me?'

'Yeah well, just 'cause you're an arsehole doesn't mean I don't think you're good at your job.'

'Thanks,' said Gethin. 'I suppose. Got to go now, junction up ahead, but I'll call you when I get back to the office.'

Gethin ended the call, and settled back in his seat, trying to bring back to mind what he remembered about the Morgan Hopkins case. And also wondering why Cat should throw him this juicy bone. If there was one thing twenty odd years with Catriona had taught him, it was always to watch out for an ulterior motive.

* * *

The Last Resort Legals office was in the Coal Exchange, the faded centrepiece of the Cardiff docks. A century ago it had been the place where the first million-dollar cheque was written. Over the years of the city's decline it gradually emptied out, turned into an occasional rock venue and a dilapidated HQ for any number of fly-by-night businesses. Last Resort was actually one of the more long-term tenants, but any time they were more than a month away from bankruptcy, Gethin counted his blessings.

The firm's other two full-time employees, Bex and

Lee, were standing outside the office in the early autumn sunshine, vaping and chatting as Gethin approached.

'Nice hair,' he said to Bex.

Bex was rocking a blue and blonde bob. Gethin was fairly sure it was her own hair as, while Bex was partial to a wig, they were always clearly identifiable as whichever 80s legend Bex was impersonating that night in the tribute band she fronted. And he was struggling to think of an 80s legend with blonde and blue hair. Toyah maybe – but who in their right mind would book a Toyah tribute act?

Bex did a little pirouette – she was a surprisingly graceful mover for a big girl.

'How was Karl?' asked Lee. 'And his lovely fiancée. She was there too I suppose?'

'Oh yes,' said Gethin. 'She was there all right.'

Lee rolled her eyes. 'Gives me the creeps she does. Worse than him.'

'I know what you mean.'

'Bet she wasn't too happy about the postman.'

'Not happy is right. She wants us to get him hypnotised.'

Bex laughed: 'She really is a maniac.'

'Sure is. But it's all billable, so why not? Either of you two know any hypnotists?'

Lee shook her head and grinned, her gold tooth glinting in the sun.

'I do,' said Bex. 'Guy on Cathedral Road. I went to him once to try and stop smoking.'

Gethin stared meaningfully at the vape in her hands. 'Not much good then?'

'Fuck off, it's better than fags, Geth. It didn't totally work like, but he was good at hypnotising. I was out in no time and afterwards I felt like I'd been smoking some really good draw, all light and spacy.'

'Fine. Can you give him a bell, see if he undertakes this

14

kind of work? And if not maybe he knows someone who does?'

'No worries.' Bex stuck her vape back in her handbag and led the way back into the office down a sulphurous green corridor with barred windows that had, like most of the communal parts of the Coal Exchange, the air of a long-since decommissioned mental hospital.

* * *

'Anything happening?' asked Gethin, once Bex had squeezed herself in behind her desk and started checking her email.

'Nothing much. Couple of possible leads. I've forwarded them on to you. Looks like we might have a result on the Donaldson case.'

This was another lowlight of the current roster. A death by dangerous driving case that had landed a pissed-up accountant in prison. Last Resort had been working on getting it reduced to plain dangerous driving.

He turned to Lee. 'Nice work on that.'

'Cheers. Lucky it was only a Muslim the twat ran over, otherwise we'd have had no chance.'

Gethin started to laugh then realised Lee wasn't making a joke of it. She was genuinely pissed off by this particular example of the injustice of the world. Mostly she kept up an effective mask of blanket cynicism, but every now and again she let it drop and Gethin could see the anger there in her black eyes.

He sighed. 'Fucking world we live in, eh? But guess what, for once I've got some good news.'

'Uh huh?'

'Morgan Hopkins.'

'Fucking hell,' said Bex, 'you're kidding. They want us on that? How come?'

'You won't ever guess,' said Gethin. 'Catriona just called

me about it. Apparently she knows Hopkins and his family from her rehab thing.'

'You two getting on better then?'

'No, that's what's weird about it.' He paused. 'Maybe she just wants to make sure I'm earning.'

His colleagues were divided on the subject of Cat's desertion. Bex was hopeful she'd come back, once she'd seen the error of her ways, and they'd be okay. Lee was more of the opinion that Gethin should have given her a slap and moved on. At least that's what she said. As ever with Lee, it was hard to know for sure whether she was joking or not.

'Anyway, got to be good news for us. So, Morgan Hopkins, what do we know?'

Two

GETHIN WAS TEN MINUTES LATE picking Hattie up from her friend Alys's house. The mum, Martina, was fine about it. She was German, worked in the theatre on the admin side and seemed, dare he say it, very efficient. Nice too. She had been more friendly with Catriona than him, before the shit hit the fan, but she had been careful not to say anything that suggested she was taking sides. Instead she just helped out. They had an arrangement in place that Hattie went there three nights a week after school.

Gethin felt bad turning up late, like he was taking her for granted. And bad for Hattie too. She needed all the stability he could offer and picking her up late was poor.

Not that she seemed to mind. Sitting in the passenger seat for the short drive up the hill to Gwaelod Y Garth, she was happily burbling away about the school play and which part she should audition for.

'D'you think I'd be better as Hermia or Titania?'

Gethin struggled to bring *Midsummer Night's Dream* into focus: 'Titania is the Fairy Queen right?'

'Obviously! And Hermia is like the young princess who's in love with Lysander.'

'Okay, that sounds like a good part.'

'Yes, but Titania gets to sing a song.'

Hattie's love of singing was undeniable but even her doting father had to admit to some reservations when it came to her ability to stay in tune. 'I still think Hermia sounds good for you.'

'Yeah me too.'

Gethin stuck the car into first gear to make it up the steep incline that led to their house. The upside-down house as everyone called it, because the bedrooms were on the lower floors, with the living room up above. It was all to do with the way the house perched on the side of the valley.

Once inside Hattie disappeared into her room. Gethin yelled after her to do her homework and not just spend all evening Snapchatting her friends or whatever. He was sure she was taking no notice, but you had to show some intent at least.

Gethin himself headed for the living room and poured himself a large glass of a nice Spanish Albarino and stuck an old Lucinda Williams album on the stereo, enjoying the fact that Cat wasn't there to look disapprovingly at his drinking and tell him to turn the music down.

Did he want her back? Not that there was any sign of her wanting to come back, rather the reverse. Right now, with a new case in the offing, he felt like he could be fine without her. Maybe even better off. He could find someone else. Enjoy the thrill of the chase, start a whole new chapter. Other times though, the sleepless four in the morning times, he felt like his world was shattered and he couldn't put himself back together again. Not without Cat. He didn't want to raise his daughter alone. He didn't want the thrill of the bloody chase. He just wanted her back, wanted his life back.

Inevitably, just as he was enjoying the absence of Cat, he remembered he needed to call her back about Morgan Hopkins... She picked up after three rings. No hello, she just went straight to business, the way that in previous times she'd have issued a list of instructions for domestic matters.

'So I've talked to the sister. She's called Linda and she wants to come to see you at your office tomorrow morning. Here's her number. You have a pen?'

Gethin dutifully picked up a biro and took down a mobile number. 'Did you mention our fees?'

'Well I don't know how much you'll charge her, do I? You've never bothered to let me know how you run your business.'

Gethin declined the invitation to an argument. First, there was no point. And second, he didn't want to rile Catriona till he'd taken delivery of this particular bit of new business.

'Thanks,' he said. 'I'll call her now.'

Gethin turned the music back up loud, let Lucinda's righteous anger wash over him.

At the end of Lucinda's Stonesy thrash, 'Guitar Strings and Bleeding Fingers', he turned the music off and sat down at the desk he'd recently moved into a corner of the living room. Then he dialled Linda Hopkins' number.

Linda turned out to be one of those Valleys women who had little trouble giving vent to their opinions. And it took him a while to get a word in edgeways. Eventually he persuaded her that it would be better if she saved up her thoughts for the following morning. She arranged to come in at 11 and Gethin sat back in his typing chair. It looked like he had a client and a case worth fighting for.

* * *

Later that evening, once Hattie was in bed sleeping/watching YouTube videos, Gethin started typing up an account of the case as he understood it.

It began with a woman called Kelly Rowlands, a heavily tattooed twenty-four-year-old, living in the Valleys village of Abertridwr, just north of Caerphilly – not more than five miles from Gethin's house as the red kite flies.

Kelly had a colourful love life. She had had an ongoing relationship with Morgan Hopkins, an older man who lived a couple of streets away. She was also sexually involved with a policewoman called Leanne Batey and, if that wasn't enough, she was alleged to have been seeing Batey's brother Ryan as well. He was a copper too. There were also – or so Hopkins' defence had claimed – any number of casual pick-ups. Even the suggestion that she was taking paying callers.

On 10 March 2015, someone – or, conceivably, two or more someones – had choked Kelly to death, then beaten her dead face to a pulp. The post-mortem injuries inflicted on Kelly suggested an extraordinary level of rage. Either before or after the murder the killer had ransacked the house, as if looking for something.

Gethin swallowed as he typed out the grim details of the violence. Even after all his years in the business it still shook him, the depths to which we are capable of sinking.

Suspicion had initially fallen on the policewoman, Leanne. She was the last known person to have seen Kelly. And her skin had been found beneath the dead woman's fingernails. However, she had been alibied by her brother Ryan. Apparently the Batey siblings had been having a takeaway together in her flat when the call came in that there was a murder in Abertridwr. Gethin underlined this bit. Brother and sister coppers alibiing each other! That really wasn't worth the paper their statements were printed on.

And to make matters yet murkier Ryan's own fingerprints had been found all over the house. This was explained away by the fact that he'd been the first officer to arrive at the scene but still he seemed to have put his hands in an awful lot of places at a time when you'd think he'd have been careful not to damage the crime scene.

The possible involvement of one or other of the

Bateys – that, surely, was the starting point for his own investigation. The police, it seemed to him, had pretty much given up investigating as soon as they got Morgan Hopkins in their sights. He just fitted the bill so nicely. And, most importantly, he wasn't a copper.

He was older than Kelly. A jealous, controlling individual according to his ex-wife. He was an alcoholic whose efforts at recovery frequently went off the rails. Worse still, he had two previous convictions for violent offences. Both were basically pub fights when he was a much younger man, but still. And he had no alibi worth speaking of. He said he'd had a row with Kelly and that had tipped him off the wagon. He claimed to have been at home with a bottle of whisky and a *Game of Thrones* box set – 'binge-watching, like'. Just to put a cherry on it, he had been heard mouthing off in the Four Feathers, their local pub, telling his mates that Kelly was a right slag and was going to get what was coming to her one of these days.

Gethin wasn't too fazed by any of this. The depressing fact was that most genuine victims of miscarriages of justice were there because they fitted the part. That was why the police had arrested them and that's why the jury had convicted. If you looked the part as much as Morgan Hopkins did, then it was no great surprise that you got blamed for bad shit that happened in your vicinity. Didn't mean he'd done it. It just meant that coppers were lazy. And so were the general public. They saw Hopkins' ugly mug on the front of the *Sun* with a headline calling him an animal, they didn't think twice about it.

On the upside the forensic evidence was weak. Hopkins' fingerprints were in the dead woman's house, but then they would be. He wasn't denying that he'd had a relationship with Kelly. Apart from that there was a microscopic bloodstain found on one of Hopkins' shoes and some complicated business about Hopkins' blood on a lottery ticket. That had probably played well with the jury but Gethin knew – and judges were coming to realise – that DNA contamination was a very real problem. Basically it would be easy to argue that a police forensics officer had a tiny amount of blood on their hands from handling the dead woman's blood-soaked clothing and they had transferred an invisible spot of that blood on to Hopkins' boot. Shouldn't happen but it did.

Gethin circled this piece of information. If he could discredit the forensic evidence, that would open the door for him to demonstrate the possibility that one of Kelly's other lovers was responsible – Ryan or Leanne Batey, most likely. He read over his notes and closed up his laptop, feeling a familiar buzz.

Three

'You think he did it?'

Lee was sitting with her feet up on the conference table, drinking a can of Coke, her eyes hidden behind dark glasses and her skin a paler shade of brown than usual. It had been her partner Monica's birthday the day before and they'd clearly celebrated long and hard.

'That's not the point, is it?' said Gethin.

'Geth, I do understand the bloody job. I'm just curious, 'cause I dunno about this one myself.'

'To be honest, I've no idea. There's plenty of stuff looks bad for him that's for sure. Then again there's other things look good for him.'

'The coppers?'

'Yeah, the coppers. Alibiing each other as well.' Gethin thought of something. 'You ever seen her about, the woman copper, Leanne?'

'What? You think I knows every dyke in Wales?'

Gethin shrugged: 'That's what you told me.'

'All right, fair point, and I did have a good look at her photo, but I can't say for sure. There's a lot of girls look a bit like that. In the old days it was a dead giveaway, a buzz cut, but now there's millions of people have it. Businesswomen like. I'll have an ask about though, in the Kings, see if there's any goss.'

Bex had been on her phone through all this, but now she put it down and turned to face the others. 'Deano says he knows the other copper, the bloke.'

23

That was good news. Deano was their part-time field investigator and Gethin had hoped he might know something. Deano had a wide assortment of dubious friends and acquaintances.

'He say anything about him?'

'Yeah, he said he's an absolute cunt.'

Gethin laughed. 'Well, he's in the right job then.' He didn't entirely mean it. Most coppers were decent, hard-working, blah blah. It was just that when you worked on miscarriages of justice, inevitably you came up against the ones who weren't. You came across the bent, the slipshod and the irredeemably thick. And once you took on the case, the coppers were the enemy. Never more so than in the last big case they worked. One which had left its scars on all of them.

It wasn't going to be easy trying to investigate the Bateys. Leanne might be easier to get to as she wasn't a copper any more, didn't have the same level of protection. Getting to Ryan, though, was definitely going to be a challenge. He picked up his phone to give Deano a call, discuss their strategy.

But just then the intercom buzzed and, rather than let Linda Hopkins try to navigate the Coal Exchange's labyrinthine corridors by herself, Gethin headed for the front door.

Linda Hopkins turned out to be somewhere in her forties: smart dyed-blonde hair, a business lady suit and a determined expression. Gethin figured her for a floor manageress at Debenhams, something like that..

He led her inside, introduced her to Bex and Lee, then sat her down at the conference table.

'Well then, what can you do for us?'

Gethin looked her in the eye, hoping to project trustworthiness. 'There are no guarantees, Linda, I'm sure you realise that. But I have looked over the case, as have my colleagues, and we are all convinced that Morgan's trial – okay if I call him Morgan?'

Linda nodded. 'It's his bloody name, isn't it?'

'Indeed.' Gethin winced. Was he sounding irredeemably pompous? 'As I was saying Morgan's trial was obviously unsatisfactory. And I'm confident that, at the very least, we can demonstrate grounds for appeal. After that you're in the hands of the judges and, again, we can't guarantee what a judge is going to do. What we can guarantee is that we'll work every angle, shake every tree and find every bit of evidence there is to help Morgan's case. How does that sound?'

Linda sighed. 'Well, at least you're not promising the moon like all the other bloody shysters I've talked to about all this. How much do you charge?'

Gethin was good at dodging this particular question. 'It really depends. We'll talk now about the case and put together a strategy and there'll be a couple of different ways we can go within that. There will be a cheaper option where we just focus on the basics and then there will be a more expensive option where we go all out and follow every avenue we can. Initially it would be for a two-week period then we'll have a conference and decide what more needs doing. How's that sound?'

'Fair enough. But don't worry, Morgan might look like he doesn't have a brass farthing but he was doing all right. He bought himself a bunch of houses up and down the valley, rents most of them out but there's a couple he was doing up to sell and he's told me to flog one of them and use the money for this. Not doing him any good inside, is it?'

'True enough,' said Gethin. 'I'll get the plan over to you later today and if you're okay with it, then we'll get started right away.'

'Okay. Catriona says you're the best and I trust her. Is

there anything else you need from me? I've got to get back to work in a bit.'

'Did you know about Morgan's relationship with the dead woman?'

'That skank, Kelly? Sorry, shouldn't speak ill of the dead, but that's what she was. Yeah, I knew about it all right. Told him to leave her alone, he could do better than that. But he wouldn't have it, said I didn't understand, said she wasn't like everyone thought she was.'

'Everyone?'

'Yeah. She was one of those girls everyone knew, everyone gossiped about. In Abertridwr anyway.'

'You know where they met?'

Linda snorted. 'In the pub of course. Four Feathers.'

'I thought Morgan had stopped drinking?'

'Doesn't mean he didn't go to the pub though. And he was always relapsing. But this was when he was still properly drinking. Must have been two, three years ago.'

'Oh,' said Gethin, 'so it was quite a long-running thing, the two of them?'

'Yeah, I suppose.' Linda looked instantly stressed. 'He was nuts about her, infatuated like. Don't know why, she was pretty enough, I suppose, if you don't mind all the tattoos and piercings and that. But I couldn't see there was anything special about her. There's loads of girls like that. Go in to town on a Friday night...' She tailed off, shaking her head.

Gethin frowned. This was not really what he wanted to hear. It all sounded guilty, guilty, guilty. His thoughts must have shown on his face.

'He didn't do it, you know.'

Gethin raised his hands in an attempted display of innocence. 'I didn't...'

'Yeah, you did. Of course you did. I did too, at first. I heard someone had smashed Kelly's face in, and I thought oh my God, Morgan, what have you done? But then I went to see him and I asked him straight out and I know he's innocent. I'm his big sister, I've seen him trying to lie to me since he was born and he never managed it. If he'd killed her I'd know, believe me.'

'Okay,' said Gethin, 'that's good enough for me. But to be honest it doesn't make much difference to how we go about things. If you're going to get someone acquitted you need to know how the prosecutor thinks. You look at the case as if you're trying to prove he's guilty, and then you notice all the little things that don't add up, all the gaps in the evidence. And I can assure you, from what I know already, there's plenty of gaps and plenty of unanswered questions.'

'All right,' said Linda. 'You just get him out, okay?'

* * *

After he'd shown Linda Hopkins out of the Coal Exchange, Gethin got the three of them to thrash out a strategy. The question was which threads to pull, and in which order. First off, there would be the substantial task of going through all the material that had been disclosed by the prosecution, all the witness statements and so forth. Then there was the forensics. They could potentially commission an expert to report on the evidence against Morgan Hopkins. It looked thin to Gethin, but he needed that verified.

Finally, there was the matter of the other suspects. Generally Gethin didn't like this approach: it reeked of desperation, trying to find someone else to point the finger at. The whole point of an outfit like Last Resort was to prove their guy was innocent, not to prove some other guy or gal was guilty. But in some cases – and this was definitely one of them – it was a valid enough approach. It wasn't like they were going to have to look far to find viable suspects.

They quickly drew up a shortlist. First up was the policewoman, Leanne Batey. Though, according to one of the news stories, she'd subsequently left the force. The case against her was pretty straightforward. She had admitted having a sexual relationship with the dead woman and had seen her on the day she died. DNA tests had shown that there were bits of Leanne's skin under Kelly's fingernails when she died. Leanne claimed this was down to passionate lovemaking. But it could just as easily suggest a fight. Gethin could find no suggestion that her fellow coppers had asked Leanne to show them the scratches on her body that Kelly was meant to have made.

Second up was Leanne's brother and fellow cop, Ryan Batey. He had denied knowing the dead girl other than by sight. He further claimed that he'd never been into her house before he showed up in a professional capacity after her death. As for the matter of his fingerprints being all over the place, he had apologised for the poor police work, but blamed it on being freaked out by what he'd found there. Which, to be fair, did make sense. None of the Last Resort team liked him for it as much as his sister, but he was definitely still a person of interest.

The other obvious suspect should have been Kelly's estranged husband, Aston, but he had a pretty cast-iron alibi. He was in Parc Prison at the time, doing three months for possession with intent to supply.

'Anyone else?' asked Gethin.

'Could have been a punter,' said Lee. 'Sounds like she was doing business.'

'Yeah, we should definitely follow up that angle. That it?'

'Hope so,' said Bex. 'I reckon that's plenty to be getting on with.'

Gethin sat back and considered the task ahead. 'Looks like about two weeks work for all three of us, plus the forensic report. Bex, you want to type all that up and send the quote over to Mrs Hopkins? Soon as she okays it, we can get moving.'

Four

GETHIN LEFT THE OFFICE EARLY that afternoon. He drove a half-mile or so up Dumballs Road, past the new gated blocks of private flats which had replaced the old factories. John Williams Steel and Currans, where the young Shirley Bassey had gone to work age fourteen, packing chamber pots. He parked on Callaghan Square and walked into town, en route to meet Andy Moles. Andy was an old mate who worked on the local paper crime beat, so Gethin figured he'd be a good source of gossip on the Hopkins case. He was jumping the gun really. He knew he should wait till the money had been agreed before starting work, but what the hell. Finally he had a case with the potential to take his mind off the devastation of his private life, and he just wanted to throw himself into it.

Andy Moles was stood at the bar of the City Arms, over the road from the Stadium, with a half-empty pint of a very dark beer in his hand and a copy of the *South Wales Echo* on the bar in front of him. Andy was a short, fat bloke who had lately decided to make up for the disappearance of his once curly hair by adding a bushy new beard.

'Pint?'

'Mineral water, please,' said Gethin, 'I'm driving.'

'Suit yourself.' Andy ordered another pint for himself, plus the water.

Gethin frowned at his glass, wondering why he'd turned down the offer of a real drink. He could drive perfectly well after a single pint. And then he got it: part of him was still anticipating Cat's disapproval if he came home with beer on his breath. Christ, it was ironic. She'd spent all those years treating him like he was an alcoholic any time he opened a second bottle of wine, and now she was seeing a bloke who mainlined vodka for breakfast. Maybe that was his mistake, trying to please her. Maybe she'd have liked him better if he'd just done as he pleased.

'Are we here for a chat or are you just going to stare into space for the next hour?'

'Sorry, mate, stuff on my mind.'

Andy nodded. 'I heard about Cat. Shame.'

'Yeah well. We'll see.'

This was about as close to a heart to heart as Gethin had ever had with Andy Moles, so they both fell silent while Andy finished off his first pint with one long swallow.

Gethin cracked at the sight and ordered himself a pint of the weakest pale ale on offer, clinked glasses with Andy and got down to business.

'Morgan Hopkins.'

Andy looked at him sharply: 'Are you on that? I hadn't heard.'

'It's not confirmed yet, but I think so.'

'Who's paying you? The sister?'

'Yeah but it's his money as I understand it. So, what d'you think?'

'Can of worms. You know what everyone reckons, don't you? Who really did it?'

'I dunno,' said Gethin, 'the copper? Leanne?'

'What I'm hearing is, it was the brother.'

'The one that gave the alibi? I can see that's obviously dodgy, but what's his motive?'

Andy gave him the kind of smirk that only twenty years of crime reporting in South Wales can produce, the kind of smirk that makes everyone in its vicinity feel dirty. 'Word is he was doing her too.'

Gethin frowned. This wasn't even hot gossip, it had come out at the trial. Maybe he was wasting his time talking to Andy: 'Yeah, I heard that rumour. You reckon it's true? '

'Don't think she was fussy, not after the first bottle of Blossom Hill anyway.'

Gethin started to laugh then stopped himself, remembered they were talking about a dead woman. Another couple of weeks of working on the case and he'd probably be joking away with the rest of them, but right now he wanted to maintain a little respect.

He was about to ask if there were any more concrete rumours about Ryan Batey that he needed to know, when he felt his phone buzz. A message from Bex. Good news, Linda Hopkins had got back to them straightaway. She'd pay 50 per cent up front on Monday morning. Gethin returned to his pint with renewed enthusiasm.

Andy had obviously received a message as well. He was scowling at his phone and tapping away. 'Got to go, Geth. Two kids been arrested for terrorist offences over in Riverside.'

'Christ,' said Gethin, 'depressing, innit?' Cardiff seemed to have acquired more than its share of back bedroom jihadis in recent years. 'Before you go though, you know anyone I should talk to about all this?'

Andy thought about it. 'Not as such. You could try asking about in her old local.'

'Where's that then?'

'The Four Feathers, up in Capeldewi.'

Gethin nodded; that was the same place Linda Hopkins said Morgan had met Kelly.

'Ask for Vic, the landlord.' Andy heaved his bulk off the bar stool. 'Mention my name. I'd watch your back though. It's a bit of an unfriendly local, the Four Feathers.'

* * *

31

Gethin picked Hattie up at half five then announced a change of plan.

'You're going over to grandad's tonight, love, I have to work. Hope that's okay.'

'Of course it's okay. I love going to his house, it's really cool. And he's teaching me to play chess.'

'Great. We'll swing by the house and pick up your stuff.'

They drove up the hill into Gwaelod Y Garth in companionable silence, Hattie engrossed in her phone. Gethin hoped he could take her perkiness at face value. She was obviously determined to put a brave face on things and show him that she was absolutely on his side. He loved her for it, but it made his heart ache. How long could they keep it up? How long could she put up with being shuttled from Martina to grandad to babysitter? How could he ever be mum and dad both?

Back at the house, while Hattie was assembling her overnight bag, Gethin took the opportunity to call Cat and check the weekend childcare arrangements.

Normally she sounded aggrieved when he called her, ready to start a row at any moment, so Gethin instinctively steeled himself for the fray. This time, though, she sounded different. There was no aggression, just a quiet, defeated tone as she assured him that yes, she was okay to show up at 12.30 the next day, Saturday, and yes, she'd be fine to give Hattie lunch.

Gethin hesitated, wondering whether to say anything, then decided there was nothing to lose: 'Cat, are you okay?'

'Yes, sure,' she forced out an unconvincing half-laugh. 'Been a long week, that's all. And I haven't been sleeping much, to be honest.'

In the early days of her desertion Gethin would have read only one thing into a remark like that – that she and Nils were screwing each other's brains out all night long – but there was no hint of gloating in her voice this time, just exhaustion. Was she starting to have regrets? Well, even if she was, he didn't feel like being too sympathetic. She'd made her bed, and if she found it hard to sleep in, that was her problem.

'Have you spoken to Linda Hopkins, then? Actually scratch that, I know you have. She told me. So you're going to take the case?'

'Looks like it. If you want me to say thanks again, then here you go. Thanks very much. Don't know what I'd do without you.'

'Oh Geth, you don't have to be so...' She trailed off. 'I suppose you do.' Another pause. 'Look, Morgan's a good man, okay? He may not look like it, but he is. And I know he didn't do this thing.'

Gethin stared at his phone, surprised. Whatever else she was, Cat was an experienced psychiatrist who knew full well that the most unlikely people were capable of the most appalling acts. What on earth made her so certain that Morgan Hopkins wasn't one of those? He was about to say something when Hattie appeared, coat on and backpack in hand. He told Cat he had to go and led the way down to the car.

* * *

Gethin's father, former high court judge Anthony Grey, lived in an architect-designed modern house overlooking the Bristol Channel, between the Edwardian resort town of Penarth and the retirement bungalows of Sully.

For years, after his mother died, it had been a gloomy place, less a home than a bunker, a place for the Judge to hide away from the world. A high wall protected it from the stares of passing walkers on the coastal path. In theory, in the architect's intention, this was counterbalanced by a huge upstairs window offering views over the Channel for miles in all directions. On a clear day you could see both the Severn Bridge, twenty-odd miles to the north-east, and Minehead, a similar distance to the south-west. But for years the curtains had been kept closed and the only inhabitant was apparently happy to brood alone in the gloom. Lately though, the Judge seemed to be returning to the world.

In particular he'd shown a new interest in his granddaughter, and it was one she was keen to reciprocate. Her maternal grandparents were fine, but had retired to the Isle of Mull and so, with Gethin's mother dead, she was keen to see more of the one grandparent she had to hand. Which was just as well from Gethin's point of view. He needed all the help he could get with looking after her.

They parked in the lane and Gethin pressed the buzzer. The front door opened into a big dining–living area, which was now full of light on what was turning into a lovely autumn evening.

'Take your bag up, dear,' said the Judge, 'then help yourself to a drink. I have some apple juice in the fridge for you.'

'Thanks, Grandad,' said Hattie and bounded up the stairs.

The Judge gave Gethin a thoughtful look, as if he was examining a new witness in the dock. Examination completed, he nodded to himself.

'Do I detect a new case? You look better than of late.'

Gethin rolled his eyes. 'Well spotted, your honour. Though I might observe that I told you I needed to be out this evening for work.'

'A fair point. Can you tell me which well-funded reprobate has engaged your services this time?'

'Morgan Hopkins.'

The Judge raised his eyebrows. 'I confess I was wondering if that one might come your way. Interesting case.'

'Yes, I suppose. As long as your definition of someone choking a woman to death is "interesting".'

The Judge raised his eyebrows. 'I'm sorry, I rather thought I was talking to a professional.'

Gethin put his palm up in surrender. 'Yes, sorry, I'll get off my high horse. You're right, it is interesting. My guy is plausible for it, but so are about half a dozen other people. Have you heard much about it?' Gethin knew the Judge still met up with a bunch of fellow legal types every Thursday lunchtime at his club. If there was gossip floating about – and there was bound to be with a case that had aroused as much local interest as this one – he was likely to hear it.

The Judge gave him a tiny nod, accepting the apology. 'It's the dog that didn't bark.'

Gethin thought about that: 'Nobody's talked about it?'

'Well, some people have, of course. But not the ones who actually know anything. Llew hasn't said a word.'

Llew was the judge who presided over the case, Llewellyn Richards.

'And Vickers has barely said anything either. And normally when he loses a case like that he's blaming all and sundry after the second large whisky. Not after this one.'

Vickers – Harry Vickers – was Morgan Hopkins' barrister at the trial. 'So what do you make of it?'

'They don't like it. The verdict.'

'Any thoughts as to why?'

'The police involvement, I suspect. As you say, Mr Hopkins fits the bill very nicely. On the other hand having two serving officers alibi each other in a case like that, well people are going to wonder, aren't they? But you're not going to spread that sort of gossip around the club, not with a chief constable sat at the table.'

'I suppose not,' said Gethin. In past years he would have gone on a rant then – asking how anyone expected justice to be done in this city when the senior cops and the senior lawyers and the judges all sat down to dinner together, were all quite literally in the same club. These days, though, he supposed he too had mellowed, or just lost the energy to fight against the status quo. He'd reluctantly come to accept that he was better off keeping his powder dry for battles he might just have a chance of winning. And rather than rail against his father's cronies he would simply take advantage of them.

'I'll need to talk to Vickers. Do you think you might put in a word?'

'Of course,' said the Judge, then turned his attention to Hattie, who had come back downstairs wearing a unicorn onesie.

Gethin gave her a goodnight hug and told her to be ready to be collected at 11 the next morning. 'Your mum's coming to see you at 12.30, remember?'

Hattie pantomimed retching and Gethin smiled, but felt a wave of sadness. He didn't want Hattie hating her mum. He wanted things to be back how they were. Though one of the many things his work had told him was that that never happened. Once you'd been imprisoned for something you didn't do, you were never going to go back to being the person you were before. And once your mother walked out on you, it was never going to be the same again, even if she walked back in.

On which cheery note he said goodbye to the Judge and pointed the car in the direction of the Four Feathers in Capeldewi.

Five

TO REACH THE FOUR FEATHERS Gethin had to retrace the route back home. But instead of turning off for Gwaelod Y Garth he carried on up the A470 to the next junction.

As he did so, it struck him how rarely he drove north from his house. Gwaelod Y Garth was technically in the Valleys. It perched on the western side of the Merthyr Valley, but to all intents and purposes it was a suburb of Cardiff. Its inhabitants were largely professional people like Cat and himself.

Everything to the north was different. There were no mines left on the valley floor – it was all retail and light industrial parks these days. Sure there were still some jobs out there, but the focal points had gone. There was still a strong sense of community in these little towns, strung out along the hillsides, but it was one based on a shared sense of loss and displacement. The industrial workforce, once the shock troops of the British labour movement, were reduced to part-time jobs in Aldi or Screwfix.

Gethin turned off the main road, took a couple of right turns and started following a lane climbing up the eastern side of the Merthyr Valley. At once he was surrounded by clear evidence of the other great change to have taken place in the Valleys over the past thirty years. How green they were now, these valleys. How little trace there was of the smoke and slag that Gethin remembered from his childhood. Just a few hundred yards from the main road, he was surrounded by nature, green and impassive.

Humans may have mastered this terrain for a while, but it was fast returning to its prelapsarian state. It was both reassuring and slightly chilling to realise how fleeting are the works of men.

At first sight the Four Feathers was an unlikely candidate for Kelly Rowlands' local. Gethin had been expecting a classic estate pub, some glorified prefab built in the 60s, or a knackered old town pub with knock-off Sky Sports and two steaks for a fiver. This looked the kind of place you take the family to for an overcooked Sunday lunch and disappointing pint of real ale, but put up with because of the location and, if it was the summer, because you got to sit outside and try to ignore the fact that the so-called beer garden was also the car park.

It was hard to ignore the car park on this early autumn evening though. There were two cars parked at right angles to each other, their doors open, surrounded by half a dozen young men. Once Gethin turned his engine off he could hear the relentless 4 on the floor thump of industrial dance music coming from their car speakers. When he emerged into the evening air he could feel the bass frequencies shaking everything in the neighbourhood.

It looked like the Four Feathers was a wolf in sheep's clothing. And this was just the car park. Gethin took a deep breath and opened the front door, wondering what mayhem lay inside.

It was a definite anti-climax: hardly anyone there and something thoroughly miserable about it. Sometime in the past, probably the 1980s, there'd been a refurb, doubtless in the hope of attracting families and making it a food pub. Thirty years on, though, the fixtures and fittings all looked knackered, there was a smell of ammonia coming from the toilets and stale beer from the carpet. That was the worst part of the smoking ban: now you knew what a pub really smelt like. The Four Feathers reeked of failure. Gethin wouldn't be surprised if he came back in six months and found it boarded up like half the pubs in the Valleys these days. There was no one eating and no sign of any menus, just a bloke at the bar chatting to the barman and an old couple sat in silence next to the fruit machine.

Despite the lack of customers it took the barman a good thirty seconds to tear himself away from a discussion of Jose Mourinho's failings as Man United manager. He was probably no more than thirty years old but he had the pinched, undernourished face of a man who'd lived on chips his entire life and latterly combined them with fags and vodka. His arms were covered in the kind of crude ink that suggested prison rather than a tattoo parlour. God knows how he'd got the job, Maybe he, like the pub, had known better days.

'Help you?'

'Half of Bass, please.'

'What?' The barman stared at him. Gethin wondered if it was his failure to order a pint. He tried again.

'Half of Bass,' longer pause, 'please.'

'Fraid it's off, mate.' The barman reached over to the pump and turned the little sign saying Bass round to the back to signify it was no longer on offer.

Gethin considered asking if they had anything else on draft, then decided to save his breath. He peered past the barman to the fridge, checking what bottles were on offer. The barman returned immediately to his conversation and Gethin had to wait for his moment to interrupt the football talk again by asking for a bottle of Becks.

The barman very slowly made his way over to the fridge, extracted a bottle of bland but drinkable German lager and plonked it down on the bar.

'Four pounds, mate.'

Gethin wondered what he'd done to attract this level

of rudeness and overcharging. He liked to think he fitted in most places. His permanent uniform of jeans and plaid shirts, plus his mop of shaggy hair, caused most people to take him for some kind of ageing muso, not a part of the legal industry.

Ah well.

'Are you Vic?'

'Nah.'

'Is he about?'

'Don't work here no more.'

'All right then.' He took a breath then ploughed on. 'Maybe you can help me. My name's Gethin Gray from Last Resort Legals. I've been employed by Morgan Hopkins' family to look into his conviction. He used to drink in here didn't he?'

'Yeah,' said the barman. 'He did. The bastard.'

'You think he's guilty?'

'Course he's fucking guilty. Came in here threatening her with all sorts, night it happened.'

'You heard him?'

'No,' said the barman. 'I was away at the time but everyone heard him. So now you know. How about you drink your little bottle and piss off out of here.'

Gethin held his hands up in surrender. 'Look if you don't want to talk to me, that's fine. All I'm trying to do is find out the truth.'

The barman shook his head in disgust. 'What you want to do is find some bullshit rumour that'll get Hopkins an appeal.'

Gethin was starting to feel angry now. Mostly with Andy for sending him off on this pointless excursion. He could be home with Hattie now, watching bad TV and drinking a glass of good white wine. The Four Feathers would be just out of sight and blissfully out of mind over the opposite brow of the valley. Instead he was wasting his time arguing with some retard in a stained Umbro sweatshirt. Enough already.

'Fine,' he said, 'if you don't want to talk about Morgan Hopkins that's up to you.' He turned round and was about to head out to the car when he saw the old couple in the corner looking at him with interest. For their benefit as much as the landlord, he had one last try: 'Look, if you know stuff that helps prove Hopkins is guilty then tell me about it. It'll make my job a lot quicker. 'Cause, believe it or not, I really am just trying to find out the truth. I don't want to waste my time trying to help a guilty man.'

Even as he trotted out this line, Gethin found the spectre of Karl Fletcher flashing across his brain. Christ he was a hypocrite. 'I mean I'm just an investigator. Innocent or guilty, I get paid the same. So if you've got anything...'

'Yeah, I bet you get paid all right, you vulture.'

The voice came from behind him. Gethin turned round and saw two of the lads from the car park coming through the door. Oh great.

'Okay, you don't want to talk to me, I get the message.' He made his way towards the door, doing his best not to look intimidated by the guys in the doorway. Neither of them showed any inclination to get out of his way so he skirted round them ignoring the sotto voce 'wanker' as he passed by.

Once out of the door he felt momentary relief, then saw that the rest of the lads were now draped around his car, all of them giving him the hard stare. None of them said anything, or if they did he couldn't hear them over the continuing electronic dance onslaught.

Gethin found himself irritated and scared at the same time. He considered facing up to the four guys, all of them looking like the kind of tossers who put you off ever going to the gym.

One of them spat ostentatiously across Gethin's windscreen.

'Oy,' said Gethin, 'you mind?'

'No,' said the guy, flexing his muscles under his Superdry T-shirt, 'don't mind at all.' Then he gobbed on the bonnet.

'Christ's sake,' said Gethin, half under his breath, and then turned to go back into the pub. No use in fighting with the monkeys when the organ-grinder was in the neighbourhood.

Back inside everyone stared at him. The two young guys gave him their best hard looks. One of them made a chicken noise which made his mate crease up with pretend amusement.

'You got a problem?' asked the barman.

'Yeah,' said Gethin, 'you could say that. You don't want to talk to me, that's fine, but you tell your boys to leave my car alone.'

'Not my boys,' said the barman, 'they're just concerned citizens. Don't like people coming up here and stirring shit up, just to make a few quid.'

'That's what you want to think, go ahead. But just call them off now or...'

'Or what?'

Gethin pulled his phone out of his pocket, 'Or I'm dialling 999 right now – getting the police to sort it out.'

As he was saying this Gethin had made the basic mistake of turning his back on his adversaries. One of the young guys must have crept up behind him, because next thing he knew he was caught in a bear hug and his phone had been ripped from his hand. Then the guy who'd taken the phone let him go and waved the phone under his nose.

'What are you going to call them with now, bruv?'

For the first time Gethin started to feel frightened. Were

these retards really going to give him a kicking, just for showing up and asking some questions? There was no way he was going to fight his way out of this situation, so he figured he'd better use his supposed skill with words instead.

He focused his attention on the landlord and ignored the lad with his phone. 'You think beating me up is going to make me go away? All it does is make it look like someone's got something to hide.'

'Or maybe we've had enough of people coming up here, treating us like we're a bunch of rednecks.'

Gethin just managed to stop himself from saying that getting all *Deliverance* on his ass wasn't exactly the way to dispel that particular prejudice. Instead he looked round at the old couple, still sat by the fruit machine, but now looking a lot more awake than they had earlier. Now they looked like they were on *Gogglebox*, watching something particularly interesting.

'Would you mind calling the police for me?' he said.

Some hope. The old couple looked at him with utter loathing.

'Call the police?' said the old lady. 'I wouldn't piss on you if you were on fire.'

Gethin took an involuntary step back, startled by the level of hostility.

'You know who this lady is, you're talking to?' asked the landlord.

'No.'

The landlord shook his head in disgust. 'This is Mrs Marinelli – Kelly's nan. You think she wants people coming here raking everything up again?'

Ah shit, Gethin saw the whole thing now. He turned back to the old lady. Maybe not that old, now that he was actually looking at her.

'I'm really sorry, Mrs Marinelli,' he said. 'I had no idea,

of course, and the last thing I want to do is cause you any grief. So maybe it would be best if I left right away.'

Mrs Marinelli looked at him with naked contempt: 'Yeah, fuck off and don't come back.'

Gethin didn't wait to be told twice. He started heading towards the door. Then he remembered his phone and looked over at the guy who'd taken it off him. He looked ready to square up for a fight.

'Can I have my phone, please?'

The lad shrugged, then chucked the phone down on the floor so it bounced up and hit Gethin on the ankle. He reached down to pick it up and the guy got there first, kicked it further along the floor, forcing Gethin to crawl after it on his hands and knees.

'Gayboy.'

His hand was about to close on the phone when another boot slid in and kicked it further away. There was a second lad joining in the fun now. He started to get to his feet and try to take control of the situation, hoping he didn't look as scared as he was.

The first lad kicked his legs from under him before he could make it back up. He was lying on the floor then, the two blokes moving towards him with big mean grins on their faces. He looked over at Mrs Marinelli, like she was the Roman Emperor ready to give him the thumbs up or down. There was absolutely no sign of mercy in her expression, just an avid stare, like watching Gethin Grey get a good kicking would go some small way to make her feel better about her own loss.

The first lad was just drawing his foot back ready to deliver the first blow, when Gethin heard the pub door opening behind him.

Everyone froze, waiting to see who the new arrival might be.

Gethin couldn't see who it was from his position on

the floor, but he heard her voice behind him and felt an immediate relief:

'What the fuck is going on here?'

Gethin twisted round and he could see her now. Lee, standing there in the doorway, looking at the two lads with casual contempt.

'Who are you then?' asked the first lad, but he pulled his foot back and allowed Gethin the chance to scramble to his feet.

'None of your business,' said Lee just standing there in the doorway, casual as you like in the face of these two tall, aggressive blokes, despite the fact that she was all of five foot three. Gethin had no idea how she managed it. He supposed it was the lack of fear in a situation in which you're expected to be fearful. A small black woman walks into a rough white pub and immediately owns it. It shouldn't work like that.

Clearly the old lady took the same view. 'What?' she said to the lads. 'Are you just going to let him go?'

The second of the two lads, the one in the Superdry top, was shamed into activity.

'Oy,' he said, making a move towards Gethin. 'You're not getting out...'

He didn't get to finish his sentence as, in a blur of motion, Lee went from utterly relaxed to flying through the air, driving a leg into Superdry guy's gut, followed by an elbow to his face, and then he was on the floor with Lee standing over him, her right boot hovering over his balls.

'Maybe you should say sorry.'

'Sorry,' said Superdry.

'How about your mate? You got something to say.'

'No,' said the bloke, who had taken several paces back towards the bar.

'How about you, missis?'

Mrs Marinelli just shook her head in disgust.

'Fine we'll just stroll out of this dump, then.'

'Yeah, like hell you will.' The friendly barman had decided it was time to join the party. He had come round to the front of the bar and he had a baseball bat in his hand and brutality in his eyes.

Gethin looked round at Lee. She still seemed supremely unphased. He wondered if she was armed.

'Nice,' said Lee, 'I likes a man with a big bat.' She followed that with a theatrical eyeroll. The old feller couldn't stop himself snorting with laughter, though Mrs Marinelli gave him a hell of a look.

The barman kept on coming.

'Fine,' said Lee, 'you hit me with a bat. Or you can try to anyway. But you know who you're going to be answering to?'

The barman slowed up. 'What are you talking about? Him?' He sneered in Gethin's direction.

'Nah. Kenny Ibadulla.'

That barman stopped moving immediately. He stared at Lee, obviously trying to figure out whether she really was connected to Cardiff's best-known gangster. It didn't take him long to decide it wasn't worth finding out. Stories of stuff Big Ken had done to his business rivals were legendary in pubs like this.

'Just fuck off,' he said, but the baseball bat was now dangling limp by his side.

'What I was suggesting,' said Lee, giving him a smile of absolute contempt. 'C'mon, Gethin, pick up your phone and let's leave these good people to their evening.'

Gethin did as he was told, picked up the phone and led the way out of the pub into the car park, now shrouded in dusk. The lads were still there, their terrible music still shattering the peace. With Lee next to him, though, they moved aside to let him get into his car. He did his best to ignore the fact that it had all manner of liquid spilt on it: lager, tomato ketchup, Coke. No doubt one of them had pissed on it somewhere. Thankfully the windows had all been tightly shut. Lee's car – or rather her girlfriend Monica's car – was parked next to it, totally untouched of course.

'Well, thanks for that. But... how come you came up here?'

'Bex told me where you were. And I knows this place, knows the sort of person comes in here, like. So I thought you might need a hand.'

'Yeah,' said Gethin, feeling momentarily unmanned that he should have needed Lee's help, but then accepting that there were precious few men who made you feel half as safe as Lee did. 'So thanks.'

'No worries. Might be an idea we get out of here though.'

'Yeah course, what are you doing now?'

Lee shrugged. 'After last night? Quiet night in. And I know what you're doing next.'

'Oh yeah, what's that?'

'Getting your car washed. See you on Monday.'

Gethin laughed and got in the car, turned the windscreen wipers on so he could see to drive, then got the hell out of Dodge, a volley of abuse following him as the car park lads recovered their bottle.

Without thinking about it, Gethin took the road that carried on past the pub and, within a couple of hundred yards, he was coming into Abertridwr itself, the place where Kelly Rowlands lived and died. There was a mixture of pre- and post-war terraced houses. A big pub on the corner called itself the Royal Hotel, though it was hard to imagine Meghan Markle stopping by any time soon. Still, it seemed just about open, unlike the bingo hall and the nearby pubs at the bottom of the hill, in what ought to be the town centre. The only thing open there was a chip shop, while the only business that looked remotely prosperous was the undertakers, and the most activity was at the bus stop, where a bunch of twelve-year-olds were mucking about.

Sometimes Gethin drove through these leftover towns and villages along the old coal seams and viewed them with sadness and compassion. This evening, though, after his reception in the Four Feathers, he just felt like nature had best get on with its reclamation project as fast as possible.

Just then his phone started beeping frantically. He pulled over to see what was going on. There were a dozen messages coming in one after another, plus a bunch of other notifications. He must have been out of signal up on the mountain. He had a quick scan through.

The first of them was from Andy at the newspaper. It said 'Best you give the Four Feathers a miss, mate. Vic's left and he says YOU WILL NOT BE WELCOME!!!' True fact, thought Gethin, even more fed up now he realised that – if his mobile network had just been capable of beaming a signal to the top of a hill – he might have avoided all the shit he'd just been through.

The next half-dozen messages were all from Hattie. The first five detailed her complete panic at having thought she'd lost her homework. The sixth message announced that all was well, after all. The other message was from Bex. It said she was out with an old friend, and 'she was big mates with Kelly R'.

Gethin texted back a simple 'Oh, yeah?'

Bex replied at once. 'Def – we're at the Tramshed, if you want to come down?'

Gethin thought about it. He had nothing else to do.

'Be there in half an hour.'

Six

GETHIN DROVE OUT OF ABERTRIDWR through Caerphilly and on to the A470 towards Cardiff. When he hit the lights on Manor Way he realised other motorists were staring at him and he remembered that his car was covered in all kinds of crap, so he swung down on to Western Avenue and into the carwash by the big Tesco. Normally he found carwashes, the big automated ones, strangely satisfying. There was a sense of being cocooned from the world by the giant rollers. Today, though, after the Four Feathers experience, it just seemed menacing. He felt for a moment as if the rollers were going to crush him, collapse the car roof on top of him.

But when the rollers stopped rolling, and he was able to drive out in a nice clean car, he felt his mood lift. This wasn't that unusual. He'd expected to feel a lot worse when Cat left, but much of the time he was oddly cheerful. He was enjoying being able to live by no one's rules but his own. Happy to feel that sense of adventure back in his life. At least for a little while.

Ten more minutes and he was parked just down the road from the Tramshed – an old tramshed that had been converted into a gig venue and bar. Plus, of course, a load of flats. It had been billed as an 'Arts Centre' while they were building it, but in practice it was basically just a mid-sized venue specialising in tribute bands and semi-has-beens – or 'heritage acts' as they like to call themselves. So, several nights a week, you could either see an 80s band – The Specials say – with one

49

original member trying not to look too depressed about it, or you could see some bunch of Herberts pretending to be The Specials. You got more jumping about and fake enthusiasm if you went with option two.

Gethin, being something of a music snob, looked down on the whole lot of them. Not Bex though. Bex supplemented her meagre earnings from Last Resort by appearing in a whole range of tribute acts and, sure enough, when he walked into the bar he spotted her over in the corner wearing a blonde wig.

'So who are we tonight then?'

Bex rolled her eyes: 'Didn't you see the poster, Geth?'

Gethin turned round and checked the poster on the door. 'Blondish' were on tonight. Evidently Bex was channelling Debbie Harry. Albeit a rather more substantial version than the original.

'Debbie,' he said, 'you look amazing! When are you on?'

'Half an hour or so. I'd better go backstage and get ready. You sit here and have a chat with my friend Chrissie.'

Chrissie was a bit older than Bex, probably fortyish though it was hard to be sure with all the tattoos and purple hair and black eye make-up she was sporting. She was wearing a Crass T-shirt and fishnet tights under a black leather skirt. The same standard issue punk rock gear that people had been wearing for Gethin's entire life. Quite sexy though, he couldn't help thinking.

'Hiya.' Gethin thought he should get straight to the point. 'Bex says you knew Kelly Rowlands.'

Chrissie gave him a bit of a look. 'Nice to meet you too! Look, you want me to tell you about Kelly, least you can do is get us a drink first.'

'Oh God, sorry. Had a bit of a day. What would you like?'

'Pint of cider.'

'No worries. How about you, Bex?'

'Nah, I'm all right. Got a bottle of prosecco backstage. My rider, darlings. See you afterwards. That's if you're staying for the show, Geth?'

'Er, yeah, maybe.' Gethin was suddenly flustered.

When he handed over the cider Chrissie gave him a good looking over. 'Have I seen you around somewhere?'

'Don't think so. Not recently anyway.'

'I'm not talking about recently.'

Gethin's turn to have a close look. He tried to imagine a younger, less tattooed Chrissie, her hair some other colour. Still didn't ring any bells. Her voice didn't give much of a clue either. She had a slight accent, a touch of lower-middle-class north Cardiff, like most of the girls he'd grown up around. 'Sorry,' he said. 'You look a bit familiar but I don't really know…'

'Never mind then. So what do you want to know about Kelly?'

'Not sure really. Whatever you can tell me, I guess. How do… how did you know her?'

'My tattooist, Ted, she used to work for him.'

Gethin got out his phone, opened up a memo. 'Where's that then?'

'Blood and Roses – it's in Roath.'

Gethin took down the name.

'Kelly was the receptionist and we got talking and that. And we're both into the same kind of music so I started to see her around at gigs and stuff and sometimes she'd stay over at mine rather than get the last train back.'

'And what was she like?'

'Wild.' Chrissie's eyes were gleaming. And something about the way she said it made Gethin wonder if there had been something between them, or at least whether Chrissie had fancied her. 'Not all the time, but when she wanted to go for it, she really went for it. The rest of the time she was… She was kind, you know. She used to talk about training to be a vet, did you know that?'

Gethin shook his head.

'Yeah she was full of plans Kell, and even at Ted's place she was great with the clients, because you know it hurts quite a bit and some people get well stressed when they're there, but Kell could always calm them down, make them feel better.' Chrissie paused. Her voice choked up. 'That's what she liked to do, make people feel better. And I suppose that's what got her into trouble too.'

'How do you mean?'

'Sex. All of that. Kelly didn't like to say no, you know. And she didn't see why you had to keep it to yourself, or just you and your bloke.'

'Oh,' said Gethin, 'I see...'

'Yeah, that's how she was. Just free. And wild, like I said, and now some bastard killed her ...' Chrissie started crying then, gulping her cider and crying.

Gethin didn't say anything, just sipped his Guinness and waited for her to get over the wave of grief.

'And after what happened before too. It's just wrong – how can someone so lovely have that happen twice?'

'Sorry, what happened before? I don't know...'

Chrissie wiped her eyes, but her voice still quavered as she answered. 'Her baby died. A couple of years ago. Her little boy, Ossian. He was only eighteen months old and he got meningitis. The bloody doctor didn't realise and... and he died.'

That was too much for Chrissie. She broke down in tears again while Gethin sat there, mumbling how sorry he was.

'She would have been a great mother, you know. Just 'cause she liked to go out doesn't mean she didn't look after Ossian properly, 'cause she did.'

Gethin wanted to follow up on this, to ask how Ossian's dad fitted into this story, whether Chrissie knew him at all. But before he could say anything more there was an announcement piped into the bar from the main hall. Blondish were about to start. Chrissie wiped her eyes and stood up. 'Listen mate, I came out tonight to enjoy myself, so if you don't mind we'll leave it there.'

'Sure.'

'You coming in?'

'Why not,' said Gethin, ordering another pint.

* * *

As Bex gave it her all on an acapella intro to 'Heart of Glass', Gethin found himself staring at one couple in particular – the guy in a New Order T-shirt, the woman in a smart dress with a fancy leather jacket on top in a vain attempt to make it a bit more edgy. When had it become the norm for women to dress up on a night out and men not to bother?

Anyway, when the band kicked into the circular disco riff, the woman started dancing wildly, while the guy just nodded his head like he was a professional rock critic or something. Then Chrissie, who'd been right down the front, started dancing with leather jacket woman and you could just tell they'd known each other forever and Gethin got a flash of recognition. The two girls together. Years and years ago. Maybe from Clwb Ifor or the Square Club or Sam's Bar. He wasn't sure but there was definitely something there. He felt a prickling sensation under his skin. The Kelly Rowlands' case was coming into focus, its tendrils straying into his world. Maybe Kelly herself had been in this very room.

'Yeah, quite a few times in fact,' confirmed Chrissie after the show. 'Stiff Little Fingers definitely, the Undertones as well, I think. You want a drink?'

They were back in the bar waiting for Bex to join them. Gethin hesitated; he'd already had a couple of pints.

'Just a mineral water. I'm driving.'

Chrissie gave him a look: 'It's Friday night, mun, have a proper drink for Christ's sake. Just leave your car and get a cab home.'

Gethin thought about it. His instinct, born of ingrained habit, was to say no, don't be ridiculous – it'd cost a fortune and anyway what would Cat think? It still took a moment for him to remember that what Cat thought was no longer of any direct relevance. And if he wanted to get pissed with a girl in leather and fishnets and waste fifteen quid on a cab home then that was up to him.

'Fair enough,' he said, 'pint of Guinness then.'

They sat down at a table and Gethin sensed that now really wasn't the time to ask more questions about Kelly, so instead they made chitchat about music and, while he still couldn't exactly place Chrissie in his past, he was able to establish that they'd both been at the REM show in the 80s, out at the old Ocean Club, so she had to be roughly his age, on the far side of forty.

Bex joined them and Gethin noticed that his pint had mysteriously evaporated so he went to the bar and bought another round and when he sat down he heard Bex telling Chrissie that it was nice to see him out.

'Did I tell you his wife left him? Oh sorry, Geth, hope you don't mind me saying?'

'No,' said Gethin, 'can't hide from the truth.'

'True that.' Chrissie clinked her glass against his. 'You married long?'

'Twenty years, give or take.'

Chrissie whistled. 'Shit.'

'Yeah.'

Bex chipped in: 'The guy she's gone off with, he was in a band wasn't he?'

How did Bex know that? He must have told her, he supposed. 'Yeah.'

'Which one,' asked Chrissie, 'anyone I'd remember?'

Gethin said the name of the band. 'He was the singer, Nils Hofberg.'

'Oh wow,' said Chrissie, her eyes widening, 'I do remember him. Right poser wasn't he?'

Gethin laughed, 'Yeah, you obviously do remember him.'

Half an hour later the three of them were walking over the bridge into town in search of another drink. Chrissie and him were already well on the way and Bex was buzzing a bit from the show and – Bex being Bex – probably keeping an eye on him. The fact that Bex was the best part of two decades younger than him had never yet stopped her from acting like his mother. And God knows he'd given her plenty to worry about over the years she'd been working for him. The gambling debts. Oh God, the gambling debts. He had to be careful not to let temptation claim him tonight, once he was in his cups. He would leave town when Bex did, that would be the ticket.

As they came off the bridge into Wood Street it started to hit him, the whole 'Town on a Friday night' thing. How long was it since he'd been out and about in the city centre on a weekend? Years, probably. It just wasn't where he went any more. A decade or so back Town had really changed, on the weekends at least. It had turned into a giant rolling stag and hen party. It had stopped being somewhere you went for a meal or a show, became somewhere you only went to drink and dance till all hours and pull till you puke or puke till you pulled.

'C'mon, Geth, where are we going?' Bex in his ear.

'I dunno, Urban Tap House?'

This was one of a sprinkling of new-fangled craft-ale places on Westgate Street, on the edge of town, just opposite the Millennium Stadium. Gethin figured he'd probably feel less like somebody's lairy dad there than in most places.

The three of them elbowed their way into a corner of the

bar and Bex went off to get some drinks. The sound system was blasting out some old Goth stuff which delighted Chrissie. Then Bex reappeared with a pint of some sort of pale ale that he could immediately tell was way stronger than he'd usually drink. He thought for a moment of taking it back, but the place was absolutely rammed so he started drinking it anyway, well aware that no good was likely to come of it.

Sure enough, by the time he was halfway through the pint, he was treating the women to a diatribe about what a great place the Tap House had been, back when it was the old Glamorgan Council staff club and populated by half a dozen elderly drinkers. So when Bex spotted some mates on a hen, she jumped at the chance to go off to chat with them. Which left Gethin and Chrissie on their own. For some reason Gethin found himself asking her about her tattoos, and she started telling him in detail about each one of them. By the time she'd got to the leopard on her left shoulder he realised his pint was empty and he got another one for himself and a double vodka for Chrissie and then she was turning round and lifting the back of her T-shirt up so he could see yet another tattoo.

This one, just below her left shoulder blade, was a picture of Frida Kahlo. It was quite well done. For starters Gethin had no trouble recognising who it was, but it did make him wonder why you would want anyone's face tattooed on your body, no matter how much you admired them. He was a big fan of the work of the LA singer-songwriter Jackson Browne, for instance. But it hadn't ever occurred to him to have Jackson Browne's face tattooed on his back.

'Cool,' he said. And then, feeling that was hardly response enough to such a painfully acquired portrait: 'Why Frida Kahlo?'

'Oh,' said Chrissie, smiling, 'you know who she is.'

Gethin nodded, basking in her approval. Even though,

truth be told, it was pretty hard to avoid recognising Frida Kahlo these days. Cat had liked her stuff for ages and was always complaining about how ubiquitous it was becoming, how trivialised. The final straw had come when she'd seen Theresa May wearing a Frida Kahlo broach at the Tory party conference.

'Yeah,' Chrissie carried on, 'I just love her, she is so badass and beautiful. She is so strong but she makes this beautiful work. I mean, it's like she's proud of being a woman, of women's work, and she's not trying to be like a man but she wants to live on her own terms. And that's, you know, how I'd like to be.'

Gethin could see the emotion welling up in Chrissie, felt like she was telling him something important about herself. Drunk as he was, he wasn't sure how to process that. She seemed to be opening her heart to him – but maybe that's what she always did to whoever was around after a few drinks. Or maybe, just maybe, she really liked him.

Did he like her? Well she was definitely looking more attractive now than at the start of the evening. He didn't like tattoos much, or at least he didn't think he did, but maybe he did and, well, he did like the curve of her quite sizeable breasts, he definitely did like that and actually, underneath all the eye make-up, she was really quite pretty.

He put his pint down and leaned in to give Chrissie a hug, 'cause that's what her little speech seemed to ask for, not sure whether he was also going in for more, but before he knew it her face was angling up at his and his lips and her lips had only one place to go and well, he felt like he was back in the Mars Bar way back when – young, free and single.

Seven

The next morning was rough.

Gethin woke at six feeling like he hadn't slept at all. Headache, urgent need to piss and an immediate sense of alarm. What had he done? What had he said? Had he really spent the night snogging the woman with the tattoos in the corner of the Tap House? Oh God he had. And not just snogging either. Snogging and taking cocaine. Shit.

Taking cocaine was the second worst thing Gethin was prone to do under the influence of drink. The worst was gambling, the vice which had done so much to disarrange his marriage. It was almost impossible – without actually killing yourself – to spend as much on coke as Gethin was able to gamble away. But still it was not a good idea. It made for poor decision-making.

Chrissie, then – had that been a poor decision? The smile that came unbidden to his face suggested not. They'd had them some fun, him and Chrissie – in the Tap House, then later still in Clwb Ifor and outside Clwb Ifor on the fire escape where they had done the kind of things that Bill Clinton didn't count as having sex but pretty much everyone else did. Cat definitely would. But then it was none of her business. Not now. Well bloody hell, it had been a long time since he'd done anything like that.

Did he feel guilty? He examined his conscience, found it lurking somewhere underneath his hangover. It seemed okay at first, but there was something nagging at him. Something Chrissie had said when they were out on the fire escape. Oh God, now he remembered. She'd told him she had a boyfriend. Jesus, what had he got himself into?

He buried his head under the pillow and struggled to get back to sleep, finally dozed for a while. Inevitably there was a nightmare – burglars coming into the house. He had to stop them before they got to Hattie's room. He woke with the fear fresh in his mind. Hattie, was she okay? Then he remembered she was at his dad's place. Then he further remembered that Cat was coming to pick her up at 12.30, so he would have to fetch her first. Then he further, further remembered that he had left his car outside the Tramshed. Oh dear God, what a complete screw-up.

How long before he had to get up? He could maybe stretch it till nine. God knows he could do with another hour's kip. But it was no good, sleep wasn't interested. Instead his mind rolled over the night before from its dodgy beginning in the Four Feathers to its libertine finish in Clwb. It was irresponsible, adolescent, all of that. But as he finally gave in to the inevitable and hauled himself under a hot shower he found himself singing – *Hot dog, jumping frog, Albuquerque*. It obviously wasn't the start of some big romance – bearing in mind the boyfriend thing – but it had been fun. How long since he'd felt that unpredictability? That he'd woken up having to figure out the night before. How long since he'd had choices?

He got out of the shower, made a pot of coffee while listening to 6 Music, relishing it all the more because he knew Cat hated it. Then he walked down the hill to Taff's Well station. A twenty-minute stroll and, on a fine morning like this, he enjoyed it. He got the train to Cardiff Central, walked over the bridge to reclaim his car and drove out to Sully.

Hattie wasn't quite ready so Gethin accepted a cappuccino from his dad's fancy coffee machine. He saw the great pile of Saturday newspapers on the breakfast table and felt one of those powerful hangover blasts of melancholy. Suddenly he was back in Cyncoed in his childhood home, his mum making the breakfast, his dad hidden behind the *Daily Telegraph*. He mostly avoided thinking about his mother, how much he missed her.

'I mentioned your case to someone this morning,' said the Judge, providing a welcome interruption as he placed Gethin's coffee in front of him.

'Uh huh?'

'Yes, Tom Drysdale had something interesting to say.'

Gethin frowned. 'I don't remember seeing his name anywhere in the paperwork.'

'He wasn't involved in that case. He acted for Kelly Rowlands in another matter.'

'Really?' Gethin was interested now.

'He was suing her local health trust. Apparently she had a child who died.'

'Yes, that's right.'

'Tom acted for her and the court found in her favour, not long before she died. Awarded her over two hundred thousand pounds compensation, apparently.'

'Blimey.'

'Before you get too excited, the Trust was appealing the case, and anyway she was planning on giving it all to a meningitis charity. Tom wasn't clear what the latest developments were.'

With this new piece of information buzzing around his head, Gethin drove back home, only half listening to Hattie burble on about how her friend was becoming a vegan and she was thinking of doing the same. His hangover was in full retreat now and he was looking forward to the rest of the day when he pulled into the driveway at ten to twelve, and found Cat already waiting outside, a right face on her. His good mood evaporated at once.

'You're late,' she said. 'Where the hell have you been?'

'I'm not late, you're early. And it's no business of yours but Hattie stayed over at dad's last night, didn't you, love?'

Hattie nodded and glowered at her mum before making a break for the house. Gethin could feel a row coming with crushing inevitability.

'You coming in?' he asked. 'Do you want a coffee or are you heading straight out? Hattie, are you ready to go out with your mum?'

'I'll just be a minute,' said Hattie, 'I need to have a shower.'

'Why didn't you have one at Grandpa's?' asked Gethin.

'His shower's weird. Anyway, I won't be long.'

Gethin made a 'hey what can I do' gesture, but Cat didn't look impressed. 'Fine,' she said, 'I'll come in then.'

Inside Gethin busied himself making a coffee for Cat and a tea for himself. Any more coffee and he felt like he might collapse. The hangover was making a triumphant return. And now he had an angry Cat to deal with. He turned to face her, the conciliatory coffee in his hand.

'Sorry,' she said.

He almost spilt the drink. Cat was never sorry about anything.

'I didn't mean to be rude. I was just worried, you know, when I rang the door and you didn't answer.'

'I was just fetching Hattie.'

'Yes, I know that now. I was just... I don't know. I don't like not knowing what you're doing. Where you both are... I just... I don't know what I thought.'

Gethin stared at her. What did she mean? Did she think he was seeing someone else?

As ever when he saw Cat these days, he didn't know what to say, what to feel. He didn't really trust himself to say anything, so he just handed her the coffee instead.

Cat took it and made a visible effort to pull herself together. He stared at her, his faithless wife. She was, he had to admit, looking great. She'd changed her hair, dyed it all the way blonde, got rid of the encroaching grey. She had revamped her make-up: bold red lipstick, something clever around her eyes. Gethin had a limited understanding of make-up. Her clothes were different too. Younger, trendier. Topshop or Zara, he guessed, not the sensible grown-up places she used to go. And it worked for her. She was still as slim as ever. She didn't look like she was trying too hard or anything. She just looked great. Maybe he'd been holding her back. Maybe they'd been holding each other back.

He was just about to ask if she was okay when she started talking.

'How's the Hopkins case going? Have you started work?'

'Sort of. They're not a friendly bunch, the locals.'

Cat snorted, 'Tell me about it. Who've you met?'

'No one much. Just been to the local pub and, as it was my lucky day, the dead woman's nan was in there. You can imagine how pleased they were to see me.'

'I suppose they like feeling that the guilty man's been locked up for it.'

'Always the way,' agreed Gethin. And it was. In fact it was one of the trickiest features of investigating miscarriages of justice: dealing with the victims, or the victims' families if it was a murder case. They always wanted to believe the guy in prison was the guy who did it. Otherwise it was unbearable.

'You have any idea who might actually have done it?'

Gethin's turn to take a moment. 'Well, the two cops are the obvious ones, I suppose.'

'Yes, of course. But I might have another name for you.'

'How come?'

Cat sipped her coffee. 'You know I said I met Morgan through the rehab group. Well, there was a lot that came up in that particular group. And you know I can't really talk about all the things people say in that situation. I have a duty of care of course. But let's just say it's quite a small world, and everyone knows everyone's business, and Kelly's name came up a few times. Morgan mentioned her and so did this other guy.'

'Another local guy?'

'Not exactly. He's a lecturer at the University of Mid Glamorgan.'

The university was just a mile or two away, in Treforest, the next mining town up the valley. 'Any particular reason you think he's dodgy?'

Cat frowned and shook her head. 'Not really. It's just... It sounds stupid I know, but he makes my flesh crawl. And I know he'd had some kind of affair with the dead girl. He said so once.'

That made Gethin pay attention. Whatever Cat's faults she wasn't prone to hyperbole and she spent her whole working life dealing with all kinds of fucked-up individuals, so if this guy made that much of an impression – and he'd been involved with Kelly – then it was definitely worth checking him out.

'I'll look into it. Can anyone go along to the group?'

'Yeah, if they've got an addiction problem. You'd fit in fine.' She gave him a tight smile. 'Just check the website.'

'What website?' Hattie came into the room, changed into her weekend finery.

'Nothing, love, just work stuff. How does lunch in Carluccio's sound?'

Hattie couldn't repress a slight smile. She loved Carluccio's, thought it was dead sophisticated.

While she put her coat on, Gethin and Cat stood awkwardly by the door.

'How's Nils,' he asked, just to emphasise the chasm between them, give it its name.

'Great,' said Cat, 'he's got a part in this new Welsh TV

series, a Scandi-noir type thing. He plays a villain.' She failed to repress a smile at this.

'Oh yeah? I bet.'

* * *

It was odd being in the house alone. Gethin didn't like it. With Cat gone it was feeling less and less like a family home. Just a place two people slept and ate and used as a base before going off to school or work. It needed more love. Perhaps he should buy some flowers.

He really did have to get to grips with the moving on thing. He'd been expecting Cat and Nils to crash and burn. For Cat to come back with her tail between her legs. But there was no sign of it. Time to get his act together.

He tried to settle to some work on his laptop, researching the case. He decided to see what he could find out about Leanne Batey, Kelly's lover. He needed to find out what had become of her now she was no longer a copper. There were plenty of hits, but all of them just led back to the same old news stories. He kept on scrolling down the references till he found one link that stood out. He wasn't sure if it was her at first. Sure she had an uncommon name, but this was quite an unusual thing for someone to do. Especially a one-time cop.

The link in question was to a site for puppeteers. There was a long list of UK puppet shows and theatres, divided up into children's and adult shows. Halfway down the list of adult-orientated puppet shows he found the name Leanne Batey attached to an outfit called Puppet Freaks – 'the wildest puppet show you'll ever see!'. There was a link through to a website, but when Gethin clicked on it there was only a holding page. He tried googling 'puppet freaks' and got a whole lot of disturbing images, but nothing helpful, so he tried again with 'puppet freaks' and 'Cardiff' and this time he got a link to a page on the Wales Online site.

It was a piece on alternative ideas for hen nights. 'Why not go to a freaky puppet show? Leanne Beethoven's puppet freaks are a long way from the end of the pier. Valleys girl Leanne loves to shock with this show that's strictly for adults only.' There was a contact number and address at the bottom of the piece. The address was familiar. The TextileWorks. It was an old factory full of artists' workshops; he'd gone there once, looking for a present for Cat.

Could it be the same person? It seemed likely. Presumably Leanne Beethoven was just a kind of stage name for Leanne Batey. He considered phoning the number but decided against it, didn't want to give his hand away over the phone. Better to turn up there sometime in person. He knew what policewoman Leanne looked like – the picture had been in the papers plenty of times in connection with the trial. Next time he was passing TextileWorks he'd go in and see if she was around.

Next he tried to see if he could dig up anything on the brother, Ryan. This was less successful. It looked as if he'd played rugby for the South Wales Police a few years earlier, but that was about it.

He had a similarly fruitless stab at finding a Facebook page for Ryan Batey but it looked as if he either didn't have one or it was set to private. Which made sense if you were a copper.

He got up to make a cup of tea and, just as the kettle was boiling, he heard a car pulling up outside. And then Hattie was back, chatting about how she'd seen this boy from school in town, and how embarrassing that was because she was with her mum, and anyway would it be okay if Amy came over for a sleepover? Gethin closed down his laptop and got on with being a parent.

Eight

MONDAY MORNING AND GETHIN, BEX, Lee and Deano were sat round the conference table discussing the case. Bex raised her eyebrows at him as she sat down, but thankfully refrained from any references to Friday night. Instead she had some good news – the money had indeed gone into their account. Then Gethin updated the others on the fiasco at the Four Feathers.

'Just bad luck,' said Lee, 'her nan being there like that. I'll bet if you go back they'll be dying to tell you all about it.'

Gethin nodded, accepting the point. He still didn't much relish the prospect of a return visit. He looked round at Deano, who was fiddling with his Apple watch. He looked younger somehow and Gethin wasn't quite sure why. Then he got it. Deano had trimmed his beard so it looked a lot neater. Maybe we'd passed peak hipster. 'How about Ryan Batey then? You had any luck catching up with him?'

Deano looked up, making it seem like a major effort. 'Nah, I usually see him at the gym, like, but he hasn't been there the last few days. Someone said they thought he was on a stag.'

'Ah right. Any chance of finding his address? I know it'll be tricky.'

Deano tapped the side of his nose. 'One step ahead of you, boss. I didn't know before, 'cause he's just one of those guys I see around. Don't like him much – he's dead arrogant and you don't really know what he's got to be so arrogant about. Typical copper, though, to be fair. Anyway, so I goes up to Charl who's on the reception and I give her some crap about how I borrowed an iPad off him and I need to drop it round his house but he forgot to tell me where it was. And Charl, she's obviously not supposed to give out that kind of info, but we were at primary school together and she likes me and that, so she just digs in the computer and writes it out for me. Looks like it's one of those new blocks off Dumballs Road.'

'Nice one, might be worth popping round there this evening. Should be back from a stag by Monday night, I'd have thought.'

'Fine,' said Deano. Then his watch beeped. He looked at it, stood up quickly and headed out the door with his customary lack of interest in letting anyone know what he was up to.

Gethin watched him go, then turned to the others: 'How about you, Lee? Any word on Leanne? Picked anything up on the grapevine?'

'You talking about the lesbian grapevine, Geth? The hand-knitted purple one?'

'You know what I mean.'

'Whatever. And yeah, I did ask about a bit in the Kings. Nobody seemed to know the copper. There's one or two knew the dead girl. Apparently she was hard to miss with the tats and that.'

'Anything interesting?'

'Not really. Don't think any of them knew her properly.'

'Fair enough. We do need to find Leanne though. Bex, can you see if you can find an address for her on the net?'

'Sure.' Bex started tapping away.

Gethin thought about mentioning the puppet theatre thing but decided not to. He'd go and check it out in person. 'Any ideas, Lee?'

'Tell you what, Geth, I reckon the best thing I can do is head up to Abertridwr and have a bit of a nose around, see if anyone knows anything they didn't want to tell the coppers. Lot of people don't have much love for the law up there.'

Gethin looked at her askance. 'And you think they'll talk to you?' He felt a bit bad as he said it, the implication being that places like Abertridwr were chock-full of racists who wouldn't talk to someone who looked like Lee, but there it was.

'Course they will. Got family there, haven't I?'

'Really?'

'Yeah, it's where my mum was from.'

'Oh,' said Gethin, 'right.'

Lee didn't talk much about her mum. As far as Gethin knew most of Lee's childhood had been spent in a children's home. Her mum hadn't wanted to keep her. Or maybe she'd been taken away by the social services. He wasn't quite sure and never liked to ask. But if Lee was cool with going up there...

'Fine then, you have a nose around. And Bex?'

'Yeah? Oh hang on a mo, phone's going.'

Bex went off to answer the office landline.

'How about you, boss?'

'I'll get on with sorting out a forensic expert and...' Gethin knew there was another lead he wanted to follow up: 'Cat told me about a rehab group Morgan Hopkins was in. She said there was another guy in the group who struck her as a serious wrong 'un.'

'Sounds promising. So you and Cat are talking again?'

'Kind of. She's still with the dick though.'

'You want him taught a lesson, boss? 'Cause I can sort it for you any time.'

Gethin laughed. The first time Lee had mentioned she could have one of her dubious associates break Nils Hofberg's legs he'd been sorely tempted, but reluctantly accepted that it would only make things worse. And if Cat found out...

Right then there was the beep of a text coming in. He looked at his phone. Cat. Jesus, it was like she'd wiretapped his thoughts. The text was about the rehab group. There was a meeting at three that afternoon, in a community centre in Treforest. 'Don't worry. I'm not leading it any more' she added, along with a winking emoji. Hmm, they were back on emoji terms, it seemed.

Gethin relayed the news to Lee.

'Good one,' she said. 'Why don't you go along and have a look? I'll head up to the ancestral homelands and start shaking the trees.'

As Lee left, Bex came back into the conference room, holding a piece of paper.

'Looks like we've got another job, Geth.'

'What is it?'

'Another phoner.'

Gethin nodded. Phone evidence was a big feature in modern-day trials. And there'd been a whole bunch of cases thrown out of court recently because the police hadn't bothered to disclose all the evidence on people's phones. Rape cases particularly. Made a big difference when there was a whole bunch of texts between the accuser and the accused.

'So who's the unfortunate victim of institutional incompetence then?'

Bex looked down at her notes. 'Feller called Tyrone Horan, scrap metal dealer out by Wentloog.'

Which information pretty much guaranteed he'd be from Traveller stock. 'Oh yeah, what's he been done for?'

'Selling stolen goods. He had about a mile of copper cabling used to belong to BT. Cops had a big crackdown last year – called it Operation Copper for a laugh, you remember?'

'Vaguely.'

'Anyway, what our boy Tyrone says is that he was set up. An undercover copper went on and on at him to buy this cable, claimed it was totally kosher. The second he handed over the cash half a dozen squad cars show up like they're busting Al Capone.'

Gethin nodded. It all sounded perfectly plausible. 'And the relevance of the phone?'

'He reckons there'll be loads of text messages on there from the undercover copper. He says he told his brief at the time to check it out, but didn't get anywhere. Police just claimed there was nothing of interest on the phone.'

'Fine, sounds like he's got a case. And he might even have a few quid for us?'

'Yeah, obviously he asked if we could do a no-win no-fee and I told him we didn't play that way. So he said he could put a couple of grand down and see how we go.'

'Fair enough. Can you get on to his brief, get things going?'

'Yep, will do.' Bex paused. 'Looked like you were having a good time with Chrissie.'

'Uh huh,' said Gethin, suddenly embarrassed and trying to figure out how much Bex might have seen.

'Yeah she's great, Chrissie. Only I'd be a bit careful if I were you.'

'Oh yeah.'

'Did she mention she had a boyfriend?'

Gethin nodded, feeling like a guilty schoolboy for all that he was nearly old enough to be Bex's dad.

'Well they don't live together or anything, but he's a right psycho by all accounts so...'

'Right,' said Gethin, swallowing. 'Ta.'

'Cool, just thought you'd better know.'

With that Bex headed off to work the phones and Gethin settled down to reading through more of the trial records from the Kelly Rowlands case, using the information there to add to the timeline of the last days of her life. It was only when he'd been engaged in the task for a couple of hours that something struck him. Or rather the absence of something. Where were the phone records? There were some edited quotes that came up in the police interviews with Morgan. He was asked about texts he'd sent Kelly. But where was the full record of the messages on Kelly's phones? Maybe there was nothing else of interest there. He wanted to see for himself, though, before taking it on trust. He bashed out an email to Hopkins' brief, Harry Vickers, first explaining that they were now on the case, and second asking if he had the complete phone records and, if so, could he mail them over?

* * *

The Treforest community centre was a typically squat 1990s building on the edge of an industrial estate. The number of women exiting pushing buggies, as Gethin tried to make his way indoors, confirmed that its primary function was still providing childcare. On the front door there was a poster advertising 'Tumble Tots'.

Gethin went up to the receptionist: 'I believe there's a rehab group session here?'

The receptionist, a cheery young girl with badly dyed hair, nodded enthusiastically. 'Yes. Getting It Together. They're in room three – down there on the right.' Then she looked over his shoulder and called out. 'Hey, Steve, got someone here for your group.'

Gethin turned round to see a bloke in his late thirties, who looked more like a sports coach than a mental health professional. The guy, Steve, stuck out his hand. Gethin was about to explain who he was and what he was doing, when it struck him that that was highly unlikely to do any good. No one was going to encourage you to invade the privacy of their clients, were they?

'So what's your problem?' asked Steve. Then he broke out in an annoying grin. 'Don't worry, just a joke. I'm Steve

Ridley. I run the group here. You're interested in coming along, yeah?'

'I think so,' said Gethin. 'I have,' he took a deep breath, 'I have a gambling problem and, well, it's a struggle not giving into it so, I thought...'

'That's a very brave decision. And welcome, you've come to the right place...'

'Gethin.'

'Good to meet you, Gethin. You'll find this is a very supportive group. So why don't you come with me and meet everyone.'

Gethin followed Steve along the corridor and into room three. Inside were a bunch of blokes and a couple of women sat on plastic chairs. The blokes were mostly keeping as far away from each other as possible, while the two women had their heads together chatting. At the back of the room there was a makeshift tea counter, sporting a couple of those thermos jugs that reliably keep coffee lukewarm and a plate of bourbons. There was another gaggle of addicts standing in front of it, all looking like they wished to Christ you were still allowed to smoke indoors.

'Hiya,' said Steve, as they walked in. 'How's everyone? As you can see we have a newcomer with us today.'

A few of the group turned round to inspect the new arrival.

'I'm Gethin,' he said.

'Hi, Gethin,' said one of the bunch standing by the tea bar, a tall, bald man with serious glasses and a neat goatee. 'Can I pour you a cup of this appalling tea? I'm afraid there's none of the repellent coffee available this week.'

Gethin figured this had to be the Prof. He accepted a tea then Steve suggested they all sit down and do some quick introductions.

First up were a couple of interchangeable middle-aged guys, Bryn and Darren. Both of them looked the wrong side of sixty but Gethin had a nasty suspicion they might really be his own age.

Then came the first of the women: a mumsy-looking woman with blonde highlights and make-up failing to quite cover up the red patches on her face. 'I'm Theresa.'

Gethin did his best to give her an encouraging smile.

Next in line was the presumable prof. 'Hi, I'm Philip. And just in case you're wondering what my problem is, I'm afraid I'm just a common or garden alkie.'

Two more guys. A skinny young man in his twenties, who looked exactly like you expected a Valleys junkie to look. One thing Gethin had learned in life – nine times out of ten you really can judge a book by the cover.

Then came a guy probably in his early forties, wiry and sharply dressed in a good suit with a smart shirt but no tie, and his hair cut in a style Gethin associated with the cooler sort of footballer: short back and sides, longer on top but heavily gelled with a severe side parting. He radiated self-satisfaction and Gethin hated him on sight. 'I'm Mark,' he said: a northern accent. 'And yeah, I'm here because I'm told I have a sex addiction.'

Gethin wondered if Cat had got it wrong. At first impression this guy was the one to watch: there was something really off about him, the obvious passive-aggressive resentment.

Finally, the second woman spoke up. She'd been sitting at a subtle but distinct distance from the rest of them, her head down so her hair covered her face. 'I'm Ella,' she said, 'and I hope you'll have a good experience here...' Her voice, a gentle drawl with a slight accent, Australian perhaps, tailed off and Gethin noticed with a jolt that she was beautiful – a picture book pre-Raphaelite damsel with long gently curly red hair and the palest of skin. She was way too delicate-looking to be in the room with this bunch of fuck-ups.

And now it was his turn.

'Hi everyone,' he said, 'I'm Gethin and I'm a compulsive gambler.' It was weird saying it out loud. He'd imagined it in the past, going to a meeting – Gamblers Anonymous or whatever – and saying those words. He'd read a few books by ex-alcoholics over the years and they always went on about what an amazing moment it was, when you came out and said it. And now here he was saying it and it was like he was two people at once – one of them was an actor playing a part, a slick undercover detective type. And the other was him, Gethin, a compulsive gambler who'd fucked up his life. And suddenly, out of nowhere, he was welling up.

Steve waited a beat for Gethin to compose himself: 'Well, you're welcome here, Gethin. None of us are going to judge you. Just one question: how long have you been clean, as it were?'

Gethin thought about it. 'Three months, more or less.'

'Well done. Are you ready to share some of your story with us? There's no pressure. If you just want to be in the room and let the others talk, then that's fine too. This is a safe space. No one is going to make you talk about anything you don't want to.'

'Oh right, okay. Well I won't go on. I expect you all know what it's like. Started out recreationally then it got compulsive yadda yadda.' He paused. 'It wasn't like I did it all the time, but when I did there was no stopping me. I'd just carry on till I'd lost everything, till I'd fucked up everything I could. I don't know, does that sound familiar to any of you?'

There were a couple of grunts and a 'yes absolutely' from the Prof.

'I suppose I didn't think of it as an addiction really. 'Cause it wasn't like I did it every day. I wasn't going in the bookies, playing the fixed odds machines. I've never played online poker in my life. Too smart for that, you know.' He tried a little laugh that was meant to be self-mocking, but it came out a bit loud and hysterical. 'It was just something that happened occasionally. I can go years in between... Till it was... too... too...'

'Like you're saving it all up.' It was the woman, the beautiful one, Ella. 'I know how that feels.'

'Yeah,' said Gethin, 'I suppose you're right.' She was too. Day by day he was mostly a pretty calm person. He drank but rarely got drunk, took drugs even more rarely, give or take the other night with Chrissie. He had never been a compulsive womaniser, also ditto with Chrissie. Up till just lately he'd had Cat, and that was enough for him. All good, right?

Except every so often he'd feel this kind of subterranean pressure building inside him and he'd get the itch, the casino itch. The urge to take whatever money he had, or his bank would allow him access to, and risk it all gambling face to face. The cliché about gamblers is that really they want to lose and Gethin knew it was true of him. But why did he do it? It wasn't like he was unhappy in his life. In most ways he loved his life. And yet again and again he'd risked screwing it all up. He'd relied on Cat to pick up the pieces, keep the family together.

'So what happened to bring you here?'

It was Steve asking the question. Gethin looked around, realised he'd been lost in his own thoughts and immediately felt guilty, like he was taking up their precious time dealing with their problems, while he was just an impostor. Except he wasn't.

'My wife left me,' he said. There was a chorus of sympathetic murmuration.

And then the session moved on. One of the alkies – Darren or possibly Bryn – started talking about how he'd nearly had a relapse. A collective sigh of relief and some rote positive feedback from Steve. Then Theresa launched into a long story about nothing very much and Gethin found himself zoning out, only coming back to the scene in front of him when he realised the baton had been passed to Mark the northern sex addict.

Mark leant forward with his hands clasped together. 'Okay, as most of you know I'm pretty cynical about how much use any of this is. Sorry, Geraint' – he looked over at Gethin who gave him the sort of smile you give people you've taken an immediate dislike to and who can't even get your name right – 'maybe it'll work for you. But since I'm here I may as well talk about what's going on with me.'

Steve gave him a nod of approval.

'So it's the students again. Just like usual.'

Gethin sat back in his chair, realising he'd made a mistake. Clearly Mark was the Prof, not the guy who acted like a prof. He was pretty happy with this discovery.

'First off I want to stress that I haven't done anything. But it's hard. They come for their tutorials and they're so bloody eager, have such faith in my knowledge, and they so much want my approval... Anyway, this girl was visiting my office discussing her geography essay. This particular one was about climate change in South America – it's always about climate change these days – and this girl, this Olivia, she was so passionate about it all, how terrible it all is, and she expected me to be just as passionate, as I'm the one who told her about all this terrible stuff going on in the world. And she's all noble and outraged and nineteen, and me, I'm just looking down her top and I can see that she has these amazing breasts and all I'm thinking of is...'

There was a cough at this point; Ella, Gethin thought, and he was profoundly grateful for it, because it stopped Mark's flow, before he got any more carried away.

Then the other guy, the one he'd originally taken for the Prof, Philip, stepped in. 'Mark, you know we have to be careful how we talk about our vices here. We need to hold them at a distance, not get swept up in their intoxicating powers.'

'Sorry, sorry, you're right.' Mark took a deep breath. 'Obviously you can all see what I'm getting at. I had this girl in my office and all I wanted to do was make a move, which I would have done in the past.' He held his hands up in a gesture of apology. 'Don't worry I'm not going to tell you about all that again – but the point is I didn't. And you know what stopped me? He paused for effect, looking around the room but held it a little too long.

'Tell us, Mark.' Steve the coach.

'There was something Morgan said to me once, right here in this room.'

Morgan? He had to be talking about Morgan Hopkins, Gethin figured. Certainly there was a new kind of hush in the room, a definite tension. He was sure of it. He leaned forward to hear what came next.

'He told me not to be such a wanker!'

The room erupted in laughter. But when it finished there was an awkward silence. Gethin decided he could get away with filling it.

'Who's Morgan?'

The group exchanged glances then Steve stepped in: 'He used to be part of the group.'

Gethin wondered whether to push further but decided against it. Instead, Steve took the chance to bring the meeting to an end. 'Though as ever we have the room for an extra half-hour, so if any of you want to stay and chat, that's fine. I'll see you next week.'

Everyone stayed silent till Steve left the room, Gethin flashing all the way back to his schooldays, waiting for teacher to leave so the mischief could begin. Most of the others filed out pretty quickly though.

Gethin caught Philip and Ella smirking at each other as Mark left.

'He really ought to find himself another job,' said Philip. 'It's like an alcoholic working in a pub.'

'One more complaint and he'll be out of a job and unemployable,' added Ella.

Philip handed out fresh cups of tea and the three of them stood around the urn.

'So what brought you here, Gethin?' asked Philip

'Um, like I said in the meeting,' started Gethin, a little nonplussed.

'No, sorry, what I meant was where did you hear about us? Not Gamblers Anonymous was it? I don't think I've seen you there. I have a certain history in that department too.'

Gethin thought quickly, He'd been going to say it was Gamblers Anon if anyone asked, so thank Christ Philip had saved him from that pitfall.

'It was my psychiatrist actually.'

'Who's that?' asked Ella. 'I mean you don't have to say, it's just that between us we've seen most of them.'

'That's fine,' said Gethin. 'It's Catriona Douglas.' Thankfully Cat used her maiden name for work. 'She thought I could benefit from sharing my issues in a group setting.' Well, that was true all right.

'Oh, that sounds like our Catriona,' said Philip. 'You know this whole group was her idea?'

'No,' said Gethin, 'I don't think she mentioned that.'

'She's very discreet. It's such a shame she doesn't have the time for us anymore. We miss her, don't we, Ella?'

'Mm hmm,' said Ella, not sounding completely convinced, Gethin thought.

'Steve can't quite measure up really, can he? You know he used to be a rugby coach?'

Gethin didn't say anything just smiled, pleased that his characterisation of Coach Steve had been on the money.

'Yes, he loves all that motivational stuff. Him and

Morgan, always looking for a snappy slogan. "Getting It Together", our ridiculous new rubric. That was one of theirs.'

'They knew each other, you know.' Darren joined in their conversation. 'Outside of here, I mean.'

'Really?' said Ella, 'Steve and Morgan? I never heard that.'

'Yeah, they both played for Tonteg. Morgan was in the scrum, Steve was fly half. He goes to visit him every month apparently.'

'Sorry,' said Gethin, hoping he could pitch it right, 'this is the guy who used to be part of the group, yeah?'

'That's right,' said Darren, 'Morgan Hopkins, he is. You must have heard about him. The murder case.'

Gethin caught Philip giving Darren a look, like 'why don't you shut up about this?', but too late, he had his opening now. Anyone would have a few questions on hearing that sort of news.

'Christ, yeah I heard about that on the news. Wow. I mean he was found guilty, right?'

'He's not guilty.' Ella, quietly.

'Oh?' Gethin turned to look at her but she avoided his eyes, just stared unhappily off to one side.

Philip took charge, as was clearly his wont. 'This isn't really a subject we should be discussing here. The whole point is just to be in the room without the outside world impinging. We only know of each other what we bring to the room. You don't know what I do for a living. I don't know what you do for a living, do I, Gethin?'

Was he suspicious? Gethin decided to play it straight. 'Yeah sorry, this is all new to me. I don't really understand how it works, but I'm sure I'll pick it up.'

Philip nodded and ostentatiously drained his tea, like time to go folks. Ella followed his lead.

Nine

OUTSIDE THE COMMUNITY CENTRE GETHIN checked his messages. There was a missed call and a text from Lee.

He phoned her back and she picked up immediately.

'Hiya, Geth. You got to come over.'

'Over where?'

'Abertridwr. Where are you?'

'Treforest.'

'Get here quick as you can. Meet me by the clock, there's someone I want you to see.'

Abertridwr on a warmish autumn afternoon. This time the shop had customers. There were school kids mucking about outside the chippie. As he drove across the main junction, looking for somewhere to park, he saw Lee standing by the town clock, sucking on a vape.

There was a space outside Londis, so he pulled over.

She opened the passenger door and slid into the seat. 'Bloody hell, Geth, I've got a weird lead for us.'

'What are you talking about?'

'You'll see, just drive up the high street and take the second left.'

Gethin did as he was told, went past a pub and down a standard issue Victorian terrace: two-up two-downs built cheaply and quickly for the influx of miners and somehow still standing 130 years later.

'Over there.' Lee was pointing to a house halfway along the terrace. Gethin parked opposite. The house in question had evidently once been a little shop, having a big front window that marked it out from its neighbours. The other thing that distinguished it was a banner hung across the window saying 'The Church of the Unpoisoned Mind'.

Gethin looked round at Lee and raised his eyebrows.

'That's where she lived. Kelly. Inside there is where she was killed.'

'Jesus. So what's with the weird sign?'

'That's the thing. I don't suppose I've ever mentioned my cousin Dennis?'

'No. To be honest you don't talk a whole lot about this bit of your family.' Or any of her family, really. Lee lived in the present.

'So I'm back here this morning, going to see my mum and getting the usual welcome. Like "What the fuck are you doing coming here and making me feel all guilty again?" So then I tells her not to worry, I'm not after the family silver – like there's any of that – and I started asking about the Kelly Rowlands business and obviously she's dying to talk about all that, loves a bit of gossip my old ma, but it's all the same old bollocks from the trial, nothing new as far as I could see, like. But then she says: "You know your cousin Dennis is living in the house now?" And I'm trying to remember who the fuck cousin Dennis is and then I remember he's the religious nutter used to go to chapel five times a day, and spent the rest of the time hanging around outside the primary school giving books to the older girls.'

'Wow,' said Gethin, 'he sounds like…'

'A total nutter, yeah. But don't take my word for it. Let's go visit.'

Lee led the way over the road, rang on the doorbell to no audible effect, then banged on the door.

After a few seconds the door opened and Gethin got his first sight of Lee's cousin.

Cousin Dennis was close on six foot, tall for the Valleys, dressed in black trousers and black jumper. He was a little overweight and of absolutely indeterminate age – he could be anywhere between thirty and sixty. He had a big completely bald head and a shiny, unlined face – looked a bit like an albino pumpkin.

'Oh,' he said, staring fixedly at Lee. 'Oh.' He looked perturbed at first, but then his face broke into a strange genuinely childlike grin and he giggled delightedly before saying, in a child's sing-song voice, 'I know who you are. I know who you are.'

Lee gave him a look, like she was prepared to tolerate this up to a point.

'So who am I then?'

'You're the harlot's daughter. You're the one cursed with the blackness of sin.'

Gethin had seen Lee break a man's arm once for less than that, but on this occasion she just seemed amused. 'Well it's a relief that there's someone around here brave enough to say what the rest of them are thinking. You going to ask us in then?'

'Yes, of course,' he giggled again. 'You can join my congregation.'

Dennis led the way inside and into the front room.

It was dark there. The window was covered up by a sheet, and the light switch failed to respond when Gethin tried it.

'Sorry,' said Dennis, 'it's been cut off.' He walked over to a Welsh dresser, set against the far wall. It was covered in candles and seemed to have been converted into some sort of altar. Dennis fussed around finding some matches and lighting the wicks. As he did so Gethin looked around, his eyes adjusting to the murk.

The sheet covering the front window bore a painted slogan. 'In JC we trust.' On the side wall, above the fireplace, was a painting that looked to have been done by a moderately talented child. It depicted a white-bearded individual with the initials JC beneath it. Next to it, pinned to the wall, was a series of newspaper cuttings, all of them featuring Jeremy Corbyn. JC himself, presumably.

Lee had evidently spotted them too. 'Hey, Cuz,' she said, 'is this the church of St Jeremy then?'

Dennis didn't answer at first. He had just finished lighting the candles and was admiring their effect. Then, apparently satisfied, he gave Lee his alarmingly open grin one more time.

'Not quite, daughter of sin, but nearly. Jeremy is indeed a saint, but he is not the Messiah, he is a modern-day John the Baptist, preparing the way of the true Messiah, whose identity the world will soon know.'

Gethin stared at Dennis. Trying to decide whether he was being remotely serious or whether this was just some bizarre wind-up. Then he noticed the wall just to the right of the fireplace. In the extra light provided by the candle he could see there was a splatter of rust-coloured drips. At first he was just depressed by the level of housekeeping neglect that had allowed these stains to remain on the walls. Then he felt a prickling along his spine and an awful suspicion forming in his head.

'These stains,' he said, pointing at the wall.

'The blood of the harlot,' said Dennis and giggled again, the sound now less childlike, more flat out crazy.

'Dennis,' said Lee, 'you fucking psycho. That's her blood. You haven't just left it there?'

'So others might learn. Learn the wages of sin.'

'You what?'

'Don't worry. She died in purity.'

Lee gave Dennis a death stare but he didn't appear to notice.

'She refused fornication at the last. She sacrificed herself to the male evil.'

Gethin was starting to feel faint. The oddness, to put it

mildly, of Dennis, the blood on the wall, the flickering light of the candles, at least one of which seemed to be scented with something unpleasant.

'Is there somewhere else we could sit,' he said, waving his hand at the room, 'away from all this?'

'As you wish,' said Dennis and moved towards the door.

Before he left the room Gethin took a quick look at the makeshift altar. There were more pictures on display. Jeremy Corbyn again. The missing child Madeleine McCann. A still from the old silent movie of Joan of Arc. There were also a couple of books, displayed with their covers facing outwards. One was called *The Streetcleaner* and had a picture of the Yorkshire Ripper on the front. The other was called *Pornography: Men Possessing Women*, written by Andrea Dworkin, a feminist writer Gethin dimly remembered. A colour picture lying on the floor caught his eyes just as he was leaving. It was Jodie Foster playing a child prostitute in *Taxi Driver*. He placed it face down on the altar, and couldn't repress a shudder as he came out into the hall.

The back room was set up as a dining room with a little kitchen beyond. In the absence of electric light it was horrendously gloomy. To make matters worse the walls were covered in a toddler's primitive drawings, a reminder that Kelly had once had a little boy.

The dinner table was covered in a mess of newspapers and magazines, plus the odd pizza box and empty chocolate biscuit packet. Dennis walked over to it and started digging into one of the piles of paper. His hand emerged bearing a clutch of letters.

'These are hers,' he said. 'I need to pass them to the next of kin, but I'm not sure who that is.' He gave Lee a searching look. 'Do you know?'

'Not sure,' she said, 'probably her husband, if she was still married, but I'm not sure. Geth?'

'As far as I know she was. Can I have a look?'

Dennis frowned and held on tight to the letters. He held them out towards Gethin but wouldn't let go. Several of them were serious-looking A4 envelopes, probably legal matters of one sort or another. 'Would you like me to pass them along?'

Dennis shook his head firmly. 'They are my responsibility. I will carry out my duty. Thank you for explaining it to me.'

The three of them stood there in silence for a moment and Gethin became uncomfortably aware of a faint smell of rot in the air. Rationally he knew it couldn't possibly be Kelly's dead body, but once the thought had entered his mind he couldn't shake it.

He looked round at Lee to see how she was faring. She wrinkled her nose at him.

Part of Gethin just wanted to bolt but another part was starting to wonder if Dennis might have something useful to tell them. Or indeed whether he might have had something to do with her death. It was hard to think of him as a potential murderer. He looked pallid and puny but ultimately he was still a big bloke and, however out of shape, he was bound to be stronger than a small woman like Kelly.

'You mind if we go outside?' Gethin said, eyeing a small back yard just visible from the dining room window. 'I think your cousin here could do with a smoke.'

Lee rolled her eyes at this but didn't complain. Once they were out in the back yard, Gethin started to feel a little less freaked out.

'So, Dennis,' he said, doing his best to sound casual, 'did you know Kelly Rowlands then?'

Dennis peered at Gethin as if seeing him for the first time. 'Excuse me, who are you?'

'I'm Gethin, I'm a legal investigator.'

Dennis seemed a bit panicked by this piece of news, and looked round at Lee.

'He's my boss.'

'Oh,' said Dennis, 'thank God for that. I was worried he might be your boyfriend, that you might have strayed from the path of purity.'

Lee stared at her cousin, baffled, then she laughed. 'Well I've never heard being a dyke called that before.'

'Oh but it is,' said Dennis, very earnest. 'It is the only alternative to the way of sin. If only Kelly had listened to me. If she had just stayed with that nice policewoman then none of this would have happened.'

'So you did know her?'

Dennis turned back to Gethin. 'Of course. Everybody knew Kelly. She was our golden girl. That's what my mother called her.'

'So when did you see her last?'

'I don't know. Not long before…'

'What? The same week? The same day?'

Dennis looked stricken: 'I don't like you. Please stop asking me questions.' He turned back to Lee. 'I won't talk to him. I'll talk to you but not now. I'm feeling upset. Can you both leave now?'

Gethin was in two minds whether to push harder or retreat, but before he could decide Lee took charge.

'No worries, Cuz. I'll see you soon. And say hello to your mum.'

'No.' Dennis giggled again. 'I don't think I'd better do that. She doesn't approve of you. She's old-fashioned about that sort of thing.'

Lee led the way back through the dining room and into the hall. By the front door Gethin noticed a big pile of copies of the Andrea Dworkin book on pornography. Dennis must've seen him staring at them: 'That's the good book. Would you like one?'

'No thanks,' said Gethin.

'That's a shame. You can learn a lot, I'm sure.'

And then Gethin and Lee were back out on the street, crossing the road to the car.

'Fucking hell, Lee. Has he always been like that?'

Lee didn't answer. She just pointed at the car. The windscreen was shattered.

Ten

GETHIN DROPPED LEE OFF AT Treforest station. He'd offered to drive her all the way back home, but it was so unpleasant sitting in the car with the wind whistling into their faces she said she'd sooner catch the train, thanks very much. Gethin wasn't arguing. It meant he would be able to pick Hattie up a little earlier than normal, then get home and call the emergency windscreen people to come and fix up the car.

On the short drive over the hill, they discussed Cousin Dennis some more. Lee confirmed that he'd always been a weirdo, but had struck her as completely harmless. Then again she'd only met him a few times before.

Gethin was really struggling to make sense of him. His instincts were to go along with Lee, see him as just a harmless nutter. But there was definitely a weird obsession with female sexuality. And, weirdest of all, he was actually living in the house where it happened, with the dead woman's blood on the walls. Then again, surely the actual killer wouldn't be crazy enough to squat in the house in which he had committed the crime.

They decided not to rule out Cousin Dennis. Lee would go back there in the next few days and see if she could get some more out of him. Find out what he was doing on the day of the murder, if possible.

Lee caught the train and Gethin drove up the side of the valley to Gwaelod Y Garth.

He parked the car outside the house, then walked

around to Martina's to pick up Hattie. He didn't want to show up there with a missing windscreen. When he arrived Hattie and Alys were apparently working on some project for school and absolutely needed another fifteen minutes. Martina asked Gethin if he'd like a cup of tea 'or maybe a glass of wine?'

Gethin hesitated. He felt very much like a glass of wine after the afternoon he'd had, but he wasn't sure whether the offer was one of those that were made simply out of politeness, and that you were meant to refuse. He didn't want Martina to think he was some sort of alkie either. On the other hand he really did want a drink; Cousin Dennis and the brick through the windscreen were surely excuse enough.

'A glass of wine would be great actually, but only if you've got a bottle open.'

'Always!' said Martina with a big smile. 'White okay?'

'Sure.'

Martina went over to the fridge and pulled out a bottle, unscrewed the top and poured out a couple of glasses. She passed one to Gethin then chinked her glass against his.

'Cheers.'

'Cheers,' said Gethin and took a big slurp, while trying to think of something to say. A worry assailed him. Was Martina interested in him? Christ he hoped not. It was weird being effectively single again. Especially since the roles seemed to have reversed a bit in the intervening twenty years. When he'd got together with Cat, way back when, it was still pretty much a matter of blokes chasing after girls. Now though, in the age of internet dating, there were loads of middle-aged blokes getting off with younger girls, and an increasing pool of women Gethin's age who'd been dumped by their partners and were on the lookout.

Cat hadn't been gone a week before a neighbour he barely knew – name of Bethan, had a daughter in the same class as

Hattie – came round with a casserole: 'I didn't like to think of you all on your own without any home cooking'. Gethin had been outraged at first – why did she assume he couldn't cook? – then confused. It was Hattie who'd pointed out that Bethan was a single mum and obviously on the lookout.

So now he was on the alert. And he knew Martina's husband was two years gone. He was a pro-vice-chancellor at the uni in Treforest. He'd wandered off with someone in the marketing department apparently.

But just because she was single again, and not necessarily happy about it, didn't mean she was after him specifically. Sometimes, most times surely, a glass of wine is a glass of wine. Definitely that's how he'd play it. And anyway he'd just thought of something to ask her about.

'Have you ever come across a geography lecturer at the uni called Mark? Snappy dresser, one of those footballer haircuts?'

Martina thought about it, then screwed up her face in obvious distaste. 'Yes,' she said, then paused, 'Mark Lewis. He's not a friend of yours, is he?'

'No,' said Gethin, 'not at all.'

'I don't like him. He's one of those guys, you know. You hear rumours about him and students. Though he is very active in the union, so I guess he's not all bad. He's a friend of Cedwyn's, so perhaps I'm a bit prejudiced.'

Cedwyn was Martina's estranged husband. Gethin offered up what he hoped was a sympathetic grin.

'So why do you ask? Is he in trouble?'

'I just met him in the course of an investigation I'm working on.'

'The Kelly Rowlands murder? Cat told me you were working on it. I hope you don't mind?'

'Not at all,' said Gethin, registering that Marina and Cat were clearly still in touch.

'So is Mark involved in some way?'

Martina looked eager now, excited. 'Not as far as I know. I mean I'm sure he's not. It was really just a chance encounter. Please don't think he's a suspect or anything.' Christ he was probably making it worse with all these denials. Chances were it would be all over the uni by lunchtime tomorrow.

He made a heavy-handed attempt to change the subject. 'So how is Alys getting on at school? Does she hate the new English teacher as much as Hattie?'

* * *

As they walked back along the lane Hattie went quiet before asking a question with obviously forced casualness.

'What do you think of Martina, Dad?'

'Well, I think she's very nice.' He paused then, watching Hattie's eyes widen. 'But I'm not romantically interested, if that's what you're wondering.'

Hattie actually sighed with relief. 'Oh thank God for that, Dad, I mean it would just be so embarrassing if you were, like, with one of my friends' mums, I mean God. I just saw the two of you there drinking wine and I was a bit worried.'

It was Gethin's turn to go quiet then. What to say? On the one hand, he didn't want Hattie to think she had some kind of say as to who he dated, surely that was his private business. But on the other hand, it sort of was her business too. He was going to have to be careful.

'Look, love,' he said eventually, 'I'm not looking for a new relationship. As far as I'm concerned I'm still married to your mum so...'

'Hah. She's such a bitch!'

Gethin managed to resist the temptation to agree and put on his best stern voice instead: 'Don't call your mother that.'

'Well, she is.'

91

Father and daughter both fell silent this time. It was only when they were coming up the final incline to the house that Hattie spoke again. 'I think he's evil.'

Gethin looked at her, surprised and wondering who she was talking about. Morgan Hopkins, maybe? Perhaps she'd been finding out about the case. Or had she heard him talking to Martina about Mark Lewis? No, that didn't make sense. 'Sorry, who's evil?'

'Stupid Nils, of course. I think mum's afraid of him.'

'What d'you mean?'

'The other day when she took me out, we were in Carluccio's and her phone rang and it was him and I could see on her face that she was all scared and tense when she was talking to him. She kept apologising for something. She was like totally different to when she talks to you on the phone.'

'Oh, Hattie, love. They probably just had a row or something. I'm sure she's not afraid of him. I've never seen your mum afraid of anyone.'

That seemed to satisfy Hattie, and once back in the house she went off to her room happily enough. Gethin poured himself another glass of white wine and pondered. He tried not to think too much about Cat and Nils, how they were together. Mostly he tried not to think about it because he assumed it must be the sex that was the thing. What else would have made Cat skip out on her family? Well, there was anger and boredom, of course. They might have made her leave him. They might even explain why she first started seeing Nils. But leaving the house, going to live with Nils, that was something else and what else could explain it except sex?

But what Hattie said about her being afraid, could that be true? Nils was such a selfish prick that surely they'd have rows – when they weren't having the mind-blowing sex. He tried to imagine Cat being scared of Nils, then quickly banished the thought; it was too emotionally confusing. He didn't want to feel sorry for Cat – in some ways she was getting what she deserved. And yet part of him felt like leaping to her rescue, going round and threatening Nils, beating Nils to a bloody pulp.

* * *

Settling back to work, Gethin returned to the transcripts of Morgan Hopkins' trial, beginning with the prosecution case. He made notes as he read, looking for any little details that hadn't made it into the press coverage. When he finished he organised his notes into a summary.

Kelly Rowlands had been murdered on a Sunday night around 11 pm. Morgan Hopkins had come over in the morning and they'd had sex. Kelly had spent the afternoon at her mother's house nearby, having Sunday lunch. She returned home around six. Her neighbours had heard her come in and start listening to loud punk music. Her next-door neighbour said this was something she was prone to do if she was a bit down and had had a few drinks. 'And there was no point in complaining, she'd just tell you to fuck off. So I just turned the telly up and tried to ignore it. She always apologised the next day, like.' This hypothesis was borne out by the post-mortem which identified a significant level of alcohol in Kelly's blood, roughly a bottle of wine's worth.

The key question was who else was in the house that evening? The prosecution alleged that Leanne Batey had come round at seven pm, but had left by eight thirty. The two women had had sex but Leanne had left soon afterwards, having had a row with Kelly. There was a witness who'd seen Leanne arrive, but no one saw her leave. The next-door neighbour had initially told the police she had heard two women arguing, shouting at each other, later that night, around 11pm. But in a subsequent statement she had agreed that she might just have heard Kelly shouting and that it could have been a man she was shouting at. She might not have made out the man's voice, as a deeper voice was less likely to cut through the general racket. Gethin underlined this section. If she had heard two women arguing – and surely she would know the difference – then that would put Leanne Batey in the house hours later than she claimed. He definitely needed to talk to her.

Then there was the question of the male visitor. According to the prosecution Morgan Hopkins had arrived at the house between 10 and 10.15, entering via the back door. He – or at least somebody – had been seen approaching the house by a passer-by, one Malcolm Bennett. Morgan had stayed in the house for as long as it took to murder Kelly, then left without being observed. This eyewitness sighting was crucial to the police case, but really the description Bennett gave the police could have been anyone: a six-foot male in a hooded coat. The police hadn't even bothered setting up an ID parade. Really all Bennett had seen was a man approaching the house around the time of the murder. Inside the house there was DNA belonging to Morgan, but so what? He was an on-off boyfriend of Kelly's, that wasn't under dispute. Leanne's DNA was under Kelly's fingernails, for God's sake. And Ryan's fingerprints were all over the place. But of course they'd alibied each other so nothing to see there.

Which left the matter of the scratchcard. There was a lottery scratchcard – a £1 million Monopoly Card to be precise – found lying next to Kelly's body. There was Kelly's blood all over it. No one thought much about it at first. It was assumed that Kelly had dropped it on the floor. She wasn't the most punctilious of housekeepers. It was only later that the cops decided to trace its origins. A hard-working plod figured out from the number that it had been sold at the Londis in Abertridwr on or around the day of the murder. And the woman on the till said they didn't sell that many of them, as they cost a fiver a go, but there was one bloke who always bought one every Friday – Morgan Hopkins.

The cops went back to Morgan then and asked him if the scratchcard was his. He made the mistake of denying it. A mistake because there was a hair stuck to the card and a DNA test matched it to Morgan. This really was the heart of the case against him. His scratchcard was covered in Kelly's blood and he had lied about it.

Gethin could see how that would sway the jury. On its own it wasn't much. All it did was place Morgan at the house sometime on the day of the murder, which he'd already admitted. He could have dropped the scratchcard earlier in the day – and indeed that's what he claimed he had done, once he'd been busted on his initial lie – and it could have been sitting there until Kelly was killed and her blood dripped all over it. The lying though, that made him look guilty, no doubt about it.

Gethin sat back in his chair thinking about it. Mostly, by the time he'd got this far into investigating a case, he had a pretty good sense as to whether his client was guilty or not. With this one though, he really wasn't sure. He'd been dreading that moment when you're reading through court papers and you have to accept that you're working for a guilty man. Of course he knew how to rationalise it – everyone deserves a proper defence, all of that – but it was a dispiriting feeling, trying to get a guilty man off on a technicality. The exception was drugs cases. You didn't want to get Gethin started on Britain's drugs laws. The sooner Britain stopped treating drugs as a criminal matter the better. But the same didn't go for the murderers, the rapists, the wife beaters and all the rest of them. Those were the jobs that kept you awake at night, when you started to suspect you were working for a guilty man.

And conversely, of course, when you were sure your client was innocent, that gave you a buzz of righteousness. And sometimes a crushing sense of powerlessness. But which category did Morgan Hopkins fit into? Had he done it? Next thing would be to meet the man himself, look him in the eyes.

Eleven

MORGAN HOPKINS WAS ONE OF the first out of the door for the visiting hour. It took Gethin a moment to recognise him. The Morgan Hopkins in the photos he'd seen was a flash type in smart casual, football hooligan designer wear. A six-foot Jack the Lad with tattooed arms and a cocky grin. This guy looked older, greyer and thinner. It was only the big Celtic cross on his left arm that reassured Gethin he definitely had the right man. Two years in prison and Morgan Hopkins looked broken.

That wasn't always the case. Gethin had spent more than his fair share of time in visiting rooms like this one. Sitting on one side of a table that had been bolted to the floor, talking to someone who claimed to be innocent. Some of these guys didn't mind being inside, as far as Gethin could see. They quite liked the routine, the way you didn't have to think for yourself, didn't have to worry about paying the rent or doing the shopping. Some of them liked the camaraderie of it, like being on an extended lads' bonding trip. Morgan Hopkins wasn't one of them though. He moved slowly and when he said hello his voice was low and slightly robotic. Gethin figured they probably had him on some sledgehammer antidepressants.

'How are you doing?' said Gethin, once Hopkins was sat opposite him.

Hopkins didn't say anything for a while, busied himself sorting through a selection of crisps and chocolate bars Gethin had bought from the snack bar.

Gethin took further stock of his client. He was wearing a faded pink Paul & Shark polo shirt. It probably looked cool once, but now it was faded and ripped and paired with prison-issue trackie bottoms, never a good look. It was one of the first privileges you earned inside, wearing your own clothes – it took about three months of keeping your nose clean. The prison gear was awful – grey track suits that had been worn by a hundred men before you and were handed out in random sizes. Boxer shorts too, which really didn't bear thinking about. It was all part of the dehumanising process.

So of course most cons preferred to wear their own stuff as soon as they were allowed, definitely when they were meeting visitors. You could pretty much wear normal clothing. The main exception was football tops which were banned in order to stop the inmates rioting. But Morgan Hopkins simply looked like he'd stopped caring.

'How d'you think I'm doing, mun? I'm in bloody Belmarsh, aren't I?'

Gethin did his best to look properly sympathetic. And he was. He hated Belmarsh too. For starters it was a pain in the arse to get to, all the way round to the furthest south-east end of London. But there was something particularly depressing about it too, which was weird because it was quite new, built in the 90s, and the visiting area was lighter and airier than most of its kind. And yet it was just irrevocably dismal. The old school prisons, the ones in Cardiff and Swansea – or Wormwood Scrubs, where Gethin had served six months, half a lifetime back – at least they had a bit of style, bizarre though it might sound to say it of a prison. They were properly grim with their big, scary walls and all that. Belmarsh, though, was like the out-of-town shopping centre version. Modern and theoretically user-friendly but grindingly soulless.

'Having a rough time of it, then?' said Gethin redundantly.

'What d'you reckon? People calling me a rapist, calling me a murderer. When I ain't. I never raped her, never killed the silly cow. Fucking cops fitted me up.'

His words were angry but his tone curiously blank, like he was reading a script. Gethin was now convinced there was some serious medication going on.

'So who do you think did it?' He hoped the question would cut through the fog.

'The copper,' said Hopkins. There was immediately a little more vigour to his voice. 'Ryan. I reckon he found out about Kelly and his sister and he went nuts.'

Gethin nodded. It was a theory he had entertained himself. Made sense. He wondered whether Deano had managed to talk to Ryan yet. He was a decent investigator, Dean, but he tended to do things his own way and in his own time.

Hopkins didn't seem to have any more to add so Gethin changed the subject. 'You know my wife,' he said.

Hopkins stared at him, confused. 'Do I? Sorry, mate, I'm a bit shit on remembering things at the moment.'

'It was her who put you on to me,' Gethin said. 'Cat, Catriona from your rehab group.'

'You're Cat's husband? Fuck, no one told me that.'

Gethin wondered why Cat hadn't mentioned it. Maybe she thought it would seem more professional if she didn't. That they'd think she was just trying to get work for her husband or something. 'Yeah, that's who I am.'

'Lucky feller. She's amazing, your old lady. Wish she worked here. Maybe I wouldn't have done it...' He trailed off, frowning and staring at his feet.

'Done what?'

'Didn't she tell you?'

Gethin had a nasty feeling he knew what was coming.

'I did something stupid. Tried to... you know.'

Christ.

'I'm sorry, man. Did you get some help?'

Hopkins shrugged. 'Could say that. Doc put me on the happy pills. Can't remember my own name but at least I'm not a danger. To myself.'

Well, no wonder his family wanted him out of there. But it was a worrying piece of news. For starters it didn't play well with the not guilty narrative. It was generally guilty types who killed themselves in prison.

'You mind telling me what brought it on? You getting grief from people inside?'

'Not really. Mostly people leaves me alone. Had a bit of bother with one lad first week, but it's not like I've never had a fight. You've probably seen my record. There's a lot of nutters in here – all the fucking gangbangers and that – but they don't bother with me. It wasn't that, it's just... Well it does your head in getting a life sentence for something you haven't done. You start off feeling like it's all a dream. And then you realise it's a nightmare and you can't get out of it for twenty years. Imagine that, a nightmare that lasts twenty years. Wouldn't you want to get out of it any way you could?'

Gethin swallowed, his own sorry memories of doing time threatening to flood his brain. 'Look, we're going to get you out. Prove you're innocent. That's what I do, Morgan. I'm good at it.'

'That's what Catriona said.' Hopkins' voice, which had seemed briefly animated when he was talking about his predicament, was now slow and slurring again. He stopped and rubbed his eyes. 'Sorry, mate, these fucking pills make me sleepy all the time. You want anything else?'

'Just anything that can help with your defence. You haven't thought of anyone could help with your alibi have you?'

Hopkins shook his head. It wasn't surprising. His alibi was simple and believable and hopeless. He'd been in the pub earlier in the evening – mouthing off about Kelly – and then he'd left about an hour before Kelly was killed. Hopkins said he'd gone home alone and watched TV. As people do. But alibi-wise it would have been a lot better if he'd just stayed in the pub.

'You didn't make any phone calls did you? On your landline?'

Hopkins stared at him. 'Who uses a bloody landline these days?'

That was a fair point. And if he'd made calls on his mobile they might be able to get a rough geographic location, but seeing as he only lived round the corner from Kelly it wouldn't prove anything.

'How about Kelly? Did she ever say anything to you about being scared or anything like that? Someone threatening her, that sort of thing? Leanne maybe? Or Ryan?'

He could see that Hopkins was on the edge of drifting off, really struggling to answer the question. The words, when they came, were slower and slurrier than ever. Gethin had to lean right forward to catch them

'No, I wish. She mentioned Leanne once or twice, 'cause I asked her when I heard the rumours. Sounded like she really liked her. Definitely wasn't afraid of her.'

'How about Ryan?'

'I dunno, mate, I don't think she ever mentioned him. And anyway she wasn't the sort to see the bad side in people. Kelly, she wasn't like that. She was always positive. It's weird she... well I knew she was putting it about a bit, right, but she didn't chat on about it. When you was with her, you was with her, you know what I mean... She was a fucking lovely girl, mun...'

Hopkins subsided into silence. Gethin watched as a single tear made its way down his cheek. He signalled to the officer on duty. It was definitely time to go.

He leant forward and tapped Hopkins on the arm. He

jerked forward, staring at Gethin wildly, like he'd just woken from a dream.

'She was seeing someone else.'

'You mean Leanne?'

'No not her. I just remembered. Last time I saw her.'

Another pause. The prison officer was walking towards them. Gethin tried to move things along. 'Did she tell you she was seeing someone else?'

'No. There were marks.'

'What d'you mean?'

'On her arse. Whip marks. I never saw them before. I'd seen bites and stuff, but nothing like that. It was somebody new.'

And then the prison officer was there and it was time to go.

As he began the long drive back, crawling around the M25, a CD by Shelby Lynne and Allison Moorer on the stereo, Gethin wondered about his client. Was he guilty? He didn't think so. Though the suicide attempt couldn't be ignored. As for the business about the whip marks, he had no idea how seriously to take it. To be honest it had seemed like something Hopkins had dreamed up in that moment. But you never know. He could check the post-mortem, see if there was any reference to whip marks.

Mostly though, what he thought about Morgan Hopkins was that he was a broken man. Whether he could be fixed, even if he was released, remained to be seen. Not many victims of a miscarriage of justice were ever the same again. Far too many of them were dead within a few years of release. Maybe Cat would be able to help Morgan if he did get out. But that was getting ahead of the game. First he had to do his part of the job. Get Morgan Hopkins the hell out of Belmarsh.

And then a track called 'Every Time You Leave', an old Louvin Brothers country ballad, came on and Gethin found himself thinking about what Hopkins had said. About Kelly's body. Seeing the evidence of other lovers – the bites, the whip marks – and he wondered what that must be like. And what he might find if Cat ever came back to him. What would be written on her body?

Twelve

BACK HOME THAT EVENING, HATTIE allegedly doing her homework in her bedroom, Gethin gave his investigator a call.

He could hear pub noises in the background when Deano picked up. 'You drinking or working?'

'Working.' Deano worked part-time in his mate's hipster gin bar.

'Won't keep you then. Just wondering if you'd seen Ryan yet?'

'Nah, looks like he's still in Tallinn. Stag do I mentioned.'

'It's bloody Tuesday. What kind of stag do carries on till Tuesday?'

'Dunno. Coppers, they're a law to themselves. One thing I did clock, there's a lot of people asking for him.'

'Oh yeah, why's that?'

'Dunno for sure boss but I reckon Ryan has a load of body building gear, the dodgy kind. Dishes it out to his bros, I reckon.'

'Steroids?'

'Yeah maybe, that kind of shit anyway.'

'Well keep an eye, might be a way of getting him to talk to us if he's into something like that.'

'Sure. I've got to go. I'll be in touch soon as I catch up with him.'

Gethin hung up. He had hopes for Ryan Batey. A murder like this one had all the hallmarks of jealousy – nothing like jealousy for turning people into monsters – and who are you more likely to be jealous of than your sister? Talking of whom, he badly needed to find Leanne Batey. He called Lee – she had nothing. Bex hadn't found an address on the net either. Coppers tended to guard their privacy, for obvious reasons. He was left with the wild card option. He could stop by the TextileWorks in the morning, and see if Leanne Beethoven, puppeteer, was one and the same as Leanne Batey, copper.

* * *

And she was. Leanne Beethoven was quite obviously the policewoman called Leanne Batey, immediately recognisable from the newspaper coverage of the case. At the same time she wasn't quite what he expected. Not that he'd had a very clear idea of what a copper turned puppeteer would look like – a sort of butch Goth was his best guess.

She wasn't a butch Goth. The woman he'd found – once he'd navigated his way past the assorted ceramicists and terrible abstract painters who mostly inhabited the TextileWorks – was tall and blonde. She had a short haircut that looked like she'd done it herself without looking in a mirror, and a slightly stooped posture like she was embarrassed about her height. She looked arty, but in a practical sort of way: jeans and a paint-flecked smock. When Gethin spotted her she was sat at a worktable, concentrating hard on a puppet.

She jumped when he said hello and blushed pink as he asked if she was Leanne Beethoven, the puppet show person. God knows how she'd coped with life in the police. This woman looked like she'd have trouble saying boo to a goose, even if you'd cooked it first. If he hadn't known she was thirty-two, he'd have put her at mid-twenties, tops.

'Hiya, sorry, I'm just working on something. How can I help you?'

Gethin was slightly taken aback by her strong north Cardiff accent. Her appearance had him expecting something more middle-class boho. He wondered whether to come clean and decided not to. This Leanne Batey looked like she'd freak out completely if he did.

'I was just thinking about my daughter's birthday. She's going to be thirteen and I was thinking a puppet show could be fun, if it wasn't too childish. You know how sophisticated thirteen-year-olds are.'

Leanne Batey gave a polite half-laugh, while her expression suggested she had no idea what he was talking about.

Gethin ploughed on: 'Yeah, so have I got this right? I read on the internet you do sort of spooky puppet shows?'

She frowned. 'I don't do spooky. I don't know where you read that. Adult is what I do. LGBTQ stuff, you know?'

Gethin nodded, feeling more confident now that he'd got the right woman. 'Would that be good with teenagers then? My daughters' friends are all very, er, LGBT friendly.'

The puppeteer raised her eyebrows. Gethin wondered if that had sounded weird. He blundered on, feeling his cheeks get as red as hers. 'I suppose they get it all from social media. I wouldn't have known what they were talking about at her age. Anyway, do you think your show would be appropriate?'

She shook her head decisively. 'Sorry, but it's adults only, what I do, so I'm afraid I can't help. You could try Herky Jerky in Bristol, they're really good.'

'Thanks.' Gethin half turned to go, then shuffled awkwardly on the spot, trying to think of an excuse to prolong the conversation. 'What's that you're working on?' he said, pointing at the puppet lying on the workbench.

'That's a dog.'

Gethin leaned over to take a better look. It was indeed a dog, a snarling Staff rendered in impressive detail. He whistled in genuine appreciation of the craftswoman-ship.

'So is that for a show then?'

'Yes.' Leanne clearly wanted to leave it there, but Gethin just carried on staring at her and not saying anything and she finally capitulated. 'I'm doing a modern-day Punch and Judy show.'

'Oh fantastic,' said Gethin. 'I've always thought there was something pretty adult about Punch and Judy.'

Leanne laughed, not much humour in it. 'Yeah you could say that.'

'Have you done any of the other puppets then? Could I have a look at the stars?'

Leanne sighed. 'I suppose.'

She reached under the table and brought out two large puppets, a good two feet high. One was obviously male and one female. Punch was wearing tracksuit bottoms and a muscle T-shirt and a whole lot of tattoos. Judy was in punky leathers and more tattoos. The male was the spit of Morgan Hopkins and the female was obviously Kelly Rowlands. Morgan's face was contorted with fury. Kelly's face was riveting, a mix of terror and desire. How Leanne had managed to convey so much on a painted puppet head was amazing.

'Wow,' said Gethin, 'they're very realistic.' He waited to see if she was going to say anything about them. As he did so he peered closely at the puppets, increasingly unnerved by the disjuncture between the meekness of the woman herself and the ferocity of the work. A line from a Dave Rawlings song – 'Short Haired Woman Blues' – flitted through his head. *With her hair cut like a farm boy/and her cards so close to her vest.* This Leanne Batey was evidently rather more than the shrinking violet she presented as. Could she have battered her lover to death?

Leanne didn't speak till the silence became really

oppressive. Then she gathered up the puppets while muttering, 'I suppose', again.

'Did you use models for them?' he ventured.

Leanne Batey stared at him then, like she was trying to work out whether he knew who they were. Gethin kept a poker face.

'Not really, just from memory. Now if you don't mind, I've got to get these finished ready for the show.'

'You've got a show coming up?'

Leanne looked like she wanted to kick herself. 'Yeah, but it's private.'

'What? A party?'

'No, a charity thing.'

'Oh great,' said Gethin, all fake sunny enthusiasm, 'which charity?'

'Rainbow Valley,' said Leanne, 'now please, I need to get on.'

'Sorry, of course.' And Gethin wandered off, ostentatiously stopping at other workshops as he went along in an effort to throw her off the scent. Now he'd found her, he needed to figure out a strategy to draw her out, maybe provoke her into saying something that undermined her alibi. It struck him that if one of the siblings really was the murderer, then the other one must have very strong suspicions. And Leanne Batey didn't look like she would stand up to much of an interrogation. Getting the chance to interrogate her, though, that was going to be the tricky thing. If they went too early she'd just lawyer up and say nothing.

On his way out of the TextileWorks he said hello to a big red-bearded guy called Padraig, who had a sculpture studio there. He used to buy weed off Paddy, years back. But when he reached the exit he turned round and saw Leanne Batey staring straight at him, biting her lip.

* * *

'You ever heard of Rainbow Valley?' he asked Lee when he arrived at the office.

'Dunno, was it a kids' TV show?'

'No. Well, might have been. This one's some sort of LGBT charity, offers support to kids in the Valleys.' He'd just googled it.

'Sounds like a good idea. Never heard of it though. Why are you asking?'

Gethin told Lee and Bex about Leanne Batey and her Punch and Judy show. 'She's doing some sort of private show for this charity.'

'So we'd better go along then, see if it gives anything away.'

'Yeah, that's what I was thinking. You want to give them a ring, see what you can find out?'

Lee frowned briefly. Gethin could see she was on the point of objecting to being given all the lesbian stuff to do, like that's all she was capable of, but then she just shrugged. 'Fine, I'll get on it now.'

Gethin had hardly got started on drawing up a list of action points when Lee stuck her head round his door. 'Puppet show's on Friday night. At the Muni, Pontypridd. Apparently it's specifically for people who have experienced violence and discrimination because of their sexuality. So I told them that was me all right and I'm on the guest list. They said I could bring my carer too.' She winked at Gethin.

'Great work,' said Gethin and stuck the info in the diary.

Thirteen

GETHIN STOPPED OFF AT THE big Asda by the M4 junction on his way home. It was never a task he relished, but they were running out of basic necessities in the house.

So there he was, engaged in the glamorous task of stocking up, figuring out whether a pack of sixteen toilet rolls worked out cheaper than two packs of nine rolls that were on special offer, when he heard a voice saying hello. It was the red-haired woman from the rehab group.

'Hi,' he said, 'it's Ella, isn't it?'

'Yeah, and you're Gareth?'

'Close. I'm Gethin.'

'Oh God, I'm really sorry,' she blushed and stood there looking embarrassed.

'Well, nice to see you, I'd better…'

'I thought it was you. You live round here, I suppose.'

'Sort of. Gwaelod Y Garth.'

'Oh nice. Up on the hill. I bet you have amazing views.'

'Uh yeah, I do actually.' He had almost said 'we do' but the words that came out of his mouth were 'I do'. Why was she talking to him? There was no need, under standard British etiquette rules, to have a conversation with someone you've barely met when you see them in a supermarket. Maybe she wasn't from these parts – there was a definite hint of an accent as she talked, perhaps more American than Australian as he'd previously thought.

'How about you? Are you local?'

'Just like you, sort of. I don't think anyone actually lives here' – she waved towards the retail park and motorway interchange outside the supermarket – 'do they?'

'No,' said Gethin, giving her his best polite chuckle.

'I'm in Whitchurch actually.'

'Ah, right,' said Gethin. To a local this could mean one of two things. Either she lived in Whitchurch, a middle-class north Cardiff suburb, or it meant you were an inmate of the neighbourhood's best-known building, Whitchurch psychiatric hospital. If a Cardiffian says 'so and so has gone to Whitchurch' then you'd assume that was what they meant. Maybe she was an inmate and just coming up to the rehab group on day release or something. That might explain a few things. Why she stopped strange men in supermarkets, that sort of thing.

She must've seen something in his face. 'Not the hospital, Gethin. Well, not anymore.' She paused, obviously working herself up to say something. 'Listen, could we go for a coffee in the café here? There's something I'd really like to talk to you about.'

Gethin checked his watch. It was still an hour before he had to collect Hattie. He'd been planning to get a bit more work done when he got home, but really, was he going to refuse a cup of coffee with pre-Raphaelite Ella? Maybe she was coming on to him? Surely not – a woman who looked like her wouldn't need to come on to anyone, would she?

* * *

When they'd sat down with two so-called lattes in the newly rebranded Asda Café, she began. 'It's really weird seeing you here. I was just taking about you to Philip.'

'Uh huh,' said Gethin, feeling immediately uncomfortable.

'We were just on one of his history walks. There's this old murder case from the 60s he's obsessed with.'

'Oh right.' That figured – Philip came over as your classic local history bore. 'But you were talking about me?'

'That's right,' said Ella with a bit of a gulp. 'I hope I'm not out of order here, but you didn't really come to the group for support, did you?'

Gethin hesitated. He thought he'd done pretty well there. Maybe he should just deny it. On the other hand she didn't seem angry, so maybe he should come clean and find out what she wanted. While he made his mind up, he decided to play for time. 'Well, I do have a problem with gambling...'

Ella stared at him. 'Yeah, I believe you. But that's not why you came, is it?

'I'm sorry,' said Gethin, still stalling.

'It's about Morgan Hopkins and the girl isn't it? I saw your eyes light up when she got mentioned. Isn't that true?'

Christ, thought Gethin, he was well and truly busted. 'Well...'

Ella cut him off. 'You're Cat's husband, aren't you?'

He couldn't think what to say, just stared at her, mouth open like a guppy.

'So Philip was right,' said Ella, smiling now.

'What do you mean?'

'He said he was pretty sure he'd seen you with Cat somewhere.'

Gethin sighed. It was a small world, Cardiff.

Gethin capitulated. 'Yes, you're right. I am an addict, that part is true, but I am also an investigator and I'm looking into the Morgan Hopkins case. And Catriona is my wife and she did suggest I look into the rehab group. I'm very sorry if you feel I've violated your privacy.'

'Oh no. Normally I would be upset, obviously, but in this case... Well I trust Cat and it's so awful, what happened to Morgan. I really can't believe what's happened to him. And just wondering whether I might know who the real murderer is, it's driving me crazy...' She paused, smiled at Gethin again. She really was very pretty, it took him a moment to reconfigure his thoughts.

'So, do you think anyone in the group might have something to do with…'

'Well, Philip and I have discussed it and there's one person we're both suspicious of.'

'Do you mean the Professor, Mark?'

'He's just a lecturer, but yes, Mark. You must have seen it too.'

'Well, nothing very substantial. Do you have a reason to suspect him?'

'That's the problem, we don't know anything. I see how he is, how he talks about women, how he talks to me, how he looks at me. I know he met Kelly, the dead girl. He told us so after Morgan was arrested. He said he had met her at some punk gig. He's always going to gigs and stuff. I've seen them once or twice. He always stands at the back on his own with his arms folded, like he's in charge or something, like he's someone important.' She shook her head and made a face. 'Can't stand it, that sort of arrogance.'

'Yeah that's what Cat – Catriona – said too.'

Ella clapped her hands. 'There you are! Will you tell her hello from me?'

'Um sure, though. We're not really together at the moment. We're having some… difficulties.'

'Oh,' said Ella, 'I'm sorry.' She frowned and bit her lip. 'Is that why she left us too?'

Gethin couldn't think what she meant at first, then realised she was referring to the rehab group. Never underestimate the self-centredness of people 'in recovery'.

'I dunno, maybe.' He thought about it. Maybe it was the case. Maybe Cat felt like the way she was living with Nils meant she no longer had the moral authority. 'Yes, I guess it could be part of the same process. Her midlife crisis.'

'God,' said Ella, then laughed. 'Funny, you never imagine

your therapist having any problems in their own life.'

Ella lapsed into silence and they just stared at each other for a few seconds, the silence growing bigger and more awkward till Ella started to stand up.

'Sorry to take up your time, Gethin, I guess I'll see you on Monday. You will come back?'

'Of course,' said Gethin, 'I mean, as long as you're okay with it?'

'Absolutely. Philip and I will do our best to help, give Mark the opportunity to show you what he's really like. He doesn't need much encouraging. I'll talk to Philip about it beforehand.'

'Oh,' said Gethin, feeling a stab of disappointment. 'Are you two seeing each other?'

Ella laughed. 'Well, not like that, we aren't. It's very much frowned upon, you know, having a relationship with someone you meet in a rehab group.'

Gethin wondered if he should take that as a warning or an invitation.

Fourteen

THURSDAY MORNING DEANO WAS OUTSIDE the office having a smoke when Gethin arrived. He was still sporting the short beard but now he'd shaved off his moustache. The result was a look pitched somewhere between devout Muslim and professional footballer. Deano's styling tended to move back and forth between street and hipster. Today he was definitely street.

'Bit early for you,' said Gethin.

Deano rolled his eyes. 'I'm a busy guy.'

'Oh aye. Any sign of yer man Ryan?'

'That's what I want to tell you about. You got any coffee?'

'Nothing decent. Let's go round to the caff.'

Nata & Co, a Portuguese bakery and café, was just around the corner and functioned as an ancillary office for Last Resort. They ran into Bex inside, getting her morning pastries and she came over to join them at the back table. Deano started talking while he was waiting for his cappuccino to arrive.

'I've just seen him,' he announced.

'In the gym?'

'No, after. I was walking through town, needed to go into my bank, and I'm passing the Laguna Hotel, when out walks Ryan, practically bumps into me. It took him a second to recognise me and I could see he was half tempted to do a runner. So I blocks him off, like, and he has to say hello. "What's happening, Deano," he says and I tell him

115

I'm working the Hopkins case and I've been looking for him for the last week.'

'He's not happy, as you can imagine. So he's like "good luck with that seeing as the guy who did it's in prison" and then he starts walking off down towards Greyfriars. So I walks with him, like I'm a bloody reporter or something, asking him questions, and he's telling me to fuck off and stop being such a nosy prat, and then we get over by the Slug & Lettuce when a car comes up alongside like it's being following us, a really flash fucking Jag, and it pulls over in front and Ryan just gets in the passenger seat and they drive off, me still trying to ask him some questions.'

'So he didn't tell you anything about where he'd been?'

'No,' said Deano, 'but here's the interesting thing. You know who was driving the car? Whose Jag it is?'

Gethin tried to think of an obvious candidate but couldn't come up with one. 'Who?'

'Only fucking Jake Sanchez.'

'Jake Sanchez,' chipped in Bex, 'that wanker.'

'Yeah,' said Deano, 'that wanker.'

Jake Sanchez was a Cardiff City footballer who'd been the subject of a high-profile rape case a couple of years earlier. He and two of his meathead teammates had been arrested after they'd taken some girl back to a hotel room in Stoke and done all kinds of shit with her without bothering to ask permission first. There'd been the usual trial by social media and so forth but when it got to court the jury didn't buy it. The girl was well known as a football groupie, she'd had a load to drink. They obviously felt she basically deserved it. So Jake Sanchez was free to get paid some ludicrous amount of money every week to head balls away from his penalty area. But people didn't have to like it.

'So what's that all about, you reckon?'

Deano thought about it. 'They probably met down the

gym. Both love themselves you know. Spend the whole time doing weights in front of the mirror.'

'Strong bloke is he, Ryan?'

Deano made a face. 'He's got a lot of muscles. Dunno if he's actually strong. Reckon I could take him easy.'

Gethin didn't doubt it. Deano didn't have super muscled arms or giant abs or whatever, but he was lean and wiry and absolutely fearless in a fight. 'So what should we do next about him?'

'Well, if you've got a witness, boss, show them the photo. Can't say I'd be unhappy if it was him. Those guys, the way they're always chatting shit about women, it's pathetic.'

Bex chipped in. 'You think Sanchez could be involved?'

Gethin and Deano looked at each other, then both shook their heads.

'Can't see it really,' said Gethin. 'Surely someone would have noticed if he'd been seeing Kelly. Not a lot of flash Jags in Abertridwr.'

'Ryan might have called up that night,' said Bex, 'told him to come round and join in with Kelly. It's what these guys do, innit. Like to have their bros along to cheer them on. Probably can't get it up otherwise.' She wrinkled her nose in a show of disgust.

'Maybe,' said Gethin. 'It's worth keeping an open mind on it at least. Be a hell of a story, that's for sure.'

* * *

Back in the office Bex had a message from Mrs Kendall, wondering about the results of the hypnotism. Gethin had completely forgotten to do anything about it, what with all the excitement. So he passed Lee the task of trying to persuade the postman that he should take part and then booking a hypnotist. Ideally she could use Bex's guy in Cardiff, but realistically she'd probably have to find somewhere near where the postman lived. Lee gave him a bit of side-eye, but said she'd get on with it.

Meanwhile Gethin typed up a summary of what they'd learned so far on the Hopkins case, hoping it would shed some light on what to do next. He considered the key alternative suspects. The problem was that the more guilty seeming any of them were, the less evidence there was against them. And vice versa. Take Leanne Batey for instance. In a way she was the obvious suspect. She'd admitted to having sex with Kelly on the evening of her death. There was no witness to her leaving the house when she said she did, and her only alibi came from her brother. And yet, having met her, Gethin found it hard, if not impossible, to imagine Leanne beating someone to death.

Then there was brother Ryan, perhaps the most frustrating of the lot. Everything about his behaviour felt dodgy, and his fingerprints were in the house, but he had both an alibi – albeit provided by his sister – and a perfect excuse for his prints being there – he was the first officer on the scene. And 'cause he was a serving copper, there was no obvious way of exerting any pressure. If only they could find some evidence that Ryan had known Kelly before she died, that might change things.

And then at the other extreme there was Mark the Prof. Absolutely no evidence against him, just Catriona's not-to-be-undervalued instinct. And Gethin's own dislike. Again, they absolutely had to find some concrete evidence. Something to put Mark in Abertridwr with Kelly on the day of her death.

So what evidence could there be? An eyewitness would be ideal, maybe the one who'd seen a man approaching the back door of Kelly's house around the time of the murder. In the trial the prosecution had made that seem like a positive identification of Morgan, but it wasn't really. The witness had said he was about the same size as the guy he'd seen, but it was dark and the guy had his hood up so he couldn't say he remembered the face.

The defence had tried suggesting the hooded man could have been Ryan Batey, but the witness failed to identify him, and anyway Ryan was alibied by his sister. Maybe it would be worth trying again though. Wouldn't put it past the coppers to have used a completely unrecognisable picture of Ryan. And while he was at it he could show the guy a picture of Mark the Prof. Had to be worth trying. Gethin went through the file till he found the original witness statement, complete with name and address. Malcolm Bennett, Coldstream Terrace, Abertridwr. He put the info into Google and there was his man, listed in the phone book.

He called the number and a woman answered – middle-aged to elderly with a Valleys accent.

'Hiya,' said Gethin, 'is Malcolm there?'

'No,' said the woman, 'he's out with the dog, who's this calling?'

Gethin left a message for Malcolm to call him. The case was frustrating him. Lots of possibilities but nothing solid. Maybe something would crop up at tomorrow's puppet show, he thought, then laughed at himself. It was coming to something if you were hoping a puppet show would break open a case.

Fifteen

GETHIN ARRIVED AT THE SHOW late and fed up. Everything was moving too slowly for his liking. He couldn't get hold of the eyewitness, Malcolm Bennett, while Ryan Batey seemed to have vanished again. And then the whole of Friday daytime had been spent pissing about trying to sort out a hypnotist for the Karl Fletcher case. It looked like they'd finally got something set up for the following Tuesday in Birmingham, but really, what a waste of time.

And then he'd had to rush back to pick up Hattie from Martina's place and deliver her to his dad's for the night. Hattie didn't complain exactly, but he could see the disappointment in her face when he announced that's what was happening.

Just to add the icing on the cake, as he arrived at the Muni he got a text from Lee saying she had to look after Monica's kids and couldn't make it. Wonderful, he thought; if he couldn't even get into the show after all that, he was really going to lose it. Thankfully nobody seemed too bothered about his LGBTQ credentials; they were obviously just happy that anyone showed up.

That was something of a relief, but on the other hand, before the puppet show even started there was a good hour's worth of talks on the wrongs of domestic violence and how it could be combatted. And there Gethin was, sat in the back row on his own, two empty seats on either side of him as an almost exclusively female crowd kept their distance.

Finally, at eight thirty, the lights dimmed. An old girl group tune started playing. Gethin got what it was after the first few bars – 'He Hit Me (And It Felt Like a Kiss)' by The Crystals. Kind of an obvious choice, but it made the point. He had a vague memory of seeing Courtney Love playing it live. Maybe that was the same night in Newport that Kurt Cobain was meant to have proposed to her.

Then the music faded down and the lights came up on an apparently standard issue Punch and Judy show. Punch/ Morgan swaggered around the stage asking if there were any fit women out there wanted some of his big stick. He waved the traditional stick about, except this one was painted pink and frankly obscene. The audience tittered nervously.

When there were no takers from the audience, Punch made a noise of disgust and said he'd have to settle for old Judy again.

'Judy!' he shouted, and up popped the female puppet, quite obviously Kelly Rowlands, in her punk clothes and dyed black hair. As tradition demanded, Punch began by asking Judy for a kiss. She fought him off for a bit, but then he whacked her with his giant stick/penis and the audience gasped. He hit her again and again while making orgasmic groans.

By now the audience, Gethin not the least, were starting to squirm in their seats. There was no let-up though. Punch kept hitting Judy till she briefly revived and asked if Punch wanted to see the baby.

'Nah,' said Punch, 'get your mum to look after her. I want my oats.' Then he went back to hitting her. At first there were groans from Judy – disturbing ambiguous groans that could be pleasure or pain or both – then she flopped to the ground and Punch exited stage left, whistling.

A moment later the policeman entered the stage. He was identifiable too – at least to anyone who knew him or had studied his photo as carefully as Gethin had. This was Ryan Batey dressed in an old-time police uniform. He pulled Judy/Kelly off the floor.

'Oh thank God,' she squeaked, 'you've come to save me.'

'No I haven't, you stupid slag,' said Ryan, 'I bet you were asking for it.' Then he gave her a couple of whacks with his truncheon and left the stage. Judy sat halfway up and sobbed quietly.

By now the tension in the room was unbearable. There was complete silence apart from a couple of sobs as everyone waited to see what would happen next.

What happened next was a part of the Punch and Judy tradition that Gethin had completely blocked out of his childhood memories.

The Devil entered from stage left. He was a traditional Devil – there was no hint of a modern face. On seeing Judy/Kelly he cackled and brought out his own pink stick, even bigger than Morgan's, and started beating her with it. The puppeteer set up a rhythm: the Devil beating and cackling, Judy whimpering. Finally she fell silent and the audience sighed in relief as it looked as if the Devil had had his fun and exited the way he came. But seconds later he was back and had a very realistic knife in his hand, the stage lights glinting off it. He bent over Kelly and stabbed and stabbed and stabbed and stabbed. There was no sound at all apart from a woman in the audience sobbing uncontrollably. And then the stage went black.

Another song started to play – Nina Simone singing 'I Loves You Porgy' – and gradually the lights came up again. The audience left quickly, almost tripping over each other in their eagerness to escape.

Gethin just sat there, trying to make sense of what he'd seen. Did Leanne know who Kelly's murderer was? Did the Devil have a name? He needed to ask but he wasn't sure whether he would have a chance this evening. There was a group of women hanging around by the stage, presumably her friends, waiting to talk to her once she emerged from whatever makeshift dressing room the community centre had to offer.

And then he noticed another man hanging around by the exit. He didn't recognise him at first, because his face was obscured by a strange hooded top, more Da Vinci Code monk than sportswear. But then the house lights came all the way up in an obvious signal that it was time to go home, and Gethin saw his face. It was Lee's strange cousin, Dennis. He was about to walk over and say hello when Dennis saw him. His face creased with fear and he immediately took flight through the exit door.

Gethin thought about running after him but decided against it. He would definitely need to pay another visit to Dennis's bizarre church soon, though. Instead he decided to sit and wait for Leanne to come out. First, however, an officious janitor came over and asked him to get moving. He was slowly making his way towards the exit when Leanne appeared from backstage. She looked pale and tired and sweaty, like someone who'd just run a 5K up and down the sides of the valley, as a bewildering number of Gethin's neighbours seemed to like to do of an evening. She spotted him there, lurking in the background, and frowned as she tried to remember who he was. She gave him a slight noncommittal wave before turning towards her group of friends – all of them obvious lesbians to Gethin's eye – and they started congratulating her and pulling her into a series of hugs.

Gethin decided this was probably the worst possible time to reveal that he was not, after all, someone trying to book a puppet show for his daughter's birthday. He would go back to the TextileWorks soon and come clean, see whether she had any real information or whether she was just traumatised by what had happened and trying to work it out through puppetry. He suspected the latter but needed to know about the former.

* * *

Forty minutes later he was in the Wetherspoon on the City Road in Cardiff. More precisely he was outside the 'Spoons, in the beer garden with Bex and Chrissie plus a couple more girlfriends of Bex. All the girls were drinking rosé out of wine glasses that probably held the best part of a pint. Bex was wearing a bunch of ribbons in her hair. Gethin identified them as part of her Madonna outfit. She must have had an early evening gig and come straight to the pub.

After a while of doing his best to join in the general banter that had broken out once Bex announced that he was her boss come to join them, Gethin managed to get Chrissie into a side conversation.

Seeing her again, now stone cold sober, Gethin found it hard to imagine that they'd got up to all the stuff they had. She really wasn't his type at all. He wasn't exactly sure what his type was, but it surely wasn't forty-something punkettes. Fortunately Chrissie seemed to be feeling the same. She made a couple of pointed remarks about her boyfriend maybe coming along later, and then they were both able to relax a bit.

Chrissie started reminiscing about the nightlife of twenty years earlier. She brought out her phone and showed him a Facebook page dedicated to Maddison, the crucial indie club of their youth.

They stared scrolling through the old photos that had been uploaded by half-remembered scenesters, looking for people they both knew.

'I definitely remember him!' said Chrissie. She was pointing at a spotty herbert with dyed red hair, wearing a mohair sweater.

'Yeah?'

'Oh yeah. Shagged him once, round at my nan's house.'

Gethin must've looked at her funny because she quickly added: 'I was living there for a bit and anyway she wasn't in!'

Gethin held his hands up. 'I wasn't judging, honest. What's his name?'

'Mike. Mikey. He's still around, I think. Saw him on Queen Street a few years ago, outside Zara. He's bald now. Shame.'

Chrissie kept on scrolling. A picture jumped out at Gethin.

'Hey, stop there.'

'Why?' said Chrissie. Then she looked more closely at the photo, a group shot with two guys in the middle, arms around each other's shoulder. 'Oh my God, is that you?'

It was indeed Gethin and the guy he had his arm around was his best friend in the world at the time, Nils Hofberg.

'You were actually quite cute.' Chrissie brought the phone up to her face to study the picture more carefully, then let out a shriek of exaggerated excitement. 'And that's him, isn't it?'

'Nils Hofberg? Yeah, it is.'

Chrissie smiled, a definite bad girl's smile. 'Did I mention I shagged him too?'

Gethin's turn to laugh. 'You and half Cardiff.'

Chrissie pretended to look hurt. 'Oh, I thought it was true love!' Then she joined in the laughter. 'Yeah, he was a right twat. And...' Her face fell. 'Christ, did Bex say your wife's gone off with him?'

'Yeah,' said Gethin.

'Oh I'm sorry, mun. You must be really fucked off by that.'

'Yeah. Really, really fucked off.'

Chrissie obviously couldn't come up with much to say

about that. They both focused on their drinks till she thought of something.

'Hey, you mind if we talk about Kelly a bit?'

'No. Please do.'

'I feel like I might have given you the wrong impression a bit, like about how happy she was all the time. 'Cause she wasn't really, not underneath. You know her little boy died?'

Gethin nodded.

'That was before I really got to know her, but I reckon it changed her. I suppose that's obvious, but I didn't realise it at first. She always seemed to be so up for everything like she wanted to squeeze every last drop out of life. It wasn't till she stayed over with me one time and I saw her the next morning that I realised how bad it was for her underneath. She told me about this dream she'd had, like a recurring dream and she'd had another one that night. In the dream there's a man – he's like Jack the Ripper or something – and she knows who he is but she goes with him anyway and every time he'd get this knife out and start to cut her throat and then she'd wake up...'

'God.'

'Yeah, and you know what the worst part was?'

'What?'

'She told me she was disappointed when she woke up alive. Every time she was disappointed.'

Gethin couldn't think of anything to say to that, was just looking at Chrissie and shaking his head, hoping it was clear how saddened he was, when there was an almighty crash behind him. It was the sound of a man tripping over the doorway that led out into the garden and crashing into an abandoned pub table, sending the glasses flying.

Gethin turned round to see who was responsible. 'Well, speak of the bloody devil.'

It was Nils Hofberg: large as life and twice as clumsy.

Once he'd got over the initial shock of seeing him, he realised he should have expected it. Nils's flat was only just around the corner, and the 'Spoons was cheap and stayed open late...

Gethin couldn't stop himself from laughing. Nils had always been physically awkward. He was a liability on stage, always tripping over the cables and knocking over the amps. As he picked himself up from the floor Gethin considered the condition of the man his wife had left him for.

The last time he'd seen Nils had been outside a casino in the middle of the night and he had looked fried. Gethin had to accept that he looked better now. He'd lost weight, had his hair cut, shaved off an ill-advised beard. Cat must have taken him in hand. You could see once again the Nils Hofberg who'd been prince of the Maddison scene: tall and dark, with sharp cheekbones and bright blue eyes,

It took him a moment to spot Gethin. When he did he broke out a delighted grin. 'Hey, Greyboy, how are you doing?'

He grabbed a seat and pulled it up to the table in between Gethin and Chrissie.

Gethin couldn't believe it. It was like Nils had forgotten he was shagging his wife.

'Make yourself at home,' said Gethin, rolling his eyes.

Nils didn't appear to notice the sarcasm. He was too busy staring at Chrissie. 'Who's this then?'

Gethin ignored him, hoping Chrissie would do likewise. But Nils kept staring at her. His face seemed to sharpen, like he was coming into focus. 'Hey, I remember you, don't I?'

'Maybe,' said Chrissie, a smile breaking out.

'Yeah, I do.' Nils let out a whoop. 'Christina. It's you. How have you been, girl? You remember the fireworks?'

Chrissie's face fully lit up at that, like someone had struck up a sparkler in front of her. 'Yeah, that was a night.'

'It really was,' said Nils. Then he turned to Gethin. 'We need champagne!'

For an instant Gethin was transported back to the old days, when he was Nils's wingman. And then he came back to the present with a bang.

'Fuck off,' he said.

'Oh come on, Gethin,' said Chrissie, her disdain for Nils dissipating in the face of his cheekbones and his charm offensive. 'Let's all have a drink.'

'You've got to be joking, this pissed cunt has been fucking my wife for the last six months.'

Nils lumbered up and out of his chair. 'Her choice, dude. Nobody made her. You'd been giving her what she needed she...'

Nils didn't get to finish his sentence, as by that point Gethin had got out of his own chair and launched one of the hardest, if not the most accurate, punches of his adult life. It caught Nils on the shoulder and was enough – given his already tenuous hold on equilibrium – to knock him over.

Gethin stood over him, wrestling with the temptation to put boot to face. Then a Wetherspoon's bouncer saved Nils's remaining good looks by bundling Gethin out of the emergency exit and on to the street with instructions to fuck off and never come back.

Sixteen

BEX STARTED CLAPPING WHEN GETHIN entered the office on Monday morning. Lee, coming in just behind him, looked bemused.

'What's that about?'

'Geth decked Cat's boyfriend in the pub Friday night.'

'Really,' said Lee, looking amazed. 'You hit the cunt?'

'Yeah,' said Gethin, trying to look cool about it, like he was always decking geezers in pubs, 's'pose I did.'

'Well about fucking time,' said Lee and engaged him in a complicated fist bump routine that Gethin got about half right.

'What happened to you afterwards?' asked Bex. 'I ran outside and had a look for you, but there was no sign.'

'Nothing much,' said Gethin, 'there was a taxi outside so I took it.'

'Fair enough. And how was your weekend after? Cat say anything?'

'No,' said Gethin, 'not a peep.' He'd been disappointed by that. He kind of wanted to have Cat giving him a hard time for beating up her boyfriend but sort of secretly admiring him for it. But she turned up Saturday lunchtime to take Hattie out for lunch as per the new usual and she hadn't said a thing. Probably Nils hadn't told her. Too embarrassed. Or maybe he didn't even remember it, fucked up as he was.

Apart from that the weekend had been okay. Lots of ferrying Hattie to and from friends' houses. A week's

129

worth of household chores; laundry and cooking. The first few weeks after Cat left, he'd felt resentful about all that, but now he quite liked it, having stuff to do, a nice bit of mindless drudgery. Sometimes it even helped with his work. He'd be halfway through loading the dishes when something to do with a case would become clear.

Not this weekend though, not this case. This one still seemed to lead in about four different directions at once. His phone had rung as he'd brought in the washing on Sunday afternoon. It was his dad reporting on another conversation he'd had with Kelly Rowlands' lawyer in the compensation matter. Apparently the appeal had dragged on and on, but the Trust had finally capitulated and there was a large cheque going to be on its way to someone: 'The next of kin presumably.'

This news had pricked his interest. Someone was standing to benefit from Kelly's death. Who would her next of kin be? Her mother? Her ex- (or was he?) husband? Had she left a will? The Judge had said he'd see what he could find out. If it was the ex-husband, Aston, that would be a thing – he'd have 200K's worth of motive. But he'd been inside at the time. Could he have commissioned her murder somehow? Maybe got someone he'd met in prison to do it, make it look like a sex thing? It seemed fantastical but it was worth checking out.

He told Bex and Lee about this latest development and they both agreed with Gethin that it was hard to imagine a three-time loser like Aston successfully hiring a hitman. But Bex said she'd check the probate records, see who the next of kin was.

Bex had a couple of bits of news, both phone-related. On the upside it looked like they had the cops bang to rights on setting up Tyrone Horan over the stolen copper deal. It was just a matter of engaging a new brief on Horan's behalf and putting in the paperwork for an appeal. Less usefully it turned out that the reason there was no phone evidence in the Kelly Rowlands case was that no one had ever found her mobile. Presumably the killer had taken it with him.

'Or her,' said Gethin. 'I'm definitely not ruling Leanne Batey out of this.' He proceeded to tell Bex and Lee about the puppet show. And as he neared the end of the story he remembered something.

'That weirdo was there, Lee.'

'Which weirdo might that be? I knows far too many.'

'Your cousin. Squatting in Kelly's old house.'

'Dennis. He was at the puppet show? That is weird.'

'That's what I thought. You fancy paying him a visit this afternoon?'

'Sure,' said Lee. 'I still don't think he did it though. Don't think he has it in him. You get a vibe, you know, from people, what they're capable of. Karl Fletcher, for instance, perfect example. You don't have any trouble at all imagining him killing someone, know what I mean, Geth?'

Gethin nodded. It was one of the many unedifying features of representing Karl Fletcher, that sense of latent rage you got from him. But could you always tell? He very much doubted it.

'Vibe or no vibe, he was acting really weirdly. We need to check him out.'

'Yeah, like I said, that's fine. I'll borrow Monica's car.'

'No need,' said Gethin, 'I'm going back to that rehab group this afternoon, I'm still quite liking this Prof feller for some kind of involvement.'

'You sure?' said Bex. 'I know you said Cat thinks he's dodgy but is that really all you've got?'

'Not quite.' Gethin told them about meeting Ella in the supermarket, how she was suspicious of Prof Mark too. Even as he was telling the story, though, he found himself wondering if the real reason he was so keen to go back was just to see Ella again.

'Fair enough,' said Bex, 'no harm checking him out some more then.'

'Exactly. So, Lee, I can drive you to Abertridwr on the way and you can get the train back. Actually, while we're at it...' He turned round to Bex. 'Have we heard anything back from the neighbour, Malcolm Bennett?'

'No,' said Bex, 'you expecting to?'

'Dunno,' said Gethin, 'I left a whole load of messages, but maybe it's best if we go up there and knock on the door while we're at it. Two birds one stone, all of that.'

* * *

Malcolm Bennett opened his door at the second knock. 'Who are you then?'

He was a short but pugnacious looking gent of seventy or so, with tight-cropped steel grey hair. Gethin would have bet money that the dog he could hear barking indoors would be an equally scrappy looking creature. A terrier maybe.

'I'm Gethin Gray from Last Resort Legals. We're looking into the Kelly Rowlands murder and I'd like to ask you a couple of questions about the evidence you gave.'

'Oh aye?' The door remained half open but Malcolm Bennett's face in the gap was now joined by his dog. Gethin was right in the generality but wrong in the specifics. Not a terrier but a Boxer. And not the friendliest looking pugilist Gethin had seen either. He sensed Lee tensing up next to him. She was not a big fan of large canines.

'Yes, just a couple of things really. I was hoping you might be able to show me exactly where you were when you saw the person.'

'I told the police already. I don't know why I should tell you.'

Gethin ploughed on. 'And I have a couple of photos to show you in case you might recognise him...'

'Shouldn't think so, it was bastard dark at the time.'

'You never know. Can we come in or do you want to come out?'

'I'll just stand here. My house, innit?'

'Fine,' sighed Gethin and reached into his shoulder bag to bring out the photocopies he'd prepared.

The dog started barking furiously at that and Lee stepped back a couple of paces. It didn't come all the way out though, so presumably Malcolm had him in some sort of grip.

Gethin produced five colour photos. One of them was Ryan Batey, one was Mark the Prof, the other three were random faces taken from the university staff page to bulk up the numbers and not let on exactly who the suspects were.

Malcolm took the pictures in one hand. Then he reluctantly accepted that he couldn't hold the dog, the door and photos all at the same time, shut the door on the dog and stepped outside, seemingly oblivious to the furious barking behind him.

He looked at the faces carefully. 'Never seen a one of them. Like I said to the cops, it was dark and the fellow was wearing a hoodie.'

Gethin thought of something. 'A hoodie? Like a sports hoodie?'

Malcolm looked at him. 'Actually, I dunno, there was something a bit funny about it…'

'Was it a bit like something a monk would wear? That sort of hood?'

'Aye,' said Malcolm, 'it was. It was exactly like that.'

Gethin brought the interview to a close quickly after that. Malcolm still couldn't be bothered to take them round to where he'd seen the hooded man – 'just in the alley round the back'. But Gethin didn't make a fuss. He was in too much of a hurry to tell Lee what he'd figured out. Maybe figured out.

'You know who wears a hooded top, looks like a monk's cowl?'

'No.'

'Your cousin Dennis. You know, the one who wouldn't hurt a fly.'

'I s'pose,' said Lee. 'I'll have another word with him.'

Gethin was very tempted to go along with Lee to see Dennis, but there wasn't time. He left her to revisit the Church of the Unpoisoned Mind and drove back over the hill to the Treforest community centre and the Monday afternoon meeting.

* * *

Gethin walked in on a row. Mark the Prof and Philip were at the heart of it.

'Safe spaces,' Mark was saying. 'What the fuck are they supposed to be? Life is not a safe space, is it? We are all going to die – sorry, maybe I should put a trigger warning ahead of that in case any of my students' mummies and daddies had failed to inform them of this salient fact. Sorry, kids, when I said we are all going to die, what I meant was that some so-called experts – disproportionately middle-class white males – are of the so-called scientific opinion that we are all going to die, but really isn't that just a conspiracy against differently abled and gendered people who are being murdered every day by the fascist KKK government? And this "we're all going to die" thing may just be a cover-up. Is that how it's going to be in your lovely safe fucking space?'

'Mark,' said Philip, in a voice of such studied reasonableness that Gethin couldn't help suspecting he was using it deliberately to wind angry Mark up even further, 'what I was saying was that this meeting, this place, needs to be a safe space for us. No one is saying the world is safe – God knows we are all here because we realise it's full of danger – but right here, right now, we need to be safe in order that we can heal, in order that we can help each other to heal. We can't do that if people are bringing violence and anger here.'

It looked like Mark was about to tell Philip where to go with his sweet reasonableness but right then Coach Steve arrived and everyone calmed down like a bunch of schoolkids.

The pause gave the group a chance to acknowledge Gethin's arrival as well. Mark, oddly enough, was particularly friendly – perhaps hoping to enlist Gethin as an ally against namby-pamby PC culture – while beautiful Ella made rather a show of barely remembering him.

They waited a few minutes before getting started. Everyone was there apart from Dafydd who'd cried off with a stinking cold. But it wasn't long before Philip chimed up.

'Steve,' he said, 'I think we need to address the question of sexual harassment within the group.'

Steve looked first surprised and then thoroughly alarmed by this. 'How do you mean? I haven't seen anything...'

'Well no,' said Philip, 'that's the point. As men we don't even realise we're doing it. We just sort of own the space and carry on regardless.'

Gethin bit back the temptation to say 'isn't that what you're doing now, mate?' because he could see the effect all this was having on Mark. You could practically see the steam coming off his head. And anyway Philip stopped there and said, 'Here I go mansplaining it all. Anyone else have something to say about this? Any of the women here? Theresa? Ella?'

By now it was clear to Gethin that Philip was doing this deliberately. Of course Theresa didn't say anything but Ella sat forward in her chair to make a contribution.

'Thanks, Philip. I don't want to make a fuss, but...' she paused to sweep her hair back off her face. Gethin found himself struggling to actually listen to the words coming out of her mouth and not just stare at her. 'But I must say I have felt uncomfortable at times here in the last year. There have been conversations that, as a woman, I find very difficult...' Her voice was quiet and she paused again, what looked like a smile flickered across her face, probably just a nervous grimace. Gethin glanced round at Mark. He was staring at Ella with avid lust. Gethin very much hoped his own face didn't look like that.

She carried on: 'To be honest, I've been thinking about this and I think the problem is really around sex addiction. I know it's an important issue and everything, but as a woman I feel like I'm the thing certain people here are addicted to. It's just a bit different – we don't have a line of cocaine or a bottle of whisky or a roulette wheel sitting on one of these chairs, joining the discussion, but that's how I feel when certain people are talking. Like I'm a bottle of whisky they want to grab hold of, rip the top off and drink their fill.'

'Whoah,' said Coach Steve, 'let's, er, let's just stop there and take a moment.'

It was, for once, a useful intervention. Angry Mark looked ready to leap out of his chair. But whether to hit Philip or sexually assault Ella, it was hard to say.

Coach Steve had his eyes flickering this way and that, trying to figure out whether to address Ella's concerns or placate Mark or somehow both. He took a deep breath and then like a ten-stone scrum half running straight into the giants of the opposition pack, he waded into the centre ground.

'Ella, I hear what you're saying. And I believe that Catriona, when she was running this group, did lay down some pretty clear guidelines around this, that there should be no question of anyone feeling threatened or harassed. Is that right?'

Ella nodded. Mark snorted.

'So I'm not clear whether you're wanting to make an official complaint about anyone in particular – in which case we may have to stop this here for today – or whether you're just making a more general point.'

'Neither,' said Ella, 'I'd just like a certain person to stop staring at my tits every time he speaks to me.'

'Okay,' said Steve with a forced chuckle, 'I hear you. All of us, we need to make sure we're respectful at all times. This is a space where we can bring some pretty difficult stuff, but it must also be a safe space.'

'Oh for fuck's sake,' said Angry Mark, 'not you too. Just because I'm honest about my problems. I like sex, all right? I'm told I like it too much. But I never lied to anyone about it. Before I got married we agreed it would be an open relationship – I could do what I wanted, Sooz could do what she wanted. Was it my fault if I did and she didn't? Apparently so if you ask her. And my bloody students, half of them come here dying to get a lecturer into bed 'cause they're all too grown up to go out with anyone their own age, the sort of little geniuses who end up at the University of Mid Fucking Glamorgan. So why the fuck shouldn't I give them what they want? You don't see them complaining about it I can tell you. Best sex they've ever had, that's what they all say. If it wasn't for that fucking jealous cunt Sian Moulson I wouldn't be here, going yes sir, no sir, three bags full, I'd be in bed with one of them right now. But instead I have to take shit from this dickless wonder' – he pointed at Philip – ''cause he doesn't have the guts to tell Little Miss Perfect here that he wants to get into her pants. Go on mate, give it a go. It's what she wants, innit. Look at her – nothing wrong with her that a good shag wouldn't sort out.'

He broke off from his tirade as Coach Steve was now on his feet and looking apoplectic. 'All right, hold your horses. You don't need to throw me out, I'm going. I realise I have broken the fucking code. I know I've made this an unsafe space. Well boo hoo and fuck the lot of you.'

Mark was halfway to the door when Philip called after him in a clear voice: 'Is this how angry you were with Kelly?'

Mark turned and stared at Philip. 'I don't know what the fuck you're talking about.'

Then he turned back and headed out the door, muttering what sounded like 'fucking weirdo' as he went.

Coach Steve tried to retrieve the situation, but it was hopeless. Any semblance of order had gone out of the window and everyone was talking amongst themselves about what a creep Angry Mark was. Gethin was doing his best to listen in to three conversations at once, hoping for some relevant gossip on Mark and Kelly, when his phone buzzed. It was a text from Lee.

'Get over here now' was all it said.

He made his apologies and got out of there. As he was leaving, Philip asked if he could have a word, but Gethin told him this was most definitely not the time. 'Looks like something may have come up.'

'Don't suppose you can say?'

'No,' he said. Then, as discreetly as he could, he jotted down his phone number on the back of a flyer and handed it to Philip: 'Call me later.'

'Okay,' said Philip, 'it's just that, well you saw how he was. I'm worried what he might do next.'

Seventeen

GETHIN TOOK THE WINDING ROAD up the far side of the valley, cursing each time he had to back up to let an inordinate number of cars come down the hill in the opposite direction. He checked the time on the dashboard. Just after three – had to be the primary school run. To make matters worse another car, a brown SUV, came hurtling up the lane behind him and had to screech the brakes to avoid ploughing into the back of Gethin's trusty Nissan. He craned his neck backwards to see what kind of wanker was driving it, but couldn't see a thing thanks to the stupid tinted windows.

As a result of all that it was nearly half an hour after the initial phone call that Gethin made it to the Church of the Unpoisoned Mind. He knocked on the door and Lee opened up. She let him through to the back room where Dennis sat clutching a cup of instant coffee, looking obviously upset. Lee and Gethin sat across the kitchen table from him. Dennis looked down at his mug, refusing eye contact.

'Cousin Dennis has something to tell you,' said Lee. 'Come on, tell my boss what you told me.'

Dennis still refused to meet Gethin's gaze but he started mumbling something into his chest. Gethin leaned forward to catch it.

'It was me that Mr Bennett saw. He didn't recognise me because I had my hood up. I was just going for a walk.'

Lee chipped in. 'C'mon, Dennis, be a big boy, you

weren't just going for a walk were you? You were going somewhere in particular.'

Dennis flinched, then carried on mumbling, now in the third person.

'Dennis goes out walking sometimes. Dennis is the Good Shepherd. Dennis is the Karma Chameleon. Dennis looks after his flock. Dennis was worried about Kelly. Dennis wanted to make sure she was all right. Dennis knew a place where he could see her. Just out there.' He pointed in the general direction of the back garden.

Lee rolled her eyes at Gethin. 'I'm sure.'

Dennis ignored the barb, just kept mumbling on.

'Dennis saw her. She was dancing. She was an angel dancing. And then the devil came.'

'You what?' said Gethin. 'Are you saying you saw the murder?'

'I saw the devil. He did the devil's work.'

'You saw him kill her?'

'I saw him do the devil's work.'

'Can you describe him this devil?' tried Gethin.

'He had the mark. The devil's mark.'

'Uh huh. Did you see his face?'

'Dennis saw his face. But he didn't see Dennis.' He laughed: a weird high-pitched cackle.

'Do you think you might be able to identify him if I showed you his picture?'

Dennis looked up at this. 'You have the devil's picture?'

Gethin reached into his bag to show Dennis the picture of Angry Mark he'd shown the neighbour, Malcolm. He couldn't find it. Malcolm must have held on to it. He got out his phone but there was no 3G to be had. Christ's sake, he'd have to go back outside, find someplace with a signal, download the photos and come back.. 'Tell you what. How about I come back in ten minutes with some photos and you can tell me if you recognise any of them?'

'That could be okay,' said Dennis. Then his voice changed, went from a mumble to a preacher's declamation: 'The devil is at war with woman. The devil hates woman. The devil is misogynist. The devil is a rapist...'

'Okay,' said Gethin, then nodded to Lee to follow him outside. She didn't need much encouragement.

The 3G sputtered into life just as they reached the car. Before Gethin could start downloading photos he saw a message from Bex: 'COME NOW Ryan Batey is here and he's kicking off.'

He showed it to Lee. She made a face. 'Let's get back. Dennis can keep for a bit.'

* * *

By the time they made it back to the office, Ryan had gone. Bex was obviously shaken though.

'He came in and he was absolutely steaming, threatening us with all sorts. Said if we didn't lay off him he was going to put us out of business, said he had connections. Usual bullshit really, Geth, it was just he was so angry, veins standing out on his forehead. I really felt like if I said one word wrong he was going to punch me. And he's a big fucking guy. So sorry for texting, you know I wouldn't normally...'

'No,' said Gethin. And it was true, Bex was the most unflappable of people. If Ryan Batey had scared her, then he must have been in quite some temper.

'Did he say anything useful? About his alibi?'

'He was just ranting. Started storming around the place picking up papers, looking for anything with his name on it and chucking them all around the floor. I've picked them all up now, don't worry. But that's when I texted you. And then I was trying to calm him down and getting nowhere, when his phone rang and he went out into the hall to answer it so I couldn't hear anything. Then he came back

141

and said he was going but we'd better back off or else.'

'Almost like he's got something to hide,' said Gethin, and the others laughed and then they crowded round Bex's monitor to decide which photos they should show Dennis. Ryan Batey had obviously just promoted himself to top of the list. Angry Mark the Prof came next. They decided to include Morgan Hopkins too. Though it seemed unlikely that Dennis wouldn't have known who he was. Those were the three obvious candidates, though Leanne couldn't be completely ruled out.

* * *

It took over half an hour to make it back to Abertridwr, crawling through the rush hour traffic. Gethin had to make yet another call to Martina, tell her he was going to be late. She said that would be fine, but suggested they might have a chat when he got there. Lord.

Finally they pulled up outside the house and Gethin picked up the folder with the photos.

Lee knocked on the door. No reply. She knocked again, harder. Still no reply. She banged like hell and shouted through the letter box. Still nothing.

They looked at each other.

'He didn't say anything about going out, did he?'

'No,' said Lee. 'Tell you what, let's have a look round the back.

Lee led the way along the terrace, turned first right and right again into the lane that ran behind the houses. It was easy enough to tell which one was Kelly's place. For one thing the back wall had crumbled so you could see straight in to the back garden and for another there was a sheet hanging in the back window with the spray-painted legend 'Pornography = Sin'.

Lee clambered over the remains of the wall into the garden. Gethin hung back at first.

'Oh for God's sake,' said Lee. 'It's not like Dennis has any right to be here. He's just a squatter.'

'Fair enough,' said Gethin and followed her over the wall. Lee was already trying the back door. At first he thought it was locked as nothing seemed to happen, but then Lee gave it a bit of a shove and it opened up.

The kitchen and dining room looked and smelt much as they had on their previous visit, neglected and rotten but unchanged. The front room though, was a mess, the sofa was shoved back against the wall, a table was overturned, there was paper everywhere. The makeshift altar had been torn down and its contents distributed around the floor. There had either been a fight or Dennis had had a spectacular meltdown.

'What d'you reckon?' asked Gethin.

'Dunno,' said Lee. 'Could be Dennis, but he seemed all right before, didn't he?'

'Maybe he was scared what would happen if he recognised one of our photos.'

'S'pose,' said Lee. 'Well, we'd better find him then.'

Before they left they had a quick look upstairs. Dennis appeared to have been camping in what must once have been Kelly's son's room as it had a child's bed and a wall with a badly painted mural of a sunrise on it. There was a sleeping bag laid out on the floor and a filthy pillow and a multiband radio next to it.

As he stood there Gethin felt himself overwhelmed by a wave of terrible sadness. This overgrown child living in a dead kid's room surrounded by the aftermath of a brutal murder, horrified and fascinated by the adult world of sex. It was just unbearable. He wanted desperately to see Hattie, to hold her in his arms, to make sure that she grew up happy and untouched by the darkness.

'Fuck, let's get out of here.'

Lee needed no encouragement and they hurried back out

of the house the way they came. Picking his way through the garden, Gethin felt his foot land on something that felt different to the rest of the rubble. He looked down and saw that it was a phone. An old Motorola flip phone. He picked it up, opened it. There was a generic picture of a sunset. He clicked on to the contacts list. There were precious few of them, which suggested it might well be Dennis's, but none of the names was familiar. He looked at the call list. There had been a couple incoming and outgoing an hour or so earlier. Probably worth checking out.

He waved the phone at Lee.

'Probably Dennis's. Let me take it. I'll check the numbers, see if I know any of them. And if he calls up because he's lost it, then probably best if he speaks to me.'

Gethin handed her the phone and led the way back around the houses and into the car. He dropped Lee at the station then put his foot down, driving recklessly through the country lanes, needing to see Hattie as soon as possible.

* * *

Hattie seemed absolutely fine when he arrived at Martina's place. She was hunched over a laptop next to Alys, sharing a pair of headphones and laughing at something on screen. Martina, however, looked tense.

'Shall we have a look at the garden while the girls are finishing up?' she said, with obviously forced cheerfulness. He glanced over to see if Hattie had picked up on this, but thankfully not.

He followed Martina outside, bracing himself for a lecture on how he had to sort his life out, how he couldn't expect Martina to look after his daughter for him. But it wasn't that.

'I saw Cat today,' she said, 'we had lunch in the park.'

'Oh yes? How was she?'

Martina frowned. 'I don't really know. She looked great, I must say, but there was something about her.' She paused.

'What sort of thing?'

'Like she had to be careful what she said to me.' She paused. 'You know this guy Nils she's seeing, don't you?'

'Yes,' said Gethin, still tentative and momentarily distracted by thinking what an odd phrase 'seeing someone' was. Cat and Nils were doing a fuck of a lot more than seeing each other, that was for sure.

'I don't like to say this, but do you think he's a violent man?'

Gethin thought about it.

Was Nils violent? You could see getting him in a fight easily enough – idiot that he was. But so what? Look at Gethin himself – hadn't he punched Nils just a few days ago – still didn't mean he would hit a woman. Surely he would have hit Cat when she told him she was going off with Nils, if he had any of that in him. As far as he was concerned it was a completely different order of violence, hitting a woman if you're a man. Could Nils cross that line?

'I don't know.' he said. 'Maybe.'

Martina nodded like he was confirming her suspicions. 'Whenever I mentioned him she seemed to flinch. Do you know what I mean?'

Gethin nodded, though he found it hard to imagine Cat that way. 'It might just be that she was embarrassed about the whole thing.'

'Sure. I expect you're right. I just wanted to tell you though,' said Martina putting her hand on his forearm.

Gethin let it lie there for the minimum amount of time before he felt it would no longer be rude to move his arm away. 'Thanks. I'm not sure what I can do though. If I asked her if there are any problems with Nils, what's she going to say?'

Martina stared at him 'Do you still love her, Gethin?'

He grimaced.

'I know it's hard right now, but I think you do. So if you love her, talk to her. Tell her she can come back. I don't believe she's happy the way things are.'

'Okay,' said Gethin, 'I'll try to talk to her.'

'Good,' said Martina, leading the way back indoors. 'She needs you.'

Yeah maybe, thought Gethin as he drove Hattie home, but did he need her? That was his question and even as he pondered it he found a woman's face coming into mind. Not Cat but Ella.

Eighteen

BACK AT THE HOUSE GETHIN saw that he had messages from Lee and Bex. He waited till Hattie had headed down to bed before calling them back. He got hold of Lee first.

'Any news on the mad monk?'

'No. It's his phone all right, because one of the numbers is for my Auntie Reet, his mum. But she hadn't seen him. Asked if he was at his church. When I told her no, she sounded worried, then she said he might be out on one of his walks. I asked where he would go. She said he usually just walked around the town. Peeping in windows I expect. So I had a bit of a wander about, but no sign of him.'

'Was there anything else on his phone? Any texts?'

'No texts but there were three phone calls he seems to have made just after we were there. Two outgoing, one incoming. I tried them all but they went straight to voicemail, no messages or anything, so right now I've no idea who they were.'

'Well keep trying,' said Gethin, 'and let me know if you find out anything at all. It doesn't feel right to me, him going missing like this. You don't reckon Ryan could have something to do with it?'

'Don't see how, boss. He was in our office at the time, wasn't he?'

'Yeah. Suppose.'

'Don't worry,' said Lee, 'I'm on the case. I find anything out at all, I'll call you.'

After he put the phone down, he tried to figure out

whether Ryan could have been involved in Dennis's disappearance. True he was in the office when they left Dennis, but if he'd driven up there straightaway he might just have had time. Except why would he have suddenly decided to do that when he was in the middle of threatening Bex? Because he stopped after he got a phone call. Could Dennis have phoned Ryan? Or could somebody else have called Ryan about Dennis, told him that he was in danger of being identified? But who could have done that? No one except him or Lee. It really wasn't easy to see how Ryan could be involved. Unless it turned out that one of the numbers on the phone they'd found belonged to Ryan. Definitely something to check out in the morning.

Next up he called Bex back. She picked up and apologised for the noise, then went off to turn the TV down. 'You've interrupted *The Affair*, Geth.'

'Sorry, but you did ring me. What's it about?'

'I had a message from Chrissie. She wants you to give her a ring. She's got an idea about someone you should talk to about Kelly Rowlands. Hang on.'

Bex went quiet, then read out Chrissie's number. Gethin noted it down on the back of an electricity bill.

'I think she likes you, Geth.'

'Uh huh.'

'Yeah, especially since you decked that twat the other night. Women like a bit of that sometimes, you know. Like to see a man asserting himself.'

'Thanks for the tip.' Gethin let the sarcasm show just a little. Then he said goodbye and called Chrissie's number, hoping it wasn't too late. She picked up right away and sounded happy to hear from him

'Hey, Gethin. How's your hand?'

'Bit sore actually. It's not what I usually do, you know, that sort of thing.'

Chrissie laughed. 'I could see that – you looked like one of my little boys trying to hit his big brother.'

'Oh right.' Gethin felt a bit hurt by this, even though he knew it must be true. Had he been aiming at a more mobile target than Nils Hofberg he'd never have connected. All he'd done was have a wild swing. A lucky punch.

'Bex said there was someone you think I should talk to.'

'That's right. You need to talk to Ted.'

'Ted?'

'Kelly's boss, Ted the Piercings.'

'Right, yes, of course.' Gethin was annoyed with himself for not thinking of Ted before. He tried to remember if there'd been any mention of him in the court documents. Whether there had been a police interview. Surely they must have talked to him, but maybe they got nothing.

'Yeah, I was talking to him this morning – he's doing a new piece for me – and we were talking about Kelly – that's what the piece is, a sort of little memorial for her – and when I told him there was a new investigation going on he was surprised and said he thought Morgan Hopkins was guilty and what did I think? And I said it seemed like it was pretty doubtful and then he went all sort of thoughtful and said in that case there was something that had been bothering him a bit. And I said what's that and he asked if I'd seen Kelly's private photos. And I said no, what do you mean? And he said he'd come in the shop early one day and Kelly was there already and she obviously wasn't expecting him because she was looking at some photos on her PC and he couldn't help seeing one of them and it was her in some sort of heavy S&M scene. And he'd sort of coughed or something to let her know he was there and then she'd clicked out of the photos but he could see it was part of like a big gallery or something and then he'd made a joke about it, some remark about seeing her secret photo stash – they had quite a flirty sort of relationship – well I mean it's that sort of place. When you're piercing dicks and clits every day you can't be too private about stuff can you?'

'Suppose not,' said Gethin with an involuntary horrified snort. 'So does he know where she stored these photos?'

'Not exactly, but he said there might be a way of finding out, 'cause she was looking at them on her work PC and it's still there, so maybe there might be a trail in the history. Anyway, he said if you want to call in, you were welcome to have a look.'

'Great, thanks – I'll call him in the morning. Thanks very much for the tip.'

'You think it might be important?'

'Maybe. Depends who's in the photos, I suppose.' Ryan Batey, he thought. That's who he'd like to see. Though Angry Mark would work fine too.

'Oh, that's great.' Chrissie hesitated. 'Listen if you'd like me to come down to Ed's and make the introductions or whatever, then I could do that tomorrow if you don't mind coming at lunchtime.'

'No need to put yourself out,' said Gethin, deliberately oblivious to the possibility that what Chrissie really wanted was to see him again. 'I'll be fine to go over there, and anyway I probably need to do it first thing, as I've got quite a lot going on tomorrow.'

'Oh right.' She sounded a bit disappointed. 'Well if you do end up going later, just let me know. And give me a call anyway, I'd love to know if you find out anything.'

* * *

Blood & Roses Tattoos & Piercings was on Clifton Street, between an African women's charity and a kebab shop. Clifton Street was a half-mile or so east of the city centre and people these days tended to say it was in Splott. As far as Gethin was concerned it was in Adamsdown. Splott only started once you crossed over the railway line. When Gethin was young everyone in Cardiff knew these demarcations: the point at which Canton became Llandaff or Roath became Cathays. Cardiff was different now, a young city full of newcomers who didn't understand the profound differences between the old communities. Now they were all merging into one unholy mess of attempted gentrification.

Blood & Roses had a biker slash Goth vibe, old school and slightly scary. Gethin had never been much drawn to bodily modification. He did have one tattoo, a rose high up on his back. He got it in the week after he came out of prison, as a sign of spiritual rebirth or something. But it hurt and he quickly went off it; didn't like the permanent reminder of a temporary emotion.

If the outside of Blood & Roses – all red and black – looked a little forbidding, it was nothing compared to the guy who came to the door when he knocked. The guy had a shaved head, black eyes, a long grey beard and arms the size of hams covered in writhing snakes. They were well done, the writhing snakes, but Christ, why would you want to look down at yourself and see that every minute of the livelong day?

'Are you Ted?'

'Yeah that's me.' The scary man's voice was surprisingly high and slightly camp. 'Are you the lawyer?'

'Yeah,' said Gethin. It wasn't strictly true. He wasn't a qualified lawyer, the prison sentence had seen to that. He was a mere paralegal, though he knew a good deal more about criminal law than most of the idiots who had helped his clients end up in prison. He didn't think Ted looked like the kind of person who would be too bothered about the niceties, though.

'Well, come in then.'

Gethin followed Ted through the anteroom, lined with photos of Blood & Roses' handiwork and featuring a reception desk and a blood red velvet sofa. Gethin didn't really get piercings at the best of times. He'd had a single earring for a while when he was younger but that was it. The photos on the wall, though, he just couldn't imagine why anyone would want to do that to themselves.

'Why on earth?' he asked Ted, pointing at a picture of a penis with no fewer than three Prince Alberts running through it.

'Lots of reasons,' said Ted, looking vaguely offended.

'Ah yeah, I suppose,' said Gethin, remembering that while Ted seemed like a reasonable enough bloke, he did have half a dozen piercings on open display. God knows what other bits of him would set off a metal detector. 'Just not my thing, you know.'

'Fair enough,' said Ted.

'Why do you think people go in for this stuff? I mean, what attracted you to it, for instance?'

Ted thought about it for a moment then laughed. '*Doctor Who*, I suppose. When I was a kid I always wanted to be a Cyberman. Iron Man as well. I always wanted to be more than just flesh and blood. Didn't you?'

'Not really,' said Gethin and followed Ted through a door at the back which led them into a white room, a bit like a dentist's surgery. He tried not to focus on the various alarming tools laid out on the counter next to the steriliser.

'Nice place,' he said, just to be polite.

'I like it. Cleanest parlour in Cardiff. Everyone says so. Anyway, you're not here for a piercing are you, mate? Don't fancy an ampallang, do you?'

Gethin was about to ask what that was, then clocked the grin on Ted's face and figured he could probably guess. His thighs involuntarily closed together.

'No? Fair enough. Yeah, so joking apart – there's the PC.' He pointed at a bog-standard Dell desktop set up at a desk in the corner.

'Right. So what exactly did you see?'

Ted booted up the computer while he talked. 'Not that much really. It just looked like home-made porn, an S&M set-up with a girl tied up on the bed. I wouldn't have said anything – I mean I don't care what people are into, wouldn't get far working here if I did! – except it was clear the girl was Kelly and she freaked out a bit when I came in. Obviously she hadn't heard me and wasn't expecting me back for a while. So she was all like oh my god oh my god I can't believe you just saw that and she clicked out of the photo and that just took her back to a whole gallery and I've got pretty good eyesight – you have to in this job – and I could see it was like a dropbox folder. Then she clicked out of that and said she was really embarrassed – and some pervy guy had just sent her a bunch of photos. So, anyway, I did my best to make a joke out of it and once she'd calmed down she had a laugh too and I never mentioned it again and nor did she. Not that she was around much longer...' He fell silent and Gethin saw his cheery face turned dark and pained. 'It was only a few weeks later that cunt killed her. Fuck's sake.'

Ted sat down heavily in the chair in front of the PC. Kelly's old chair, presumably. He put his head in his hands and took some deep breaths. Gethin just stood there, trying not to look at any of the photos on the wall.

Finally Ted brought his head back up. 'You don't think it was him then, Hopkins?'

'I can't be certain,' said Gethin, 'but I don't think so.'

'Well that makes me feel like a twat. I should have mentioned this stuff before, maybe it's important.'

'Could be,' said Gethin. 'But didn't you talk to the police about Kelly?'

'Not really. Not worth speaking of. First time they came they obviously thought I was a suspect. But I'd been at a body art convention in Birmingham all weekend and there were about a thousand people saw me there, so they dropped that. Then I hardly heard from them at all. Not till they came back and asked if I'd done that guy Hopkins' tats and I told them to fuck off, I do better work than that. But they seemed certain he was the guy, so I just sort of forgot about it. Got on with mourning her, you know.'

'And they never asked to look at your computer?'

'They didn't really ask anything about what she did here.'

The police never failed to amaze Gethin with their laziness and lack of curiosity. 'So did you recognise the guy in the photos with Kelly?'

'Not in the one I saw. You couldn't really see him, just Kelly. I guess he was taking the picture. But maybe if we can find the rest of the photos he'd be in there. You want to pull up a chair?'

Gethin fetched a stool from the other side of the room and pulled it up next to Ted. He watched as Ted navigated to the Dropbox site online and held his breath when Ted clicked on 'login'. Would the computer have saved Kelly's details?

'Yes,' said Ted, 'fucking yes.'

They were into Kelly's Dropbox. There was a folder simply called Photos. Inside that were a number of sub-folders each of them simply identified by date. Ted tried one and just got a bunch of pictures of a family gathering. Several featured a happy Kelly cuddling her little boy.

'Christ,' said Ted under his breath and quickly exited the folder. The next one he tried was mostly shots of some gig – the kind of pictures everybody feels compelled to take these days and nobody actually looks at afterwards because they're so boring.

The next folder was the one. There were half a dozen pictures in it and they all featured a naked Kelly tied to a bed. Gethin really didn't want to look at them; there was something very wrong about looking at someone's private sex photos at the best of times, but knowing the woman in question had been savagely murdered a few weeks later was just too horrible. For a moment he thought he was going to throw up. He steadied himself. The photos were evidence. If he could identify the man in the picture, he might have a real suspect. Kelly's death might be avenged, or at least explained.

Ted was clearly feeling something very similar. 'You know what, mate,' he said, 'I'll leave you to look at those. Don't want this stuff in my head. Cup of tea?'

'Thanks.' Gethin was unable to repress a momentary smile at the very British oddity of having this ostensibly scary bloke with his tattoos and piercings making a nice cup of tea when things got rough.

He shifted closer to the screen and took hold of the mouse. Willed himself to see the photos as simply factual and not sexual. The first two didn't feature the man at all, no handy reflection in the mirror, no nothing. The third photo most certainly did feature the man, but just his thighs and the base of his penis as the rest of it was buried in Kelly's mouth. The fourth and fifth pictures once again featured the guy's penis, which was poised to enter Kelly. It was a pretty standard size body part but distinctive in that it had some sort of piercing – a small barbell type thing – running through it. Gethin's thighs clamped together at the sight of it. The final photo was just Kelly on her own again.

'Shit,' said Gethin, 'there's nothing. Unless you can identify a bloke by his dick.'

'Ah really? I'm sorry about that. I was hoping… Do you think it might be significant that he doesn't show his face in the photos?'

'Dunno. Could be.' Gethin suddenly found himself feeling thoroughly depressed. Poor Kelly. What had she got herself into? Except that wasn't quite right. She didn't look like a victim in the photos, not scared or anything. As far as you could tell she was into it. Maybe there was no link at all between the guy who tied her up and the guy who stoved her head in.

He was jolted out of this train of thought by the simultaneous arrival of a mug of tea and the local news headlines coming on the radio. The second item jumped out at him. 'The body of a man has been discovered close to the River Taff near Treforest.'

Gethin had an awful feeling he knew whose body it might be.

Nineteen

GETHIN MET LEE OUTSIDE THE pub on the Treforest industrial estate. It was as close as they could get the car to the spot where the body had been found. A quick call to a friendly copper provided a rough location for the body – right next to the River Taff, close to the footbridge. Lee just had time to stop off before heading up to Birmingham for the hypnotherapy appointment.

They walked down the side roads towards the river, passing a recently closed-down furniture warehouse and an obscure outpost of the Welsh Assembly Government, before coming to the river. The path carried on to the footbridge which would take you over to the Treforest estate railway halt. To the left of the footpath was an area of scrubland stretching south alongside the riverbank. Access to this was closed off by a line of police tape. An ambulance was parked alongside.

A couple of coppers were standing next to the makeshift barricade. Gethin approached them.

'Can you tell us what's going on here?'

'Sorry, mate,' said the taller of the two coppers. 'We're just conducting an investigation, so if you don't mind moving on.'

'Yeah I can see that, it's just that I think I might possibly know the person concerned.'

'Did I say anything about a person? If you wouldn't mind...'

Gethin was wondering whether to start getting semi-official when he saw four guys carrying a stretcher towards them. Gethin and Lee stepped back from the police line and watched as the stretcher came closer. There was obviously a dead body on it but it was enshrouded in a bag. At least it was until one of the bearers stumbled as they transitioned from the scrubland to the pavement and the legs started to pop out. Just enough for Gethin to glimpse a pair of baggy jogging bottoms and cheap black work boots. Had Dennis been wearing them last time they'd seen him? He was pretty sure he had. Lee nodded her agreement.

Gethin was about to have another word with the coppers on the line when he saw another obviously more senior officer coming up the path towards them. Gethin didn't know him personally, but he recognised him at once. The Cardiff police didn't have a lot of black senior detectives, so this guy, Deryck Davies, was something of a celeb, always getting wheeled out for the cameras. He looked like a grumpy bastard whenever Gethin had seen him on telly, and he was none too cheery right now.

He scowled at Gethin from a way off, making it very clear that any attempt at conversation would not be welcomed. Lee didn't seem to have read the memo though.

'How you doing, Deryck?'

Deryck stopped and stared at her. He was in his forties, at a guess, shaven headed and lean, looked strong like a runner or a rower.

'Lee Ranger,' he said, 'what the fuck are you doing here?'

'Nice,' said Lee, 'you don't see me in years and this is how you greet me. You think your Auntie Cass would be happy about that?' Her accent, which was always Cardiff at root, could swing north to the Valleys twang and south to docks Jamaican at will. Right now it was veering heavily towards its southern pole.

She turned to Gethin to make the point clear. 'He's a docks boy, Deryck, only he don't like people to know.

Funny thing is they guess it anyway. Can't imagine why.'

Deryck stared back at her. 'Maybe some of us don't want to boast about coming from a place full of thieves, pimps and drug dealers. Maybe some of us have ambition.' Then he shook his head and cracked a smile. 'Good to see you though. You still living up by Cass?'

'Yeah.'

'Tell her I'll come visit soon. Tell her I'm busy at the moment. Like now.' He made to move off, then paused and looked at Gethin. 'I know who you are, don't I? The miscarriage of justice guy. And you're working for him, right?'

'Right,' said Lee.

'So what are you doing here? Waiting to see if I fuck this one up and arrest the wrong guy? Or is there something I should know about?'

'Depends,' said Gethin. 'Are we right in thinking that it's Dennis Hillyer you found?'

'You might be. Why?'

'Because he's involved in the case we're investigating and he's gone missing so...'

'And what case might that be?'

Gethin could see the detective, Deryck, trying to make connections. He'd probably figure it out for himself soon, but for now Gethin still had some limited negotiating power.

'How about you tell me what happened to him, as much as you know, then I'll tell you why we're interested?'

Deryck laughed, no humour in it. 'How about you tell me what you're doing here wasting police time and I don't arrest you for being a nosy twat?'

Gethin wasn't sure whether or not the threat was serious but decided he didn't have much to lose by playing straight. 'All right, he may have been a witness in the Morgan Hopkins case.'

The copper winced like he had a sudden sharp headache. 'Should have thought of that. Abertridwr address. Nobody told you your man was bang to rights then? Suppose it doesn't matter – as long as you get paid you can piss about raking up a load of old shit that needs to be left to moulder away. So this Dennis was going to lead you to the killer, was he? Except he went out for a bit of extracurricular and got his head kicked in.'

'You what?'

Deryck shook his head: 'That's more than enough. I got a job to do, so if you don't mind fucking off.'

Gethin was prepared to leave it there. He had a definite sense that you really didn't want to mess with Deryck. Lee had other ideas though.

'He was my cousin,' she said, a little catch in her throat. Gethin stared at her, wondering if it was real or laid on for Deryck's benefit. As ever, he wasn't sure.

Deryck stared at her: 'You what?'

Lee shrugged. 'I don't know what you're looking surprised about. Bet you've got a bunch of white cousins somewhere and all.'

Deryck pursed his lips, thought about it. 'All right, I'll believe you. And it will all be on the news soon enough. Nothing to it really. It's a bit of a cruising ground here, at night. Your cousin picked the wrong guy and he decided to work out his issues on his head. With his boots. Poor fucker.' He paused again. 'Don't worry, I'll find the bastard.'

Deryck stalked off towards the ambulance and Gethin and Lee looked at each other and came to a swift wordless decision that there was no more point in hanging about.

They walked back to the pub car park. Across the road a coach with the Cardiff Blues logo on it was pulling into the turning opposite. There was a sports ground down there somewhere.

'What do you reckon?' asked Gethin, once they were back in the car.

'Well I don't think it was some random queer-basher, that's for definite.'

'No,' said Gethin, 'me neither. But your mate seems to like it.'

'He does, doesn't he? Or maybe he just doesn't like the Morgan Hopkins case. None of them do. Soon as you've got a copper in the frame they lose all interest. No way he wants to link Dennis to all that.'

'Yeah, that's how it feels. You want to go back to the house?'

'No point. Cops will be all over it.' Lee made a face. 'His poor mum. Let's get moving. Got to be in Birmingham in two hours.'

'Fine.' Gethin set the controls for Cardiff Central and started to drive.

'So are we agreed that whoever killed Dennis killed Kelly?'

'Got to be, Geth. I don't believe in coincidence. Specially not with murder.'

'Fine,' said Gethin. 'I'm with you. And how about this theory: Dennis was murdered because someone knew we were going to show him some photos, so whoever killed him must have been one of the people in the photos.'

'Or someone who thought they might be in the photos.'

'Fair point.'

'Or just someone who saw us talking to him. A neighbour for instance.'

'Fair point again. But still that's a start.'

* * *

Back in the office, Bex told him she'd been trying to discover who was due to inherit Kelly's estate – and any possible compensation money – but no luck as yet.

'Looks like either no one's sorted out the probate, or there's a row going on about it. It's been nearly a year so it should be sorted, but some people just don't get round to it...'

Gethin thought about it. He couldn't see how it was going to be of much relevance, whoever Kelly's heir was. There was no chance it was going to be Ryan or Angry Mark. 'Okay, dig a bit more when you have time. Meanwhile d'you mind having a look through Kelly's photos?'

Bex looked less than enthusiastic at the prospect but brought the folder up on screen while Gethin retreated to his office to try and think things through. He decided that for the moment there were three viable suspects – the Batey siblings and Mark the Prof.

Of the three, Leanne still struck him as the one least likely to have been the actual murderer. He simply couldn't imagine her doing it. But her puppet show suggested that she might, at the very least, know more than she'd told the police. And then something else struck him. What if Leanne was Kelly's heir? That would be a game-changer all right. He figured Lee was the most likely person to get something out of her. He'd send her down to the TextileWorks in the morning. Meanwhile she was up in Brum on her ridiculous hypnotism mission, but she had taken Dennis's phone with her and promised to call in if she found anything interesting.

Ryan Batey still looked a much better bet. The murder had all the hallmarks of being carried out by an angry man and Ryan was definitely an angry man. The problem was that he appeared to have gone to ground again. Deano was on the case, said he'd drop round in five to give them an update.

That left Mark the Prof. He was another angry man and he had known Kelly, but rationally he was a longshot. And yet Gethin couldn't shake the sense that he felt right for it.

So he started working Google, seeing what he could dig up.

The answer was nothing much. All he could find was the university profile, a bland document detailing Mark Lewis's qualifications and interests. Apparently he was fond of kayaking. And lived to inspire young people with a love of geography. He wasn't on Facebook. Or, if he was, it had to be under a false name. A lot of people with public-facing jobs – teachers, doctors, etc – did that. He wondered if Ella might know anything. She'd given him her number when they met in Aldi, so no harm in firing off a text. No ulterior motive, of course.

Unsure what to do next, he called Lee, who stepped out of the hypnotherapist's waiting room to give him an update. 'Okay, like I told you, Dennis made or received three phone calls after we saw him. The first call was incoming and lasted two minutes. I've rung the number but there's no reply and the voicemail has been deactivated. Then there's two calls he made himself, right after he'd received the other one. The first number there was no reply. There is a voicemail but it doesn't give the name or anything. I haven't left a number for now. The other one didn't answer either – nobody picks up these days if they don't recognise the number calling them – but this time there was a name on the voicemail. It's Leanne Beethoven.'

'Christ,' said Gethin. 'Did you leave a message for her?'

'No. I thought we'd better have a plan first.'

Before he hung up Gethin got Lee to give him the two mystery mobile numbers. He called Bex into his office and read out the numbers to see if she'd noted any of them down in their researches so far. She was efficient like that. And she had a hit on the second one.

'Got it, Geth, that's Ryan Batey.'

'Bloody hell,' said Gethin. 'So Dennis gets a call from

persons unknown. Then he calls first Ryan and then Leanne Batey. Soon afterwards there's some kind of fight out back of the house, and then he shows up dead a couple of miles away.' Then it struck him. 'Ryan got a call while he was here, didn't he?'

He got Deano on the phone right away: 'You had any luck with Ryan?'

'No. He won't answer calls or open his door. I tried the gym again this morning. Mate of his there reckons he hasn't been around there because he's training with the Cardiff Blues. Ryan is pretty good, used to play for the South Wales Police.'

Gethin flashed on seeing the Cardiff Blues coach that morning. 'Do they train up in Treforest?'

'Yeah,' said Deano, 'think so.'

Could be a coincidence, Gethin thought. But given that Dennis had called Ryan just before his abduction, maybe not. Ryan knew that area from training up there, maybe he knew there was a quiet spot by the river. 'We really do need to speak to him.'

'Yeah, boss, I'm on it.'

'Might be worth doorstepping Jake Sanchez, see if he knows anything.'

Deano said he'd give it a go, then hung up.

Gethin turned to Bex: 'You found anything?'

'Sort of. I mean I couldn't see anything with the guy's face in it.' She made a face. 'I mean whatever floats your boat, but really... Anyway I had a look at the metadata on them and they weren't taken with her camera. Best case scenario: the bloke emailed them to her in a zip file. So if we can find her email account...'

'Okay,' said Gethin, 'that should have been disclosed to the defence, all her email communications, but surely they'd have noticed something like that.'

'She might have had a whole bunch of email accounts.'

'True, see what you can find out. Anything else of interest in her photos?'

'One thing, Geth. Dunno if you're going to like this or not.'

Bex clicked through a couple of folders till she found what she was looking for. Then she passed the laptop over for Gethin to have a look. There was a whole series of photos taken at gigs. Mostly they were just the usual crap pictures of bands that people never take another look at, but some of them had Kelly with friends. Gethin peered at them, looking for someone he recognised.

'Keep going,' said Bex.

Gethin kept going and there it was – just after a photo of a band he rather feared might be Stiff Little Fingers – a selfie of Kelly with her arm around a man Gethin knew all too well: Nils Hofberg.

'Fucking hell.' Gethin stared at the photo, trying to assess the relationship between the dead Kelly and the all-too-alive Nils. There was no obvious sign that it was anything more than a casual snap. Kelly looked quite excited. Probably someone had told her that Nils used to be sort of famous, but there was no kissing, no hands where they shouldn't be. Probably just another coincidence and barely even that. Kelly went to loads of gigs and Nils used to hang out in those places, looking for fresh meat. Still, it was troubling, the way this case seemed to circle ever closer to Gethin's own life

'Do you think it means anything?'

Gethin made a face. 'Don't think so.' Before he could say any more he felt his phone buzz. He looked down and saw that Ella had replied to his text.

'Must talk to you. Call soon as you can.'

Twenty

GETHIN PICKED ELLA UP FROM her work. It turned out she was another academic. Which made sense of what she was doing at the rehab group. Probably most of them were connected to the university in some way or other. It was the biggest employer thereabouts. And doubtless chock-full of addicts. Obvs, as Hattie would say.

Her office was on the ground floor of a terraced house just adjacent to the main university buildings. She was waiting for him outside, wearing a pale yellow sundress that was respectable enough for a work outfit, but not by much. Gethin felt immediately self-conscious, transported back to his younger self.

He pulled up alongside her, but as he manoeuvred into a parking position she tapped on the passenger side window and indicated that she wanted to get in.

'Can't talk here,' she said, 'too many ears. Let's go to the pub.'

Gethin looked at her, surprised. 'Are you okay with a pub?'

'Yes of course,' said Ella. 'Oh, I see what you mean. Don't worry, I don't have a drink problem. I mean, strictly speaking I should avoid all stimulants et cetera et cetera, but it's really not my issue.'

'Oh right,' said Gethin. 'Bunch of Grapes okay?'

'Perfect,' she said, 'we can sit outside.'

Gethin headed back down the hill, then turned left towards Pontypridd. 'So what is your problem? Sorry, I should have remembered from the meeting.'

'I don't mind. I know what yours is. Well, if it was true, what you said.'

'Afraid so. That stuff was all too true.'

'So it's pills for me. Benzos, you know?'

Gethin knew, more or less. Valium and all that. 'Any one in particular?'

'Lorazepam. That's the one. Takes the pain away.'

Gethin looked over at her, wondering what the pain was she needed taken away. He was trying to think of something appropriate to say when he saw Ella frown and lean forward towards the speakers.

'Hey,' she said, 'turn that up.'

The CD was playing so quietly Gethin hadn't even realised it was still on. It was Gillian Welch, her second album, *Hell Among the Yearlings*. He turned the volume up and let the words flow over them – *Forget my sins upon the wind / My hobo soul will rise* – before getting to the titular refrain, 'I'm Not Afraid to Die'.

When the song ended Ella leant forward and turned off the CD player. 'I supported her a few times, you know.'

Gethin looked at her in frank amazement: 'Seriously?'

'San Francisco twice, Portland, Seattle. Olympia too, I think.'

'So what were you doing?' Gethin asked, the question coming out all wrong in his surprise.

She laughed. 'Playing the guitar and singing my songs, what do you think? I'm not a bleeding stand-up comedian, in case you were wondering.'

Gethin laughed: 'I'm just surprised, you know.'

'Well I have had a past. I didn't grow up wanting to be a lecturer in performance studies at the University of Mid Glamorgan, that's for sure.'

'Right, of course not.' Gethin laughed. So Ella really wasn't just a pretty face. 'I'd love to hear about your music.'

'Okay' she said, a hint of a sigh, 'but there's something we need to talk about first.'

They had turned off the main road and were following the lane that led to the Bunch of Grapes, nestling alongside the old canal. Gethin parked outside the front door and led the way into the pub.

There was a regular locals' bar on the left and a decent gastropub area to the right, with a beer garden beyond. Gethin headed for the main bar, ordered a bitter shandy for himself – selected as having the right balance between work, pleasure and responsible driving – and a medium glass of rosé for Ella.

Once they were sat down on the terrace, well away from anyone else, Ella explained what was up.

'I got this email today.' She handed Gethin an A4 printout. The message was short and to the point. 'Keep your fucking nose out or I'll carve you up.'

Gethin looked at the address. It was a random string of letters @outlook.com.

'Christ, that's awful.'

'Yes,' said Ella and now they were sat opposite each other, he could see that she was very pale and her hands definitely trembling.

'Any idea who could have sent it?'

'Only one. Mark Lewis. I mean who else? Who else knows we're looking into what happened, me and Philip. And you too now. You haven't been sent anything like this, have you?'

Gethin shook his head.

'No, course not, how would he know your email address? He'd know mine all right, 'cause we've all got university email addresses.'

That made sense. Though Gethin thought it was a stupid thing for Mark to do, if it was him. If he had killed Kelly, then it just drew attention to him.

'You sure it couldn't be one of your students? Or even another lecturer? There's not any work thing going on that someone might be angry with you about, is there?'

'I can't think of anyone. I mean I'm not interested enough in anyone's business – or my students frankly – for anyone to tell me to keep my nose out. Most of them would be happier if I did put my nose in every now and then.'

'And you think Mark knows you're suspicious of him?'

Ella frowned. 'He knows we don't like him. And there's a few things Philip has said. I can see how he might have guessed.'

'What d'you want to do about it? Go to the police?'

'I don't know. I'm worried it's not enough. People get death threats the whole time on Twitter and stuff. I don't imagine the police would take much interest, would they?'

Gethin thought about it and tended to agree. 'They wouldn't do much. Do you feel safe where you are?'

'I suppose so. And actually I feel better just telling you about it. I called Philip and I think he's teaching all afternoon and then I texted you and now I think maybe I'm getting it out of proportion.'

'Okay,' said Gethin, 'but be careful. Keep an eye out for anything untoward going on and if there is anything – call me.'

'Thanks.' Ella sat there silent for a while, then made a visible effort to put her fear aside. 'He'd be crazy to do anything to me, wouldn't he? It would be so obvious who it is.'

'That's right. It really would. If it is him, he's just trying to scare you. That's all.'

Ella nodded to herself. 'Fine, okay. Let's talk about something else.'

'No problem,' said Gethin. 'Why don't you tell me about this musical career of yours?'

'Career!' said Ella. 'I wouldn't call it that.' But then

she gave him her potted history. How she'd always played guitar and written her own songs ever since hearing her parents' Simon and Garfunkel records at an impressionable age, and she'd sung at open mics and so forth in Swansea when she was young and then she'd gone to university to do American Studies and that had included a year at Berkeley, across the bay from San Francisco, and during that year she started playing in the coffee houses.

Gethin stopped her there. He had an unhealthy degree of knowledge of West Coast rock. Too young to remember it in real time, he was a sucker for the California hippie ethos. 'Which places did you play?'

'Oh God, in Berkeley it was the Freight and the Starry Plow. That's where I really started out. Then in the city I began playing at the Hotel Utah a lot, that was a cool place, and then you know, all sorts, punk clubs, Methodist church halls, wherever.'

'Wow,' said Gethin, thoroughly impressed and frankly jealous, 'that sounds brilliant. Who else was around?'

'Oh lots of people, everyone, no one, I don't know. I was just so into what I was doing I hardly noticed. I played with Freedy Johnston a few times, that was pretty cool.'

'So did you get a record deal?'

'Kind of. I got signed by some indie label who'd broken through a few acts. That's how I ended up playing with Gillian. The label sent us out on some important supports. But then, just as I was about to start making my album, they went bust. And – maybe this is something about me – it was like I saw it all slipping away through my fingers and I felt like there was nothing I could do to stop it. Which was stupid really. I saw all these other people starting to properly make it and well... Let's just say that's when I started to develop some bad habits. Some bad boyfriends too, that didn't help.' She laughed. 'Bad habits and bad boyfriends – that's the road to hell, right there, Gethin.'

He laughed with her but was struck that, even as she was talking about things going wrong, there was a light in her face that was mostly absent. He thought he could see flashes of the young woman she must've been, playing her songs in San Francisco punk clubs.

'Did you ever make a record then?'

She made a face. 'Yeah, I did make an album. But it was too late and I was bored with all the songs and I'd never met the band that my so-called manager got to play on it and it was just a disaster...'

'You mind telling me what it was called?'

'Oh God, you're not thinking of listening to it, are you?'

'Maybe.'

'I suppose you'll be able to google it anyway.'

Gethin gave her the smile of a man who liked nothing better than running down obscure albums on the internet.

'Fine. It's called *Three Cliffs Bay*. By Ella Tregaron.'

'After the beach? Really playing up the Welsh angle.'

'Exactly. I think people liked it at first, my being Welsh, but in the end they didn't know what to do with me. So I ended up coming home. But they really didn't know what to do with me here, the music industry people. Some girl from Swansea Bay, but she spent the last decade in San Francisco Bay. Doesn't make sense. For ages everyone kept asking me why did you come back? Like they couldn't imagine why anyone would ever come back from California to this. And I just mumbled something about being homesick and the hiraeth, and after a bit everyone lost interest. No one over here has ever been interested in my music so now this is me. "Ella Tregaron, half-hearted purveyor of spurious dreams of an artistic career to kids with indifferent A-levels".'

Gethin waited a beat before replying, let the bitterness lie there and wither. 'So why did you really come back?'

Ella brushed her hair away from her eyes. 'Now that is a good question. You know what you're doing, don't you, with this investigating? You know what to ask.'

Gethin didn't reply, just waited for her to answer. Interview technique rule #1 – never fill in the silence.

'So I had a miscarriage. Six months. With the last of the bad men. And I came home to mum to lick my wounds, so I thought. Only it was worse than that, I couldn't stop crying for a month. And then I found something that could make me stop crying. The little blue pills. And the next two years after that, I barely remember them. That's what the benzos can do, take your pain away and everything else with it. Till I woke up in a crashed car two years ago.'

'Ah shit, I'm sorry.'

'Yeah, me too. Sorry for what might have been. There's a lot of us around, you know, people who thought they were going to be somebody and then they weren't. You have to get on with it anyway and try not to be bitter. But it's hard sometimes, you know. Have you ever read Caitlin Thomas's autobiography?'

'Dylan's wife? No, I never did.'

'Well it's the title that always gets me. She called it *Leftover Life to Kill*. And that's how it feels mostly, being back here.' She stopped there and slapped herself across the face. Quite hard, with a definite crack. Gethin was glad no one was close by, in case they thought he'd hit her.

'I'm sorry,' she said, 'burdening you with all this. One thing I have learnt in this rehab is it doesn't do to dwell on your past. It's all about moving on. And mostly I can do that, or at least I can fake it, but sometimes it all comes back. You know, I never listen to music these days. Because that's the worst.'

'God.' Gethin was touched and appalled and wondering if it would be okay if he took her hand to comfort her. 'That's awful.'

'Yeah it is,' said Ella, and as if anticipating his move she leant forward and took his right hand in her two hands and held it for a moment. 'And then I heard Gillian singing in your car and it reminded me. Made me think of everything I've lost.'

She squeezed his hand then and let go. Gethin stared at her across the table, drinking in her beauty and feeling like all he wanted to do was rescue her. Even as he thought this, an alarm bell went off somewhere in the back of his mind. That's what Catriona always said about him, that he had a messiah complex. That's why he worked on miscarriages of justice, because he wanted to be the saviour. The great white saviour, that's how she put it, and she had a knack of making that sound like a bad thing.

'Do you think you might go back to it one day?' he said at last.

'What? America?'

'I suppose that might be part of it, but I was really thinking of music.'

'I don't know, Gethin. Mostly I think I'm happier without it. Because when I hear it, let alone play it, I get like this.' She raised a hand to eye level and Gethin could see the tears there, just a few of them trickling down towards her perfect cheekbones.

'I'm sorry,' said Gethin. 'Would you like another drink?'

'I don't think so. Not in this mood. I'm really sorry, but would you mind dropping me home? My car's there – I don't like to drive if I don't have to, not since the crash – so I come in and out on the train normally, but I just feel a little shaky.'

'Sure,' said Gethin. Then he realised he wasn't at all sure what time it was and there was Hattie to collect. He checked his watch. It was only just after six. Plenty of time to drop Ella off, as she only lived in Whitchurch. 'Whereabouts are you, exactly?'

'Not far from the hospital. Appropriate huh?' She smiled and Gethin smiled back. 'Let me just freshen up and we'll get going, if that's okay with you?'

'Fine.' Gethin watched her walk through the beer garden and into the pub. There was nothing about the look of her he didn't like.

While she was gone, he checked his phone and noticed a missed call from Lee and a message asking him to ring her.

She picked up immediately. 'What's happening, boss?'

'Not much, about to collect Hattie. How did the hypnotism go?'

'Surprisingly good. I'll tell you later. While I was sitting around there, I had a thought. Bex sent me a link to those photos of Kelly, the S&M ones.'

'Uh huh.'

'Well, you can't see the bloke's face, right, but you can't half see his cock?'

'Yeah,' said Gethin, wondering where on earth she was going with this.

'So he's got this barbell right through the middle of it. And I could be wrong, Gethin, but I don't think there's millions of blokes walking around with one of those in their pants.'

'You think we should get all the suspects to whip their tackle out so we can have a look?'

'Up to you, Geth, if it tickles your fancy. But no, what I was thinking is there's not a lot of places you can get something like that done. In fact, far as I know in Cardiff, there's only the one and that's where Kelly was working. Why don't we ask the feller there if he knows who he's done those for and see if any names match up?'

'Shit,' said Gethin, 'you're right. Why didn't I think of that?'

''Cause you're not the brains of the operation. You're just the eye candy for the ladies. Now you want to call him or shall I?'

'Leave it to me,' said Gethin, 'and thanks.' Then he saw Ella walking towards him, her face washed, fresh red lipstick applied, ready for the world. 'Okay, gotta go.'

Twenty-One

ELLA LIVED IN THE FANCY part of Whitchurch, a tree-lined street of thirties semis. Gethin asked her if she was feeling okay about being there on her own, after the email business. Even as he said it he hoped she didn't read anything into that. Or did he? Maybe he was hoping she'd invite him inside. Make sure the locks were working on her bedroom windows, that kind of thing.

But not only did she not take it as an attempted seduction, it seemed to take her a few seconds to work out what he was talking about. The threatening email appeared to have receded to the back of her mind. Odd, but then Ella Tregaron was an odd one, through and through. He was just waving her goodbye when she leaned in through the driver's side window and kissed him on the side of the mouth.

'Thanks,' she said, 'for everything.'

Gethin drove back up to Gwaelod Y Garth, barely seeing the roads or the traffic around him. Ella Tregaron was all over his thoughts. The touch of her lips, the smell of her perfume, the green of her eyes. He wondered what her music sounded like. He would look it up as soon as he got home. He really hoped he liked it. It would be awful if he didn't, would puncture the daydream he was starting to form, the one in which he coaxed her back into making music, in which she made this amazing album and started to play live. In which she went to SXSW, the big showcase festival in Austin Texas, and she was the word-of-mouth hit. And he'd be what? Her lover/manager? Together they'd tour the US, visit all the places he'd always wanted to go: Montana, Wyoming, Louisiana.

He was a hundred yards past the turning up to Martina's house before he came to and remembered what he was meant to be doing. He U-turned and parked at the side of the house, picked up Hattie and then he was driving up the hill to the upside-down house – his daughter telling him about her friend's birthday party that was happening on Saturday 'and will it be all right if I go for a sleepover?' – when he saw a familiar car parked outside the house. Cat's Hyundai.

'What's mum doing here?' asked Hattie.

'I dunno. Let's find out.'

Cat was waiting for them upstairs in the kitchen diner. She had made a pot of coffee. Cat liked an old-school cafetiere, plenty of weak coffee rather than the occasional strong one that Gethin favoured.

She was looking pale and tense. Before he could say anything she started in: 'I'm sorry, I know I'm not meant to be here. I meant to ask you before coming over and I know this isn't my house anymore.' Her voice cracked on this last, like she was about to start crying. 'I'm sorry. I just wanted to see you. I just need to give my little girl a hug.'

She walked towards Hattie, holding her arms out.

'Oh for God's sake, Mum,' said Hattie. But she let herself be hugged and Gethin stood there watching them, the two people he was closest to in his life. One of them more his responsibility than ever, the other now estranged from him.

After the hug finished Cat wiped a tear from her eye. 'Love, d'you have some homework to get on with? I need to have a chat with your dad.'

Hattie grunted her assent and headed off. Gethin and Cat stood there, staring at each other across six foot of dining table and a hard-to-fathom distance of mutual suspicion.

'So why are you here?' asked Gethin, deliberately

brusque. If Cat wanted to cry on his shoulder she was going to have to earn the right.

'Oh, Geth,' said Cat, 'I'm sorry.' And then she sat down at the table and put her head in her hands. Gethin walked over to the kitchen counter, put the kettle on. He didn't say anything, just waited for Cat to tell him what was on her mind.

'Gethin,' she said eventually. 'I think I'm going mad.'

'Uh huh,' said Gethin, busying himself with the kettle. 'You want a cup of tea?'

'No, I'm all right.' She waved her coffee cup towards him to demonstrate her all-rightness, in the matter of caffeine intake at least. 'Oh, Geth, I don't know what to do. All I want is to come back and make it right. That's why I came over. I wanted to ask you to forgive me. Beg you both to have me back. But then I was sitting here, where I used to sit every day of my fucking life. And after about ten minutes, when you don't show up, I'm thinking about him again. Him. Geth, I just can't let go of it. Of him. That's why I think I'm going mad.'

Gethin was just trying to figure out how to respond to this, without giving in to sheer rage, when the door opened and in stormed Hattie. Clearly she'd gone no further than the other side of the door and was absolutely ready to express her own rage.

'Mum,' she shouted, standing across the table from where Cat was sitting and staring down at her. 'I can't believe you. You prefer him, that, that horrible person over us. Well just go away. Go away and leave us alone. I don't care if you're going mad, you're just...' she was losing it now, rage giving way to tears. 'I hate you. I really, really hate you.' And with that she burst into tears and ran out of the room.

Cat got up, made to follow her downstairs, but Gethin blocked her way. 'No. You've done enough damage. And she's right. Just leave us alone.'

It was Cat's turn to start crying, But Gethin really wasn't having it. He just stood there with his arms folded, waiting for her to stop. Finally she came to a halt and let out a little whimper. 'I'm sorry.'

That was enough. Gethin didn't want to hear any more. What the hell was that supposed to mean? What was he supposed to say? Oh, that's all right then. 'Fine, you're sorry. So what? Ach...' he couldn't restrain himself any longer: 'Go, get out, fuck off back to him.'

She looked up then, stared at him. And her eyes widened. 'Oh God,' she said. 'Is that lipstick on your mouth?'

Instinctively Gethin raised his hand to his mouth, felt a smear of Ella's lipstick there. 'None of your business,' he said. He could have explained that it was nothing, just a social thing, but he didn't. He liked the idea of making Cat jealous and he liked the memory of Ella's lips brushing against the corner of his mouth.

'No,' she said, 'I suppose it isn't.' And with that she got up and left, looking so small and hunched as she went that Gethin almost called after her. But he didn't.

He walked outside into the garden, watched her car make its way down the hill, and thought about how sad it was, and then he mowed the lawn, practically hurling the Hovercast over the grass in his anger at first. Gradually the familiar repetition of the act started to calm him and, by the time he'd finished, his mind was back on the Ella Tregaron daydream and he was happy to let it linger there.

Inside he stuck an old Lemonheads album on the hi-fi and sang along to 'It's a Shame About Ray' as he made tea for Hattie and himself.

As they ate he tried to talk to Hattie about her mother.

'She does love you, you know.'

'Not as much as she loves stupid Nils.'

'That's not true. She loves you much more than that.'

'Why isn't she here then? Why did she leave us?'

'Because...' Gethin cast around for an answer that didn't explicitly refer to sex. 'Did you hear what she said about thinking she was going mad?'

'I didn't mean to. I mean I did. I just want to know what's going on...'

'Of course you do, love. Anyway I think that's the truth: your mum's gone a bit mad.'

'Oh my God. Does that mean she's going away for ever?' Hattie looked ashen now.

'No, love, nothing like that. Adults have these things sometimes, sort of moments of madness. And they pass. In fact I think maybe your mum's getting better. That's why she came over. When you're really mad you don't even realise it. The fact she's saying it means she's getting better. Do you see what I mean?'

'I think so. Do you mean you think she will come back?'

'I can't say for definite, but I think so, I think she probably will want to.'

Hattie bit her lip and stared at him. 'But would you want to get back with her, Dad, after what she's done? Cheating on you.'

Gethin didn't want to lie to Hattie, but nor did he want to shatter her fragile hope. 'Let's just see what happens. One thing you must remember: whatever happens between me and your mum we'll always love you most of all. Okay?'

'Okay,' said Hattie, but her eyes were hooded and suspicious.

Gethin decided not to dig this particular hole any deeper and moved the conversation on to Hattie's schoolwork. She had to prepare an argument for the debating club. She'd been charged with arguing that Brexit was good news for Wales and was finding it hard to come up with much.

'I don't really understand why people in Wales voted for it, like everyone in the Valleys did, didn't they, Dad?'

'Not everyone but most certainly did. A lot of people are

angry because they feel the government doesn't care about them. So if they see a chance to change things they grab it.'

'Even if it's not a very sensible change?'

'That's right, people aren't always sensible. And they don't always want sensible things.' Even as he spoke, he wondered if it was Brexit he was talking about.

* * *

Supper over, Hattie went off to her room to write up some notes and Gethin remembered he was meant to be phoning Ted the Piercings. He fished out the Blood & Roses business card and dialled Ted's mobile number. He picked up on the third ring.

'Who's this then?'

'Hi, it's Gethin from Last Resort Legals. I came round this morning...'

'Sure, what can I do for you?'

'I've been thinking about those photos. The man in them had quite an unusual penis piercing, didn't he?'

'Yeah an ampallang, wasn't it?'

'So I was wondering if you might have done it? And maybe, if you did, that's how Kelly would have met the guy.'

''Course,' said Ted, 'I should have thought of that. I mean I have done a fair few of them over the years. I wouldn't say I recognise that one – no one's got a hard on when you're sticking a hole through it – but I could have a look through the records, especially if it might have been recent. Tell you what, I'll have a look through my records in the morning and call you back.'

'Fine, thanks' said Gethin, then took himself over to his PC. Time to google Ella Tregaron.

There wasn't that much. A brief Wikipedia entry ('This article is a stub. You can help Wikipedia by expanding it.'). A deserted Facebook fan page. A Discogs.com listing that included her one CD and a couple of earlier singles, plus a contribution to a Fred Neil tribute album. It looked as if her heyday was before the internet had really got going, and there didn't seem too much in the way of a cult following. He looked for her on Spotify but she wasn't there. He tried YouTube next and hit gold – three songs from the album had been uploaded. Each had view counts in the high hundreds and a handful of comments, most of them along the lines of 'saw her back in the 90s, lovely voice, whatever happened to?'.

Gethin took a deep breath and clicked on the first of them, a song called 'Crescent Moon'. He really wanted it to be good.

And it was... pretty good. She sounded, Gethin thought, quite a bit like a country-folk singer called Nanci Griffith. Gethin had bought one of her records back in the 90s, but found it just a bit too winsome. And the same went for Ella Tregaron. It was all a bit dreamcatchers and herbal tea for his taste. He was more of a Lucinda Williams, fags and whisky, kind of guy.

He tried the next one, the album's title track, 'Three Cliffs Bay'. This was better. It foregrounded Ella's rather good guitar playing and singing, and the bland backing band didn't show up till the second verse. The song itself had an authentic sense of longing for home, for the summers of childhood, paradise lost.

He decided to leave the third track for another time. Instead he sat back in his chair and wondered what he thought. Being honest with himself he had to acknowledge a slight disappointment. He'd hoped to be bowled over, to fall in love with a great talent. Instead he heard some talent, all right, but rather more potential than delivery. Maybe Ella was right to have given up. Following your dreams wasn't always a recipe for happiness, that was for sure. Look at Cat.

Twenty-Two

TED THE PIERCINGS CALLED GETHIN first thing, just as he was preparing to head out.

'Okay, I've been back through the last eighteen months and I've got seven ampallangs in all.'

'Great,' said Gethin and scrambled around for a pen and paper.

'There's a few we can probably rule out right away. We're not looking for a black guy, are we? Or a pensioner?'

'No,' said Gethin, wondering what sort of OAP suddenly decided his life wasn't complete without a bolt through his bits.

'Great. Well that's two down. And we can probably forget about the next two as well.'

'How come?'

'Two of our queer customers. Not sure even Kelly could have converted either of these guys. So there are just three left.'

'Can you give me the names?'

'Feel a bit uncomfortable. Privacy and all, but here goes.'

Gethin tensed, wondering if Nils Hofberg's name was going to be amongst them.

'There's Peter McCardle from Llanishen. Oh hang on, that's Pete the Pirate, he's covered in tats as well. It definitely wasn't him. There's a James Despenser from Canton. Don't really remember him, to be honest. Not a regular anyway, so you might want to check him out. And there's Mark Lewis, address in Pontypridd. Another one I don't know.'

It took Gethin a moment to process this and then he felt like punching the air. Mark Lewis from Pontypridd, just near the university. That was angry Mark the Prof – had to be –what chance was there it was someone else with the same name?

* * *

Gethin was driving across town to the TextileWorks, where he was due to be meeting Lee to corner Leanne Batey in her lair. As he drove he wondered what it meant if Mark Lewis was the guy in Kelly's photos. It could be nothing much – he was a guy who'd had sex with Kelly. She was a girl who liked sex, so it wasn't the most exclusive of clubs. But he'd sent her those photos just a few days before she died, so it made sense that they'd be seeing each other again. If only crazy Dennis had lived long enough to ID the guy he saw with Kelly that night. But even without that, there were definite grounds for suspicion. Gethin told himself to cool it down – not to let his dislike of Angry Mark colour his judgement – but there was no question Mark Lewis was right in the frame.

Lee was already waiting outside the building when Gethin arrived. She was wearing rolled-up jeans and a black crop top with the word Queen written on it in big white letters. And a New York Yankees baseball cap pulled low over her eyes – the whole thing managing to make her look, as per usual, like an unholy mix of forty-something lesbian and fourteen-year-old boy.

'You ready, boss?'

'Sure,' said Gethin, 'but guess what, you were dead right about the piercing. It's only Mark Lewis – the guy in the rehab group.'

Lee looked properly impressed. 'Fucking A. Shall we go find him now and have a word?'

Gethin had been thinking about this. 'Not yet. If we

don't have any other evidence against him, and we let him know we've seen the photos, then he'll just come up with some bullshit alibi. We should try and see what we can find out first.'

'Fine. In that case let's go see the puppet dyke.'

* * *

Leanne Batey/Beethoven was sat in her unit, bent over a table, sewing a costume. She looked surprised when she saw Gethin and Lee approach, but not especially fearful.

'What did you think of the show?' she asked as they got close.

Gethin was caught on the hop. He'd been hoping Leanne might not have recognised him. Clearly his attempt to pose as a possible client hadn't worked. 'It was… extraordinary,' he said finally. 'I've definitely never seen anything like it.' Which was the truth.

'So are you still hoping to book me for your daughter's birthday then? This your wife, is it?'

Her tone was obviously sarcastic. Clearly she'd seen right through Gethin. She had been a police officer after all. Well, there was no point in pretending any longer.

'Sorry about all that,' said Gethin. 'I was just, you know, trying to check you out. I'm Gethin Grey and this is Lee Ranger, and we're from Last Resort Legals and we're looking into…'

'The murder of Kelly Rowlands.' Leanne finished Gethin's sentence for him, then turned her head to get a good look at Lee. 'I've seen you around, haven't I?'

Lee gave her a good long look back: 'Probably. Was your hair longer before?'

'A bit.'

'Thought so. You knows Patsy from Merthyr, don't you?'

Leanne nodded.

'Okay, then I do remember you,' said Lee. 'All right, Geth, you can carry on. We've finished sniffing each other's arses.'

'Do you mind if we ask you a few questions?'

'If it'll make you go away then fine. But I've got nothing more to tell anyone about Kelly's murder. Everything I know I said in court.'

'Really?' said Gethin. 'I saw your show, remember. Doesn't look to me like you think they've got the right man.'

'I never said they did. Because I wasn't there. That's all I know. I wasn't there, Ryan wasn't there...'

Gethin was sure he detected a change in tone between 'I wasn't there' and 'Ryan wasn't there'. He decided to file it away.

'So of course I don't know for sure who did it. I hope they got the right guy – that fucker Hopkins – but I don't know for sure. And it worries me, I don't mind admitting it. It worries me that there might be someone out there who could do what he did to Kelly, could do it again...' Her voice tailed off. She looked down at the costume she was sewing. 'I loved her, I think.'

Lee picked up the baton. 'But did she love you?'

Leanne looked immediately stricken.

'I don't want to speak ill of the dead, love, but she put it about a bit, didn't she? And she liked the fellers too. Liked a bit of rough stuff, didn't she? You give her any of that, did you?'

Leanne's face went from stricken to horrified. 'No, no, I wanted to get her away from all that. I hoped she'd get over that. She wanted to... I know she wanted to...'

Gethin flashed on a connection – saving Kelly through the power of lesbianism – and decided to run with it.

'Tell us about Dennis then.'

Leanne just looked confused. 'Dennis? Who's that?'

185

'Dennis who moved into the house after she died. Dennis the monk. Dennis who came to your puppet show. Dennis who called you two nights ago.'

'I'm sorry, I have no idea who you mean,' said Leanne, looking genuinely baffled. 'You say he phoned me, this person?'

'Two nights ago for approximately three minutes.'

Leanne did a very good impression of someone trying to remember something, before suddenly getting it. 'Oh yeah, I did get a call the other night, but I had no idea who it was from.'

'Uh huh,' said Gethin, 'so what happened?'

'This guy called my number – I have no idea how he got it but he seemed to know who I am. Except he seemed to think I was still in the police. And he told me he had important information about the Kelly Rowlands case and then something about how some people were going to come and show him photos, but he didn't know if he should trust them or not.'

'So what did you say to all that?'

'Nothing much. I told him to call the actual police. I mean, no offence, but ever since the murder I've had all sorts telling me all kinds of shit about who they think did it and I've had a bellyful to be honest.' She paused again. 'Did you say he came to my show?'

'Yes, he was wearing a weird sort of hoodie, a bit like a monk's cowl.'

'I do remember him. He came up and talked to me afterwards. Very intense. He was starting some sort of charity, I think, to help abused women. Is that the guy?'

'Yeah, that was Dennis.'

'Okay, so that's how he had my number. He told me he wanted to book my show to appear in his church. He has a church, yeah?'

'Sort of,' said Gethin. 'You do know he's been murdered?'

Leanne was horror-struck: 'Christ, no.'

'He called you, then he called your brother, then he went out and that night someone murdered him. Beat him to death at a cruising spot by the Taff.'

'What? He called my brother?'

'That's right,' said Gethin. 'Probably made the same sort of call he made to you.'

'Oh no,' said Leanne. This piece of news seemed to completely wipe her out. She was clutching on to her knees and rocking back and forth.

'Have you heard from your brother in the last couple of days?'

'No I haven't,' said Leanne, 'and I'd like you to go now, please.'

'Do you think your brother may have had something to do with Dennis's death?'

Leanne didn't answer, just kept rocking.

'Do you think your brother could have killed Kelly Rowlands?'

Leanne reared up and screamed at them. 'Just fucking go.'

* * *

Standing outside the TextileWorks, Gethin tried to decide what to do next.

'Ryan or the Prof. Which one do you think we should focus on first?'

Lee stared down at her feet and kicked a stone along the pavement before answering. 'Way I see it, Geth, we start with who killed Dennis. As it stands to reason whoever did that also killed Kelly, right?'

Gethin nodded.

'And the Prof guy, we've got no reason to think he knew anything about Dennis.'

'No reason as of yet. He may have done, for all we know.'

'Okay he may have done. But Ryan the cop, we know he knew Kelly and we know he was the last person Dennis spoke to before he went out. So I reckon we starts with him.'

'I agree. Obviously he's none too keen to talk to us. And we can't just walk in the station and ask for him. But what I'm wondering is whether his mate Jake Sanchez might be involved? He's got form for that kind of thing, after all. Him and his mates raping that girl. Sorry "allegedly raping that girl". Maybe he was there with Ryan Batey. Maybe the two of them could have been there when Kelly was killed. Maybe they really took it too far, that time. What d'you reckon?'

'Like it, boss. No one saw two guys though, did they?'

'No, but then it looks like the person the witness saw was Dennis, not the murderer. So, if no one saw the actual killer, then it could just as easily have been two guys as one. Worth checking out anyway.'

'Sure,' said Lee, 'and he should be easy enough to find. They'll have training every day. We can try and brace him at the training ground or follow him home, wherever that is.'

'Sounds like a plan.'

They were just about to drive off when Leanne Batey came out of the TextileWorks, and started walking north, towards Llandaff Fields.

'Tell you what, boss,' said Lee, 'how about I follow Leanne, see what she's up to, and you see if you can track down Jake Sanchez.'

Twenty-Three

GETHIN WAS SAT IN THE car park of the Vale Resort, waiting for Andy Moles's mate to show up and get him into the training facility, when Lee rang.

'So I followed our girl, right. Guess where she went?'

'No idea.'

'To see her therapist. Place on Cathedral Road. She must have got herself an emergency appointment or something. She looked dead twitchy all the time she was walking over there. So what do you make of that?'

'Not much. She was upset, I suppose, by talking to us.'

'Exactly. And why is she upset? Cos she is hiding something. Hundred to one on, Geth, the puppet girl knows something. Reckon we should go and see her again. Soon.'

'Yeah fine,' said Gethin, his attention distracted by the arrival of another car. The driver was a middle-aged guy in sun specs wearing a bad suit. Had to be Andy's mate. 'Got to go, Lee. Speak later, yeah? And good work.'

Gethin got out of the car and introduced himself to the guy. He was indeed Bryn Daniels, sports reporter for the *South Wales Echo*.

'You're Andy's mate. Hard luck!'

'Yeah,' said Gethin, 'somebody has to be.'

'If you say so. So you want a word with Jake, right?'

'If possible,' said Gethin, who was still trying to figure out exactly what he was planning on asking Mr Sanchez. Where were you on the evening of 10 March, 2015?

'Well, I can get you inside, but after that you're on your own. Doubt you'll get a word out of him. None of them like talking to reporters unless they're being forced to, and he's the worst of the lot. Not totally surprising mind, given that all anyone asks him is whether he's a rapist.'

'You think he was guilty?'

'Yes and no. I think him and his mates did what she said, passed her around like a piece of meat, probably scared the shit out of her too. But I reckon she said yes. At the start anyway. Then afterwards, the way they treated her, she thought she'd get her own back. Get a bit of compo and all. If it was my daughter I'd want him castrated but it wasn't and the jury found him innocent so I'll just get on with doing my job. All right, Jake, tell us about the gaffer's new defensive strategy. Hi, Jake, tell me about that goal-line clearance that bounced off your arse. Do you practise that in training?'

Gethin laughed. 'Don't envy you that. Mind you, should meet some of the people I have to deal with.'

'I'll bet.' Bryn led the way towards the training ground entrance. He was just waving to the feller on the door when a big guy in a fancy tracksuit came barrelling out, a pissed-off look on his face.

'All right, Jake?' called out Bryn. 'You playing Sunday? Any message for the opposition, maybe?'

'Ask the gaffer,' said Jake Sanchez, not breaking stride as he passed them.

'Can I ask you about Ryan Batey?' shouted Gethin.

That grabbed Sanchez's attention. He stopped, turned around and gave Gethin a death stare. 'No you can't. And who the fuck are you anyway?'

He looked at Bryn accusingly: 'He with you?'

Bryn stepped back and shook his head. 'Nothing to do with me.'

'I'm Gethin Gray from Last Resort Legals. I have a couple of questions I want to ask you.'

'Fuck off,' said Jake Sanchez, and walked off fast in the direction of a line of flash motors.

Gethin thought for a moment of getting in his own car and following him, before rejecting it as a palpably stupid idea on the grounds that a) Sanchez's motor would be three times as fast as his and b) there was absolutely no way he wouldn't notice Gethin pursuing him down the narrow lanes that led to the Vale Resort. Instead he had a better idea.

'Charmer, isn't he? You don't happen to know where he lives, do you?'

Bryn gave him a look, then shrugged. 'You didn't hear it from me but he's not far away. Got a big spread just outside St Hillary. On the road to St Mary Church. You can't miss it. Just look for the massive fucking gate and railings.'

* * *

Bryn was right. Jake Sanchez's country pile was easy to spot. Big gold railings. Ten-foot-high gates, topped by some serious looking security equipment. Gethin kept on driving slowly past, till he found an opening in the hedge on the other side of the road and he was able to pull up next to a farm gate.

What to do? He could try ringing on Sanchez's entryphone, but he was pretty sure he knew exactly how that would go. And out here in the Vale – the network of little villages that were becoming Cardiff's very own commuter belt – there was no way of watching the house itself, no neighbours to chat to. He was just about to call it a day when another car pulled up in front of Jake Sanchez's gate. Gethin recognised the driver at once. Ryan Batey as he lived and breathed. The big doors swung open and Batey drove in.

Gethin gave it a minute then drove up to the gate himself and pressed on the entryphone.

'Who is it?'

'Gethin Gray from Last Resort Legals. Is that Mr Sanchez?'

'What do you want?'

'I want to talk to you and Ryan Batey about the late Kelly Rowlands.'

'Ryan's not here.'

'Yes he is, I just saw him drive in.'

There was silence then. Gethin figured the two men must have been having a quick consultation. Then the gate swung open.

Gethin drove up towards what must once have been a regular Welsh farmhouse, but now looked like something that ought to be sat beside an Algarve golf course. There were pillars, there was a swimming pool and a tennis court, and if there wasn't a home cinema somewhere inside Gethin would have been very surprised indeed. He parked the car in front of the ridiculous six-column porch arrangement and rang on the bell. He was half expecting a butler in full evening dress to open the door.

It wasn't a butler though, it was a professional central defender with a very big and powerful right fist that he proceeded to drive straight into Gethin's gut.

Gethin fell to the ground gasping for breath and trying to curl up into a ball before any further violence was perpetrated on him. Next thing he knew, someone very strong was picking him up into the air and he was being held upside down, still struggling for breath, while his car keys fell to the floor. A second person entered his field of vision then. Presumably Ryan Batey, though he could only see his legs. Then this person picked up Gethin's keys and squeezed the fob, and the guy carrying him walked round to the back of Gethin's car, his ageing Nissan Primera, and shoved him into the boot. And then the lights went out and his world shrunk to 180 litres of Japanese engineered storage space.

Gethin lay there, still desperately trying to get his breath back from the punch to the gut, and then to keep from hyperventilating due to the whole being locked in his own car boot thing. Meanwhile some part of his brain could hear talking outside the boot and then the sound of the car door opening and closing and someone turning on the ignition. And then they were off.

Where in God's name were they taking him? Surely Jake Sanchez and Ryan Batey didn't actually intend to kill him. He felt his spirits lift microscopically at that realisation. The pain was wearing off a little and the boot was big enough for him to lie down, not exactly in comfort but not in acute discomfort either. So it could be worse. Then an unwelcome inner voice chipped in – 'What if they did kill Kelly? Then they might have a very good reason to get rid of you and your pesky suspicions.' He started to feel around him in the boot in search of something he could use to defend himself. The odds weren't great against his two big, fit abductors but every little helps, apparently.

It wasn't easy to search the boot, as the car kept lurching around bends, suggesting they were still in the lanes rather than out on the main road. He wasn't sure whether that was reassuring or not. He tried to remember what he had in the boot. A windscreen wiper wasn't going to be much help, that was for sure. There ought to be a jack somewhere. That would be worth having, but he couldn't lay his hands on it. Then he remembered it was in the well with the spare tyre. The problem with that was that the well was covered by the boot carpet and he was lying on top of said carpet. He tried to pull away at the edges, to work it loose then pull it under himself, but it was no good. The car lurched round a particularly tight bend then, and Gethin whacked his head on the side of the boot. It hurt and he felt like curling up into a ball and resigning himself to his fate. He felt, quite honestly, like crying and calling for his mummy.

No, he couldn't give in. He must have a plan. He tried to organise his body so that he'd be able to spring out as soon as the boot was opened. It didn't feel remotely like it was going to work. He dug into his pocket and got hold of his house keys. He could hold them in his hand the way women were told to when walking home at night. It was better than nothing. Though not much. Then, as he dug out his keys, his fingers touched his phone. Oh for God's sake, why hadn't he thought of that before?

He pulled it out of his pocket, manoeuvred himself around so he could look at it. He pulled up the phone and called 999. Surely the police would be able to track his signal. He waited for the operator to pick up. Except there was no ringing tone. He must be in one of the Vale's many mobile phone black spots. Now he really did feel like crying at the unfairness of it all.

He tried to remember where the blackspots were. Along the coast mostly, in his experience. Where were they going? He lay there staring at his phone, waiting for some precious bars of signal to arrive. They didn't, though. Instead the car started to bump along what felt like a farm track and then to move very slowly indeed before coming to a stop.

Gethin heard the ignition turn off, the car door open and close. Then he heard the sound of another car approaching. Another car door opening and shutting. And then a conversation. Two voices, Ryan and Jake presumably, though he couldn't be sure, stressed as he was, which was which.

The first voice: 'Let's just push the cunt over.'

Second voice: 'Tempted mate, can't say I'm not.'

'Like to see his face, mind, when he gets out.'

'If he gets out.'

Both men laughed at that. Then the second voice spoke up – clearly talking to Gethin. 'Keep the fuck out of my business, right?'

Gethin didn't reply, just waited till he heard two car doors open and shut and a car drive off, a fancy high-powered car by the sound of it.

He took stock. He was locked in the boot of a car with no phone reception. Presumably he was in the middle of nowhere. He tried to listen carefully for any clue as to where he might be. There were plenty of seagulls and, perhaps – he wasn't quite sure – the noise of waves crashing against the shore. He was pretty sure he was on the coast somewhere.

First things first, he had to get out of the boot. He tried to kick his way into the back seat. He felt like it should be easy but it wasn't. Whatever catches kept the back seats in place were holding firm. He twisted right and left, trying to get maximum torsion, but still no luck. Maybe there was some way to unlock the boot from the inside. He fumbled around for the catch, then remembered he had a torch on his phone. He shone it around the lock, in the vain hope there would be some kind of catch he could flip, but no.

He twisted and turned some more looking for weak points. After a bit he identified the insides of the rear lights. Maybe he could push one of them out, but what use would that be? He slumped back into a ball, really struggling to keep it together now. Partly he was feeling hard done by, partly he was feeling like an idiot. Why hadn't he taken precautions before doorstepping Jake Sanchez? Because you don't expect professional footballers to kidnap you, that's why. But they probably get up to all kinds of shit. Don't the big teams have specially employed fixers to sort things out for them, pull some strings?

Pull some strings – a synapse finally fired in Gethin's brain. There was some kind of wire that went from the front seats to the boot and sprang it open when you pressed on the lever. It must run through the boot, surely it must. He examined the edges of the boot with his phone torch, noting uneasily that it was quickly running out of power. Nothing to be seen. Then he remembered he was lying on top of a carpet. He had to get the carpet out of the way. He took some deep breaths and started working away at the joints between the carpet and the car frame. Using his keys he managed to make first a small incision and then a larger one and soon he was ripping the whole passenger-side end of the carpet away from the frame and tortuously pulling it underneath him so it all rucked up on the driver's side. It was getting harder than ever to manoeuvre in the boot, but slowly, agonisingly, Gethin managed to locate a cable that ran along the floor of the boot and following a further desperate act of contortion he was able to pull on it hard and then like an absolute bloody miracle the boot sprang open. This time tears just sprang from his eyes unbidden. He'd actually done it. He'd opened the boot.

He rearranged himself and started to clamber out and then abruptly stopped. Oh dear God. All he could see, once he stuck his head out, was nothingness and then he looked down and saw a sheer drop of 100 feet or so. And even as he peered over what was evidently a cliff edge, he felt the car tremble and he flung himself backwards into the boot.

He took a moment to get his breathing back to normal. Then, trying to move as little as possible, he put his head up again and looked out. He registered the sheer drop below him then looked to left and right. Over to his left he could see a lighthouse. He knew where he was now. Nash Point. A beauty spot. Him and Cat had brought Hattie here a few times. The thought calmed him. People came here all the time with their kids and they didn't fall over a cliff.

Very slowly, very carefully he opened the boot to its full extent, making sure to keep his weight as far back as possible. He got one leg out, then thought he could feel the car starting to move so he pulled it back and then, in one desperate move, he flung himself headfirst over the side of the boot. He caught his back leg on the side of the car and hit the ground unevenly. He started to roll towards the cliff edge, just a couple of feet away. He flung his arms out trying to grab on to something, anything, and merciful fate provided salvation in the shape of a hardy shrub, a strong and hardy shrub. He stopped rolling, gained control of his momentum and started to crawl back from the edge. Then he lay there on the ground for what seemed like forever, shaking and staring up at the sky.

Twenty-Four

NINE O'CLOCK THAT EVENING GETHIN was sat in his living room drinking red wine with Lee and replaying the events of the day. He was still feeling decidedly shaky and when Lee had offered to drive him home from the office that evening and help out a bit he'd been happy to accept.

Somehow he'd driven from Nash Point to the office, feeling on the edge of panic all the way. Bex and Lee had known something was up at once and he'd just collapsed and let them take charge. Bex had called Martina and arranged for Hattie to sleep over, and then Lee had driven him home and tipped red wine down him, and now he was finally starting to feel calm enough to decide what to do about calling the police.

'Trouble is,' said Lee, 'it's your word against two of them. And one of them's a bastard copper.'

'Exactly. And most places there's CCTV, but not out there.'

'Only good thing I can think of is if they reckon they've scared you off then maybe we can turn this to our advantage, like.'

Gethin thought about that. If he didn't go to the police about what had happened, then Jake and Ryan might well assume he'd been scared off.

Just then a text message popped up on his phone. It was from Bex. 'Check the BBC Wales news,' it said, 'there's been an arrest.'

Geth did as he was told. And there it was: 'Forty-two-year-old lecturer Mark Lewis has been arrested in connection with the murder of Dennis Hillyer'. There wasn't much more to it than that. But that alone was plenty.

He showed it to Lee. 'Christ,' she said. 'Looks like it's a change of plan.'

* * *

Gethin found out some more about the arrest first thing the next morning. He'd offered Andy at the newspaper a generous drink in return for any info and he'd called back around eight thirty with the inside story.

'Turns out the cops found one of those clip-on IDs they give you when you go into an office, and it had the lecturer geezer's name on it and there were bloodstains as well. So they're being tested now and if there's a match then it looks like yer man's bang to rights.'

'How come they took so long to arrest him if they had something that blatant?'

'Apparently it was pretty well hidden in the undergrowth. Plus, Mark Lewis is a pretty common name, so they had to make sure they had the right one.'

'Do you know if he's talking at all? Has he confessed?'

'Apparently not. Just asked for a lawyer and kept his mouth shut.'

Driving into the Bay, Gethin started to feel a wave of anxiety. Kept flashing back on the day before. He felt as if he was simultaneously driving his car and locked in the boot. To distract himself, he tried to focus on figuring out the implications of the new arrest. If Mark Lewis, the angry professor, really had killed Dennis, then how had it come about? It surely had to be because he feared that Dennis was about to identify him. But how had he learnt that? There were two possible explanations he could think of. The first and most likely was that the mystery phone number Dennis had called had belonged to Mark. That, however, begged the question of why Dennis would have called Mark. How would he have had his number?

The other possibility was that Mark had been aware of Gethin's investigation, had somehow followed him to Dennis's church. He had a flash of memory – a big car following him over the hill from Treforest to Abertridwr that day. Could that have been Mark? Or could it have been Jake Sanchez? No, that made no sense. He felt like his mind was scrambled. Maybe he had PTSD or something. Maybe, rather than calling the cops, he should be calling a therapist.

He was still feeling distracted and out of sorts when he arrived in the office. The rest of the team were little better. Bex was knackered from having travelled to Haverfordwest the night before to sing with Fleetwood Mock. She was doing the Christine McVie parts. She was actually a pretty decent piano player, Bex. Lee was plain grumpy: there'd been another drama with one of Monica's kids when she got home.

Gethin brought them up to speed on the Mark Lewis news.

'There's one problem, though, from our point of view.'

'What's that?' asked Bex.

'The cops are only interested in Mark Lewis for killing Dennis. It looks like they've got good forensics, so they don't care what his motive is. And, as we know, the last thing they want to do is reopen the Kelly Rowlands case.'

Lee nodded. 'We needs to find the links and stick them under the coppers' noses. If they've got this guy cold for killing my cousin and we can show the links to Kelly, they have to allow an appeal for Morgan.'

'Exactly. Let's hope so anyway. So what have we got?'

'The piercing?'

'That's not 100 per cent yet, but it looks pretty likely. Trouble is I've had another look at the pics and I can't see anything else to identify who the guy is apart from his dick. And even if he does have a bloody great bolt through it, it's not easy to make it stand up in court...'

Gethin paused, having realised what he'd just said. Both Bex and Lee were in stitches. He gave it a minute then carried on.

'All right, ladies, that's enough. So what I reckon is that it's good corroborating evidence, but we need more. Someone who can make the link between Mark and Kelly, or even the link between Mark and Dennis.'

'Just thinking about that, boss,' said Lee. 'I'll go and have a word with my Auntie Reet – Dennis's mum – I ought to see how she is doing anyway and find out if she knows anything about Dennis and this Mark guy knowing each other.'

'Thanks. Have you tried the number again, the one from Dennis's phone?'

'Yeah. Just rings out.'

'All right, well good luck with the mum and I'll try the rehab group. There's a guy there who reckons he saw Mark and Kelly together. Bex, you get on to Morgan's brief, tell them what's going on.'

Gethin retreated to his office with a cup of tea. He didn't have Philip's number but he figured he knew somebody who did.

Ella picked up on the third ring. The second he heard her voice he had the thought flit across his brain that he really, really wanted to have sex with her. He didn't say that though. Instead he got straight to the point and asked for Philip's number.

'I want to ask him about the time he said he saw Mark and Kelly together.'

'Yes, yes of course. We can't believe it. Listen he's right here. Hang on.' Gethin could hear Ella talking to Philip. 'Can you come up here? We could meet you in the university canteen.'

There was no need, really. Gethin could have got all he needed over the phone, but the chance to see Ella again tilted the balance. 'Fine. See you there.'

* * *

Twenty minutes later Gethin was sat in the canteen with Ella and Philip. Philip Gomer, senior lecturer in history, to give him his full title. They were all drinking tea and discussing the sensational turn of events.

'So the first I knew of it,' said Philip, 'was when I saw a couple of cop cars parked outside the main reception area. I was thinking "Oh God, which of the Media students has been busted for drug dealing now?" – dunno why it is but Media Studies seems to have more drug dealers per head than any other degree.'

Gethin laughed and Philip carried on. 'So I decided to go and see what was going on – I'm incorrigibly nosy, I'm afraid – and there were two coppers walking down the corridor with Mark in between them. I couldn't believe it. I asked if anyone knew what was going on and right then the vice-chancellor comes barrelling up and he's talking to the coppers and anyway, to cut a long story short, it looks like Mark's been arrested in connection with the murder of that lad who was killed down by the Taff the other night.'

'Must have been a shock.'

'Definitely. I must say I'm, am finding it hard to process. I've never liked Mark – that's no secret, we have a certain history – but to think he could have done something like this.' He shook his head in slightly stagey disbelief. 'What do you think, Ella?'

'No, I agree. I'm just staggered. I know he's something of a sexual predator, but I had no idea he was interested in men as well as women. Just shows how little we understand of other people. Don't you think, Gethin? But maybe you know more about it?'

Gethin hesitated. He didn't want to give too much away at this stage. 'I dunno... It's just possible there may be a connection between the dead man and the Kelly Rowlands case.'

'Seriously?' Philip looked like he'd just won the lottery but was trying not to let on.

'Let's just say it's possible the dead man may have been a witness to something that went on around the time of the murder.'

'Jesus,' said Ella, who just looked shocked. 'That's just horrible. I know we've talked about Mark possibly being involved in that murder, but I suppose I never really believed it deep down. But if this is true...' She wrapped her arms around herself. 'The thought that I'd been sitting in the same room as a murderer, telling him all my shit and him staring at me the whole time. Oh God.'

'Let's not get ahead of ourselves,' said Gethin, 'best we see what evidence the police have against him before anything else.'

At this point Philip announced that he had to head off to a lecture. He arranged to meet Gethin that afternoon to tell him more about Mark Lewis. And then he was gone, leaving Ella and Gethin alone at the table. They both hesitated before starting to speak simultaneously.

Ella laughed and said 'After you.'

'I was just going to say I listened to some of your music.'

'Oh my God, what did you think?'

'I really liked it.'

'No, come on what did you actually think?'

'I did like it. The songs, your singing. Okay, some of the production sounds a bit dated but... you're really good.' He felt fake as he talked, hoped she couldn't tell. Maybe he should say what he really thought, that it was kind of okay with some genuinely promising elements. Sure, and put the kybosh on any chance of, er, intimacy. The classic dilemma: whether to flatter and stand a chance or tell the truth and lose that chance. Either way you ended up feeling a bit wrong. Still, in for a penny...

'Is there any more stuff I can listen to – live shows or anything?'

Ella laughed again. 'Okay, no need to overdo it. I know how good I was and I was quite good. If I'd stuck with it maybe I could have been more than that...'

She tailed off and Gethin decided to jump over the cliff.

'Would you like to get a drink this evening?'

'Yes,' she said, without missing a beat, 'I'd love to.'

They agreed to meet at the Gwaelod Y Garth Inn just down the road from Gethin's place at nine that evening. Leaving the university, Gethin felt momentarily exhilarated until he remembered he was a single parent. And in dire need of a babysitter.

'Bex,' he said, then, 'any chance you could do me a huge favour?'

Twenty-Five

AT TWO O'CLOCK THAT AFTERNOON Gethin drove into the car park of the Four Feathers in Capeldewi, the same car park that had seen his car drenched in lager and piss the last time he'd visited. It wasn't his idea to meet there but Philip had suggested it, said he'd had a hard few days and he was badly in need of some fresh air, so if Gethin didn't mind they could combine a talk about Mark Lewis with a hilltop walk. The walk part of it sounded good to Gethin too.

'Just as long as we don't have to go into the pub,' he'd said and Philip had laughed and said, 'Oh, it's all right once they know you.'

Gethin hadn't been entirely convinced by that, but on a weekday afternoon the car park was empty and the pub itself appeared to be closed.

Philip turned up a couple of minutes later, driving an old Range Rover. He jumped out of the car, shook hands with Gethin then got out his walking boots. Gethin looked down at his DMs.

'Think these will be all right?'

'You'll be fine. I just like to have the right gear, bit anal like that.'

Gethin laughed and tried to ignore the arrival of one of his occasional cravings for a cigarette, while Philip very carefully laced up his boots.

Then he was done and leading the way out of the car park and past the village church till they came to a track leading gently uphill. Soon they'd left the world of cars and Valley towns behind in favour of a scrubby atmospheric plateau, populated by sheep but studded with the odd abandoned mattress or burnt-out car as a reminder that this was working countryside, not a specially designated beauty spot. Considering they were no more than twenty minutes from the centre of Cardiff, it was amazing how remote it felt, even more so to see that they had it all to themselves.

Philip had kept determinedly silent until they were properly away from civilisation. Gethin didn't mind too much. He was enjoying the views and the peace, but he was about to start asking questions when Philip seemed to anticipate him.

'So you want to know about Mark and Kelly?'

'Uh huh. I'm looking for anything we can take to the police, to show that if Mark Lewis did kill Dennis, then it was to cover up the fact that he'd already killed Kelly.'

Philip shook his head, looking sorrowful. 'I can't believe it, I really can't. I've never liked Mark. I think he's an arrogant sexist twat, basically. And I know Ella and me were talking about the possibility that he could have murdered Kelly, but to be honest I never really believed it. I suppose I sort of wanted it to be true, just because I dislike the man, and you know how it is in the self-help groups, your feelings get magnified. But it was almost like a parlour game, Cluedo or something. Did you, Professor Mark, kill Miss Kelly in her front room with a lead pipe? And now...'

He tailed off, gave Gethin a theatrically mournful look, 'And now it seems like he might actually have done it. And instead of focusing on all the negative things about him, his boorishness, his sexual boasting, I keep thinking that he was just another colleague, used the same coffee machine, taught the same students. It's just so bizarre. Don't you think? Or are you used to this? I suppose you've met quite a lot of murderers?'

Gethin thought about it. 'I've met a few. Though pretty much all the ones I meet say they're innocent.' He thought of Karl Fletcher and shuddered inwardly. 'But I know what you mean. You sort of expect them to have horns or a crazy stare or something, but generally they seem pretty normal and, talking to them, you have to make a kind of conscious effort to remember what they've done before you get too friendly.'

'Right,' said Philip, 'and it really looks like Mark killed this guy, Dennis?'

Gethin didn't want to say too much. 'It looks like they have some pretty solid forensic evidence.'

'Okay. This is all I know. I was in the Bunch of Grapes one afternoon...'

Gethin immediately saw himself sitting there with Ella Tregaron. He forced himself to concentrate on what Philip was saying.

'I was there on my own, just having a beer and catching up on some marking and in comes Mark Lewis with this punky little girl, looked young enough to be his daughter. Though apparently she was older than she looked, but anyway. I just thought "Oh yeah here's Mark with another of his students – social media campaign waiting to happen".'

'He had a reputation for that, then?'

'Yeah absolutely. Well, that's why he was in the rehab group. The university told him it was a condition of keeping his job.'

'Right, so walking out the other day was quite a thing.'

'I suppose he thought the vice-chancellor's bark is usually worse than his bite. But maybe he knew things were getting out of control.'

'That makes sense, I guess. So did you know who Kelly was, that time you saw them together?'

'No, he didn't introduce me or anything. Didn't even

notice I was there. Was only after she was murdered and I saw her picture in the paper that I realised who she was.'

'Did you think of going to the police when you realised?'

Philip looked sheepish. 'No. Of course I think now that I should have done, but it seems tenuous and obviously the poor girl had quite a few relationships. And then they arrested Morgan, so I didn't see any point.' He paused. 'And I suppose I was worried that it might look like personal jealousy or something, us both being on faculty at the same place. And it wasn't as if anything untoward happened.'

'Really?' asked Gethin. 'So you just saw them together once, that's all?'

''Fraid so,' said Philip.

Gethin couldn't help feeling irritated. If that really was all Philip had, then why the hell had he dragged him out here for a hilltop hike? 'Nothing about the body language then? They weren't having a row or anything?'

Philip frowned. 'Not really.' He screwed up his eyes as if trying to visualise the scene. 'Well he was kind of all over her. Squeezing her hand and actually, yeah, I think I did hear her say something like "Easy tiger" to him at one point.'

'Anything else?'

'No, I'm sorry.'

Gethin had another thought. 'Did Mark ever mention, maybe in one of the sessions, anything about having piercings? Unusual piercings.'

Philip looked shocked. 'Oh, my lord. No, I don't think so. But really I've no idea and, come to think of it, he may have made one or two sort of jokes about his sex life which hinted at something like that. They just went over my head at the time. Or I just thought he was joking. I mean it's another of those things you hear about but you can't imagine anyone you know actually doing – murdering people, piercing your, er, privates.'

It was oddly prissy, the way he said 'privates'. And

Gethin was starting to get a little exasperated with this walk. He checked his watch ostentatiously. 'I really should be getting back now.'

'No problem,' said Philip, 'but just indulge me a little. If we just head on another fifty yards there's the most remarkable view.'

Gethin assented. He had walked all this way, so he might as well get the benefit of the view. And it was quite something: you could see north towards Merthyr and the Brecon Beacons beyond, and directly in front of them you could look east towards the Black Mountains. He was pretty sure he could see the Sugarloaf. He leaned on a dry stone wall and took it all in, let the revelation of nature calm his troubled soul for a while. But after two minutes of that he was ready to head back.

'Beautiful,' he said to Philip, aware of his banality but using it deliberately to discourage detailed conversation. It didn't work though. Philip pointed downwards, not towards the far distance but the valley immediately below them. You could see Abertridwr to the right. Philip, though, was pointing to the next village along, over to their left.

'You know what that place is?'

'No.'

'It's Senghenydd.' Philip waited for Gethin to respond. When he didn't, he carried on. 'What do you know about Senghenydd?'

Gethin tried to think. A word popped into his mind. 'Wasn't there a disaster?'

'You could say that,' said Philip. 'In fact there were two disasters. One in 1901 which killed 81 miners. Another in 1913 which killed 440 people, the worst such disaster in British history.'

'Christ.'

'Yes, quite. Do you know why they happened, these disasters?'

Gethin shook his head, wondering what on earth had possessed him to go on a walk with a local history-obsessed lecturer,

'Firedamp. It's a mixture of hydrogen and methane. Highly explosive. They had the finest coal here – steam coal – but alongside it came the firedamp. If you had too much coal dust in the air – and you generally did – it could ignite just like that. It happened, like I say, in 1901 and 81 miners died. There was one survivor. Baron Merthyr didn't change anything, though, the man who owned the pit here.' He paused. 'Sorry as you can see, this is rather a hobby horse of mine. But for a good reason, I think. You mind if I go on?'

'All right,' said Gethin, his tone now verging on the rude. He needed to get back to work. He turned away for the view and started heading back to Capeldewi. If Philip wanted to continue his lecture, he was going to have to do it while walking.

Philip took the challenge in his stride: 'So after the first disaster and another one that happened in France there were laws brought in. New safety standards had to be put in place by January 1913. Baron Merthyr – William Lewis his name was, local man – he didn't bother. And on October 14 the mine blew up. Four hundred and forty dead.'

'Jesus,' said Gethin, picking up the pace but still struck by the scale of the disaster.

'Quite. And would you like to guess how much the colliery was fined for not doing the safety work?'

'Go on,' said Gethin, imagining it now, the mining village below a hundred years earlier, the explosion and the terror and the families up above, waiting and despairing.

'They fined the colliery £10. Ten fucking pounds.'

'Jesus.'

'It's not much, is it, £10? An old sixpence for each life.

Of course the royal family chipped in. You can always rely on them to show concern for their loyal subjects. Shall I tell you how they contributed?'

'Okay.' Gethin could appreciate that this was a genuine outrage he was hearing about, but did Philip really have to deliver his lecture in quite such a patronising tone?

'Well they didn't bother coming down or anything, but there was a royal wedding coming up. So they put their wedding presents on display and charged the hoi polloi to come and look at them – and then gave the money to the disaster fund. Marvellous, eh?'

'Really?' Gethin pondered this as he walked. As a general principle he tried to avoid getting angry about politics. He wore a battered carapace of cynicism that allowed him to keep on going. Last Resort Legals struck the odd blow for justice. But now and again the injustice of the world did get to him. And this was one of those times.

'What a bunch of cunts,' he said.

'Yes,' said Philip, 'that they are.'

The two of them fell silent then and carried on walking back the way they came. And after a little while Philip changed the subject.

'Ella said she went for a drink with you the other day.'

'She was pretty shaken up after she got a threatening email' – Christ he'd forgotten about that, he should definitely follow up, see if it could be linked to Mark Lewis – 'so we went for a quick one in the Bunch of Grapes.'

'Oh, she took you to the Grapes.'

Gethin thought he detected a note of jealousy. Maybe Mark did have a point about Philip's feelings for Ella. He decided to tread carefully.

'My choice actually. I mean it's the best pub around isn't it?'

'Oh of course, I forgot you lived locally. I hear she told you about her music.'

Gethin was sure of it now: Philip was definitely interested in Ella Tregaron and definitely not very happy that she'd been getting close to him.

'She mentioned it.'

'So what did you think?'

'Pretty good,' said Gethin. 'I mean it's always a bit odd hearing people's music when you've already met them. Sort of hard to separate the song from the person.'

'I suppose it might be for some people,' said Philip, about as sniffily as he could without actually sniffing. 'I think it's pretty extraordinary, her facility for melody and especially her lyrics. So literate, so superior to all that terrible rubbish you hear now, the Stereophonics or whatever. I don't listen to anything more recent than Vaughan Williams most of the time, but Ella Tregaron, she's something special. Though maybe you don't see that?'

How was he supposed to answer that? He just went with a vaguely positive grunt and was relieved to see that they were almost back at the car, approaching the churchyard.

'Shall we have a quick look in here?' Philip opened the churchyard gate.

'As long as it's quick,' said Gethin, in a tone that he hoped conveyed the fact that his patience was running thin.

Philip led the way to the area of the graveyard furthest from the church. The building itself was evidently very old, Norman probably, and many of the gravestones were ancient and indecipherable, but in this corner they looked relatively recent and their inscriptions were all too clear. Victims of the Senghenydd disaster. Philip stopped in front of one and stared at it.

Gethin wandered from grave to grave, acknowledging the deaths. He was just about to leave when he stopped in front of one last gravestone. When he saw a woman's name, he nearly didn't bother looking any closer – only men died in the Universal Colliery – but something pulled him towards it and he read on, fascinated and appalled.

'This monument was erected by public subscription,' it began. 'In honoured memory of Annie Dorothy Fletcher, beloved daughter of William and Alma Fletcher of Abertridwr who died 12 August 1908 yielding up her life rather than her virtue aged 19 years.'

Below this grim declaration there was a motto: 'Blest are the pure in heart for they shall see God.'

Twenty-Six

GETHIN TOLD ELLA ABOUT THE inscription as they sat outside the Gwaelod Y Garth Inn, enjoying the Indian summer evening.

'Oh my God,' she said, 'someone tried to rape her and she fought back, so he killed her. You don't imagine something like that happening in a little mining village.'

'No,' said Gethin, wondering why not. 'Maybe it's because we like to keep our stories simple. Mining villages populated by working-class heroes, mining by day, choir singing and studying by night, while their womenfolk are towers of strength...'

'You're right,' said Ella, 'but men are always men, aren't they? There is nowhere safe if you're a woman. Not really.'

'Not ever?' asked Gethin. 'Do you always feel in danger?'

He looked at her and realised it was a stupid question. She was lovely and somewhat fey. Of course there were men who would want her, whether or not she wanted them.

Ella just gave him a sad smile and a shake of the head.

'It's okay, I don't want to exaggerate it. It's not red alert all the time. And some places really are safer than others. I lived in Oakland for a while and everyone who lived there was on permanent alert. When I'm here at home, it's mostly fine. But does it affect every decision I make? Where I sit in a café? What I wear to teach my students? Of course it does.'

'Right,' said Gethin, trying to look concerned, which he was, but also trying desperately to think of a subject less guaranteed to nix any chances of a romantic outcome to the evening.

'So,' he said, after what he hoped was a suitable pause, sufficient to suggest that he had been properly affected by her little speech. 'Do you miss it, California?'

'Yes. No. Sometimes?' Ella leaned across the table and took his hand. 'Do you really care?'

'Not really,' said Gethin, the touch of her hand sending a wave of excitement through him. They looked each other in the eye and this time Gethin was absolutely sure that the woman opposite him wanted the exact same thing he wanted and he leaned forward and she leaned forward and then they were kissing. In his eagerness his lunge had sent his pint glass flying. He was dimly thankful that it was nearly empty and there was no one else outside the pub to laugh at his clumsiness, but frankly he wouldn't have cared if there had been. He was kissing Ella Tregaron, his tongue in her mouth, hers in his and that was all he wanted the world to be.

The position he got himself in, sprawled across the pub table, was unsustainable. So he made a ludicrous cramped dance around the side of it with the ultimate aim of joining her on her bench, but keeping his lips locked on hers the whole time. It would doubtless have been YouTube gold, had someone been filming, but then he was there and for the next ten minutes that really was the whole world.

It was Ella who came up for air first, but only to say: 'Can we go to yours?'

There was nothing Gethin wanted more, but Hattie was there with Bex babysitting, so it was never going to work.

'Not really, my daughter's there. How about yours?'

Ella immediately pulled back. 'You have a daughter?'

'Yes, didn't I say?'

Ella seemed oddly perturbed by this. 'Cat never mentioned she had a daughter.'

There was something about her tone – sort of aggrieved

and disbelieving, a little whiny even – that caused Gethin to pull back too. He bit back the words he was on the point of saying – 'Of course she didn't, she's your bloody therapist, not your mate' – and managed a flat 'Well she does. We do.'

'You do,' said Ella and they could both see it ebbing away, the moment. 'I'm sorry. It's just I was forgetting about your situation, all the baggage. I don't know if I'm ready for this. Look I'd better go.'

'No,' said Gethin, 'I mean okay but... we'll see each other again?'

Ella stared at him. 'I hope so. Look I'm sorry, I'm just... I'm not quite right...'

Gethin watched her leave, then went inside and bought another pint. He came back out and watched the darkness gradually blot out the view. His heart rate settled down and he wondered if there really would be a next time.

* * *

Bex was watching a 1980s episode of *Top Of The Pops* on BBC 4 when he got in half an hour later. She gave him a good, long look then grinned. 'So nice drink, was it, Geth?'

'What do you mean?'

'Dunno. Maybe the lipstick all over your face and on your ear.'

'Oh that, yeah,' he said, rubbing ineffectually at his cheek.

'Well done you. She nice?'

'Yeah she's gorgeous.' Not happy though, he thought, but didn't say.

Bex started getting her things together.

'How was Hattie?'

'Fine,' said Bex, then hesitated before carrying on. 'I think she misses her mum a lot. She doesn't want to admit it, but she does.'

'Ach,' said Gethin, 'I know.'

He saw Bex to the door, thanking her profusely, and then sat up for a while in the living room, nursing a small whisky by way of a nightcap, and pondering. What was he to do? Try and follow through with Ella? Or did he owe it to Hattie to try and make things right with Cat? Not that that was his choice to make, as long as she stayed with Nils. These things surely didn't get easier as you got older.

A little while later, just as he was getting to sleep, Gethin remembered Nelson Algren's hard-boiled rules for life. The first was never play cards with a man named Doc. The second was never eat at a place called Mom's. Neither of these were too much of a worry if you lived in Britain, but the third one – 'never sleep with a woman whose troubles are worse than your own' – that one definitely concerned him.

Twenty-Seven

MARK LEWIS HAD BEEN RELEASED from custody without charge the night before. Gethin heard about it on Radio Wales. He was normally more of a Radio 4 man, but the roads were terrible so he'd tuned in to hear the traffic info. And there it was: third item on the local news headlines. 'A South Wales University lecturer has been released by the police without charge following his arrest on Thursday in connection with the murder of Dennis Hillyer.'

He called Andy as soon as he'd parked the car outside the office. 'You got any idea what's happened? I thought they had forensics.'

'So did I, butt. Word is he has a cast-iron alibi though.'

'I thought your copper said they had his ID right there.'

'That's what he told me. Three possibilities I can think of. One, his cast-iron alibi isn't really. Two, somebody's trying to frame him. Three, it's just a weird coincidence. Maybe he was out there one night, exploring his sexual boundaries, and he dropped his card there.'

'I suppose those could all work. Let me know if you hear anything else – especially about the alibi.'

He finished the call and went inside. Bex gave him a cheery wave and was obviously keen to give him the third degree about last night, but he wasn't in the mood.

'Mark Lewis has been released,' he told her. 'I've got to figure out what's going on.'

He sat at his desk and tried to do just that. His initial instinct was that the Prof's alibi had to be fake, but until he knew that it was, there wasn't too much he could do.

If it was real, then what did that mean? He found it hard to imagine it was coincidence. Surely somebody must have been trying to frame Mark. So who would that be?

The best answer he could come up with was Ryan Batey. He was a copper, he knew how these things worked. And last time Gethin had seen him, he'd locked him in the boot of his car. He was the man most likely until Mark was arrested. But if Mark really was innocent, then Gethin would be absolutely bloody delighted to point the finger at PC Ryan.

Just at this point in his deliberations Lee came into the office. She saw Gethin at his desk, signalled that she had something to tell him and he waved her in.

'All right, Geth? So I saw my Auntie Reet last night. She was in the pub with my mum, the pair of them absolutely fucked, you can imagine.' She shuddered. 'Awful state. Anyway, eventually I got her to focus for a minute and I told her Dennis phoned some mystery person just before he was murdered, like, and was there anyone new he'd been friends with or anything like that? He didn't have a lot of friends, Dennis, as you can imagine. And she thinks about it, like, and then she says there was some guy Dennis had been talking about, was lending him books and stuff, encouraging him with all that crazy church stuff. She said he was like a teacher or something. So I said how about a professor, maybe? And she says that's it, Dennis used to call him the Prof and then she's off on one and I finishes up my cider and gets out of there because frankly I has enough to worry about for myself without getting other people's grief all over me.'

'Well that sounds like the connection we were looking for. Maybe we can show your auntie a picture of Mark Lewis and see if she recognises him. There's only one problem.'

'What's that then?'

Gethin explained that Mark had been released from custody, and gave her the gist of his thinking as to what that might mean.

Lee pretty much agreed with his analysis. At least until they found out more about the alibi. 'So you want to have another look at this twat Ryan then?'

'Yeah, though that may be easier said than done. Doesn't take too kindly to being asked questions.'

'You didn't have me with you last time, Geth, that was your mistake. But I tell you what I think. We should go back and chat to the sister some more. Little Leanne. It's her that gave him his alibi, isn't it?'

Gethin nodded.

'Fine. Let's go see her and maybe I can use my special empathy power to get her to fess up.'

* * *

Driving over to the TextileWorks, Gethin found himself telling Lee about his drink with Ella. When he'd finished she sucked her teeth, then gave him her verdict.

'So you're into her, but you're worried she's too screwed up, is that it?'

'Yeah,' said Gethin, 'pretty much. I dunno, Lee, seems like every woman I know has some terrible history with men. Ella's ex obviously messed her up completely. And Cat – did I tell you Cat came round the other night?'

'No.'

'Well she did and I dunno, Lee, it was weird. I think she wants to come back. Part of her does anyway.'

'Oh yeah, getting bored of shagging that ponce, is she?'

'I guess.'

'So do you want her back?'

'I dunno, Lee, I really don't.'

'Can't tell you what to do, boss, except if I were you I'd

be tupping this new bird sooner rather than later. Got to take advantage of your free pass, innit.'

Gethin laughed. 'Yeah, I suppose.'

They pulled up outside the TextileWorks and Lee led the way inside. Leanne was there at her stall, sewing away. She must have seen them approaching but she kept her eyes down until they were right in front of her. Lee took the lead.

'All right, love?'

'What do you want?'

'What I want is to help keep your brother in his job and out of prison.'

'Uh huh.' Leanne was still eyes down, concentrating on her sewing. Gethin decided to back off from the conversation. He wandered off, pretending to be interested in the big colourful abstracts the painter over the way was working on. He was still close enough to hear the two women talking.

'Look, the way you and your bro are behaving, we can't help be suspicious. Take what Ryan did to Gethin the other day. Kidnapping. Gethin wants to prosecute. He didn't take kindly to being locked in a car boot. His brief reckons it could go attempted murder. If you knew anything about it that would make you an accessory.'

Leanne looked up at this. 'Fuck off.'

'Fair enough, I think that's a bit harsh and all, but you know what briefs are like. Got to be assault, though, kidnapping too. But maybe you gave Ryan a call, told him Gethin was on his trail? That makes you an accessory.'

'CPS will never buy that.'

'Maybe, maybe not. Maybe if you were still a copper, you'd get a pass, but you're not. Anyway, let's not get too obsessed with the detail because there's a bigger picture here. Your brother Ryan stuck Gethin in the boot of his car because Gethin wanted to talk to him about the phone call he had with Dennis Hillyer. So why doesn't he want to talk about that then?'

'Dunno. Ask him.'

'Well Gethin tried that, didn't he? And you know why it matters, what Ryan talked to Dennis about on the phone?'

'No.'

''Cause just before someone beat him to death, Dennis told us he actually saw Kelly's murderer.'

'What?' Leanne was interested now. 'Seriously?'

'Seriously. So that doesn't look good for Ryan, does it? There he is, right in the frame for Kelly and then he gets the call from Dennis, and next thing you know Dennis is dead. You're the one gave Ryan an alibi for Kelly, aren't you?'

Leanne nodded reluctantly.

'Very convenient that was. So are you still saying he's innocent?'

'I know he's innocent.'

'Why? Because you were with him that evening watching a movie and eating popcorn? 'Cause I don't believe you ever do that, because I don't believe you even likes him that much.'

Leanne took a moment and sighed. 'Okay, this is all going to shit, isn't it? You want me to tell you why I know Ryan didn't do it?'

'That'd be nice.'

'All right, look. The theory was I killed Kelly 'cause I was jealous of her shagging blokes or something, and you know what lezzers are like right, always killing other women over that sort of shit. Except it's happened like never in the history of the world, you know what I mean?'

Lee laughed. 'I might have given her a slap though. No one likes being cheated on.'

'Not if you're shacking up together or something. But Kelly? No way, you knew what the deal was with Kelly right from the start. Up for a bit of a laugh but nothing serious, take it or leave it. And I took it.'

'Doesn't mean you didn't get jealous,' said Lee. 'I seen it before. One girl's looking for a bit of fun, the other one falls in love. Boff, it all kicks off.'

'Sure, but it's tears and phone calls and Facebook stalking or a half-arsed overdose. Not what happened to Kelly. You ever hear of one girl murdering the other?'

'No,' said Lee, 'I agrees with you. But tell us about Ryan.'

'Well the story they were putting about was Ryan was seeing her too. But he never was.'

'He told the police he was. One of his mates too, if I remember.'

'Yeah that's the thing. He got caught in his own stupid lie. He told his mate he was having a thing with Kelly and then he had to tell the investigating officers as well before they heard it from someone else. But it wasn't true.'

'How do you know that? He probably didn't want you knowing.'

'Nah, it's not that. He's gay, isn't he? He's shagging this footballer who's dead paranoid about anyone finding out. And Ryan's nearly as bad himself. So he's going off to some hotel with soccer boy and to cover it up he tells his mates it's Kelly he's off with, 'cause you know with her reputation... And it was no big deal till someone kills her and then obviously it's a very big deal.'

'So was he really with you that night?'

'No, he was with bloody Jake Sanchez again. He was having a shag in a hotel in town when he got the call about the murder. But no way did he want to admit that. And I was just at home on my own and I knew it would save me a lot of shit if I had an alibi, so between the two of us geniuses we came up with that stupid plan of alibiing each other. Though, to be fair, it worked pretty well up to now... So there you go.'

Gethin and Lee looked at each other. Lee gave Gethin a little nod and he responded in kind.

'I suppose you realise you've broken a whole bunch of laws. At the very least Ryan's going to lose his job when this comes out.'

'Yes,' said Leanne, 'I know. It's the stupidest thing I've ever done.' She stared down at her sewing. 'It's actually a relief to tell you what happened. I dunno, I sort of want to blame Ryan for it. He was totally obsessed with what would happen to him if the truth came out. But I'm a grown-up and I've got to accept responsibility. It was all right as long as I thought they'd got the right guy for it, but ever since that poor Dennis got killed I've been feeling terrible.'

Lee reached over and gave her a quick back rub: 'Well, you've done the right thing now. We'll be in touch.'

Twenty-Eight

BEX BUTTONHOLED GETHIN THE MOMENT they arrived back in the office.

'You're not going to believe who's just called.'

'Just tell me,' said Gethin.

'Mark Lewis.'

'Christ!'

He went into his office and dialled the number Bex had given him. Mark Lewis picked up almost immediately.

'Lewis.'

'Hi, this is Gethin Gray. I'm calling you back.'

Gethin hadn't known what to expect. He was braced for a volley of abuse but no, the Prof sounded very happy to hear from him. 'Oh thank fuck. Listen, I need your help.'

'Okay, but first I have to ask you, do you know who I am?'

'Yeah, you're Gethin Gray from Last Resort Legals. You're the miscarriage of justice guy. And you've been coming to the rehab group.'

'Okay,' said Gethin again, 'did you know that all along?'

'No, at first I thought you were just another South Wales Uni staff fuck-up like the rest of us. I was pretty sure I'd seen your face somewhere and I assumed it was around the uni. But then you mentioned Catriona and I got it. I'd seen the two of you together somewhere. So then I did a bit of googling and I found out who you actually were and what you did. Which explained what you were doing in the rehab group. Snooping around looking for connections to the Kelly Rowlands affair.'

'Weren't you angry about that?'

'Absolutely. That's why I fucked off out of it. I've had enough of Philip making his stupid insinuations. I suppose it was him who got you involved. I know who the real killer is blah blah, it's Mark Lewis. Cunt. But I wasn't worried.'

'Why is that?'

'Why is that? Because I didn't fucking kill her, that's why.'

'You're worried now, though.'

'Yeah, because someone's tried to frame me for killing this Dennis guy I've never even heard of. Of course I'm worried. And that's why I'm calling you. You help people who have been falsely accused, don't you?'

'I do,' said Gethin carefully, 'but usually only after they've been convicted.'

'Well I'd quite like to try and stop this before that happens. So can you help?'

'I really dunno,' said Gethin, 'but I can come and meet you.'

* * *

Mark had asked to meet at the coffee bar in Jacobs Market on the grounds that it was a) reliably deserted and b) close by the train station. Mark was planning on heading to London for a few days until the fuss died down.

Gethin managed to find a parking space just round the corner and made his way up the steps and into the market. This was a big, old building offering three floors of mostly deathly dull antiques. In happier times he used to come here with Cat. He couldn't remember actually buying anything much though. A nice 1950s bedside lamp once upon a time. What happened to them – that happy Gethin and Cat? Was it that they had stopped doing the fun stuff

– weekend antique shopping, films and meals, and gigs? Partly it was Hattie, but other people had kids and still managed to go out and have a good time. They should have tried harder. He should have tried harder. And now? Was it too late?

Once he'd finally left the dusty rugs and collections of old postcards behind, Gethin arrived at the fourth floor. There was an art gallery taking up most of the space. Student stuff. Incomprehensible and almost certainly not worth the effort. At one end there was a café. No one there apart from a hippy girl behind the counter. Gethin couldn't see any sign of coffee provision, apart from a jar of Nescafé, so he ordered a tea and looked around, waiting for Mark to appear.

'He's upstairs, I think,' said the girl, once she'd tipped boiling water and milk into a mug on top of a tea bag and handed the elegant concoction over.

'Sorry?'

'There was a guy came in a few minutes ago. Looked like he was expecting to meet someone.'

'Okay thanks, which way's upstairs then?'

The girl directed Gethin through the gallery to a door that led to an external staircase up to the roof. This was a nice surprise. He had no idea there was a roof garden and Cardiff's city centre was sadly lacking in such spaces. The garden itself was pretty scrappy, but the views were great: stretching south to the Bay and north to the Castle and the hills of home beyond. There was no time to take it in though, as Mark Lewis was waving to him from a table over at the far corner of the terrace.

He stood up, his hand out to shake. Gethin was immediately aware of the change in the man. There was no bluster, no cock of the walk stuff, just naked worry. A night or two in custody will do that to a man, Gethin knew.

A quick exchange of banalities and they got down to business. First off Gethin got Mark to tell him about his arrest and – crucially – why the police had let him go. And, indeed, appeared willing to let him go to London. It had to be something pretty solid.

'Can you tell me about your alibi?'

Mark took a breath. 'I was with a woman.'

'Uh huh, does she have a name?'

'I'd rather not say. She's at the uni.'

Christ, he really couldn't keep his hands off the students. 'So where were you on the night in question?' The night in question – when did he start talking like a cartoon copper?

'In a hotel – a country house place up past Crickhowell, you know?'

Gethin knew. Crickhowell was a pretty market town on the eastern edge of the Black Mountains. The Green Man Festival took place near there every summer. He and Cat had gone once in the early years, but it was such a hassle going to a festival with a toddler that they hadn't fancied doing it again. Maybe he should go next year. Hattie might enjoy it now.

Mark carried on. 'Thank God they had us on CCTV arriving, and leaving the next morning. Even then the coppers tried to say I could have sneaked out in the middle of the night without her noticing and driven over to Treforest to go to some cruising spot by the railway, where I randomly decided to beat some guy to death. I mean, for fuck's sake, right? But as it happened I shot a little bit of video in the middle of the night – me and her like – and that had a cast-iron date stamp on it. So they had to let me go. Not before the whole bloody station had watched the video three times mind.'

'Well, if that's all sorted, what do you need me for?'

'Because someone is trying to frame me. They left my bloody ID card at the scene and if I hadn't had such an unbelievably good alibi, I could be going down for it. And I'm worried about what whoever it is might do next. The coppers didn't say it, and I don't know if they even realise it, but this is all to do with Kelly Rowlands, isn't it? The dead guy lived near her, didn't he? Can't believe it's a coincidence.'

'No,' said Gethin, 'I don't think it's a coincidence.' He wondered how much more to say, then decided to go for it. 'He reckoned he saw whoever it was really killed Kelly.'

'Really? Shit. How come the coppers didn't mention that?'

Gethin shrugged. 'Probably they don't know. They definitely don't want to know. You had a relationship with Kelly, didn't you?'

'Relationship! You've got to be kidding. I shagged her once if that's what you mean. I'd seen her around at gigs for a while and one night I bumped into her in the Bunch of Grapes and, well, you know how it goes, she invited me in and she was up for anything. Hell of a night. But then she started going on about how her kid died and I was out of there. Mark Lewis Rule #1 – Don't do tragic birds.'

'All right,' said Gethin, instinctively raising a hand to get Mark to shut up. 'So when was this? Around the time she was murdered?'

'No mate, months before. The fact is it wasn't for a while after she was murdered that I even realised who it was. Then I was like whoa, thank fuck I wasn't still tapping that.'

Gethin thought about this, sure there was something wrong with this picture. Then he got it. The photos Kelly had saved just before she was killed.

'Look,' he said, 'this is a weird question, I realise, but do you have any, er, unusual piercings?'

Mark stared at him: 'What? Are you asking if I've got a pierced dick?'

'Er, yeah.'

'Well I fucking haven't. Got plenty for any girl without sticking a bit of metal in it.' Then he paused and looked at Gethin. 'Why did you ask that?'

'Because someone giving your name got their dick pierced in Cardiff a couple of months before Kelly died. They got it done in the place she worked.'

'You what? That's totally insane.' He thought about it some more. 'Fuck. It's like someone's been stalking me or something.'

'Yeah,' said Gethin, wondering if he believed Mark, or whether he was just a very good liar. There was a simple way to check, but he couldn't see Mark agreeing to drop his trousers, so to trust or not to trust? Then he had an idea. Ted the piercing guy had seen the guy calling himself Mark Lewis, so he should be able to clear it up.

'Tell you what,' he said to Mark, 'you mind if I take your photo and send it over to the feller who did the piercing, see if he recognises you. I'm not saying I don't believe you, I just need to be sure, if I'm going to work for you.'

'Fine,' said Mark, not looking like he thought it was particularly fine.

Gethin took the photo and texted it to Ted with a brief message. A couple of minutes later his phone beeped.

'Never seen him before. Definitely not the guy – T'

'Okay,' said Gethin, 'that's good enough for me. I'm prepared to accept the idea that someone is trying to frame you. Now the next question is – have you any idea who that might be?'

Twenty-Nine

'No, THAT'S NOT HIM.'

Gethin was sitting in the front waiting room of Blood & Roses, showing Ted a series of photos on his phone – his shortlist of suspects for the framing of Prof Mark.

The first one was Morgan Hopkins himself. That was Gethin's idea. It struck him as possible that Morgan was orchestrating this whole business from inside his prison cell. Ted immediately found one of the many flaws in this theory.

'He's the guy who's inside for Kelly's murder, isn't he? I'd remember him all right because he's covered in tats.'

'Oh yeah, good point.' Gethin brought up another photo. Ryan Batey this time.

Ted took a little longer on this one. 'He looks a bit familiar, but I've never done any work with him. Nothing serious anyway.'

'Fine,' said Gethin. He hadn't thought it very likely, but he'd needed to check.

He struggled to keep his hand steady as he brought up the next picture then handed the phone back to Ted without comment.

Ted's face it up immediately. 'Yeah, I know this guy.'

Gethin felt a mix of dread and elation. Ted was looking at a photo of Nils Hofberg.

'I've never done any work on him though. Just seen him around, like. He used to be an actor or something, didn't he?'

'That's right. But you never did any work on him and he didn't call himself Mark Lewis?'

Ted shook his head.

Gethin sighed and played his final card. He did his best to enlarge a photo he'd found on the net.

Ted's eyes narrowed immediately. He held the phone up and squinted at it from different angles.

'Yeah,' he said, 'I'm pretty certain that's the guy. The Mark Lewis one. It's coming back to me a bit better now. I remember, the odd thing was he didn't have any other piercings, not even a tattoo, and he went straight for an ampallang. That's not how it usually works, so I made sure he really wanted to do it, and he wasn't drunk or on anything, so what the hell. I figured his money was good with me... So who is he really?'

'Oh,' said Gethin, 'he's another lecturer at the uni. His name's Philip.'

* * *

Lee was standing outside the piercing parlour, on her phone. Sounded like she was talking to the hypnotherapist they'd found to assist with the Karl Fletcher affair.

He got his own phone out and started making calls. The university first.

'Excuse me, can you put me through to Philip Gomer, please?'

'Hold on.'

A woman's voice. 'Philip Gomer's office.'

'Could I speak to Philip, please?'

'I'm afraid he's off sick today. Would you like to leave a message?'

Gethin said he'd call back tomorrow and hung up. What was Philip up to? He needed to find his home address. Who would have it? He came up with an answer speedily enough and called her number.

'Ella, it's Gethin.'

'I know.' She sounded pleased, which was good.

'Listen, I can't really talk now but...' But what? What did he want to say to her? Why hadn't he taken the time to think about this before dialling her number? 'But... it would be great to get together again soon.'

'I'd like that,' she said and Gethin felt a wave of relief followed by an equally powerful wave of anxiety. Did he really want to see her again? Did he want this to be a thing?

'Yeah me too. Right now, though, I was just calling to see if you had Philip's address?'

'Why do you want that?'

'It's just... Something strange has come up, you know, with the Kelly Rowlands case, and I need to ask Philip about it.'

'You don't think he's involved in it, do you?'

'I shouldn't think so. There's just something I need to check out.'

'But that's crazy.' Her voice changed, hardened. 'Has Mark Lewis put you up to this?'

'No,' said Gethin, 'not exactly. It's just I need to talk to him, clear this thing up and he's not at the university today and anyway it's probably best if we have a chat in private. I mean, I'm sure it's nothing but I do need to talk to him so...'

'Okay.' Ella didn't sound completely convinced. 'I don't actually know his exact address but it's the cottage right over the road from the pub in Capeldewi, you know where I mean?'

'Yes,' said Gethin, 'I know just where you mean.'

* * *

Philip Gomer wasn't answering his door. There was no sign that anyone was in. No tell-tale music, no lights on, no nothing. They could see through the window that he wasn't in the front room. On the other hand, his Range Rover was parked right outside, so Gethin gave the door another knock. It was possible Philip was elsewhere in the house, maybe working with headphones on or just plain hiding. Gethin gave the doorknob a serious workout just in case it was the former.

There was no sound from inside but a few seconds later there was movement across the road. The front door of the pub opened and out came the landlord, the absolute charmer who'd had Gethin chased out of the place a couple of weeks back.

'Fuck's going on?'

Gethin turned to face him: 'I'm looking for Philip Gomer.'

'Yeah? What do you want with him?'

Lee stepped in. 'Just a simple question, bra. D'you know where he is?'

Gethin braced himself, waiting for the guy to go off the deep end. He didn't though, he just shifted from side to side, looking worried.

'You're the lawyer came in here before, aren't you?'

'Yeah,' said Gethin, seeing no point in denying it, 'that's me.'

'Right, right.' The guy didn't seem angry at this, he just looked preoccupied, like he was trying to figure something out.

'Yeah, okay, I'm sorry like about what happened when you came in before. Bit of a misunderstanding. You mind telling me why you want to talk to the Prof?'

'Just something that's come up in the course of the investigation. Probably nothing. But if you've got any idea where he might be that would be very helpful indeed.'

The landlord looked like he was thinking about it, but then he seemed to make up his mind, turned on his heel and went back into the pub. A few seconds later they could hear the sound of bolts being pushed into place.

'Shit,' said Lee, 'what do we do now?'

For want of any better idea, they re-crossed the road and knocked on Philip Gomer's door one more time. Still no sound from inside but they did at least succeed in attracting the attention of another local, an elderly woman who appeared to have been weeding the churchyard.

'He's not there, love.'

'Oh?'

'Yes, I saw him go out about twenty minutes ago. A young lady came up in a car. She went inside and then they came out together two minutes later and drove off in her car. I was quite surprised.'

'Why's that?' asked Gethin.

'Oh well he's just a rather private person, the Professor. I'm not sure I've ever seen a young lady visiting him before. Not that I'm nosy, you understand, but I'm often in the church – I'm the warden see – and so I can't help noticing what goes on.'

Gethin gave her an appreciative smile. 'Didn't happen to see what she looked like, this young lady?'

'Oh she was very attractive, lovely red hair. But she seemed a bit stressed about something. He's not in trouble is he, the Professor? Or is it a family matter? You think she might be a relative, the young lady?'

Gethin didn't think she was a relative. Gethin thought she was Ella Tregaron warning Prof Philip that Gethin was on his way. Shit. There must have been some other way he could have found the address. He should have factored in how close Ella and the Prof were. Maybe they were even in league somehow? It was an intriguing idea, though one he suspected wouldn't survive for long, if held up to the light.

'Did you happen to notice which way they went?' he asked finally.

'Back down there,' said the churchwarden, pointing

down the hill towards Treforest. 'He was driving, I remember, even though it was her car. That's men for you.'

'Yes, quite,' said Gethin. 'Thanks so much for your help.' He headed over to the car, Lee following.

He sat in the driver's seat and pulled out his phone. He dialled Ella's mobile. It went straight to voicemail. Shit. That was not a good sign.

* * *

Two hours later Gethin was none the wiser as to the whereabouts of Philip and Ella and increasingly worried. They tried the university. They drove to Ella's house. They tried the Bunch of Grapes and a couple of other local pubs. All to no avail.

Meanwhile it was time to collect Hattie from Martina's. He dropped Lee off at the station, collected his daughter and drove home, feeling pretty much at his wits' end.

His phone rang as he was making Hattie's dinner. He snatched it out of his pocket, hoping for news. But it was Cat. He debated briefly as to whether to take a call, then decided he better had.

'Cat. What's happening?'

'Gethin, I'm coming home.'

'You what? No.'

'Look,' she said, and already Gethin could hear that there was something different about her voice. Or rather, there was something familiar about it. She sounded like the old Cat, determined and sure of herself, not the new, flighty, slightly hysterical Cat, the stranger who had appeared in their lives. 'It's over. Me and Nils.'

'Oh yeah?' said Gethin, taking the phone outside so Hattie didn't overhear anything.

'I know why I did it, right. I was angry with you. I was bloody furious and there was Nils. I knew he was a wanker, I knew that, but he was a wanker who was obsessed with

236

me, and thought I was the sexiest thing on legs. And if that meant putting up with all the stupid S&M shit he'd seen on the internet, well I didn't mind much, it was such a rush. I dunno – maybe it was a bit like how you felt when you went on one of those gambling binges...'

'Maybe,' said Gethin.

'Fine, whatever. But it was something I needed. Well something I wanted and something I thought I was owed. But now I don't need it and you don't owe me anything. And I want to start again.'

'Er...'

'I'm not expecting you to say yes right now. It's going to take time. But I want to come home, I want to do my part. I want my daughter back and I'll sleep in the spare room and we will find a way. I'm sure we will. What do you say?'

'Jesus, Cat, I dunno, there's a lot going on...'

'Please.'

Gethin had never heard her sound like that, the way she sounded saying please, the need in her. It cracked the wall he'd built up.

'Look, Cat, it can't be that simple. I'm not just going to forget about this, what you've done,' he said. 'But why don't you come round tomorrow evening and we can talk properly.'

'Where am I going to go tonight then?'

'Christ's sake. That's not my problem, you'll think of something. Try the Travelodge.'

'Bastard.'

'Yeah, well,' said Gethin and he was about to hang up when he thought of something.

'Cat. There is one thing maybe you can help me with.'

'You tell me to sleep in the Travelodge and then you want my help? You're really something, Gethin.'

He decided to sidestep the argument, just rushed ahead with his request: 'I need to find Philip Gomer – from the rehab group yeah – and I was wondering if you had any ideas.'

Cat took a moment to reply, her curiosity finally overcoming her anger with Gethin: 'Professor Philip! You're investigating him? I told you he was a wrong 'un.'

'What?' said Gethin. 'No you didn't. You told me to check out Mark Lewis.'

It was Cat's turn to sound confused. 'I didn't, I mean I don't, I mean Mark's a sexist arsehole, but I never got any dangerous vibes off him. It was Philip who always creeped me out. The way he used to stare at that pretty girl. The way he used to stare at me, come to that. Urghh.' She paused. 'Didn't I say it was Philip?'

'No,' said Gethin, 'and I suppose I just jumped to conclusions. Mark and his way of talking about women...'

'Christ, Gethin, you really don't understand people, do you? Any woman could tell you. It's not the mouthy ones you have to be careful of, it's the quiet ones.'

'Oh,' said Gethin, feeling angry with himself for being wrong and Cat for being right. Just like old times.

Thirty

UNFORTUNATELY, WHILE CAT LOOKED TO be dead right about Prof Philip's dodginess, she had no idea where he might have gone. Neither was Gethin sure how seriously to take the situation. He thought about calling the police, but what could he say? A man and a woman, two single people, had driven off together in the car that afternoon. There was no way they would be interested in that.

Maybe if he said Prof Philip was a suspect in the Morgan Hopkins case – and the Dennis Hillyer case as well he supposed – maybe they'd have to take an interest then. But what evidence did he have? He'd found photos that probably showed the Prof having sex with Kelly. Well so what? Kelly had plenty of sexual partners. Nothing there to justify launching a manhunt. And maybe there was no need anyway. Maybe Philip and Ella had just gone to a hotel somewhere, waiting for the fuss to die down. Maybe they'd just panicked and run away. Maybe Prof Philip was innocent as can be. Maybe maybe maybe.

He didn't like it though. If the Prof was innocent, he wouldn't have run, he was sure of it. Where would someone like that go to hide? He tried calling a selection of Cardiff hotels, asking to speak to Mr Gomer and, when that failed, Ms Tregaron. No one had heard of anyone of either name. Dead end. By now it was getting late. He had to put Hattie to bed, had to tell her the news that her mum would be coming back. There was nothing more he could do that night. He reassured himself that Prof Philip worshipped Ella, surely he wouldn't harm her.

Lying in bed that night, he couldn't sleep. It wasn't the case that was on his mind though, it was Cat. Cat and Ella. Trying to make sense of what he thought he felt. Could he take Cat back? What about Ella? Wasn't that worth a try? Strange how Cat had decided to come back the day after he'd kissed someone else for the first time. Almost as if she'd intuited the danger. Like she was a mama lion coming back to take charge of her pride.

* * *

Ella rang first thing in the morning.

'Where are you?' he asked as soon as he recognised her voice.

'At home.' She sounded tired and strained.

'Is everything okay?'

'Yes. I'm sorry, Gethin, I know you were trying to get hold of me but I was tied up and then my phone ran out of charge.'

Gethin paused, wondered what to ask next, then decided he might as well take the bull by the horns.

'You went off somewhere with Philip?'

'How did you know that?'

'A neighbour told me. I'd been hoping to ask him some questions.'

'Yes, look, I'm sorry. After what you told me I was just so upset, I felt like I had to talk to Philip. I had to know if he could have been involved in this awful thing.'

'Uh huh,' said Gethin. He supposed it made sense. They were friends. Wouldn't he have done the same thing in her situation? 'So what did he say?'

'He said he was innocent, of course. We went for a walk on the top of the Rhondda – you know he loves to walk – and well, he was quite strange to be honest. He seemed quite down and he was talking a lot about history, he's obsessed with mining history. And then he was saying that he couldn't believe anyone would accuse him of murdering that poor girl. So really, I don't know what to say, I was quite relieved to get away. I mean I still think he's innocent, but he wasn't himself, you know...'

'So what happened after you talked?'

'I just dropped him back at his place and headed home. I should have rung you then, I know, but my phone had run down and I was just feeling exhausted with all this, so I came home and crashed out.'

'And how about Philip?'

'Well he should be at home. Haven't you tried calling him?'

'No reply.'

'Maybe you should go around there.' Ella went quiet then started talking again. 'I'm sorry, Gethin. All this business with Philip, it's not taken me anywhere good. In my head.'

'I can imagine. Would you like me to come over later?'

'No. Maybe. Honestly, I think I'm better on my own when I'm like this. It's not about you. I just need some space, if that's okay?'

Gethin said 'of course' and put the phone down and wondered whether this was some kind of land speed record for getting from the first kiss to needing space.

* * *

It was Saturday morning, but there was no way the Last Resort team would be getting any time off. First stop was Capeldewi and Philip Gomer's house. No sign of him at all. His car was gone and he wasn't answering the door. As for Ella, warning Prof Philip off like that, it was just a stupid, annoying thing to have done. There was something off about Ella, he found himself thinking.

Driving into Cardiff he tried to distract himself by listening to Bruce Springsteen. He wasn't a massive fan of the Boss, but since Cat had left him he found himself reaching regularly for the breakup album, *Tunnel of Love*. The opener, 'Ain't Got You', with its familiar but irresistible groove, had him singing along, but then he made the mistake of fast forwarding to the big hit single and even as he sang along he found himself ruminating on the question poised in the chorus, *So tell me what I see when I look in your eyes / Is that you baby or just a brilliant disguise?*. Who could he believe in? Cat? Ella? The more he thought about it all, the less he knew what to do.

His mood was scarcely lifted when he arrived at the Coal Exchange to find a couple of weekend workmen drilling into the ceiling of the corridor right outside the Last Resort office.

'You got a hangover, boss?' asked Lee as he came in.

'Nah, just a bad night. Bad morning too.'

He filled Lee and Bex in on the overnight developments. They agreed that Philip still looked pretty damn suspicious, but there wasn't too much they could do till he showed his face again. Meanwhile Lee took the chance to update Gethin on the Karl Fletcher case. Unbelievably enough, the postman had remembered seeing a blue car when he was under hypnosis, and not just any blue car but a blue Audi as driven by Karl's brother. Mrs Kendall was over the moon. They just needed to come up with some ideas as to how to prove that this blue Audi was actually Karl's brother's blue Audi.

'Fine,' said Gethin, 'tell her we'll call up every CCTV camera we can for a 30-mile radius and then we'll mount a thorough investigation into the brother's alibi. Tell her it's a full month's work at the usual rate and see what she says.'

'Nice one,' said Lee, then Bex stuck her head around the door and told him he had a phone call.

It was the Judge. 'Gethin,' he said, 'I had an interesting phone call this morning.'

'Oh right.'

'You remember you asked if I might be able to discover who the compensation payment in the matter of Ms Rowlands' medical negligence would be paid out to?'

'Uh huh.' Gethin had completely forgotten, but he was all ears now.

'Well, Tom Drysdale tells me that there's been quite a tussle. Her legal next of kin is apparently still her estranged husband, a Mr Aston Rowlands. Is that right?'

'As far as I know.'

'Indeed. But Ms Rowlands' mother, a Mrs Pugh, claims that Kelly had made a will. Apparently she was determined that the compensation money should go to a meningitis charity and she'd told her mother repeatedly that she had put this in her will.'

'Okay.'

'Well it would be okay, except there's no sign of any such will. The mother has searched high and low without success and apparently the payment has now been made to Mr Rowlands. All two hundred and forty-five thousand pounds of it.'

The phone call over, Gethin sat back and considered this piece of information. Could it be that they were following the wrong thread. Most motives for murder tended to boil down to either sex or money. And Kelly's life had thrown up plenty of possibilities on the former side. But maybe it was money all along. Aston Rowlands had one hell of a reason to kill Kelly. And was it so impossible to imagine that he might have persuaded some lowlife he'd met in prison to kill Kelly for a cut of the profits?

He brought Bex and Lee back into the office and they kicked the idea around some more. Everyone agreed it was a possibility, though not one that was necessarily very helpful to their cause. If some mystery man had killed Kelly in exchange for money, then they'd done a pretty good job of getting clean away with it.

'How about the Professor guy?' said Lee. 'Do you think he could have been in league with Aston?'

It was one of those ideas that sounded brilliant for about two seconds, then fell apart. How would Aston have known Philip? And of all the unlikely people to employ as a hitman... It made no sense.

It was Bex who came up with the breakthrough. 'What about the other murder?'

Gethin and Lee both looked at her.

'Dennis. Your cousin.'

Gethin made the next connection just a half-second ahead of Lee. 'When we were in the house, you remember Dennis had those papers?'

'Right. He wanted to give them to Kelly's next of kin.'

'And he asked if that was still Aston. And I said yes. Shit, what if that was her will?'

'Exactly boss. I think we may have fucked up big time. Though I don't see how we could have known.'

'I suppose not. So let's think this through. Dennis rocks up to Aston's place – wherever that is, can you find out, Bex? – and gives him the papers. One of them is Kelly's will. Aston reads it and sees that all the money is going to charity. He sticks that in the fire and, all of a sudden, he's got a quarter of a million quid coming his way. The only problem is Dennis. He may know about the will. So Aston decides to shut him up good and proper. That works doesn't it?'

'Yeah, boss,' said Lee, 'it's definitely does. Reckon we better go after the scumbag.'

It took Bex ten minutes of working the phones to come up with an address for Mr Aston Rowlands. 'You'll never guess where he lives, Geth.'

'Where?'

'The Four Feathers in Capeldewi. He's the barman.'

'You're kidding!' Christ, no wonder he'd been such an

unfriendly bastard. He'd looked like a man regularly held at Her Majesty's pleasure too. It would be a treat to wipe the smirk off that particular face.

'Well then,' he said to Lee, 'fancy another trip back up to the ancestral homelands?'

Thirty-One

THEY MADE IT TO THE Four Feathers in twenty minutes. The car park was empty, though, and the pub itself looked to be closed. This wasn't a complete surprise. Lee had been calling the number as they drove, with no reply. Maybe Aston's money had cleared already. He hadn't struck Gethin as one of those people who love their job so much that they claimed they'd be staying on, even though they'd won the lottery. No, he definitely wasn't that guy. The minute the money went live he'd be gone.

They rang on the bell. No reply. Looked around the back. The place looked completely dead. Walking back round the front, Gethin realised he was staring straight at the Prof's place. No sign of life there either. It bothered him, the two main suspects living right opposite each other. He knew well enough that most of the time coincidences are just that, but this was pushing it. Maybe Aston had been in league with the Prof, after all.

And now both birds had flown the coop. Nothing smelt right about that. And no indication as to where they'd gone. Where was the churchwarden when they needed her?

They found her in the church and, once again, she was happy to share what little she knew. She hadn't seen the Prof at all, not that she was looking or anything. As far as Aston the landlord went, he'd been keeping very irregular hours lately. But she had seen him that morning, loading some stuff into the back of his car. Not a lot of stuff, just a couple of bags, like he was going away for a few days perhaps.

They were about to leave it at that when Lee thought of another question. 'Do you remember Mr Aston having a visitor in the last few weeks, quite a tall chap wearing a funny sort of hoodie, looked like something a monk would wear?'

'Oh, I do indeed. You're talking about young Dennis, aren't you? Dennis Hillyer. The poor boy who was murdered?'

'That's right. He's my cousin.'

'Really, love? I'm sorry. You don't look much alike though, I must say, but never mind. Well, he was christened here, wasn't he? And then when I saw on the news he'd been murdered, well I was so shocked because I'd only seen him the other day.' She stopped. 'Oh my goodness, I think it might have been the very same day. Is that possible?'

'He came up here?'

'Yes, I saw him talking to Aston, Mr Rowlands, in the car park. I don't think Dennis wanted to go inside. I got the impression he disapproved of pubs. I think he was giving Aston something, some papers maybe. But no, it can't have been the same day because I remember saying to Janice in the post office that I'd seen him three days ago and that was only the day after he passed, if you see what I mean?'

'I think so,' said Gethin, 'You saw Dennis Hillyer give Aston Rowlands some paperwork two or three days before he died?'

'Yes,' said the churchwarden.

Before they left Capeldewi, Gethin had one more idea.

'Lee,' he said. 'Do you have those numbers Dennis called just before he died?

Lee did have the numbers and when they called the third of them, the one that Dennis had received from a landline, they could hear a phone ringing inside the pub. It looked very much as if Aston Rowlands had been the last person to call Dennis before his disappearance and death. The next question was what to do with this information.

* * *

Two hours later Gethin and Lee were sat in the car outside the family pub on the industrial estate, round the corner from where Dennis was killed. After some wrangling they were listening to John Martyn. It wasn't Lee's kind of thing, but she made an exception because the drummer was a docks boy called Arran.

They were waiting for Deryck Davies to show up, the DS in charge of the Dennis Hillyer case. He'd taken Gethin's call with surprising speed, which suggested he was getting nowhere with his own investigations into the murder. Gethin had laid out the bones of the case against Aston Rowlands, and the copper had jumped on it. Thinking quickly, Davies had suggested they meet at the pub and have a look through their CCTV footage of the night in question.

Deryck Davies eventually showed up twenty minutes late, just as John Martyn got to the end of an old rhythm and blues tune that the big man had transmogrified into one of his trademark slurred Caledonian soul epics.

'Wouldn't it be easier to do this in the station?' asked Gethin, as the three of them approached the pub.

DS Davies shook his head. 'Procedure mate. Red tape and getting the viewing suite tech guy to get off Reddit for a moment and halt the progress of the Incel revolution.'

Gethin gave him a look.

'Just the way it is. Anyway, if what you're telling me is right, we need to move fast. And this is the best way to do it.'

Deryck pushed open the pub doors, spotted some teenager wiping the tables and yelled at him: 'Where's the fucking manager?'

The kid scuttled away looking terrified and thirty seconds later a slightly older kid appeared, claiming to be the acting manager.

Deryck Davies, who had clearly given the police academy charm school lessons a swerve, gave him a look of utter contempt and demanded to be taken to wherever the fuck they kept the CCTV footage.

The acting manager took them through to the back office.

'Excuse me,' he said, obviously doing his best to sound authoritative but still decidedly squeaky. 'Are you with the police? I mean under data protection laws...'

'Am I with the police? Am I with the police? You have got to be kidding – I am the fucking police. You want to see my fucking warrant card, son?'

'Yes, I mean no,' said the acting manager, his face crimson, his body language screaming that right now his sole ambition was not to be in a room with DS Deryck Davies.

'Good. That's the right answer,' said Davies, giving him a smile every bit as scary as his bark.

The acting manager turned out to be quite well skilled in navigating the CCTV footage and having cued up the evening in question was absolutely delighted to fuck off out of there and leave them alone.

'You know this's cunt's car registration?' asked Davies as they fast forwarded through the footage of the pub car park.

'Yeah.' Gethin read it out, plus the make and model. Bex had been charged with finding out this information and, as usual, she'd come up trumps. Apparently she'd found a Facebook profile of Aston Rowlands posing with his car a couple of months back. It was a 2016 BMW. A nice set of wheels for a part-time barman just out of prison. Maybe he'd been selling more than bottles of Becks out of the Four Feathers.

It was dull work watching the cars come and the cars go, having to slow the footage right down each time another one hoved into view. They'd started from six pm and had made it up to six forty-five before they hit pay dirt.

Lee saw it first, the BMW nosing into the car park. They froze the frame and checked the number plate. Bingo.

The car parked out of sight of the camera, right at the edge of the car park.

'Deliberate, do you think?' asked Gethin.

'Probably,' said the DS, 'scrotes like that are always on the lookout.'

They spent another twenty minutes changing from feed to feed, trying to find an angle that actually showed them who had got out of the car. Finally they found it. A camera aimed at the bleak pub garden also picked up people on the pavement beyond. It was there that they saw two men walking. The timestamp suggested it was thirty seconds after the car parked. One man had a profile very much like that of Aston Rowlands, though it was hard to make out much detail. The other man was easier to identify. He was wearing what appeared to be a monk's cowl.

'Is that Dennis?' asked DS Davies.

'Definitely,' said Lee, 'he always wore that hoodie.'

'Good, he was wearing something like that when we found him. Okay, let's see if he reappears.'

They scrolled the footage forward, looking for anyone walking back from the river. Ten minutes later they saw someone. It was the man who looked a lot like Aston Rowlands. And this time he was on his own. Cut back to the car park camera and they could see Rowlands' BMW leaving. At one point it was clearly illuminated by a streetlight. There was definitely only one man in the car, and if it wasn't Aston himself, it must have been a twin brother.

'That good enough for you, Del?' asked Lee.

DS Deryck Davies didn't look like he enjoyed being called Del, but, given the circumstances, he took it in his stride. 'Abso-fucking-lutely. I'll get a warrant out right away.'

Gethin's satisfaction at this news was tempered by a sudden realisation. 'Didn't any of your people actually look at any of this footage before, then?'

Deryck Davies laughed, very little humour in it. 'Watched it? Yeah, someone probably did. Seeing what's there in front of their fucking noses, though, that's beyond the fucking capabilities of 99 per cent of the tossers I work with. You want to know why the detection rate's as shit as it is? Here's your answer.' He shook his head. 'Still, keeps wankers like you in business, doesn't it? Wouldn't have any work would you, if we were capable of doing our fucking jobs properly.'

Gethin laughed – one thing about DS Deryck Davies, he was an equal opportunities bastard. He seemed to hate the entire world evenly. 'Say what you think, mate, why don't you?'

'Fuck off,' said Deryck, but Gethin thought there might just be a hint of a smile in there somewhere. 'I'll let you know soon as we find him. You have any ideas – call me. Do not go confronting him. I saw what he did.'

Gethin nodded, taking that on board. He was more than happy to let the police find Aston Rowlands. By and large the cops were pretty good at running down career criminals. They all knew each other. Fellers like Aston lived in such circumscribed worlds that it was easy to find them. They'd be in one of half a dozen pubs or staying with one of half a dozen friends and relatives, the good old known associates.

He had one more question though. 'Does this mean you're reopening the investigation into Kelly Rowlands' murder?'

Deryck gave him a long, slow look. 'That'd be a result

for you, wouldn't it? So I'm sorry to disappoint you.' He really didn't look very sorry. 'Our boy Aston was in prison at the time, wasn't he? So if there is a link there, which I very much doubt, then this is how it plays out. Aston's sitting there in Parc Prison, he hears his ex is about to get 200 grand compensation for their kid dying and she's going to give the whole lot to some fucking charity. Not having that, right? So he puts the word out to one of his more mental mates – your boy Morgan Hopkins – that if Kelly gets taken out of the picture he gets a share of the profits.'

And with that Deryck Davies headed off, leaving Gethin and Lee staring at each other.

'Don't like to admit it boss, but it does make sense.'

'Yeah, in theory it does,' said Gethin. 'You haven't met Morgan though. I really find it hard to believe he'd do that. But still, I suppose I'd better make another trip to Belmarsh.'

Thirty-Two

As soon as Gethin got home he sorted out a VO for Morgan Hopkins the next day, Sunday lunchtime. His sister Linda had been booked in and she was happy to swap if it was going to help the case. Gethin wasn't at all sure it would, but nevertheless... Meanwhile he checked the radio for news of Aston being arrested but nothing.

No news of Prof Philip either. He was still lying low somewhere. Running away couldn't help but make you look guilty and yet Gethin was starting to think that maybe Prof Philip really didn't have anything to do with it, was just terrified of being arrested for something he didn't do. He still wanted to talk to him though.

Cat came over in the evening, as agreed. She arrived just at Hattie's bedtime. There was just time for a brief and horribly awkward exchange between mother and daughter.

'Jesus,' said Cat, once they were on their own in the lounge. 'I don't know about you, but I think I could do with a drink.'

Gethin raised his eyebrows. The old Cat had been a very occasional drinker. But then this wasn't the old Cat, was it?

'I have some whisky,' he said.

She smiled at that: 'I thought you might. Must've been a relief having me out of the way, able to drink what you like.'

Gethin couldn't help smiling back: 'That's for sure. Been able to indulge all my bad habits.'

That turned Cat's smile upside down. 'You haven't been gambling again, have you?'

And that did the same thing for Gethin. 'No, since you ask, I have not been gambling again.' He uncapped the bottle of Laphroaig and poured out two glasses with deliberate bad grace. He handed one to Cat, who was sat on the sofa, and took his own to an armchair way across the living room.

Cat took a good swallow of the whisky, made a face then gave a little cough to get Gethin's attention.

'So, might as well ask the big question. Are you seeing someone then?'

'I don't know.'

'Fine, if you don't want to tell me, then don't tell. I just thought it would be helpful if we all know where we stand.'

'It's not that. I really don't know. There is someone. But it's very early days...'

'Ah Christ,' said Cat, taking another hit of her whisky. 'I should have expected it. Look, I know I can't tell you what to do, not after what I've done. If you want to fuck somebody else that's your business. But can you just think about it? I mean I just wish I hadn't done it. Nils Hofberg! Jesus Christ. I dunno, Gethin, I just woke up yesterday morning and I felt like I could suddenly see straight again.'

'Uh huh.'

'Yeah, I just couldn't believe what an idiot I've been. And I'm not telling you what you should or shouldn't do but I'll just say this. I don't want anyone else to wake up one morning and feel quite as shit as I do right now.'

Gethin rolled his eyes. 'Yeah I see. This is you having your cake, eating it and then saying you feel a bit sick.'

'Yeah, I suppose. Oh Gethin I just want to come home. I'll do my penance. I'll sleep in the spare room. I won't say anything if you go out all night. I just want to be back in the same house with you. And with Hattie, of course.'

The mention of Hattie was a red rag to Gethin, partly because it was so powerful. He knew Hattie, underneath it all, desperately wanted her mum back. And really nothing mattered more than that. Or at least not much. But what about his self-respect? What about his own need for happiness? Did he just have to swallow all that? He didn't know what to say. There was nothing he trusted himself to say. He drained his whisky and stood up.

'Look, I can't take any more of this right now. I'm going to bed. You can sleep in the spare room if you want. And I'm off to Belmarsh early in the morning. Tell Hattie that's why you stayed.'

As he poured himself a glass of water to take downstairs, he saw Cat curl up in her chair, her head buried in her arms.

* * *

The drive up to Belmarsh could have been worse. Gethin listened to Radio 4 till *The Food Programme* came on, when he switched to a live Gram Parsons album that had been dug out of the archives. It was both very good and slightly disappointing. Very good because, hell, it was Gram Parsons, still Gethin's favourite alternative country songwriter. And slightly disappointing because it was heavy on the up-tempo toe tappers and light on the mysterious ballads that Gethin really loved. So after a while he switched back to the foodies wittering on about interesting things to do with celeriac.

Soon his mind was drifting away from root vegetables and on to the case at hand. There was still no news of Prof Philip. He'd tried calling Ella when he stopped for a coffee at the Membury Starbucks, and she hadn't picked up. He had felt both irritated and relieved by that. Did he want this thing they'd started to continue? He just couldn't say. Though he couldn't help noticing that not being able to get hold of her made him keener.

He made it round the M25 and through the heavy-duty Belmarsh security right on schedule. He just had time to get a couple of teas when Morgan Hopkins arrived.

He looked better this time. For starters he was wearing his own clothes: jeans and a Superdry sweatshirt. And there was a light in his eyes as he shook Gethin's hand.

'Fucking hell, butt, you've stirred things up a bit, haven't you?'

'I guess,' said Gethin.

'Linda's been telling me all about it. And the way I see it, that bloke getting killed, that's a game-changer innit. I mean, don't get me wrong, I'm sorry he's dead and everything – though from what Lin says he was a bit of a mong – but fucking hell they can't pin that on me. Whoever killed him has got to be the person who killed Kell. Got to be.'

'You haven't heard the latest then?'

'No. What's that?' Morgan stared at Gethin, new hope in his eyes.

'Looks like we know who killed Dennis Hillyer.' Gethin paused. 'And for what it's worth he wasn't a "mong", he was just a bit... unusual.'

'Yeah, sorry. So who was it then?'

'Aston Rowlands.'

Morgan sat back in his plastic chair, a big grin breaking out. 'Aston did it? Well fuck me. He was always an evil cunt, mind. Why did he do it? Did this Dennis feller see something?'

'Not really,' said Gethin. 'Well he may have done, but that's not what got him killed. Dunno if you know but Kelly was due a whole lot of compo from the NHS after what happened with her little boy. She was going to give it to charity, but once she was dead Aston stood to get the money.'

'So what's that to do with Dennis?'

'He was squatting in Kelly's house and he found her will, saying the money was going to charity. To cut a long story short Aston killed him before he could tell anyone about the will.'

'Well, that's it then. He must've done Kelly as well...' Morgan trailed off, his smile fading. 'Except he was inside, wasn't he?'

'He was. So the cops have a theory now that explains that. And I wanted to ask you about it before they do. You ain't going to like it, mind, but I'm going to put it to you anyway, because it's what the cops are thinking.'

'Oh aye?'

'They reckon it's all about the money. Aston found out Kelly was going to get the money and give it away. He wanted her dead so he could get his hands on it. The only problem being that he was sat in prison. So he got one of his mates to do her for a share of the profits.'

'And they reckon I'm that mate.' Morgan's jaw was working now and his earlier optimism had dimmed.

'You have to admit it's neat.'

'Except it never fucking happened. But then I never fucking killed her either and I'm still sat in here.'

'Did you do it?' Gethin slipped the question in quickly, hoping to catch Morgan off guard.

'Fuck off.' Morgan's reaction was immediate but not over-egged emotionally, not protesting too much. He just sounded like a man who'd had an absurd suggestion made to him.

'Sorry, needed to be sure.'

'Yeah, fair enough.' Morgan was staring down at the table, obviously mulling over what Gethin had told him.

'Could be what happened, though, couldn't it? Aston might have found someone to do it for him.'

'I guess,' said Gethin. 'Do you have any ideas who that might be?'

Morgan shook his head. 'There's not a lot of people you can call up and say "Do you mind murdering my ex for me?" You know what I mean?'

Gethin did know. There were more people than you'd like to think out there who are capable of killing someone for sex or money or both, but not at someone else's behest, that was a whole different dimension of wrong. 'You're right. And there was no sign of forced entry or anything. Seems like it must have been someone she was seeing.'

'Maybe Aston found out who she was seeing and made a deal with them to take her out.'

'Maybe,' said Gethin, 'but that's even more unlikely. You can't just go calling up someone's boyfriend and asked them to kill their girlfriend.'

'Suppose not. So have you got any idea who Kelly was seeing back then, apart from me and the lezzer?'

'As it happens I do. And it's someone you know and all.' Gethin told him about Prof Philip from his old rehab group. Morgan was properly tickled by the fact that they'd tracked him down by his piercing.

'Jesus, you wouldn't have thought he was the type, would you? And he was definitely there that night?'

'Not sure, to be honest. As soon as I found out he was the guy in the photos I went to his place to ask some questions, but he'd done a runner. Someone told him I was suspicious and he vanished.'

The smile was right back on Morgan's face now. 'You don't do that unless you're hiding something do you?' He looked up at the ceiling. 'Philip the history man, Prof Philip.' Right then a thought struck him. He looked back at Gethin. 'He was the guy, he was the fucking guy Kelly was talking about.'

Gethin looked back at him, bewildered. 'What guy?'

'About a month before she got killed, Kelly told me she was taking on a paying guest. That's what she called it. We were well smashed at the time so I didn't know what she was talking about at first. But then she started going on about how there was this kinky old guy who was obsessed with her. Said it was like that movie, *Indecent Proposal*, he offered her, like, a grand to fuck him, do some S&M shit as well. She asked what I thought and I said I'd shag anyone for a grand. And Kelly didn't have sod all money.'

'What about her job?'

'Yeah she had that, but it was only part-time.'

Gethin was annoyed with himself. He hadn't realised that. A grand for a shag was no laughing matter in Abertridwr. He could see bloody Prof Philip handing over the money too. He was annoyed about that as well. Why hadn't he spotted the darkness that obviously lay behind Philip's holier than thou manner? Especially when Cat had obviously spotted it right away.

* * *

Gethin spent much of the drive back thinking about the dead girl, Kelly Rowlands.

He figured he'd read her wrong from the start. He listened to everyone telling him what a good-time girl she was, what a happy, giving kind of person. But it suited all of them to say that, because they were all taking from her. It was only Chrissie had suggested there was more to her.

And this latest piece of information seriously rearranged the picture. She'd taken money from Prof Philip so he could fuck her with his metal dick. So he could beat her as well, the whip marks Morgan had mentioned. Christ, if Morgan wasn't such a meathead, he'd've figured out what was going on a year ago and he wouldn't be sitting there in prison.

Kelly though. Kelly was a girl who'd take a grand for sex but she wouldn't take £200,000 for her dead baby. On one level that made no sense, but on another level it made absolute sense. Kelly blamed herself. Kelly was doing penance. Gethin felt like he was in some insignificant and now utterly irrelevant way, but nonetheless a real way, starting to feel her pain. And what he wanted now, more than anything, was to bring her killer to justice.

He called Bex from the Reading services. She'd been charged with trying to track down Prof Philip. No luck. Not answering his phone, still not at the university. He tried a number he had for Deryck Davies. Got voicemail and left a message. He called Lee and asked her to try and get DS Deryck interested in finding Philip's whereabouts. 'Try and get it into his thick head that Morgan Hopkins didn't do it.'

'Do my best, boss,' said Lee.

Gethin was just coming out of the toilet when his phone rang. He snatched it out of his pocket expecting it would be Bex or Lee with news. It was Ella.

'Gethin,' she said. 'I'm really worried about Philip. Have you found him?'

'No, I was hoping you might have heard from him.'

'No, nothing. Oh God I hope he hasn't...' She went quiet. 'Could you come over, Gethin? I really want to see you.'

There was something in her voice, something in the grain of it, some encoded promise there that meant there was no way he was going to refuse. As he drove down the motorway he had an old Tom T Hall song running through his head – *I'm old enough to want to / And fool enough to try.*

Thirty-Three

IT TOOK GETHIN THE BEST part of five hours in all to make it from Belmarsh to Whitchurch. It took less than five minutes for him to make it from Ella's front door to her bed. She'd pulled him to her the moment he walked through the front door, her mouth open and her tongue seeking entry into his mouth. He had the slightest of windows in which to say no, to move his mouth away from hers. And in that second he thought of Cat back home and he remembered that he had made no promise to her, that he was still – according to his own private laws – a free man. And with that realisation all the cares and the worries and the psychic knots were cut loose and there was one thing on his mind, one woman in his arms and then they were staggering up the stairs, each pulling at the other's clothes and their own, and then the door to her flat was slammed behind them and the clothes fell in the corridor and they were on top of the bed.

Ella was a woman transformed. She'd been awkward and uncertain the last time he'd seen her, outside the pub. Now she seemed possessed by lust. When he touched her between her legs she was soaking wet. There was no question of any foreplay being either needed or wanted. He was on top of her then, the intensity swiftly moving towards unsustainable levels.

'Don't you fucking come before me or I'll fucking kill you,' she said. And then she pushed him off her, flipped over and quickly straddled him.

'Now,' she said, 'now fuck me.'

Gethin did just that. He felt her raging desire above him and found it answered in himself, felt her scratching and biting and himself the same, till he could barely tell who was doing what to whom. It seemed to last ages but surely couldn't have done. And then she was coming and he was too and then she was still coming, wave after wave, and she was drumming her fists on his chest and saying, you you bastard, you fucking bastard, over and over. And Gethin somehow knew that she was both talking about him and about someone else entirely. Some other fucking bastard.

This time it was him who didn't know how to react afterwards. He'd seen Ella one way – the bird with a broken wing – and now he was seeing this she-wolf, this leopard. Which was she really? And what had happened to change her from one to the other? What unnerved him was his sense that this Ella was the real one, that the broken wing girl was just a thrown-on persona. That it was, perhaps, how she wanted to see herself. This woman in the bed with him though, this raging virago, was the real Ella Tregaron. She even smelt different. He didn't know if he could handle her. Didn't know if he wanted to handle her. He suspected the answer was no on both counts. He suspected he was quite simply not man enough for her.

'I've got to go,' he said.

* * *

'For Christ's sake,' said Cat as he came into the kitchen, where she was busy making the chicken casserole she always used to make, 'would it kill you to take a shower? I can smell her from here.'

'Shit,' said Gethin, 'sorry,' and did as he was told. He stood under the hot water for ages, feeling utterly disoriented. How had things come to this? How could he be coming back to his family home reeking of sex? Could he simply blame it on Cat? Or was it something that had always been lurking inside him, a midlife crisis just waiting to happen?

Later in the evening the three of them continued their polite dance around each other. Cat seemed to have taken it as a done deal that she should extend her sojourn in the spare room. Later still, once Hattie was in bed, Gethin felt the urge to ask for Cat's forgiveness, or at least to tell her not to worry, that it didn't matter, that Ella was just a revenge fuck, that he just wanted them to be together again. A family again. But he just about managed to hold himself back. There was too much to take in, too much to understand and forgive on all sides, before they could really start to rebuild their marriage. Rushing too fast into reconciliation could be disastrous. Couldn't it?

Instead he talked to Cat about the case. If nothing else he was keen to get her input. She agreed that it seemed certain that Aston killed Dennis, but like Gethin, she couldn't see him employing a hit man.

'He's just seen a whole pile of money coming his way, and when this Dennis got in the way he did what he had to. I can see him as an opportunist, not some kind of Mafia boss.'

'Right. So you reckon it's Philip that killed Kelly?'

'I always suspected he could have. And all this stuff you've found out – well it's got to be him, don't you think?'

Yeah, I suppose. It's just a bit of a head-scramble. I mean the other day we were walking over the top of the valley, him telling me all about the Senghenydd mining disaster and he seemed to care so much for the victims.'

'Well, he's a labour historian, isn't he?' said Cat. 'Funny how men can have two brains, isn't it?'

'What do you mean?'

'One for the outside world, one for the private one.'

* * *

Sometime late in the night, one of the desperate hours, while he was still half in a dream of walking through Cardiff Market looking for something but he didn't know what, he felt Cat climb into the bed next to him.

He feigned sleep, but didn't resist or react when he felt her cuddle up to his back and wrap her arms around him. Oddly comforted, he fell almost instantly back into sleep, not sure whether he had sensed her sobbing as she held him.

Sometime around dawn he woke again. His phone was ringing. He reached out and grabbed it, answering without even seeing the caller ID in his haste to stop the ringing. In the second it took to get the phone to his ear, he was able to register that it was Ella calling and that Cat was still in the bed next to him. She raised her head up and stared at him as he answered the phone.

He was tempted to switch it off right away. He wasn't ready to talk to Ella about what had happened between them. Especially not at what the clock informed him was 5:57 am. But then he heard her voice calling 'Are you there?' She sounded terrified and like she was at the bottom of a well.

'Gethin, Gethin, are you there?'

'Yes,' said Gethin, aware of Cat staring at him and doing his best to ignore her. 'Where are you?'

'I don't know. I'm underground somewhere. I'm scared, Gethin.'

'What? Where underground? Is there someone there with you?'

'Philip's here and he's... He's gone mad. I think he's going to do something.'

'To you? Has he...?'

'No,' said Ella, 'to himself. I'm afraid he's going to...' She went silent for a moment then her voice came back sounding like she was trying to shout and whisper at the same time. 'Can you come here, please, come here now?'

Gethin was already climbing out of bed and starting to pull on his clothes. 'Where exactly are you?'

'I don't know. It's some kind of an old mine, except you don't go down into it.'

'Okay, but where?' God knows how many old mines there are in the Valleys.

'Lesser Garth. The old iron mine. You know where I mean?'

'Sort of. I can find it. But where exactly...'

With that the line cut out. Gethin tried calling back but no reply.

'Who was that?' Cat was wide awake now and switched the bedside light on as she asked the question.

Gethin wondered about not telling her, then remembered that she didn't know it was Ella that he'd been seeing. 'Ella Tregaron. From the rehab group. She's gone somewhere with Prof Philip. Or he's taken her somewhere. Down a mine. It's all gone mental.'

Stared at him. 'And she called you? Shit, Gethin, is that who you've been screwing? That mad bitch?'

'She's not a...' said Gethin, realising that he'd fallen straight into her trap.

Cat smiled wickedly. Looked like the old Cat. He sensed that she was positively relieved now that she knew the identity of her rival.

'Yeah, she is, you're just too bloody trusting to see it. Bowled over by all that lovely red hair and the butter wouldn't melt shit.'

'Whatever,' said Gethin. 'The point is she's stuck down a mine with someone who's probably an actual murderer and I need to find out where she is.'

'Jesus,' said Cat, 'please, please be careful.'

* * *

Before he left Gethin googled the Lesser Garth iron mines. He was already vaguely aware of their existence. The Lesser Garth was a hill no more than a mile south-west of Gethin's house. You could see it from his terrace if you craned your neck a little, but he'd never explored it. As far as he knew there were no decent walking trails and most of it was owned by a quarry company. It was just a rather dark and dismal tree-lined hulk he passed without seeing on his way to work.

Google, however, told him that there was far more to it than had previously met his eye. Iron had been mined in the Lesser Garth for millennia, but became an industrial operation in the nineteenth century. It was famous enough in its time that Victorians used to visit the mine as a kind of tourist attraction. It eventually closed down for good in the 1920s. The mines themselves were, in effect, an elaborate network of caves inside the hill, including a number of lakes. In more recent years these underground lakes had become popular with a few brave fellas who liked to scuba dive in them. Access appeared to be possible by either of two methods. You could abseil in from above, via the edge of the neighbouring quarry. There was no way he was going to do that. The other option sounded much easier. There was a long tunnel through the rock that had been dug out by the Victorians to allow the ore to be taken from the mines by horse and cart. You could walk straight into the mine complex. That was the entrance he needed to find.

Thirty-Four

GETHIN STOPPED OFF AT THE garage, just at the foot of the Lesser Garth, where he bought a torch, a coffee from a Costa machine and a large bar of Dairy Milk for sustenance.

Then he drove the half-mile or so up Heol Berry, till he was as close as he could get to the old mine. There were some no entry notices put up by the quarry owners, but there were also public footpath signs.

He got out of the car and spent twenty minutes scrambling up and down the hillside looking for a mine entrance in the early morning gloom, without any success. The closest he managed was almost falling down a huge hole in the ground that presumably would have provided a way in – if he'd had proper abseiling equipment and any clue as to how to use it.

Finally, bravely going against his masculine impulse to reject all advice when lost, he got his phone out and checked the account on the caving forum for more details as to where the entrance could be found. Apparently it was just off a turnpike that ran around the side of the hill. He walked down the slope, almost as far as the road, till he finally found the turnpike, a well-made wide path that would once have been a highway for carts full of iron ore. He followed it for three hundred yards and then he saw an opening to his right.

It was a spur off the turnpike and it led directly into the hill. The banks got higher as he walked along the path

267

until he was confronted by a huge boulder and, beyond that, a metal door barring the way into the mine.

The boulder had clearly been placed there to dissuade passers-by from attempting access, but its function was more decorative than practical. It was possible to climb over it and get to the gate itself. This looked impregnable at first sight but, much to Gethin's surprise, when he pushed it, it gave a little and there was space for him to squeeze through into the tunnel beyond. It wasn't quite as bad as he had feared. The tunnel was easily high enough to stand in and wide enough for a horse and cart. But it was also dark and wet and scary.

The longer he stood at the entrance, the less he liked it. There was a little bit of light coming from the opening behind him, but as he switched on his torch he could see scurrying movement and hear scuttling noises ahead of him. Christ.

He made his way slowly down the tunnel, doing his best to avoid the puddles and bits of rusting metal that peppered the floor. It was seriously cold too, and by the time he made it to a T-junction at the end of the entrance tunnel, Gethin was pretty thoroughly terrified.

Though not half as terrified as he was a few seconds later when he heard a scream. He dropped his torch to the floor and let out a yelp of his own. Was the sound he'd heard human or something else, a fox maybe, he wondered, as he picked his torch up off the ghastly slimy floor. And then he heard the screaming sound again, louder this time and more clearly human.

'Ella!' yelled Gethin in response.

Another scream came back at him. Or maybe it was a cry of 'yes'?

Every fibre of his being was urging him to just turn around and get back out of the darkness. The thought that his ancestors had worked in places like this stupefied him. He wouldn't have lasted a day. Another scream and this time he was sure it contained his name.

He thought it came from the tunnel to his left. Though the acoustics were weird and he was so keyed up that he wasn't at all sure. Still, he pointed his torch to his left and followed its beam. Another twenty yards and the tunnels forked once more.

'Ella!' he shouted again.

A cry of 'Gethin' came back. It had to be her and she definitely sounded nearer rather than further away. But this time he had no idea which way to go. He tried left again and the tunnel soon opened out into a chamber. He shone his torch around and saw large bits of discarded machinery dating back to God knows when. On the walls there were silvery pinpricks of light. The ore he supposed. In other circumstances he might have found something magical about it. But now it just looked sinister, like he was in the magician's cave.

Finding his way out of the chamber and back to the junction, he shouted again. This time the response sounded a little closer. He took the other path, stuck his right foot in a water-filled pothole then scraped his other leg on a piece of rusted railing as he sought to steady himself. He blundered along the tunnel which seemed to go on and on. Every so often he yelled out Ella's name and she replied, sounding more and more hysterical each time. He wondered if she was maybe trying to find him and getting more and more lost and further away as a result. He shouted at her to stay where she was. Okay, she called back.

Finally he got to the end of the tunnel and found yet another T-junction. He looked to his right and saw the proverbial light at the end of the tunnel – or at least a definite lack of pitch darkness. Then he looked to the left. That was pitch dark all right.

'Is there any light where you are?' he shouted.

'Nothing,' Ella yelled back.

The good news was her voice was definitely coming from the darkened corridor and this didn't sound that far away either.

He had another thought: 'Is there anyone with you?'

He didn't want to walk into a murderous Philip Gomer unprepared. Shit, he really wasn't ready for any such eventuality. He supposed he'd never quite been able to see Prof Philip as dangerous. Which was, he could hear Lee telling him, absolutely fucking stupid of him. So he was more than thankful when the answer came back.

'No. I'm on my own. But hurry. Please hurry.'

Gethin did as he was bid. He moved down the dark corridor, shining his light to right and left. There was an opening to his right after thirty yards or so. He shone his torch inside – no Ella but what looked like it might once have been some kind of mine office.

He called out again and this time, when the reply came back, he could tell he was getting close.

Another twenty yards or so and he heard her again.

'Is that you? I can see a light.'

'Yes,' said Gethin and then he came to a further opening and shone his torch inside and there she was, Ella, sat on what looked like an old wheel, with her knees hugged against her chest.

She stood up as soon as she saw it was him and threw her arms around him.

'Oh my God, oh my God, you're here.'

Gethin patted her back awkwardly, waiting for her to calm down.

'What's happened? Where's Philip?'

Ella took some deep breaths then started talking. 'He was here. He brought me here, said he needed to tell me something. But I think he just wanted a witness to what he... what he was going to do.' She pulled back out of Gethin's arms then and took him by the hand. 'Come on, we need to find him.'

Gethin led the way back out into the corridor. He pointed his torch one way and then the other. How on earth were they meant to find Philip in this labyrinth? 'Which direction should we go?'

'I don't know. I got lost. I left him by the pool when I went to phone you and then I couldn't find my way back.'

'The pool?'

'Yes there's a big kind of cavern with a pool of water in it. There's some light there that comes from way up above. It's like it's the bottom of another mineshaft or something. That's where he was, where I think he was going to...'

'Okay,' said Gethin, 'so there's light there?'

'Hardly any, because it's dark out, but a little bit.'

'There should be more now. It's past dawn.'

'Really? I must have been lost for hours.'

Gethin tried to remember where he'd seen the light at the end of the tunnel. It was at the next junction, he thought, if they went back the way they came. 'Follow me.'

They walked back along the corridor to the junction and, sure enough, off to their right was another passage with some now very definite light at the end of it.

'Oh my God,' said Ella, 'I was so close.'

'It does weird things to your head though, being in the dark. Didn't you have a torch?'

'No. Philip had one, but I just had my phone and then it ran out.'

The corridor was longer than it looked, and full of potholes and debris, but they clambered their way along it and then they were, as Ella had suggested, in some sort of giant cavern. There was a low-level light from above, enough to get a vague sense of where they were, but not much detail. Gethin shone his torch around and made out

271

JOHN LINCOLN

some ancient fencing designed to stop people falling into the huge dark pool that took up most of the floor area.

'Philip,' shouted Ella, 'are you there?'

'Where did you see him last?'

'Just. Just over there.' She pointed towards the far side of the pool. 'He was looking at... well maybe you'll see...'

Gethin allowed Ella to take the lead, shining his torch in front of her as she skirted around the black water. By the time they made it round to the far side either Gethin's eyesight was getting accustomed to the murk, or the daylight was getting stronger, or both. He was able to look up now and see a kind of natural skylight twenty yards or so above them. There was no sign of Philip, though.

Then Gethin shone his torch into one of the darkest corners of the ledge that ran between the water and the cavern wall. In the beam he could see a discarded coat and next to it an open laptop.

'Oh no,' said Ella. 'Oh my God, no...' She collapsed to the ground sobbing compulsively.

Gethin walked carefully along the ledge till he got to the coat. It was a man's coat, for sure. He didn't particularly recognise it as belonging to Philip, but who else's could it be? Everything pointed to him having drowned himself.

'Ella,' he said, 'what the fuck is going on here?'

She didn't, maybe couldn't, answer.

Gethin picked up the laptop. The screen was dark but he made sure not to close the lid. He made his way carefully back to the wider part of the ledge, where Ella was sitting. Then he put his fingers on the touchpad and the laptop sprang into life.

There were two photos pasted into a document. The first photo was of a woman with bad teeth, and it looked like a mug shot from the fifties or sixties. The second one was of Kelly Rowlands and was a badly lit phone snap. Underneath the photos were typed the words 'I'm sorry'.

272

'Christ,' said Gethin. 'Did he explain this? Do you know who this other woman is?' Ella raised her head and peered at the mug shot.

'It's the prostitute who died here ages ago. He was obsessed with her case. He was talking about her when I got here.'

'Uh huh. Any idea why?'

''Cause he's a batshit crazy history professor. Apparently a prostitute's murdered body was found here in the sixties. She'd been thrown in from up top. Whoever did it didn't realise there was another way in. Philip told me he wanted to die in the same place. Some sort of penance, I suppose.'

'Except he didn't kill a prostitute fifty years ago. But he did kill Kelly Rowlands two years ago.'

'I know, so weird. He kept telling me over and over how guilty he was that she had died. Almost like it wasn't directly his fault.'

'Maybe he's told himself it was some kind of accident. Just a bit of rough sex that went too far.' This was a popular defence amongst the woman-murdering classes in recent years. 'Either that or he realised we were on to him.'

Gethin had had enough. This place, the photos, the black water and the decay all around. 'Come on,' he said. 'There's nothing more we can do. Let's get out of here and call the police.'

Thirty-Five

IT WAS A LONG AND sombre morning. Gethin spent most of it sat in his car, just up the way from the mine. In daylight the landscape looked different. He realised that there was a working quarry on the far side of the hill, with an access road that was now full of police cars, ambulances and so forth.

Gethin had called Deryck Davies at seven fifty am. It had only taken him twenty minutes to get there. Gethin suspected he never slept. Davies had the air of a total workaholic. Gethin had told him what he knew and shown him the laptop. At that point any remaining cynicism on Deryck's part had vanished, replaced by a hunger.

Were they sure Philip had gone into the water, he'd wanted to know. Ella had told him she was as sure as she could be. Where else could he be?

'Hiding out in the tunnels somewhere? Maybe he's just faking it?'

The thought had occurred to Gethin too. But Ella was adamant. 'You didn't see him. He was determined to kill himself. I'm positive.'

Deryck Davies had decided to cover both possibilities. Within an hour he'd had a dozen officers piling into the iron mine with proper searchlights and climbing equipment. An hour after that the underwater search unit guys turned up. Two divers plus backup, armed with sonar machines that could provide underwater imaging.

Meanwhile Deryck and another detective, a woman

called DC Crouch, took witness statements from Gethin and Ella. Gethin had just finished his when a call came through to Deryck. It was the tunnel team and they had found something. A couple of them came back to fetch him. Gethin and Ella just got back into the car and sat there waiting. Neither of them with anything to say to the other. Gethin got out now and again to make calls – to Cat, to Lee and Bex – but Ella just sat there, either lost in thoughts or catatonic. Gethin really couldn't say which.

Eventually Deryck returned and motioned to them to get out of the car. 'Looks like your man had a regular den in there. Tent, lights, a couple of books.'

'What books?'

'Nothing interesting. Just mining history. One about early Welsh socialism. It all looks like some nutter who is obsessed with old mines. Except for one thing.'

'What was that?'

'We found a whip. Oh yes, and a pair of handcuffs.'

'Fuck,' said Gethin.

Ella didn't say anything, just went even paler than usual and, without warning, threw up on the path. She retched and retched as Gethin and the DS stood there.

'You okay?' said Gethin, when she finally stopped.

'Oh yeah,' she said, her tone harsher than anything he'd heard from her before, 'just fucking peachy'.

After that there was more sitting around. And then, around 11.30, Deryck got another call. 'The divers. They found the body. You two up to coming to identify him?'

Ella looked stricken. 'I'm sorry, do I have to? I don't think I could bear...'

'I'll do it,' said Gethin.

The walk through the tunnel was much easier now, with the spotlights set up all along the way. What had seemed like miles in the darkness of the early morning now only took a few minutes to traverse and then they were back in the cave. The daylight was pouring in from above and, mixed with the searchlights, it gave the scene an unreal filmic quality. The water itself glowed an odd metallic blue.

Next to the water was a stretcher, a body on top of it.

'You ready for this?' asked Deryck.

'As I'll ever be.'

Gethin stepped forward and a uniformed copper peeled back the plastic sheet covering the body.

'That him?' asked Deryck. 'For the record, please.'

'That is Philip Gomer,' said Gethin, 'for the record.'

And then the copper pulled the sheet back over his head and Gethin turned to make his way back, his legs feeling like jelly beneath him. As he left the cave he could hear one of the coppers saying something that made the other copper laugh. He was pretty sure he heard the words 'pierced dick'.

* * *

Gethin finally made it home about two in the afternoon. He took a long bath then crashed out for an hour before first Hattie and then Cat came home. He told Cat the basics of what had happened and she nodded and said good riddance. She didn't say anything about Ella, but he suspected the subject would be reappearing before long.

Hattie asked what was going on and Gethin gave her a sanitised version. She didn't seem too upset about it all. She was mostly interested in what a dead body looked like after drowning.

He'd told Lee and Bex that he'd be in in the morning and tell them about it then. He was just trying to relax with a glass of Rioja and a new Jason Isbell live album when the doorbell went. Cat answered it and shouted up that there was a DS Deryck Davies there to see him.

Christ, what did he want? Gethin ushered Deryck into the living room. He offered him a glass of wine but Deryck said he'd fall asleep on the spot, so he took a glass of water instead. And then he got to the point.

'How well do you know Ms Tregaron?'

What a question? How well did he know her? 'Not that well, really. I met her a few weeks ago and we have become quite close but... What's this about?'

'What it's about is that we have what you would probably call an inconsistency in Ms Tregaron's statement. In this case it's a fucking massive inconsistency.'

'In what way?'

'In the way that the pathologist is absolutely adamant that Philip Gomer's body had been in the water for a minimum of 24 hours. Ms Tregaron's story is that he was still alive at the point she called you, which was when?'

Gethin tried to remember. It was only that morning but it seemed like weeks ago. 'About five I think, maybe six.'

'Exactly. And we pulled him out of the water around midday. So by Ms Tregaron's account he spent a maximum of seven hours in the water. You see the inconsistency?'

'Of course. And the pathologist is absolutely certain?'

'He is. Don't ask me for the details – body temperature, rigor mortis, that sort of business – but he is quite sure. So your friend Ms Tregaron is either severely confused or lying. Any opinions? You must run into a fair few liars in your line of business.'

Gethin was struggling to make sense of this. 'Could she have been in the tunnels for longer than she realised? It's easy to lose track of time.'

'What, so she stepped away from the distraught Philip Gomer to call you and somehow that took her 18 hours. Does that sound likely? When did you last see Ms Tregaron before this?'

Gethin was half tempted to lie or prevaricate but managed to stop himself. 'Yesterday afternoon. About six o'clock.' He did the maths. Even if Ella had hopped out of bed and driven straight to the mine with Philip, it would still only have been 18 hours before his body was found.

'So where was that then?'

'At her place.'

'Oh aye? What were you doing there?'

'None of your business.'

'It's a murder enquiry, mate. It's all my business. Giving her one, were you?'

'Yeah,' said Gethin, 'fine. Like you say, I was giving her one.'

'Good. I like to get things clear. And then you came home to wifey and slept the sleep of the just till five or six in the morning when Ms Tregaron called you up and you jumped out of bed like a good soldier, ran down to the mine and helped her to find Prof Gomer's last resting place. How convenient.'

'It's just what happened.'

'Uh huh. You mind telling me what you were doing yesterday morning?'

Suddenly Gethin realised where this was going. DS Davies reckoned that Ella and himself were somehow involved in Philip's suicide. Perhaps he didn't think it was a suicide at all. 'You've seen the laptop, right? You know what he did?'

'Yeah,' said DS Davies, 'I've seen the laptop and I'm inclined to believe that Philip Gomer murdered Kelly Rowlands. But what I'm wondering is when you figured it out? Would have made me pretty angry if I found out something like that. Angry enough to smash someone's face in and drown them, maybe?'

Jesus, this really was where the copper was heading. Gethin tried to figure out why and then he got it. Philip Gomer's body. There must have been signs of violence.

'So I repeat. Can you tell me where you were yesterday morning?'

It took Gethin a moment to remember. But it was a blessed relief when he did. 'I was at Belmarsh, visiting Morgan Hopkins.'

He could see the irritation on Deryck's face.

'Okay. Fair enough. Thanks for your time. We'll talk again tomorrow. Don't be running off anywhere.'

Thirty-Six

GETHIN WAS STILL STRUGGLING TO make sense of what had happened when he got into work the next morning. He did his best to explain the situation to Bex and Lee: 'So the good news is it looks like we know who murdered Kelly Rowlands and it wasn't Morgan Hopkins. Which is a major score for us.'

'He definitely did it then?' asked Bex.

'Prof Philip? Certainly looks like it. He had a picture of her on his laptop and a note saying he was sorry. He was with her just before she died. Pretty open and shut. He might have tried claiming it was accidental if he were still alive. But killing himself is pretty much as good as a confession.'

'He did kill himself then?' It was Lee chipping in this time.

'Well, that is a bit of a question. I'm not sure any more. It seemed like it, all right, when I got there and we found his coat and the laptop. Ella acted like it just happened, but apparently he had been in the water for 24 hours at least.'

'So what do you think happened?'

'I don't know. My best guess is that he did kill himself. It was all like Ella said, except it happened the night before, after he went missing. I mean it's hard to read it any other way. He'd taken his coat off and written the note. How could she have forced him to do that?'

'Maybe if she had a gun,' said Bex.

'I suppose. But why and how? Doesn't make any sense.'

'Doesn't make a lot of sense that she lied to you about

it all though, either,' said Lee. 'You think she might have persuaded him she was up for a shag? He takes his coat off and then she shoves him in?'

Gethin thought about this. 'Hardly, it's cold and dark and scary down there. Be the last thing on anyone's mind, I'd have thought.'

Lee shrugged. 'Takes all sorts, but fair enough. I still don't get what he was doing there at all.'

'No, seems like a stupid thing to do. But they were pretty close and he was obviously in a state, so he calls her tells her he's going to top himself and she comes and tries to stop him.'

'Okay, fair enough, but why doesn't she report it straight away?

'Dunno, I suppose she just freaked out. Maybe she thought she'd be accused of murdering him or something, so she came up with the bright idea of coming back the next night and then calling me, pretending all the stuff that had happened the night before was happening then, so I could be a witness.'

They kicked the idea around for a while longer but no one could come up with a better explanation. Instead, Gethin got on with the rather cheerier task of calling Linda Hopkins to tell her that there was a very good chance her brother would be coming out soon. Every cloud has a silver lining and all that.

He'd just come off the phone when a uniformed copper arrived at the office and asked Gethin if he wouldn't mind coming down to the station. 'DS Davies wants to show you something.'

Butetown Police Station was only a hundred yards away. The uniform escorted Gethin through to an interview room, where he sat twiddling his thumbs for five minutes before Deryck Davies appeared holding a crappy police issue Dell laptop.

If Deryck had looked tired the evening before, he looked absolutely and completely wiped out now. Yet at the same time there was a definite manic buzz to him, a dog with a bone.

'Have you slept at all since yesterday?'

'Couple of hours in the canteen maybe.' He leaned in close to Gethin. 'No way am I letting any of these wankers here take credit for my work.'

He pulled up a chair next to Gethin and set the laptop on the table in front of them.

'We got lucky with the CCTV. The company that owns the quarry, they're paranoid about people getting into the old mines in case they injure themselves and start looking around for someone to sue.'

He gave Gethin a look that suggested he was on a level with the personal injury compensation muppets who were busy giving the legal industry an even worse name than it rightly deserved, then carried on: 'So the camera of interest is on the road.'

Gethin tried to picture it. Then he got it: 'By all the no entry signs?'

'That's right.' Deryck brought the laptop back to life and the screen was immediately full of the view of the road, Heol Berry, and the track which led up towards the old mine.

'We'll start with the night before last.' More fiddling about and Deryck brought up a shot of a car approaching the junction of road and track, then turning into the track. He paused it there.

'Okay that's four fifteen am. You see the car, that's a Range Rover and is registered to a Prof Philip Gomer. As you can see there's only one person visible in the car, the driver. It looks like a woman. We think it's Ella Tregaron. What do you reckon?'

Gethin peered at the screen. It was hard to be certain,

given the resolution, but it did look like Ella. 'Yes, I'd have said so.'

'So there's Ella Tregaron driving Philip Gomer's car up the track towards the cave where Philip Gomer's body would be found eight hours later. An hour or so later she calls you and suggests Philip is still alive. That's right?'

'Yes.'

'But actually he's been dead for a good twenty-four hours.'

'Well, if you're 100 per cent that the pathologist is right?'

'Definitely. Twenty-four hours is the absolute minimum, he said. There are no compensating factors. The water there stays at a nice even temperature.'

'So have you talked to Ella, Ms Tregaron?'

'Oh yes. We've had some long talks, me and Ella. She wasn't very forthcoming at first. But then I got my boys and girls to go back through the CCTV footage of the previous couple of days, around the time we think Prof Gomer actually went for a swim. It was a godawfully boring fucking job, I can tell you, but they stuck at it because they're all fucking terrified of me.' He smiled at Gethin, the kind of smile whose real message was that he wasn't remotely joking. 'You want to see what they found?'

'Sure,' said Gethin.

Deryck fiddled about some more. 'Okay, here we go. Friday eve 9.12 pm. Here comes the same car. Two people in it this time. That's the same woman?'

Gethin nodded. Once again it looked very much like Ella.

'How about the driver?'

Gethin could clearly make out Prof Philip.

'That's the Prof, right?'

Gethin nodded again.

'Fair enough,' said Deryck. 'But now we get to the real surprise. Just six minutes later this happens.'

Deryck moved the footage forward then let it run. Gethin saw a man walking up the road looking up at the no entry signs and the camera hidden amongst them, then turning on to the path and starting to walk up towards the mine.

'Fucking hell,' said Gethin.

'I take it that means you recognise the new arrival.'

Gethin did recognise the new arrival. It was Mark Lewis. What in God's name was he doing there? There was no way Philip would have asked him to be there. He'd bet any money that the animosity between the two men was real. So that left Ella. Ah shit, Cat was right, he really didn't understand women.

'Okay then. So we have Professor Mark Lewis entering on foot in hot pursuit of Ms Tregaron and Professor Gomer. Now let's fast forward another hour and a half.'

Deryck restarted the footage at 10.55. There was a car coming back down the track towards the road. As it passed the camera Gethin could once again see Ella in the passenger seat, but the driver was obviously doing his best to keep his identity hidden. Deryck stopped the footage then turned to face Gethin, a disconcerting smirk on his face.

'What do you think then?'

Gethin took his time, trying to see if he was missing any angles, before he started talking to the police. In fact that was a point. 'Is this an official interview?'

'No,' said Deryck, 'it very much isn't. Tell you what, why don't we go for a little stroll? I could do with some fresh air.'

* * *

They crossed over James Street and walked down Avondale Road. Past the ghosts of old pubs and corner shops, past the abandoned Hamadryad Hospital and into the deserted park that had been built there as some sort of quid pro quo in the Bay development – *We take all the prime sites for chain restaurants and executive flats, then we give you a bit of swampland to use as a park.* Gethin's mind was working overtime, trying to figure out the meaning of what he'd just seen.

'Right,' said Deryck once they were out in the open, well away from any listening ears. 'Shall I tell you how Ms Tregaron explained what happened?'

'Yes, please do.'

'So she says she had a call from Philip Gomer three days ago. He was distressed and said he had to talk to her. She agreed to meet him at Taff's Well station and he drove them to the mine where he'd been camping out for a couple of days.'

'So what was Mark Lewis doing there?'

'She said she called Mark to provide her with some backup, as she was scared about Philip's mental state. He was also there at the station and he followed them to the mine.'

'Okay,' said Gethin. 'But why Mark?' Why not me, he thought but didn't say.

'Oh, so you didn't know she was shagging him?'

'You what?'

'Oh yeah. I thought you must have known. After all, she was his alibi for the Dennis Hillyer murder.'

'But...' said Gethin. 'I thought that was a student.'

'No,' said Dercyk. 'Who told you that?'

'Mark did,' said Gethin, realising what an idiot he was. Ella and Mark. All that stuff in the group, they'd just been play-acting that they hated each other.

'Sorry to be pulling the wool from your eyes, mate. So Ms Tregaron goes into the mine with Philip and he takes her to the cave with the pool in it. And he starts confessing all and then he's taking his coat off and Ms Tregaron freaks out and runs out of there and meets Mark Lewis, who's on his way in to find her and the two of them scarper.'

'Uh huh.' Gethin could just about see it.

'And according to her she doesn't know at this stage whether Prof Phil is alive or dead. She just wanted to get out of there. And then all the next day she's not sure what to do and then she decides to go back there, and find out for sure. And she doesn't want to take Mark because he's already been a suspect in the whole business so she decides to call you instead. How does that all sound to you?'

Gethin thought about it. Tried to separate his sense of outrage at having been lied to and self-disgust at having been so gullible. 'I suppose it makes sense.'

'Yes. Just one thing I don't like about it.'

'What's that then?'

'It looks very much like Prof Philip received a blow to the head before he went in the water.'

'Could he not have hit his head on the way down?'

'Maybe,' said Deryck, 'but the pathologist didn't think so. He couldn't rule it out though. Which is lucky.'

'Why lucky?'

'Why? Because the way I see it I have two stories I can tell here. One is nice and simple. This sick pervert dragged an innocent woman into the mine, confessed to her, showed her the evidence that he had murdered Kelly Rowlands, then killed himself because he couldn't live with his guilt any more. Like I say, nice and simple.'

'Sure,' said Gethin, as Deryck appeared to be waiting for him to say something.

'And then there is story number two. I try to prosecute Prof Lewis and Ms Tregaron for murdering the Prof, despite the fact that there is no forensic evidence, no witnesses and not a cat's chance in hell that any jury wouldn't jump at the chance to find them not guilty, given that all they may have done is get a bit over-vigorous when helping a murderer to his well-deserved end. That sound about right?'

Gethin gave him a strained smile.

'So which of these stories do you think I'd sooner tell?'

Gethin considered it. He tried to imagine what might have happened there in the mine. Philip confessing to Ella, telling her what a bad man he was. Maybe she'd led him on, like that undercover copper in the Clapham Common case. Maybe she'd persuaded him it would be a big turn-on for her if he told her he'd choked Kelly to death. Whatever – one way or another the truth was out there. And then Mark comes along and does what a lot of people would do in that situation, what Gethin could imagine himself doing, and smacks him one. Philip falls on his head or whatever and they roll him into the water. Yeah, it made sense. Did he want Mark and Ella tried for murder? He had to suppress a small, bitter grin at the thought that if Deryck did take it to court and have them sent to prison, it was just the kind of case he'd end up taking on to try and get them out again. Except Deryck was right. Even if it went to court, no jury would convict.

'Option one seems pragmatic,' he offered finally.

'Pragmatic is right. I can tie it all up at my end. There's just one potential fly in the ointment.'

'What's that?'

'It's you, bruv. You with your passion for justice, you might go shooting your mouth off about how this Prof Philip was murdered. Is that likely to happen?'

'No,' said Gethin, 'not likely at all.'

Thirty-Seven

GETHIN FOUND IT HARD TO concentrate when he got back to the office. Bex and Lee were keen to celebrate. Morgan Hopkins' lawyers were hopeful of getting their man out within the week. They all went over to the wine bar around four o'clock for a couple of glasses of champagne before heading home, but Gethin still couldn't relax.

Bex called him on it eventually. 'What's the matter, Geth? We've had a major result and you're looking like a wet weekend in Mumbles.'

Gethin apologised. 'I guess I'm still getting over the whole business in the mine.'

'I don't blame you,' said Lee. 'No way I would have even gone in there. You've probably got a bit of PTSD, bra.'

Gethin laughed and said that was probably it. But it wasn't. Or at least not entirely. What was bothering him was Ella. He didn't want to charge her with murder or anything like that. He agreed with DS Deryck about the futility of that course of action. But the questions wouldn't go away. How long had Ella and Mark planned this thing? How long had she been sleeping with him? What Gethin really resented was being played for a fool.

Halfway through the second glass he got up from the table and made his apologies. Driving back home around the ring road, he regretted having drunk anything at all. He felt his reactions were slow and blurry. A car braked suddenly, just ahead of him, as traffic came in from the Leckwith junction and he only just managed to stop in time.

The shock woke him up and by the time he approached the A470 junction he had decided he had to make one more stop before heading home.

It took Ella a little while to answer the door. He knocked and rang the bell and called her number and finally he heard her coming downstairs.

She looked different he thought. Focused and active rather than fey and passive. It was like someone had thrown a switch. She looked him up and down then sighed. 'I thought it must be you. You'd better come in.'

She led the way upstairs, straight into her bedroom again but with absolutely zero trace of romantic intent. There were a couple of cases open on the bed and clothes stacked everywhere.

'You're packing,' said Gethin redundantly.

'Right,' she said, 'I'd forgotten you were a detective.'

This was new too. The old Ella had been far too ethereal for sarcasm.

'I'm leaving,' she said.

'Thought you might be,' said Gethin, giving her a bit of attitude in return. 'The cops know you're going?'

'Why should they? I haven't been accused of anything.'

'There'll be an inquest at the very least.'

'Oh,' Ella stopped sorting out her clothes and turned to face Gethin. 'Will I have to go?'

Gethin didn't actually know the answer to this but he felt like giving her a little jab: 'I should have thought so.'

'Shit.'

'Why? You're not planning on leaving the country are you?'

Ella didn't say anything.

'Christ, you are. Where are you going?'

'Back to San Francisco.'

'Really? Back to music?'

'Yes, maybe, I don't know.'

289

'Well that's great,' said Gethin, echoes of his former fantasy about Ella Tregaron coming back into play. Maybe he'd go out and see her there sometime. Then he had a further thought. 'Are you going on your own?'

Another, deeper sigh. 'No. Mark's coming.'

'Oh,' said Gethin, 'right.'

'Yeah, look, I'm sorry, I know I haven't acted well. I was just trying to be someone I'm not. All the time I've been back. I wanted to be different to how I used to be, but I can't do it anymore. I'm not a nice person, Gethin, not like you.'

Gethin was stung. 'No, you're not, are you?' And then something else struck him. It was a cruel thing to say but he said it anyway, because he was sure it was true and because he wanted to hurt her. 'That's what's wrong with your music, isn't it? You pretend to be sweet and nice, but you're not. That's why everything you do, that record you made, it all ends up being fake.'

That got her attention. 'You fucker,' she said, 'you absolute bastard.' And in that instant he felt the moment of opportunity. The chance to get to the truth of what happened in the mine.

'Tell me,' he said. 'What did you do to Philip?'

'I don't know. Look, I've been playing games. It's what I do. Sitting in those meetings, listening to those boring alkies rambling on, I started to see how many of the guys I could make fall in love with me. With Philip it was too easy. Mark was a bit more of a challenge. The funny thing was that both of them thought the other one had killed Kelly. Well, Philip thought it all along, but Mark only started thinking it after stuff started happening.'

'How about you? Did you think either of them was a killer?'

'No. I thought they just hated each other. Like I say it was all one big game I was playing. And then Mark got arrested. And I knew he was innocent 'cause I'd been with him at the time – you knew that didn't you? Yeah I thought so – so obviously someone was trying to frame him. And who else but Philip? So that's when I started taking it seriously. Me and Mark we started, well we tried to trap him. I set him running by telling him you wanted to talk to him. And then I just waited. And sure enough he called me up and asked me to come to his secret hideout – he'd been going in the mines since he was a kid you know?'

'Right,' said Gethin, thinking that made sense. He could see Prof Philip as a lonely boy, exploring the caves while the rest of his peers played football or whatever.

'So I went in there to meet him. Mark came a little way behind me for backup. Philip met me at Treforest station then he drove me up the hill. He was falling apart. He was terrified he was going to be arrested, kept saying he was sorry, how he'd failed her.'

'So what did you say?'

'Mostly I just listened. But then he started going on about how unfair it was that he should be blamed. What about Mark? He asked why they let Mark go, and I was getting so sick of him that I told him. Told him about me and Mark.'

She stopped talking for a moment.

'I know I shouldn't have, but I had no idea he'd take it so hard. It was like he was melting in front of me, he just handed me the lantern he'd been carrying and he walked off into the dark.'

'And you?'

'What could I do? He knew the caves. I hadn't got a clue where I was, I just tried to find my way back the way I came. Kept shouting out as I went and Mark found me and then we got out of there.'

'So you didn't see him die?'

'No. I had suspicions obviously, but I didn't know...

That's why I called you. I had to find out.' She seemed to be tearing up as he spoke, but Gethin was getting more than a little cynical about the many moods of Ella Tregaron. What she was saying made sense but conveniently glossed over the 24 hours between leaving the mine and going back in. Twenty-four hours in which she'd pulled Gethin into bed with her and then kicked him out again. It all sounded way too pat.

'Why didn't you call the police?'

'Oh God, I wish I had. I was just scared and Mark said it was best not to. That we'd be suspects if he was dead. Especially as Mark had already been arrested over the case and if they saw the two of us together, then they might not believe his alibi for that other murder...'

She dried up and Gethin gave her the hard stare.

'It's true. We were together. There's a bloody film of us. You want to see it?'

Gethin shook his head. 'Okay, so you didn't call in case they suspected you. And then you decided I'd be a nice safe witness. And just to make sure I'd cooperate you shagged me. Is that how it went?'

'No, God no. I was just confused, Gethin. I really like you, you must know that.'

Gethin was weary of her now. He could hardly be bothered to tell her that he strongly suspected she cared about absolutely no one but herself. 'Whatever. So you called me up and pretended you were in the mine, is that right?'

'Yeah I suppose. I was just outside.'

'Fine and then we went inside and found what we found.'

'Yeah.'

'And it looks like he killed himself right after you left him there?'

'I suppose. Look, it wasn't my fault. He's the murderer, not me.'

'Oh yeah.' Gethin thought of something. 'Did he actually confess to it?'

Ella hesitated. He suspected she was wondering if she could get away with saying he had, but her hesitation betrayed her. 'No,' she said finally, 'not in so many words.'

* * *

Driving home Gethin tried to make sense of what Ella had told him, or rather hadn't told him. He was just too tired to think clearly though. By the time he pulled into the drive, all he wanted was to crash out on the couch with a cup of tea and a John Martyn album. John Martyn never failed to soothe the troubled brow, he found. Odd really, considering that Martyn himself had, by all accounts, been a drunken brawling menace.

It was probably his mental exhaustion that saved him. He managed to let his keys drop, just as he was trying to put them in the lock. He bent down to pick them up and as a result the baseball bat that was intended for his head smashed into the door instead.

Gethin rolled to his left and scrambled to his feet. In that moment he registered his assailant's position, recognised him and started running away from him. In the same instant he rejected the option of picking up his keys and using them to unlock the door and barricading himself inside. He'd never manage it. In the following instant he registered his assailant's new position and the likely impact area of his next swing of the bat. And that's when he started running around the side of the house, running up the hill, Aston Rowlands behind him yelling something incomprehensible – just inchoate rage noise – and swinging his bat.

The road up the hill was quite exceptionally steep. Normally Gethin took it at a slow walking pace and paused regularly for a breather, under the pretext of 'stopping to admire the view'. This time the adrenaline was doing its bit and he managed to keep running all the way up the steepest section of the road. He could hear Aston panting and swearing, no distance at all behind him. He considered trying a crafty sudden stop and double-back manoeuvre, but found two immediate objections. One was that it would inevitably bring him into Aston's bat-swinging range. The second was that Cat and Hattie would be arriving back any minute and he wanted to keep Aston Rowlands as far away from them as possible.

At the top of the killer incline there was another lane, running left to right, circling the side of the Garth mountain. Neither option offered any obvious salvation, so Gethin headed left just because he was on the left-hand side of the road already.

'You fucking cunt. You fucking ruined everything. I'm going to fucking kill you.'

Aston was angrier than ever, but even as he was yelling his manic manifesto, Gethin could sense him dropping a little further back. It was wasted effort all that shouting and, judging by the coughing fit that followed it, Aston Rowlands was not in the best of shape. On the other hand he was the best part of two decades younger than Gethin, so there were no grounds for complacency.

The path started heading uphill again. No part of Gethin's body wanted to run up it, but he risked a glance behind and saw Aston there, no more than five yards behind, and somehow his mind forced his legs and lungs to do their thing and he pushed hard onwards, hard enough to open the gap to ten, if not fifteen, yards by the time he'd crested the rise and hit another flatter stretch.

He took the risk of slowing very slightly, in order to take his phone out of his pocket. Then, doing his best to keep the pace going, he stabbed at it desperately with his right thumb, first entering the code that opened up the phone, then selecting the telephone app. He missed it twice, bringing up the internet instead, then bingo, there it was, a dial pad in front of him. He could sense Aston getting closer, so he stabbed the number nine three times, then stopped looking at the screen and started pumping towards the horizon.

Aston had closed up on him significantly while he'd farted about with the phone, so it took another awful effort to regain a six- or seven-yard gap. He raised the phone to his ear. He could hear an operator asking what service he wanted, but then his foot hit a rock and he half tripped and his phone went flying. There was no way he could pick it up now. All he could manage was to regain his footing and stumble ahead, thankful only that Aston was also struggling, judging by the mix of hacking coughs and groans coming from far too close behind.

A little way up ahead, Gethin could see a rough track leading almost vertically up Garth Hill itself. Now he had a choice to make. Either keep running along the road and see if he could outlast the much younger man behind him, or make one last burst up the hill and hope to lose his pursuer on the wooded slopes. He didn't fancy either option in the slightest, was seriously tempted to just lie down on the ground and let Aston Rowlands do his worst, but his gambler's heart advised him the way it always did. If there is a risky option available, embrace it.

So Gethin made a couple of what he hoped were smart feints to left and right, confusing Aston as to his intentions, then at the last moment swerved to his right and started up the track. He regretted it at once. Each step felt like his last. It was sapping the remaining dregs of his energy, but somehow he kept on going, step after step up through the woods, just about avoiding the assortment of roots and rocks that threatened to send him arse over tit at any moment.

He was just about to come out of the tree line on to the barren ground above, when a root finally caught him and he thudded to the ground. All he wanted to do was remain there and not get up, but he could see Aston coming closer and closer, his bat ready to swing and then somehow he forced himself off the ground and into motion and the swing of Aston's bat only caught the back of his leg. But that was enough to send him crashing to the ground again, and he was waiting for the inevitable follow-up smash of bat against head when he realised that the previous swing had caused Aston to overbalance as well, and so Gethin was able to stumble once more to his feet and make it out of the last of the trees and on to open ground.

Again there were paths diverging for him up ahead. He could go straight on up the path if he had the strength. He didn't, so it was a matter of choosing left or right. He chose right, kept on running, though, to be honest, he was barely managing more than walking speed now. Fortunately Aston was no better. He was lagging twenty yards behind him now and also labouring to keep going. Gethin imagined what it might look like from a helicopter, these two out-of-shape men lumbering along a mountain path, wheezing and groaning. Something like that surreal video footage when OJ Simpson was tracked in his car getting away from the cops in slow motion in his giant Bronco.

He wasn't sure how long they kept on like this, trudging around the side of the mountain. It seemed like hours but was no doubt just a few minutes. Finally he saw people up ahead. As he got close he was bemused to see that it was some sort of hiking group, all of them Japanese at a guess. He thought about waving to them and asking for help, but he was too worried they wouldn't understand, so he kept on going, trundling past their bemused faces.

On and on they went, locked into their slow-motion death match. Then Gethin glanced down the hill and saw a couple of figures in the landscape, both of them bent to the ground, seemingly picking things out of the grass. It took a moment to process what he was seeing. Of course, it was magic mushroom season up on the Garth. There were always hippies up here, this time of year. People like that guy Padraig from the TextileWorks, the sculptor/former dope dealer feller. And then he got close and he saw that one of the two figures looked very much like Padraig. The other one looked very much like Padraig's very large dog. Once he felt himself within earshot he yelled out his name, 'Padraig, Padraig. Help, help,' and he headed down the hill.

It was indeed Padraig. Gethin had never been so delighted to see an Irish drug dealer in his life.

'Please,' he said,' help me.' And then he collapsed.

He saw what followed from a prone position. Aston ran down the hill swinging his baseball bat and screaming blue murder. Paddy said something to his dog and then there was a blur of fur and teeth and muscle flying through the air. And then Aston was on the ground and Paddy's dog was standing on his chest, making it very clear that Aston had best stay where he was, and then Paddy was asking him a question.

'What the bloody hell is going on here?'

And even as Aston started to reply, Gethin could hear the sound of police sirens, somewhere in the near distance.

Thirty-Eight

THAT SHOULD HAVE BEEN THE end of it. The police held Aston in custody overnight. He didn't say a word to them, which was no surprise. This was scarcely his first rodeo. But they got a warrant to search his car and the pub and they found a hoody with what looked like a couple of small bloodstains. There was no sign of the actual will, but the idiot had left a covering letter from Co-op Legal Services in the bin. Turned out the Co-op had a copy. Put all that together with the deeply incriminating CCTV footage and there was enough for the CPS to agree to charge him with the murder of Dennis Hillyer the next morning. Deryck Davies gave a statement for the reporters outside Central Police Station, looking well pleased with himself.

Around the same time, Gethin finally made it into work, after sleeping for twelve hours straight. Bex did her motherly thing, checking he was all right: 'It must have been really traumatic, Geth.' Lee took the piss of course: 'See what happens every time I leaves you on your own.' Even Deano dropped by to offer his congratulations.

The team were feeling justifiably happy with the way things stood. Aston was charged with Dennis's murder. Prof Philip was clearly marked down for the Kelly Rowlands murder. Surely the way was clear to get their man, Morgan Hopkins, out of jail and in turn receive a healthy bonus for their labours.

Except it didn't work out like that. Over the next few days it became clear that the police weren't interested in crediting the late Prof with Kelly's murder. After a couple of days of getting nowhere, Gethin finally managed to persuade Deryck Davies to give him an update over a quick coffee in Octavo's – a bookshop cum café round the corner from their respective offices and guaranteed to be copper free. Deryck said that they'd searched the Prof's house and there was absolutely nothing to link into Kelly's murder. He acknowledged that the photos showed there had been a sexual relationship between the two of them, but so what, he was hardly the only one.

'What about the note?'

'A note typed on a computer? Anyone could have written that. You could have written that. And what does it say? Nothing about Kelly. Looks as if he had some weird obsession with murdered women and that caused him to top himself. Or do you think your lady friend gave him a hand? Is that what you'd like me to investigate?'

Gethin had to acknowledge that it wasn't.

'So there you go. One more tragic suicide. Anyone affected by these events should call the Samaritans. Case closed.'

'Yeah,' said Gethin, 'but what about Morgan Hopkins?'

'Not my problem,' said Deryck Davies, his expression flat and unreadable, 'not my problem at all.'

Which meant that once again it most certainly was Last Resort's problem. Gethin convened a meeting in the conference room and relayed the news from DS Deryck:

'Bollocks,' said Lee.

'Poor Morgan,' said Bex, 'he'll never get out now, will he? Not if the real murderer's dead and the police aren't interested.'

'Are you sure he did kill her, the Prof guy?' asked Lee.

'That's the question, all right,' said Gethin. He'd been thinking about it walking back to the office. Thinking over what Ella had said, or rather hadn't said. That Prof

Philip hadn't really confessed as such. He'd been prepared to let it go at the time because what did it matter, as long as Morgan got out of jail? The Prof was dead. If people thought he was a murderer then so what? Now, though, the equation was very different.

'I suppose the police have a point,' he said at last. 'There is nothing to say for definite he did it.'

'Why would he have killed himself, though,' asked Bex, 'if he didn't do it?'

'Because he thought he was about to be charged, I suppose,' said Gethin, 'couldn't bear the shame of it.' Or because Ella Tregaron had betrayed him with Mark Lewis. Or, just conceivably, because he didn't commit suicide at all, because Ella and/or Mark pushed him into the water.

'Okay' said Bex, not sounding particularly convinced. 'Well, anyway, let's say he is innocent. Who else could it have been?'

'I still like the copper for it,' said Lee.

'Me too,' said Gethin. 'Trouble is he does have an alibi.'

'Don't mean to be funny,' said Bex, 'but does he really?'

'How d'you mean?'

'We know his original alibi was nonsense, right. His sister told you.'

'Yeah,' said Lee, 'but he was actually with his lovely boyfriend, wasn't he?'

'Do we know that though?' asked Bex. 'I mean we know he told his sister that's where he was, but did we actually check it out?'

'No,' said Gethin, 'you're right. We were too busy with the Prof to bother. Any ideas how we check it out though?'

'I've got an idea, boss.' Gethin turned to see Deano leaning on the door frame. He had a way of sneaking up on you, did Deano. 'Be hard to check out where Ryan was on any given day, but Sanchez is a footballer. Should be possible to figure out where he was.'

Deano started tapping at his phone. 'What date was the murder?'

'March 10,' said Lee, who had an uncanny memory for dates.

'March 10, right.' Deano tapped some more, then started smiling. 'Well, bloody hell.'

'Bloody hell what?' said Gethin.

'Bloody hell Jake Sanchez was only playing for the City against Newcastle that day. Away at Newcastle.'

'What time?'

'Four pm kick-off. Game over just after six. No way he was back in Cardiff before midnight, even with the private plane and all.'

Gethin thought about the implications of this. He came quickly to the problem. 'What I can't see, though, is what his motive could have been? When we started looking into this, we all thought he'd been shagging her, and that doesn't look likely now.'

'Can't say that for sure, boss,' Lee chipped in, 'plenty of blokes out there go both ways. Jake Sanchez for starters.'

'True, but we're going to need more than this if we're going to get your mate Deryck to reopen the case. Any more ideas?'

They kicked it around for a while, the four of them, without getting anywhere much. Deano said he'd double-check the Sanchez alibi. Lee said she'd swing by the TextileWorks and have a word with Leanne. Gethin couldn't really think of any useful line of investigation, and was relieved when Bex needed him to run through the latest developments in Operation Copper.

* * *

Gethin left work early, made some pasta for Hattie and himself and got an early night. It was when he was making her breakfast the next morning that he made the breakthrough.

301

The Aston Rowlands case was all over the local news. The radio anchor cued up the crime reporter with the question: 'So what do we know about Mr Rowlands?'

'Well, Emma, we know he is a twenty-nine-year-old man from Abertridwr. He was married to Kelly Rowlands who, as I'm sure listeners will remember, was murdered, brutally murdered, nearly two years ago.'

The anchor cut in: 'Is there any suggestion that Mr Rowlands might have been involved in his wife's murder?'

'No, Emma. A local man Morgan Hopkins was convicted of the crime and Mr Rowlands had a pretty good alibi.'

'What was that then, Nick?'

'He was in prison.'

'Oh I see. And do we know what his crime was?'

'Yes, Emma, he was serving three months for possession of banned substances with intent to supply.'

'Banned substances?'

'Yes. Anabolic steroids, I believe.'

Gethin felt like smacking himself over the head. How had he missed that? He'd known Aston was inside for drug dealing, but he'd assumed it was the usual – party drugs or smack. Steroids, bloody hell. Suddenly he could see a pattern. A pattern he liked a lot. Half an hour later he was laying it out for Bex and Lee.

'So we know Ryan's majorly into his gym drugs, right? And Aston was stealing them. So there's the connection we've been missing.'

'How do we know that?' asked Bex.

'We don't know for sure, yet, but hear me out. What does Ryan do when he gets to Kelly's place after she's been murdered? He searches the place. Remember how his fingers were all over the place. He said he was looking for evidence and forgot to wear gloves or whatever, because he was so shocked. I never liked that story.'

Lee grunted her agreement.

'Doesn't it make more sense that Ryan was actually searching for Aston's steroid stash?'

'You're right, Geth, it does.' Bex this time.

'And didn't Deano say Ryan was dealing that stuff to his mates in the gym. If we can show that that started just after Kelly died, that Ryan came into a whole truckload of pills right then, then we are definitely getting somewhere.'

'Nice, boss,' said Lee, 'and I tell you what, that steroid shit really fucks with your personality too. Boys on roids, you've got to watch them. Terrible rages.'

'Right,' said Gethin. 'So let's think it through from the top. There's Ryan. He's addicted to the steroids. His dealer, Aston, goes to prison, so he can't get any more. Decides to have a look see if he can find Aston's stash. Maybe Aston told him where to look, whatever. He goes round the house, threatens Kelly, starts searching. She tries to stop him. He smacks her about. Grabs her by the throat. Grabs her too hard because he's a muscled-up twat. He totally loses it with her. He thinks oh shit. Then he remembers he's a copper. He can get away with this. He goes outside to a phone box. Calls 999 and reports a disturbance. Then he hangs round till the call comes over the radio, and he makes sure he gets there first. Afterwards his sister comes to him, all upset, because she thinks she's going to be in the frame. Could he alibi her? Of course he could. What she didn't realise at the time was she was actually alibiing him. How's that for a story?'

'It's a good one, Geth. Totally makes sense to me. But what evidence have we got for any of it?'

Gethin thought about it some more. He was sure his story was close enough to the truth. It just felt right. It made sense of a whole lot of things that had been bothering him. But Bex's question stood. Where was the evidence?

On one level there was plenty of evidence. Ryan's fingerprints were literally all over the shop. But that wasn't news. To reopen a case you need new evidence. And by being the first cop to arrive at the scene Ryan had managed to explain away what would otherwise be damning evidence against him. So what new evidence could there be?

CCTV was a possibility. If Ryan's car was found somewhere near the house around the time of the murder, when he was meant to be having a nice curry with his beloved sister, then that would be something. But there was no way he could access any of that now. It would have been wiped long ago. The only hope was that the defence might have been given access to some footage before the trial and not realised what they had. It was a huge longshot, but he could call Morgan's original lawyer and find out.

'How about we start by attacking his alibi?' Bex cut into Gethin's reverie.

'Of course.' Not for the first time in this case, he was wondering what was going on with his ability to think straight. 'Looks like we should be able to show there was no way he was with Jake Sanchez that night. That's definitely a start.'

'Except that's not his official alibi, is it?' Lee now. 'Far as the law knows, he was with his sister.'

'Yeah, yeah. So if we could persuade her to tell the truth...'

'Exactly,' said Lee, 'and you know what?'

'What?'

'I think if we play her right, puppet girl, she might give us more than that. She might just grass him all the way up. She loved Kelly and if she thinks he killed her I think she'll talk. Brother or no brother.'

'You reckon? You think we should head round to see her now?'

'Not we, Geth. Best leave her to me. Needs someone with a delicate touch, this job does.'

Gethin smiled, an image flashing through his mind of

Lee kicking that lad in the stomach in the Four Feathers. Delicate wasn't the word for that. Brutal maybe. But she was right. She could do delicate too.

Thirty-Nine

LEE DIDN'T COME BACK TILL mid-afternoon. She looked exhausted. Flopped down in a chair in Gethin's office and stared up at the celling for a while before saying anything. Gethin just waited. You didn't want to get on the wrong side of Lee when she was in this kind of mood. Finally she sat up, looked at her colleagues and said: 'She'll do it.'

'Do what?' asked Gethin.

'Set him up for us, see if she can get him to confess.'

'Christ,' said Gethin, 'how did you manage that?'

'Just my natural charm,' said Lee, then she stopped. You could almost see the clouds making their way across her thoughts. 'We went out for lunch.'

'Nowhere too fancy, I hope' said Gethin, trying to cheer the mood up a little, but Lee clearly wasn't in a joking mood.

'No, we went to the falafel place on Cowbridge Road, she's a veggie of course. And then we talked about shit.'

'What kind of shit.'

'All the bad shit. All the shit that changes you when you're a kid. We showed each other our scars, like.'

As she talked Gethin saw her hand move instinctively to her left cheek. There was a scar there, just faint. Gethin had never asked how she'd got it. He had quite a similar one. Got it playing cricket when he was a kid. He suspected Lee didn't get hers playing cricket.

'She told me about him. Stuff he did to her when she was a kid. And when she wasn't a kid.'

Lee's pace was slowing down to nothing now. Gethin could see her working to keep up her composure, her 'seen it all, been there, done that and didn't even bother taking the T-shirt' front.

'Don't think she'd ever told anyone about it before. Lucky the place was empty.'

More silence. Finally Gethin stepped in.

'Is this Ryan we're talking about?'

'No,' said Lee, 'well, not exactly. It was her dad.' She sighed. 'Sometimes I'm glad I never had one.'

'Christ.'

'Yeah. She's been through some serious shit. Started getting into it when I told her about the alibi.'

'Told her what?' Gethin never normally had to carry on like this with Lee, prising out the details, but he'd never seen her quite so discombobulated. He wondered if she'd fallen for Leanne. That would be a thing.

'That Ryan wasn't with Jake Sanchez. That he'd been looking for Aston's steroid stash. She just went totally pale and started shaking. Then I asked her if she thought Ryan could have killed Kelly.'

'And she said yes?'

'Yeah she did. Said he was like his old man. Said she was scared of him. Not of his doing anything to her, he loves her. But what he was capable of. And that's when she told me about their old man.'

'People ain't no good,' said Gethin, quoting Nick Cave.

'No, Gethin, they mostly ain't.'

'So she'll talk to Ryan? Tell him she doesn't believe his story?'

'Yeah. Well, she said she would.'

'So, that's great, right?'

'I suppose.'

Lee just sat there, looking utterly drained. Gethin decided to dive in.

'You okay?'

'Yeah, just wonderful.' She stood up. 'Got to go.'

Gethin thought about asking her where she was going. Decided against it and tried to get back to business instead. 'Did you make a plan with Leanne, then? What would be really good is if she was prepared to record her conversation with Ryan.'

'I suggested that. She totally freaked out. I suppose it's quite a betrayal, wearing a wire with your own brother.'

'Sure, but if he has actually killed someone...'

'Yeah, yeah I know.' Lee hesitated before carrying on. 'I might go round and see her though, later on like and I can have another crack at persuading her, but I really don't think she'll be up for it. Anyway, I'll let you know, soon as. Got to go now, give the kids their tea.' And with that Lee was up and out of there. Gethin gave her a minute to clear the building then came out of his office and looked over at Bex.

'Bloody hell, Geth, what did you say to her? Never seen her looking so miserable.'

'No,' said Gethin, 'I've got an awful feeling she might have fallen in love.'

Bex looked confused. 'Who with? Oh God, not the copper?'

'Yeah the cop.'

'Really? Didn't see that coming. Didn't think she liked butch girls.'

'You've never seen her, have you? Leanne's not butch. Quite the opposite. I mean she's quite tall, but she looks like she'd blow over in a strong wind and faint if you said boo to her.'

'That makes more sense. I can see her going for a damsel in distress.'

'Yeah,' said Gethin, 'sounds like she's pretty fucking distressed, that's for sure.'

'So does she think Ryan did it then?'

'Sounds like she thinks he's capable of it. Apparently Leanne's going to have a talk with him, try and get the truth out of him.' Gethin paused. 'Is there any way we can record someone's conversation without them knowing?'

He wasn't expecting much of a response to this. Last Resort didn't have much in the way of surveillance equipment. They didn't do divorces or industrial espionage cases, so they'd never needed any expertise in that area. Bex, though, was a resourceful woman.

'What are you thinking, Geth, put some sort of bug in her house?'

'I suppose,' he said, then carried on thinking out loud. 'Lee probably knows where she lives, but how would we know where to put it? And why would Leanne necessarily talk to her brother at her place? Not going to work, is it?'

'Probably not. I mean we could get a little voice-activated recorder and maybe Lee could stick it somewhere in the house, but then we would have to get in again and remove it and well... There's a lot could go wrong, isn't there?'

'Yeah, forget it.' He thought some more. 'How about the phone? Is there some way of tapping into that?'

'I dunno, Geth, but let me find out.'

Twenty minutes later she came into Gethin's office and said, 'I think I might have just the thing.'

* * *

Eight o'clock that evening Bex, Lee and Gethin were all sat around Bex's PC in the office, staring in frank amazement at the screen. There, in real time, they could see Leanne Batey tapping out a text message on her phone, half a mile away.

Bex had downloaded the spyware app and then Lee had done the tricky part of the job. She'd gone round to Leanne's place, just down the road in Grangetown. First she'd tried and failed to persuade her to record her conversation with

Ryan, but she did manage to get her to promise to talk to her brother that evening. Then she'd made out like her own phone had run out of charge and she'd asked to borrow Leanne's to make an urgent call. She'd stepped into the garden, ostensibly for privacy but really so she could download the spyware app on to Leanne's phone. 'Didn't feel good about it, boss, I got to say.'

And then she'd come back to the office and now every single thing that happened on Leanne's phone was being broadcast to Bex's PC. Has there even been a more treacherous invention than the smartphone?

'It's like we're all carrying miniature Trojan Horses around with us,' said Bex in wonder, as they watched Leanne's message to her brother appear on screen

'Got 2 talk 2U. ABOUT THAT NIGHT'

It was less than a minute before the reply came in.

'WOT? CU on weekend'

Leanne's reply was almost instantaneous.

'No! NOW!'

Ryan replied 'Where RU?'

'Home'

'OK. Can U come to mine now? Got 2b quick'

'OK'

The team sat and watched the next spooky surveillance development as the GPS tracked Leanne's phone as it walked round the corner in the opposite direction to Ryan's place, then presumably got into a car as it started moving fast in the right direction.

'Jesus,' said Lee.

The blue dot that was Leanne's phone came to a stop on Dumballs Road, presumably to park the car, then started moving again slowly as she walked up to Ryan's building.

'Okay, so she's gone round to his place. But she's not going to talk to him on the phone now, is she? How are we going to know what she says?'

'That's the magic part,' said Gethin. 'At least we hope it is. You know what to do, Bex?'

Bex started clicking around on the screen and a few seconds later sound started crackling out of the speakers. Nothing much at first, but then the distinct sound of someone knocking on the door, then a distorted voice saying, 'come in then' and the door opening.

'How does that work then?' said Lee, looking justifiably amazed.

'The phone's got a microphone in it – all phones do – what this program does is let us turn it on.'

'Shit, I really am never carrying one of these things again.'

Two voices started to come out of the speakers, the brother and sister talking. Bex clicked some more buttons to record it.

'So what's so fucking urgent?'

'Those investigators, Ryan, they've been on and on at me.'

'You haven't been talking to them, have you? What's wrong with you?'

'Yes, but I haven't told them anything. But I'm feeling really confused, I mean I know you wasn't with Jake the night Kelly got killed.'

'What? Who told you that?'

'No one. I was just thinking about that night and how you told me you were with Jake, but I looked on the internet and he was in Newcastle.'

A pause.

'So where were you, Ry? Where the fuck were you?'

'Okay. I was at home. I just said I was with Jake to explain why I needed an alibi. But I was just at home.'

Another longer pause.

'But, Ry. Why would you need an alibi if you were just at home? You always said you were just helping me out because I needed an alibi, because, you know, me and Kelly. Obviously I was a suspect. But you, Ry? Why would you need an alibi?'

A longer pause, the sound of someone opening a door, or maybe a fridge, as afterwards there was a sound like that of a can of lager being opened and Ryan's next words were 'you want one?'

He was obviously playing for time. Clearly Leanne thought so too, as her next words were a curt 'no, get on with it.'

'All right, so here's the thing. I was round her place, Kelly's place, that evening. Her feller, Aston, he had some stuff for me, gym stuff.'

'Steroids, you mean. Jesus, Ry.'

'Yeah all right, steroids. None of your business like.'

'So that's why you were so close by. Oh fucking hell, Ry.'

Another pause, some scuffling movement. The Last Resort team looked at each other in mounting alarm.

'What? You think I killed her?'

'No, Ry, I just…'

'You just remember you don't have an alibi either. If you try telling anyone about this, I'll just say I lied to give you an alibi, because you're my big sis. You can't say a thing about me. Mutually assured destruction. You say anything, it's my word against yours. And I'm a serving officer and you're some lezzer fuck-up who farts around with puppets. Who're they going to believe?'

'I don't believe this.' Leanne's voice was high, heading for hysteria. And then the crying started. 'You killed my Kelly. I don't care what happens to me, I'm going to…'

They didn't hear what Leanne was going to do because the next sound was of a crashing blow followed by a scream and a big clunk then some ominous quiet.

'He's hit her,' said Lee, 'the fucker's hit her.'

Forty

THEY MADE AS MUCH OF a plan as they could. Bex would stay in the office, monitoring Leanne's phone. Gethin and Lee would bomb round to Ryan's place to try and stop things going any further to hell. Gethin drove while Lee had her phone clamped to her ear, in constant contact with Bex.

Thankfully Ryan's place was only a couple of minutes away by car, just down the Dumballs Road. One side was lined with warehouses, garages and cash-and-carries; the other side, the side next to the river, used to have factories and now it had gated developments of waterfront apartments.

Ryan's place was in something called Spice Trade Wharf. As far as Gethin was aware there had been precious little actual spice trade through Cardiff, but never mind, it sounded aspirational. The gates to the car park were firmly locked. No code no access. Gethin pulled up on a yellow line and was just about to jump out when Lee said: 'Hang on. Bex says she's moving. Or at least her phone is.'

What did that mean? 'Has he let her go then? Has Bex heard anything?'

Lee asked the question then relayed the answer. 'No, nothing, just a load of thudding about and then the door opening.'

They looked at each other, trying to think through the various unsavoury scenarios this could indicate. They didn't have to speculate for long though as, just then,

Gethin could hear a car starting up and then saw a pair of headlights approaching the gates from the other side.

The gates buzzed open and there was Ryan's 4x4 nosing out into the street right next to them. There was no time to react, though, before Ryan had swung out into the road heading back the way they'd come, back into the Bay proper.

Gethin tried to turn too quickly, misjudged his angles and had to make a three-point manoeuvre which lost valuable seconds. He gunned the car down the road but Ryan was already disappearing in the distance.

Lee yelled into the phone. 'Is it moving, Bex, is she moving? Oh thank God. Okay, can you see which way he's going?' She turned to Gethin. 'We're all right. Bex can track him.'

Gethin relaxed fractionally at this news and followed the directions as Lee called them out. They turned left at the top of the road. Ryan had already gone from view, but then Lee called a right turn almost immediately. Gethin could see a car up ahead. It looked like they were heading for the ring road and so it proved. One right turn and then they were over the roundabout and on to the slip road, then heading up and over the Bay. It was the route Gethin took to and from work every day. And he was so used to carrying on all the way to the motorway junction that it came as a shock when Lee told him to come off at the first exit.

If Gethin was calming down a little, Lee was the reverse. He wasn't sure he'd ever seen her so hyped up. She was muttering under her breath about all the things she was going to do to Ryan if he'd hurt Leanne. They continued over a couple of junctions before taking the long bridge heading for Penarth and Barry.

'Maybe he's going to Jake's place,' said Gethin.

Ryan wasn't heading for Jake's place though. His 4x4

was clearly visible now, three cars ahead, and as they came to the next junction Ryan swerved across two lanes of traffic and took the Penarth exit, setting off a barrage of horn blowing. Gethin blasted his own horn, then made the same manoeuvre.

Ryan took another left off the next roundabout, taking the road leading downhill to the Penarth Marina, yet another new development of waterfront housing, though this time with the addition of plentiful moorings. They followed Ryan along the speed-bump-ridden road all the way to the end. That left them with two options: a big bar and restaurant to the right and the Barrage car park on the left. Ryan took the latter option, drove across the car park until he was as close as he could get to the Barrage itself. Gethin came to a halt at the entrance to the car park, not wanting to alert Ryan to their presence till they had some idea what was happening.

The Barrage was a massive structure, a huge tidal dam that had been built in the nineties for a billion quid – when a billion quid was still quite something – and it had turned the Bay from a tidal basin – whose water level would go up and down by twenty feet in the course of the day, from deep water to an ocean of mud – into a placid lagoon; nice to sit beside in a bar, or cruise across in your yacht. Its massive walls stood a good hundred feet above the Bristol Channel. It was a known suicide spot. There was no way you could survive the fall.

'He's going to push her off,' said Lee, 'he's going to fucking push her off.'

Just then Ryan emerged from the car and opened the rear doors.

'Gethin,' shouted Lee, 'fucking move it.'

Gethin came to and accelerated across the tarmac. As he did so, he saw Ryan dragging a body out of his car. At first he thought Leanne was either dead or unconscious, but as her feet hit the ground she stumbled then stood up. There was a gag in her mouth and her wrists were tied behind her back, but she was definitely alive. Gethin heard Lee actually sigh with relief next to him. Then he was pulling up next to the 4x4 and they both jumped out of the car, yelling incoherently, anything to let Ryan know they were after him.

Ryan started dragging Leanne through the open gateway between the car park and the Barrage itself. He was only a couple of yards from the inner lock system, the deep and narrow channel between the Bay and the Bristol Channel. It could be either full of water or empty, depending on whether the last ship to travel through it been going in or out of the Bay. Right now it was empty, a long, sheer drop to shallow water and concrete. There was only a waist-high fence to stop people falling in. And now Ryan was pushing Leanne up against the fence, looking like he was about to try and flip her over.

Gethin and Lee were no more than six feet away now. So near but so far. Ryan looked certain to send his sister to her death when she managed to kick out at him. He barely reacted, just backhanded her so quickly it was over before any of them had time to register it. Leanne subsided and Lee started to charge forward, but Ryan yelled at her to stop.

'Come any closer and she's going over.'

Lee paused, swayed by the geometry of the situation. By the time she could get to Ryan with a kick or a punch Leanne would be over the fence. The backhand to her face seemed to have rendered her inert, a life-size doll in her brother's grip.

Gethin tried to take charge of the situation. 'You can't do this. We can see you.'

'I'll fucking have you both and all.'

'What? You think that won't show up on the CCTV.

316

You have any idea how many cameras there are here?'

'I'll wipe them then, I'll fucking wipe them.' Even as he was talking though, his words were losing power. He looked at Gethin and Lee, then at Leanne.

'Let her go, man. She's your sister.' It was Lee talking now. Her voice was soft and unthreatening.

He looked towards her, his eyes unfocused. His shoulders started to slump and Gethin thought he was about to acknowledge the futility of his situation, but then he seemed to snap to. His shoulders straightened and, keeping his grip on Leanne with his left arm, he dug in his coat pocket with his right hand and pulled out a gun.

'Fuck you all,' he shouted and then things started moving so fast that it was only afterwards that Gethin was able to piece together the actual sequence of events.

Ryan fired twice. Perhaps because he wasn't sure whether it was Gethin or Lee he most wanted to kill, he managed to miss them both. Gethin threw himself to the ground, regretting his decision even as he fell. All Ryan would need to do was walk over and shoot him from no distance. He tried to get up and follow Lee's example – he could hear her running for cover – but sheer weight of terror kept him pinned to the ground. He simply couldn't bear to get off the ground and make himself a bigger target.

There was another gun shot and then a scream. Gethin's initial thought was that it was Lee, that she'd been shot, but then he looked back at Ryan and Leanne and saw Leanne pulling a knife out of Ryan's groin then diving forwards and away from him. Ryan himself slowly subsided to the ground. There was a clatter as he dropped the gun, his hands going to his wound which was spurting blood at a terrifying rate.

'Lannie,' he said, 'Lannie,' his voice high and childlike. 'What have you done?'

He collapsed to the ground, curled into a foetal position,

trying to hold his stomach together. And crying, an awful keening sound that Gethin knew he'd hear in his dreams forever.

After a while, probably only seconds, Leanne got up off the ground and walked over to Ryan. She sat beside him stroking his head, while Lee called for the coppers and the ambulance.

Acknowledgements

Once again I'd like to thank my Cardiff pub quiz team – Paul, Katell, Patrick, Julie, Euros, Andrew, Gruff and the ever occasional Rob – for laughs, graveyard visits and support through some trying times. Many thanks to Ion Mills, Ellie Lavender, Geoff Mulligan, Claire Watts and everyone else at No Exit. Thanks to Jayne Lewis for copy-editing. Thanks to my agent Matthew Hamilton. And thanks to Anna Davis for sorting out the shambles that was the first draft, and for everything else.